Shadow Wolves

Jake Kaminski

First Edition

PAGE PUBLISHING, INC.
Conneaut Lake, PA

First originally published by Page Publishing 2019

This is a work of fiction. Names, characters, places and incidents are products of the author's imagination or are used fictitiously and are not to be construed as real. Any resemblance to actual events, locales, organizations, or persons, living or dead, is entirely coincidental.

ISBN 978-1-68456-621-1 (pbk)
ISBN 978-1-68456-623-5 (hc)
ISBN 978-1-68456-622-8 (digital)

Printed in the United States of America

For Marsha—Always

Acknowledgements

It's so hard to thank all of the people that contributed to this, my first novel. To begin with, I have to thank my wife, who had the patience to read and re-read every version of this story...and believe me there were too many to count! She coaxed me through days of blank pages and the times when I wasn't quite sure where the story would take me.

A sincere thought to the late Miss Catherine Miller, my high-school teacher who first lit the fire in me to write.

I would also like to send out my thanks to Dr. Alex Thiltges, who re-ignited that fire so many years later.

This novel would never have made it to press without the able editing by my dear friend John Schaller. His input was invaluable. His attention to detail and his tactful suggestions made the manuscript so much better.

Then there were the few close friends who agreed to read the manuscript at each stage of the process:

Tom Johnson, you are a big part of this. Part of this adventure is yours my friend.

Senator Mike Bennett. It was you who convinced me that I could do this thing. I think you might have been right! Thank you so much to you and Dee for your encouragement!

All of my old friends at the PD and the FBI. Thank you for your support and your companionship over the years.

To my Balkan companions who showed me both the sadness and the wonder that is the Balkans; Oliver, Andrej, Ivana and Ljiljana.

And most important, my family, Marsha, Sean, Marilyn and Ghost. You have been at my side and in my heart for over forty years. Your love and support will be with me until I leave this Earth.

Finally, I want to thank the courageous men and women who fight the evil of human trafficking all over the world. You are on the side of the angels.

Part One

Central Bosnia, 1994

We do not want churches because they will teach us to
quarrel about God. We do not want to learn that.
We may quarrel with men sometimes about things
on this earth. But we never quarrel about God.
We do not want to learn that.

—Chief Joseph, Nez Perce

CHAPTER 1

The mountains rose steeply in every direction. The mid-autumn sky was overcast, the grey sky matching the lives of the people under its bleak umbrella. Darker, pregnant clouds hung over the highest peaks, threatening snow in the upper passes. In the valley below, winter was still a month away. The Bosna River, ice-cold and crystal clear, rushed northward, its waters a lifeblood for the farms and villages sheltered within the shadows of the rugged mountain range.

The land stood unchanged, a sentry against the passage of time. Shepherds tended flocks of sheep accompanied by massive mountain dogs, their fierce companions in keeping the wolves at bay. Weathered old peasant women trudged along dirt roads with bundles of twisted sticks strapped across their stooped shoulders. The roads were dirt, the houses stone, and the roofs straw. Soft yellow light peeked out through open shutters as wood smoke curled up from blackened chimneys. The occupants of this place took their cue from their surroundings, content to live their lives as had their ancestors. There was security in living a life that never changed.

*****

The group of soldiers materialized out of the grey mist as they came over the rise in the narrow roadway. They were death walking—dark swarthy men, faces black with stubble. They did not march but swaggered, cigarettes dangling from their mouths as they moved along the roadway. These militiamen entered the tiny village led by a Toyota truck with a large caliber machine gun mounted in the bed of the vehicle. The Toyota was followed by a white Russian-made Lada, driven by a sweaty Serb in filthy green army fatigues.

Known as the Skorpions, they were a Serb paramilitary unit that had been empowered by the Serbian strongman, Slobodan Milosevic, and blessed by the Orthodox priests in Belgrade. They were tasked to wreak havoc on Muslims and Croats whenever and wherever they found them. Prior to the war, these men had been vicious thugs and violent criminals. The war had just given them the power to operate under the color of the government in Belgrade. Their name came from their weapon of choice, the famed Skorpion VZ-61 machine pistol. Invented in the sixties by the Czechoslovakia Arms Industry, it was later manufactured in Serbia. One of the most reliable weapons made for close combat operations, it was capable of firing 850 rounds per minute. A Skorpion pistol hung menacingly from the shoulder of each of the men as they approached the outskirts of the remote hamlet.

The Serbs had turned the war in Bosnia into an ethnic cleansing, creating the worst holocaust Europe had seen since World War II. The Skorpions were, perhaps, the most vicious of the Serb contingents. They had been torturing, raping, and killing innocent civilians for two years and had no intention of stopping until all Muslims and Catholics were gone without a trace. They had no moral boundaries left to cross.

The first two peasants they encountered were an old man and woman walking along the muddy road on the outskirts of the village. The man moved slowly with the help of a knobby hand-carved walking stick. The bent ancient woman led a nanny goat on a frayed rope. The old couple had been hearing stories about the vicious Skorpions for a long time but somehow thought that their little corner of the world was so unimportant that the war would pass them by. As the two vehicles drew near, followed by the large group of armed men, the couple immediately recognized the dreaded Skorpion shoulder patches. The woman let out a barely audible whimper which was lost in the sound of the diesel engines.

The lead vehicle pulled next to the couple and stopped. The elderly pair, frozen like statues in the rutted roadway, were transfixed by the hard, unshaven men with guns held loosely in their arms. The Kommandant stepped from his position in the passenger seat of the truck and walked around to the driver's side to confront the couple. He barked, "How many soldiers in the area?" The old man, lips quivering, appeared willing but unable to answer. The old woman reached out to her husband to support him but said nothing. Without taking his eyes off the Kommandant, the man extended his shaking hand sideways to pat his wife's arm in reassurance. The goat instinctively jerked backward from the soldier, pulling the woman off-balance in the process.

"I'm talking to *you*, old man!" the Kommandant shouted, obviously enjoying the fear he instilled.

The ancient couple struggled to remain in place in spite of the actions of their goat, their shared terror obvious in their lined faces. The woman's left ankle had become twisted in the mud. The goat was now bleating loudly, shaking her head and pulling the woman from her husband's grasp. The walking stick fell from the old man's grasp as he stumbled toward his wife in an effort to keep her from falling. His frail body was failing him, and he called to her, "Moja Slatki, *my sweet one*. Don't be afraid." She looked into the eyes she had known for a lifetime, tears forming on her wrinkled cheeks. Her mind flashed to her family. This war. Both her sons killed and her daughter taken, probably dead. *This man is the only thing left that matters in my life.*

The old man moved closer to his wife, struggling to regain his grip on her bony hand. The Kommandant, smirking, pulled the Skorpion pistol from his sling and let loose a burst of ten rounds into the trembling pair, dropping them into the mud. Fifty years of love and hardship ending in a pile of black clothes on the side of the road. The goat was left standing, confused, the rope still in the hand of the old woman on the ground. The militiamen stood around the lead truck and lit cigarettes, joking and acting like he had merely squashed a bug on his sleeve rather than murdered two innocent people. The Kommandant finished his smoke, moved silently back to his seat in the lead truck, and led his men into the village. They were wild dogs on the hunt.

There were only forty people living in the village. None of them were soldiers. The able-bodied men had already joined the Federation army to try to hold back the Serbian juggernaut. All that remained were women, the very old and the very young. Upon hearing the gunfire in the road, most had come out of their houses to see what had happened. The sight of the Skorpions caused some to start running for the woods. Most just stood there, resigned to their fate. The toll of this brutal war had driven hope from every one of them.

The grizzled men fanned out as they reached the center of the village. They were fierce and merciless. They walked among the villagers, kicking and punching them. Ignoring their pleas for mercy. The older people were dragged by their necks or hair into their houses, the soldiers demanding money and other valuables. Others were simply gunned down where they stood.

Two teenage girls, who had been told to run into the woods, were found hiding behind a small house. They had been too frightened to run and had stayed as close as they could to their grandparents. When they saw the Serb let loose with a full magazine into the old couple, they had cried out and were discovered. Two of the Skorpions pulled them from hiding by their long black hair, dragging them into the nearest house. When the men were finished with them, they pulled out Soviet-era bayonets and sliced their throats. Walking away, they joked among themselves while wiping the blood from the blades on their sleeves.

The Skorpions moved through the village with ruthless efficiency. Each house was ransacked and searched for weapons, valuables, and men of fighting age. At the end of the main road, a schoolhouse stood alone surrounded by a makeshift vegetable garden and clotheslines heavy with women's undergarments. The Kommandant tapped his driver's arm with the back of his hand and pointed at the isolated building. Looking to his right, he saw a middle-aged woman in tattered clothes lying on the ground and struggling in the mud to crawl away. The truck came to a stop in the middle of the road, and he shouted down at the woman through his open window. "What is that building?" pointing to the schoolhouse.

The woman froze at the sound of his voice but then resumed her crawl to the side of the road in silence.

The Kommandant exited the truck, kicked the woman viciously in her back, and repeated, "Did you hear me, bitch? What is that building?"

The woman stopped crawling and began to weep silently. The Kommandant fired one round into the back of her head. He then climbed back into his vehicle and motioned for the Lada to follow. As they pulled in front of the building, they saw that it was an old school building that now served as living quarters. Some of the militiamen moved quickly to surround the building while a group of ten entered through the front door, pistols ready.

The Kommandant was the first of the Skorpions to enter the schoolhouse. He heard footsteps skittering frantically across the floor above his head. He raised his hand and motioned for the men to remain silent. It was then that he heard hushed voices and more movement from above. The voices sounded young, but he moved forward and up the stairs with caution. At the top of the stairs, he saw three rooms on each side of the extended hallway. He directed his men methodically through each room, patiently waiting until they reached the last door at the end of the corridor. The door was closed, but he could hear muffled voices coming from the other side, voices he knew well: voices of fear. One of his men stood next to him, looking expectantly for a command. The Kommandant smiled and then nodded. The Skorpion stepped forward and smashed through the door with one blow from his massive boot.

Four of the militiamen burst through the door with guns drawn. The Kommandant followed, calmly stepping into the darkened building. The scene was exactly what he had expected—three girls in their early teens and small groups of young children clinging to each of them in terror. The oldest of the girls, Anja, stood in the center of the room. Two young girls of about five were wrapped around her legs, wide-eyed with fear. She looked at the armed men and entreated, "We are just women and children here. We can do you no harm." Looking around at the men, she tried again. "Please, we have nothing and mean no harm. *Please.*"

One of the men stepped forward and punched Anja in the face. Her nose erupted in blood as she fell backward, striking the back of her head on the wall behind her, slowly sliding downward as she lost consciousness. The blow caused the room to erupt in screams and cries from the children. A young boy, twelve years old and larger than the rest, stepped forward to protect the rest of the children. The leader's right hand flashed forward, smashing the side of the boy's head with the butt of his pistol, dropping the boy instantly.

The militiamen moved quickly through the room, knocking children out of the way as they advanced toward the older girls. Those girls who even appeared a day over twelve years old were grabbed and dragged from the room. Some of the younger children were pulled from their feet and slammed against the walls, three of them dying instantly. Two young boys were clubbed to death where they stood by a huge Serb wielding a long-handled, heavy wooden mallet.

*****

The Skorpions continued to move methodically through the village. They showed no mercy. They viciously mutilated their victims, often while they were alive. At times they removed body parts as souvenirs.

The Kommandant returned to the center of the village and looked over the remaining group of villagers. All of them had clearly been abused. Most were bleeding. Several of the women stood in the middle of the street, wearing little or no clothing, all shame lost by now. His driver looked to him and asked, "Should we order them to leave?"

"Why? Call the artillery and tell them to send some shells this way. Fuck these animals."

He took one last look at the few weeping peasants who remained alive and drove away, never looking back. The remainder of his Skorpions fell into line behind the two vehicles as they went in search of the next village.

*****

The American Ranger platoon moved steadily along the dirt road, following a mountain ridge above a valley divided evenly by a swiftly flowing aqua blue river. They were on a reconnaissance mission, searching for a group of Croatian nuns who had gone missing a day earlier. These were busy days for the multinational forces assembled in the heart of Bosnia. The world was watching as fourteen western nations stepped cautiously into the brutal war that now stretched into its third year. After years of inaction, NATO forces were now trying to stop Serbia from the systematic genocide of both the Croatian Catholic and Bosnian Muslim populations in the former Republic of Yugoslavia.

Lieutenant Evans had his two squads deployed, one on each side of the road, guns pointed outward and ready. They had been in-country for months and had witnessed the carnage resulting from the ethnic cleansing being committed by the militias. They were seriously on edge. He worried about coming under attack as they moved through the area, concerned about his rules of engagement. If they did make contact with the men responsible for these atrocities, they were going to have to follow protocols that could only have been dreamed up by a diplomatic bureaucrat sitting safely in a Brussels café.

The lieutenant pushed the rules of engagement from his mind. His concern was for his team and then for the innocents. They would do what they needed to do and somebody else could sort out the rules back at HQ. This mission had not been what he had expected when he left Fort Bragg for Bosnia. The brutality was impossible to understand. *How could these people do this to one another?* He had to admit that he had heard about this type of cruelty from his grandfather when he talked about World War II but never thought he would see anything like it in his lifetime.

As his team moved along the road, his thoughts went to the map he had memorized over the last two days. There was a village just two klicks ahead. He was sure his scouts had reached the village by now, and he should be getting some intel soon. His three forward scouts were the best the army had to offer. All were Native Americans: a Lakota Sioux, a Seminole, and a Navajo. All could track a man across solid rock and follow a blood trail with their eyes closed. It was said that the Navajo could smell a drop of blood and know if it came from a man or a woman. The Seminole was a man of extraordinary strengths. He could run all day and handle any discomfort the environment had to offer. The Sioux was something altogether different. He was quiet and highly intelligent. His combat skills were unrivaled. He had finished at the top of his class at Ranger school and was faster than lightning in hand-to-hand combat. Eighteen months deployed to Korea, training with ROK Marines, had turned him into a formidable fighter.

*****

The lieutenant looked down from his platoon's "hide" above the village. They had reached their location about thirty minutes ago. His scouts had been in position for more than an hour. They told him that the village had been attacked about three hours earlier, leaving only a few survivors. Acting on orders, the scouts had remained outside the village until the Ranger unit could arrive. From their observations so far, all that remained were a few old people, some young children, and lots of dead bodies. They told him it was bad. They had crept close enough to hear the cries of the few remaining souls, smelling the faint remnants of automatic weapon fire still lingering in the damp air. The scouts also told him that there was sign everywhere and that the Serbs had left in a northerly direction.

As a precautionary move, the lieutenant had established the observation post until he was sure there were no militiamen waiting in ambush. Satisfied that there were no hostiles remaining, he signaled his men to move into the village. The scouts were the first in, as always. They moved like ghosts through the streets, almost unnoticed by the remaining old people and children wailing over their loved ones. The Rangers followed, clearly still not used to the indiscriminate and merciless slaughter. The carnage was everywhere and totally senseless. It was beyond terrible.

Crowe, the Lakota, moved from house to house, his right flank covered by his partner, Will Price. Price was the Navajo and his tribal name was Atsa, or Eagle. The scout was born and raised in Arizona on the Navajo Nation. Crowe's left was covered by the Seminole, Isaac Factor, who looked more African than Seminole. Factor's ancestors had taken flight from slavery in Georgia and were eventually assimilated into the Seminole tribes of Florida.

As Crowe moved to the doorway of what looked like a schoolhouse, Isaac moved to the opposite side of the door, motioning with his eyes that he was ready to enter. Both men moved in unison, covering both sides of the room simultaneously. As they moved stealthily into the semi-dark structure, Price took their place in the doorway, his eyes scanning the room like a bird of prey.

What the scouts saw stopped them in their tracks. The room was littered with the bodies of women and children. Most of them had been shot multiple times; others were smashed against the wall, skulls crushed and grey matter splattered over the whitewashed walls behind them. The coppery smell of blood and the odor of feces permeated the room, causing Crowe to look questioningly at his Seminole partner. Factor's eyes flashed back at Crowe's, and the men gradually lowered their guns as they slowly moved into the hellish scene.

Factor crouched over the body of a woman who appeared to have been about twenty years old, her clothing ripped from her body and her breasts sliced crudely from her chest. It was clear that this had been done while she was still alive. His gaze moved to her face, expecting to see horror in her face, but found that her eyes had been gouged from their sockets. Looking around, this type of mutilation had been repeated on all the victims in one way or another. A cold sheen of sweat covered his jet-black face and arms. He looked back in distress to Will Price in the doorway, but Price was looking outward, covering their backs.

The Seminole rose and continued to walk slowly among the bodies, his eyes coldly watching for movement, interrupted by occasional glances at Crowe as they both silently took in the bloodbath at their feet. A faint sound came from the back of the room, rising from a pile of bodies near the back door. Both men froze and raised their weapons, separating to opposite sides of the room and moving forward at the same time. As they neared the corner, a small boy looked up from underneath the bodies of three dead children. His eyes were wide and unblinking in fear, moving back and forth from one scout to the other.

Ethan slowly placed his rifle on the floor. "Dobar dan" (*hello*), Crowe addressing the boy in his own tongue. "Ne boj se mali" (*Don't be afraid, little one*).

The boy tried to shrink deeper under the bodies surrounding him. Factor stopped a few feet away and let Crowe make the approach, watching the Sioux move toward the trembling figure like he would a wild mustang on the Dakota plains. Crowe stooped in front of the child and smiled quietly, letting the boy's pulse slow. After several minutes, Crowe extended his hand slowly and gently toward the tiny, pale face under a mop of thick, black hair. The boy's eyes flicked back worriedly at the tall black scout standing silently in the background. He waited for a breath and then pulled his tiny arm from under a bloody girl lying across his body. Slowly he reached for Crowe's coppery hand, surrendering himself to the strength of the scout.

Crowe pulled the boy gently into his arms and held him fast, rubbing his back slowly. The boy began to weep quietly…then uncontrollably, his frail little body wracked with sobs as his grief began to flow. Crowe whispered in the boy's ear in Lakota, forgetting where he was, "Hoksi, hecheto aloe" (*It is over, child*). Crowe looked silently over the boy's shoulder at Factor, both wondering again what was wrong with these white people who waged war on women and children. Price stood silently watching his brothers, his M4 rifle held across his chest. The flat planes of his Navajo visage were devoid of emotion. His eyes calmly scanned the doors and windows, his job always to watch their backs.

CHAPTER 2

One week later, Central Bosnia

The Ranger platoon had settled into a shelled-out village fifty kilometers northeast of Sarajevo, its former occupants long since displaced or dead. They had arrived at the abandoned little hamlet after finishing a week back at their base to resupply and wait for orders. Most suspected, however, that the delay was more about the generals and politicians deciding what to do in the face of the ongoing ethnic cleansing that was going on all around them. The current mandate of passive peacekeeping was doing nothing to stop the bloodshed. The atmosphere at the base had become oppressive. The mandate of non-intervention was playing havoc with morale, and the NATO commanders on the ground were aware that something had to change very soon.

The three scouts were resting on the front porch of an abandoned stone house at the edge of the village. It was quiet out here. The only sound to be heard was that of a cuckoo calling to her mate, unaware of the human tragedy that surrounded her. The men had all refrained from going inside the house out of respect for the former occupants. Isaac Factor sat on a rough-hewn bench to the left of the front door. He worked methodically on his rifle, running a cloth back and forth over the length of the barrel and talking at the same time. "What do you think the LT will do if we run into these Serbs again this time out?"

Crowe looked up from his spot in the doorway, where he sat leaning against the threshold, sharpening his buffalo hunter knife.

"Who knows? I guess HQ will decide that. How do you suppose the boss described that last village to the folks back there?"

Factor just shook his head and continued to work on his weapon. He then called over to Price, who was leaning against a post on the far end of the porch, eyes looking outward. "Hey, Will, I think you can take a rest. We're safe here. These assholes would never attack a town with real live soldiers. They prefer women and children, right?"

Price paused a second for one last scan of their perimeter and then turned to his friends, speaking directly to Crowe, "Ethan, you've spent more time with the whites than we have. What makes these people do this stuff to one another?"

Crowe thought about an answer, but Price continued, "I keep hearing this is about religion. Is this all part of the "Jesus Road" that they talk about at the mission schools? How can that road lead to this?"

Crowe listened and just shook his head silently. *This was a lot of talk from Will. The Navajo rarely spoke and almost never shared his inner thoughts.*

Will's face took on a stony cast. "You know, my father was taken by the whites back in fifty-four. He was eight years old. They just snatched him while he was tending sheep on the rez. His folks were dead already. His father had been killed on Iwo Jima, and he was being raised by his aunt and uncle. He told me that, one day, he was walking down a dirt road on the rez when a government truck pulled up and told him to get in. They took him straight to a mission school and never once asked for his uncle's permission. It was eight months before the family finally tracked my father down. By then he had been forced to take a white name."

Will was quite animated now, enough to get the full attention of Crowe and Factor.

Price continued, "His uncle went to the authorities, but they told him it was all legal. They were 'mainstreaming Indian children' per federal guidelines. The Bureau of Indian Affairs and the churches felt the only way for us to survive was to make us white. They used to say, 'Kill the Indian but save the man.' My father stayed at the school for four years. He hated it. They told him our people were savages and that they needed to learn the ways of the Europeans. Hell, they used to beat him if he spoke our language."

Crowe interrupted, "What? You can't be serious. Hell, the Navajo code talkers helped win the war in the Pacific. Nine years later, they wanted to wipe out the language? Your grandfather died a code talker."

Will just nodded yes, clearly remembering his father's words and angered at the irony and stupidity of it all.

The three men remained silent for a time, Factor finally speaking up, "Well?" The Seminole spoke with half a grin on his face, "Jesus, Will, you gonna tell us what happened?"

Price looked back at his friend. "Yeah, my dad stayed at the school, became white, and eventually ran for governor of Arizona! What do you think happened?"

Factor and Crowe both broke into quiet laughter. Crowe then added, "And I guess you were offered a spot with the diplomatic corps due to your chatty nature. Seriously, what happened?"

"Well, my father finally ran away when he was thirteen. His uncle had arranged to pick him up on the highway leading to the school, and they drove straight back to the rez. Believe it or not, nobody even looked for him again. But he rarely spoke English after that. When he did, it was only in the army. After he got back from the army, he only spoke Navajo."

The scouts turned in unison to the sound of a lone soldier running up to the porch. Struggling to catch his breath, the messenger finally spoke, "The lieutenant wants to see you guys ASAP. He's been trying to reach you on the radio. He's down at the church or whatever they call those things over here." The boy, an E-2, looked at the scouts expectantly, apparently thinking that they would jump to their feet and follow him at full speed.

Crowe nodded to the soldier, "Thanks, Private. We'll be along presently."

The private hesitated.

"I *said* we will be along in a minute." Crowe waved him away with his left hand.

All three of the men quietly and efficiently gathered their gear and readied themselves to go back into action, leaving the stone house as one, as always.

CHAPTER 3

The sky was thick with foul-smelling pollution from the power plants and factories that still burned unrefined coal twenty-four hours a day. The sulfuric mist hung above the valley to mingle with wood smoke and the damp air, enveloping every part of the countryside. One had to wonder how the Bosnians lived past the age of fifty. The combination of the dirty air and their incessant smoking should have put them all in their graves by thirty. Sadly, after three years of ethnic cleansing, the local population was numb. Dirty air was the least of their problems.

Crowe stepped across the threshold of the small stone building. The roof was almost gone, broken tiles and loose boards dangling above the heads of the men and women working in the makeshift command post. The lieutenant was standing over a small wooden table surrounded by two sergeants and some clerks. He was pointing out the location of the next probable target of the Serb militiamen. He looked up at the three scouts as they approached.

"Good to see you, men. Are you provisioned and ready to move out?"

Crowe nodded in the affirmative, "Good to go, sir." Factor and Price remained silent.

"About three hours ago, a British spotter plane reported Serb militia moving along a road just four klicks northeast of us. They think it's a group of Skorpions, maybe the same assholes who slaughtered the village last week. We're not sure which direction they were heading because the road splits just a bit north of where they were spotted." Lieutenant Evans returned his gaze to the tabletop and resumed his briefing. "According to this map, there are only two villages in the direction that they were headed. One is about twenty klicks to the left along this road, the other about fifteen klicks along the right fork, but it goes through some elevation and would be a tougher slog for them. Of course, we won't know for sure until you men pick up their trail." The lieutenant nodding to the scouts.

The young officer paused a moment, looking at Crowe for confirmation. Crowe nodded politely. "Sir, we're set to go. I guess we'll know pretty quick which way they went. But if you want my opinion, I'd say they'll take the easier road. The only thing these guys seem to want to spend energy on is killing people."

The lieutenant let out a breath and looked at his team. "They want us to find these assholes and bring them in peaceably. That's a tall order. I don't know what to say really... We need to watch ourselves on this. You scouts are to follow, but you are not to engage unless you come under fire. If you locate them, just keep me posted and wait. We won't be far behind. Understood?"

"Yes, sir." Crowe looked at the lieutenant's three young sergeants who were also probably thinking about how this would play out. Price and Factor were already moving toward the doorway when Crowe asked the lieutenant, "That it?"

The lieutenant nodded, "Watch yourselves, all of you," his voice raised so the other two scouts could hear as well.

*****

Lieutenant Evans stood in front of his platoon. He had assembled them soon after the scouts had begun to track the Skorpions. Headquarters had confirmed their orders to track down these militiamen and to force them to surrender to NATO forces. *Fucking unbelievable. Did they really think he could peacefully convince a group of homicidal maniacs to come peacefully back to a prison camp?* He sighed to himself, knowing he had his orders and his rules of engagement. For their part, the men looked pissed. They were itching for a fight. These were Rangers, the best soldiers in the world. They were not policemen. *He would have to keep a tight leash on them.*

“Listen up, men. HQ wants us to get on these combatants and run them to ground. They have about a six-hour lead on us, but I doubt they have gone all that far. I sent out the scouts an hour ago, and we should be hearing something soon. They radioed that they were following a track going northeast from here,” the lieutenant said as he pointed over his left shoulder. “Intel indicates these are probably the same group that slaughtered the village last week. We will assume they’re correct and prepare accordingly.”

One hand went up. “Sir, we gonna have a shootin’ war with these guys?”

“We fire only when fired upon, Ranger. You know that. But we’re going to be ready for what comes our way. You’ve all seen what they’re capable of, and I’m not losing any of our people for some dickhead back at HQ. Make sure you have plenty of ammo and be ready to move out in fifteen.”

*****

Crowe and the scouts moved quickly and silently across the rugged terrain, connected through their throat microphones and their ability to communicate with hand signals when needed. They had a natural trot that allowed them to run for hours at a pace that could close the gap on any man or creature not aware that they were being pursued. This trail had been easy to pick up. A group of men, led by two small trucks, was moving leisurely due northeast from the scene of the last massacre. Upon receiving their new orders, the trackers had not hesitated for a second and had begun their pursuit quickly and silently.

Crowe knelt in the roadway, studying the tracks, flanked by Price and Factor, whose eyes moved continuously over the landscape. The sign had been clear in the moist ground, and it was obvious that the Serbian thugs had no fear of being followed or confronted. They had no rear guard and walked like they owned the entire countryside. Crowe looked up from the road and looked at the dark green of the mountains surrounding them. In spite of his superb conditioning, the filthy air was making him sick to his stomach. Crowe had spent a lot of time among the whites, first at school and then in the army. But he had never seen white people live like this. *The land was beautiful, but what had they done to it? Where was the wild game?*

As the scouts followed the Serbians' trail, they found it littered with items that had been stolen from previous villages. Crowe stopped once and picked up a small golden amulet with a blue lapis crescent. He held it in his hand, the thin gold chain draped over his wrist. *These aren't soldiers. They're psychopaths.* He looked up quickly to notice that Isaac had kept going without a word as he passed Crowe, his dark eyes angrily searching the ground ahead. He looked across to his right and saw the stocky Navajo moving effortlessly ahead, showing no sign of fatigue. Ethan sighed and launched himself back into the pursuit.

*****

The Skorpion Kommandant sat in his Toyota, stopped in the middle of the muddy roadway. He looked through the movement of the windshield wipers at the tiny hamlet that lay ahead. He took his time, watching the unsuspecting peasants going about their daily chores. He was in no hurry, having traveled several klicks ahead of his soldiers. He surveyed what actually remained of the village. *Another filthy Muslim shithole.* The small group of buildings had already been shelled extensively by Serb artillery. None of the houses looked to be in one piece. He shook his head and sat back to wait for his men to catch up. His driver, a huge, thickly built man with greasy, long black hair and a scorpion tattooed on the left side of his neck, sat quietly beside him. The Kommandant had seen him in action and knew the man incapable of mercy. He was loyal, without conscience, and exactly what the Serbian strongman wanted at his side.

The driver, sensing the Kommandant's thoughts, reached behind the seat and brought out a bottle of *rakija*, the popular "moonshine" of the region. Twisting the cap, he brought it to his lips and took a long pull from the dirty bottle. He loved the way it burned the back of his throat and warmed his belly. He then took a long drag on his Russian cigarette, blew out a steady stream of smoke, and handed the bottle to his Kommandant. They would wait for the men to arrive. No sense in taking any unnecessary chances.

*****

The scouts came upon the Skorpions seven hours into their track. They watched them as they walked in small groups along the narrow dirt road. There were approximately thirty of them, ranging in age from sixteen to forty. Most had shaved heads although some wore their unwashed hair long, falling unkempt over the collars of their military jackets. None of them were clean-shaven, and most of them looked like they were walking off a two-day drunk. The American scouts had smelled the Serbs and their cigarette smoke long before they had seen them. These Skorpions were not in a combat patrol formation, if they even knew what that meant, and appeared to believe that they were invincible. They talked loudly and joked among themselves, some chugging from clear bottles of what appeared to be alcohol. The trucks were nowhere to be seen.

Ethan and his men stopped together to watch the slow progress of the Serbs and spoke in quiet whispers. Crowe leaned into the ear of his black friend, "Take the sat phone and backtrack a bit to call the LT. Let him know we have contact and see what he wants us to do. Will and I will stay with them. When you come back, take the other side of the road so we can cover both flanks."

Factor nodded silently and moved out, not another word said. Crowe felt him leave while continuing to watch the Skorpions move steadily forward. He knew there was pure evil in this world but had never before seen it walking. He tried to relax his mind, but it would not come. He froze at the sound of sudden gunfire. One of the Serbs was firing his machine gun at sheep in the pasture on the side of the road, the others laughing at his poor marksmanship. Eventually the thug found his mark, and thirty sheep fell to the ground in clouds of blood and wool. Price closed his eyes and held his breath for a moment, the senseless slaughter seeming to hit him suddenly. His father's words coming to him, *All life is sacred and cannot be replaced.*

A series of shouts from the Serbs brought his gaze back to the scene on the road. A slender middle-aged woman had been discovered hiding behind a rock in the field where she had been tending the flock of sheep. Two of the Skorpions were now dragging her back to the road over the bloody lumps of wool that had once been her sheep. When she was pulled into the midst of the militiamen, her shirt was ripped from her body and several of the men began pulling at the hem of her dress, mimicking the motion of sex with their hips. One of the leaders suddenly stepped into the melee and somehow got the group moving forward. The two men, not wanting to surrender their prize, dragged the sobbing woman along with them as they rejoined the group.

As the Skorpions resumed their trek along the rutted dirt path, Crowe and Price also moved out, silently following the rabble as they moved through the bleak countryside.

*****

The Kommandant and the driver had been waiting for an hour when they finally heard the approach of their men. They looked over their shoulders simultaneously to see the men pushing and pulling a captive female toward their position. The woman was not young, probably forty. The Kommandant snickered and watched the scene unfold. *Where did they find this one?* He smirked as one of his men dragged the woman by her long greying hair as she struggled futilely to break free and keep her balance at the same time. In answer to her efforts, the Serb pulled her roughly toward him, licking at her face, her screams only inciting laughter from the rest of the Skorpions. The struggle finally caused her to fall, only to have him viciously kick her as she lay on the ground.

The driver commented offhandedly, "Looks like the boys have been at the bottle."

A long sigh of cigarette smoke flowed from the Kommandant. "Let them have their fun."

*****

The militiamen came shuffling to a stop, gathering informally around the Kommandant's vehicle. The woman was once again pushed roughly to the ground while most of the men looked at the village ahead.

The Kommandant got out of his truck and walked to where the woman lay sprawled on the ground. "What is this?" he said, snickering and nudging her legs with the toe of his boot. The woman sobbed quietly, her tears mixing with a steady stream of blood seeping from her mouth.

"Thought it would be better to fuck her than her sheep." The one they called Vlade smirked.

"We'll set up for the night in the village. Tell the men to stay sober. Some of those UN soldier boys might be nearby."

One of the men blurted, "Who the fuck cares! The last time it was just a bunch of those Dutch faggots and they ran away."

The Kommandant smiled quietly, remembering the young boys that the UN had sent out there to keep the peace. *What a fucking joke they were. No match for his Serbian boys.* He then looked around and shouted, "Move out and set up down in the village!" Walking back to the truck and over his shoulder, he said, "And get rid of that fucking Muslim bitch!"

The trucks and the men moved out in unison, slowly working their way down the bumpy road, the vehicle rocking through the many ruts and holes. A hundred meters along the way, the Kommandant heard a single shot from behind him. He smirked to himself with satisfaction.

*****

Crowe watched as the Skorpions moved forward toward the village. The woman captive had been thrown to the ground and shot in the head by the one that had been dragging her and abusing her.

Isaac had returned, and the three scouts were now deployed just above the village, spread out in a semicircle just south of the road that led into the small group of buildings.

Crowe's voice crackled in his earpiece. "Isaac, are you seeing this? They just offed the girl."

The Navajo quietly said, "Yeah."

Crowe replied, "How many civilians down in that village?"

Price looked down to the group of buildings. He knew he had seen several old people and at least ten children playing in what remained of a schoolyard. "Too many."

The Seminole added, "The platoon is at least an hour back."

Crowe, knowing what they would have to do, did not respond right away to his partner.

Isaac repeated matter-of-factly, "They're not going to get here in time."

*****

Lieutenant Evans listened to the report from Crowe on his radio. He looked over at the sergeant, speaking in a low tone, "Fuck."

The sergeant's brows arched. "How bad?"

"It's going to kick off now. They're going to massacre the village. We can't get there in time. We're still forty-five minutes out."

The lieutenant looked at his soldiers, who had fallen out for five while he communicated with the scouts. He called out to his sergeants, "Mount up. We have to move out double-quick. Tell the men this is the real deal."

One of the sergeants looked back at the lieutenant. "What about the scouts? Will they wait?"

"I told them to wait. I don't know what they'll do. Hell, I don't know what I would do."

The second sergeant looked questioningly at the lieutenant. "What about HQ?"

"Let's just catch up to those scouts, Sergeant."

*****

Dusk was falling quickly. The cloud cover and light rain further decreased the visibility. Crowe watched as the Serbs moved toward the village. It was obvious that they did not expect any resistance, their arrogant demeanor that of those used to having their way. There was no military discipline in the ranks. Clearly, they had never seen battle with seasoned soldiers. Crowe exhaled through his nose in disgust. *No, they were much more comfortable killing women and children.*

As the Kommandant's truck passed the first stone house, two teenagers and a woman, who might have been their mother, ran from the shelter of what was probably an outhouse. One of the lead Serbs watched them stumbling across the grassy field, took a long draw on his cigarette, and then flicked the stub into the wind. He then unslung his weapon and swept a long round of bullets across the backs of the fleeing peasants. His bullets missed all but one of the group, but it caused the remainder to stumble and lose their momentum. He quickly changed magazines and emptied another thirty rounds into the survivors, killing them in their tracks. The Skorpions, to a man, were transfixed, watching the scene play out like they would a football match. When the last of the peasants crumpled to the ground, they walked ahead like nothing had happened, some chiding the shooter for needing two magazines.

Crowe looked at his team. They were spread out over a two-hundred-meter distance to the rear of the Skorpion militiamen. The scouts were all but invisible to anyone but Crowe. Crowe and Price had painted their faces black, like all Rangers, but some traditional colors were also evident as a tribute to their heritage. Factor needed no face paint. His black countenance blended perfectly into the rest of his camo. Truly these men could have been pulled through time from the great tribal warriors of the past. For a brief moment, Crowe felt an intense pride in his people—in their ways and in their sense of duty. Quickly, he took a deep breath, knowing this decision would be problematic. They had been told to stand by and not engage. If he waited, everyone in this village would die. They would be terrible deaths.

Crowe spoke quietly into his throat mike. "If we wait, they're all going to die."

No reply on the radio from his team, only silence, the scouts just looking ahead at the village.

Crowe, "I can't let this happen again, but I can't ask you to do this if you don't want to. The boss is not going to be happy. Nobody is going to be happy."

Factor was the first to respond, "Fuck it. I can't go back to the world and tell everyone I just watched this shit."

Crowe acknowledged and waited a minute. "Will?"

A silent pause, then Will spoke quietly, "Let's do it."

Crowe scanned the scene in front of him. The Skorpions were moving into the village, entering houses and chasing people into the streets. Scattered gunfire could now be heard as the thugs began their killing once again.

Crowe said, "Let's close in tight and move in together. We'll take the row of buildings on the left. A large group of them is on that side of the street, and we can face them first. With all the shooting, they shouldn't notice us hitting them in the beginning. Maybe we can cut the odds a bit."

By the time Crowe was done speaking, Price and Factor had already tightened the formation and were ready to move forward. All three had taken their assault rifles from the slings on their backs. None of them used a fixed bayonet as it affected their accuracy and hindered their ability to move their weapons quickly in close quarters. They did, however, all have very lethal bladed weapons. Each had a personal preference, and each wore them where they could get to them quickly in close combat. In addition to Glock pistols in holsters in the small of their backs, extra magazines were secured in a variety of pockets in their combat fatigue trousers and their load-bearing vests.

The scouts moved quickly into the village. None of the Serbs were watching their backs. *Why would they?* Reaching the first house, Crowe moved to the rear doorway, listening to screams from inside. He glanced out at the garden to his left and saw a Serb hunched over a young woman, moving rhythmically against her while she was bent over a small hay cart. Crowe silently moved his rifle across his back and drew his buffalo skinner bowie from its sheath hanging at the back of his neck. Within seconds, he grabbed the hair of the militiaman, pulling his head backward. The Serb, in the throes of passion, was completely unaware of the Lakota's approach until he felt the blade cut deeply into his throat. In one fraction of a second, Crowe had severed the man's throat from ear to ear. The Serb had suddenly quit moving and the girl had frozen in place, assuming he had climaxed and was finished with her. She felt a flush of warm fluid wash across her back, and then the weight of the man was suddenly lifted from her backside.

The girl slid over onto her side and saw the dark stranger with the long hair and painted face wiping his knife on his pant leg. She was in complete shock, wondering if this was an avenging angel like the ones she had heard the old women speak about. She clumsily pulled at the remnants of her clothes, trying to somehow hide her nakedness and her shame, at the same time never taking her eyes off the face of the dark angel. He paused for seconds, a certain sadness in his eyes, and then turned back toward the house, sliding his rifle from his shoulder as he moved quickly across the yard.

Factor reached a side window and observed two Skorpions put a pistol to the head of an old woman and splatter her brains against the kitchen wall. Her husband was held firmly by the second Serb, crying loudly until his wife slid down the wall in a stream of blood. He collapsed against the grizzled man who was holding him, only to have his throat slit by that same monster. As the old man dropped to the floor, the Serb bent down to slice off the man's ear. He moved the knife blade toward the man's wrinkled old head and then suddenly collapsed as a round from Factor's rifle penetrated his skull, only to be joined by his partner, who was hit with two rounds center mass, exploding his heart in that instant.

Crowe started to enter the house when he saw the two Serbs hit the ground from Factor's rifle fire. Isaac had fired through the glass and hit his targets with perfect accuracy. Once inside, Crowe was joined by Factor while they looked for additional gunmen. The house cleared, Factor started for the back door, where he found Crowe paused in the doorway. Just then, two additional Skorpions came around the far side of the house. Crowe looked up, but almost too late. As he brought his rifle to bear, both Serbs went down under a barrage of bullets from Price, who had shot them from his covering position. Crowe looked gratefully over at the Navajo, only to see Price nodding toward more shooting in the next house. The three scouts moved along the rear walls of the buildings, killing every militiaman that found in the open. They had put down at least eight and had not yet been detected, their fire blending in with the chaos of the Skorpions' massacre of civilians.

Crowe and the team had decided to hit the easy targets first as each house entry was difficult and the odds would be against them. They now had to decide whether to hit the main body, which was in the middle of the street milling around the two Serb trucks, or to try to rescue some of the innocents being tortured in the houses on the opposite side of the road. A series of desperate bloodcurdling screams emanating from a soot-stained stucco house directly across from their vantage point made their decision for them.

*****

The lieutenant could hear the gunfire ahead. Crowe had told him on the radio that they were going to engage. He didn't know what to say when the scout had informed him. He had heard the Serbs' guns and the screams over the radio. All he could do was tell Crowe that they would be there as soon as possible.

Now they were almost there, and it sounded like the village was just over the next rise. He raised his hand, and the platoon came to a stop quietly and efficiently. He motioned for the sergeants to gather up and instructed them to form up on two flanks and to get their people ready for a firefight. Two Rangers had already been sent forward to recon the situation.

The lieutenant said, "We move out in three. We'll stop below the ridge until we get intel back from our point men. Don't forget that we have three scouts down there. They should be easy to spot. They sure don't look anything like these assholes."

Each squad was assigned a SAW gunner. They carried M249 machine guns that fired 5.56 mm ammo. Each SAW gun carried a hundred-round ammo belt fed from a canvas bag. The gunner carried an additional thirty-round backup magazine. Each gunner also had a soldier assigned to carry additional ammo bags and a spare barrel for the gun if it heated up. The gunners were usually newly minted sergeants big and strong enough to haul the heavy, high-capacity machine gun. The lieutenant sent them forward with their ammo bearers in advance of the platoon, telling them to spread out along the ridge and to establish their fields of fire. The lieutenant looked ahead, willing himself to see beyond the rise in the road. He watched as his SAW gunners trotted to the ridge. *We are going to light you assholes up if we can just catch a few more minutes time.*

*****

Crowe and his men gathered behind the corner of the last house. Will took two quick *look-sees* around the corner and turned back to Crowe and Factor. "I think we can make it across if we space ourselves out."

Crowe nodded in agreement. "I'll go first. Isaac, you and Will follow at thirty-second intervals. Hopefully, with all this gunfire and smoke, they won't notice us."

As Crowe moved to the corner of the house, the lieutenant was in his earpiece. "Crowe, are you out there? Crowe?"

Crowe reached for his throat, fingers pressing tightly against the mike. "Here, boss. We are in the village on the far end of the street on the east side, about one klick from the ridge."

The lieutenant replied, "We're here now. We're just above the rise and setting up. What's the situation now?"

"We put some bad guys down on our side of the street, but they've already shot a lot of civilians. We need to get across the street ASAP. These assholes are killing people like fucking crazy."

"What's left of their force?"

"We still got lots of bad guys, boss. At least ten in the street at the trucks and maybe ten more in the houses on the west side. I think we've KIA'd about eight on this side of the street. It's a cluster fuck for sure."

The lieutenant had moved above the village and was assessing his attack plan. To Crowe, he instructed, "Wait in place for three. We are going to move together on this. The platoon will take the main force in the street, and we will flank you and give you cover from the rear of the west end."

Crowe could hear screams in earnest from the far side of the road. He looked worriedly at his partners and acknowledged, "Roger that."

The lieutenant checked his two flanks and got a thumbs-up from the two sergeants. Into his mike, he instructed "On my signal, commence firing from the SAWs. Scouts, move out when the firing starts. Squads, move out on my signal."

Crowe and Factor checked their weapons out of habit. They counted their magazines and readied for their dash across the street, Price continuously watching their backs, as natural as breathing for him.

*****

The Kommandant leaned against the side of the battered Toyota, drawing long and hard on his cigarette, savoring the rush as the smoke filled his lungs. He paused a few seconds and released the smoke in a prolonged, steady stream into the surrounding air. He had been holding his own personal court in the street as his Skorpions dragged men and women to where he stood and threw them on the ground at his feet. His machine pistol was resting on the hood of the truck, and his Soviet-made Tokarev pistol rested in a black-leather shoulder holster. The rig made him feel like a gangster from a movie he had once seen back in Belgrade.

He watched as one of his men violently dragged and kicked a peasant from the small government building on the west side of the street. The man wore an old wool coat, two sizes too big for his tiny frame. He looked to be about fifty, but who knew and who cared? *These people are shit*, he thought as he reached across his chest and fingered the Tokarev. The soldier, a tall, rangy Serb, was half laughing as he deposited the old man in front of the Kommandant.

The Skorpion leader looked down with disdain. "What the fuck is this, a pile of old clothes?" chuckling at his own joke and tapping ashes from his cigarette onto the prostrate figure at his feet.

"He says he's the mayor. He wants to see someone in charge," the militiaman replied mockingly, wiping away the old man's spittle from his coat in disgust.

The Kommandant looked down at the man lying in the mud at his feet. "Well, here I am, Mr. Mayor. What can I do for you?"

The Mayor looked up sideways at the man speaking to him. He started to say something, but his head hurt too badly. The young Skorpion had kicked him in the head several times, and it seemed to be confusing things for him. He started to form a sentence, his lips quivering uncontrollably, "I…"

The young Serb interrupted him by kicking him viciously in the small of the back, sending shock waves all the way to his brain. He screamed in agony and fell back onto his back, writhing in pain.

*****

The lieutenant looked down on the street. He was trying to decide when to open up with the SAWs when a man in a tattered suit was dragged into the middle of the street. The Serb commander seemed to be questioning him, but another militiaman was kicking the shit out of the old man at the same time. He had to wait; he spoke quietly into his throat mike, "Hold… Let's see what they are going to do with this civilian."

*****

Isaac Factor continued to pop his head around the corner, wondering what was taking so long. He could hear the screams and gunshots from across the street. He looked back at Crowe impatiently for the fourth time. Price kept watch to their rear; there was no guarantee that they had eliminated the threats behind them.

Crowe said into his radio, "Boss, we about there?"

"Hold."

Crowe exhaled through his nose and stared out at the horizon, pissed.

Another long minute passed. Crowe once again spoke into his mike, "Lieutenant, let us go. We can make it across. We wait any longer, they'll all be dead anyway."

Silence back on the radio. A pause, then, "Go then. Watch your asses."

Crowe led the team, spaced about twenty seconds apart. They moved slowly and smoothly, no jerky movements to catch someone's eye. The three scouts reached the cover of the closest building on the west side of the road. They leaned against the wall and listened just to the right side of a window, the glass thin and rippled from a time long gone. Two shots rang out, with quiet sobbing from someplace in the room. Crowe looked cautiously through the dirty glass and saw four Serbs moving purposefully around the room. An old couple lay dead on the floor, and a thirty-something woman cowered in the corner, holding a five-year-old girl protectively in her arms. She stared in horror at what was left of her loved ones, covering the eyes of her daughter in hopes of holding the nightmare at bay.

Isaac moved quickly without a word, sliding along the wall and moving to the rear of the house and a back door which lead to the room inside. Price moved to the corner of the house with a clear line of sight between Crowe and Factor. He held up his hand and counted down, three, two, one. At zero, Crowe threw himself through the side window. Simultaneously, Factor came through the doorway, his rifle sending rounds into the chests of the first two Serbs he saw. Crowe, flying through the broken glass, rolled and came up firing his Glock, placing a round in the forehead of one Skorpion and firing four rounds into the midsection of the second.

The exchange was over in seconds. The woman remained motionless, trembling and in shock, unable to comprehend what had just happened and who these new men were.

*****

The Kommandant leaned down to the Mayor, snarling, "When were the soldiers here last?" Now screaming into the man's face, "When?"

The trembling old man could not answer. He didn't even know what the man was yelling about. *What soldiers?* He tried hard to think. *Had there been soldiers? If his back would just stop hurting so.* He spoke softly, "My name is Nedim. I don't understand your question. Could you just give me a moment?"

The Kommandant pulled up savagely on the man's thick, grey hair, forcing his prisoner's jaws to slacken. His blue steel Tokarev pistol came out of the holster and into the mayor's face. The Serb suddenly pushed the muzzle violently into the captive's mouth, pulling back on the trigger as he did so. Seething, he spit, "I will only ask you one more time."

The Mayor could do nothing but make a feeble, raspy sound, his broken teeth choking him as he struggled to breathe. He tried to look up at his tormentor but could not focus, then a burst of heat in his mouth and darkness.

*****

The Serb commander let the old man fall to the ground, pulling his Tokarev back to wipe the bloody barrel on the sleeve of his jacket.

Lieutenant Evans witnessed the execution in the street. He turned and gave the command to his SAW gunners, "Light 'em up!" his face like stone. The decision made.

The center of the street became a free-fire zone. The SAWs decimated the Serbs. The trucks were destroyed. Ten Skorpions fell in the hail of the two hundred rounds that fed from the ammo belts on the top of the ridge. The remainder of the militia men either took cover in the buildings or under the trucks. The Kommandant and his driver managed to take refuge behind a stone horse trough. Those that chose the trucks died for their troubles.

*****

The Navajo scanned the room, assessing further threats. Crowe and Factor were already moving out the back door toward a small stone cottage to the rear of their position. They observed a Serb walking out of the cottage, a makeshift bag of valuables over his shoulder and a machine pistol in the other. Not wanting to alert anyone following the Serb, Crowe closed the distance, diving forward and, coming up with his bowie knife, thrusting directly into the throat and voice box of the Serb. Factor sped past him, falling on his belly in the doorway with his rifle scanning the dimly lit room. Nothing.

Factor nodded all clear, and they both turned to the rear of the next building. At the same moment, the Skorpions started to empty from the back doors and windows of the row of houses, shooting to their rear, in obvious retreat from the Rangers' heavy machine gun fire. Crowe looked to his left as the SAW gun went silent. His Ranger company was now moving rapidly down the hill and into the village. They were firing on any Skorpion that moved, dropping many who were so busy running that they could not effectively return fire toward the Americans.

Crowe and Factor took cover behind a low stone wall and started to engage the fleeing contingent of Serbs. The monsters were no longer predators but now the prey, fleeing like cowards before the Rangers. Suddenly, three men burst from a building about one hundred meters to the scouts' left flank. The Serbs were firing for effect as they ran toward the hills to the west of the village. Crowe could see that the lead runner was the Kommandant himself, along with his driver and one additional militiaman. They cleared the stone walls to the rear of the village and were moving low and quick toward a shallow ravine leading away from the action.

As the Serbs dropped into the cover of the ravine, Crowe and Factor left the protection of their wall and started to pursue, quickly and efficiently covering the ground leading to where the thugs had disappeared. As they approached the edge of the drop-off, they paused and, at the same time, heard automatic rifle fire from the building where Will had remained with the boy. Crowe looked questioningly to his rear and then at Factor.

Both scouts wanted to continue their pursuit, wanting the Kommandant to pay for this hell, but instead, Crowe reached to his throat mike. "Boss, we have the commander running west from the village. We can't pursue. Have to check our back. Can you assist?"

Not waiting for a response, Ethan and Isaac turned toward the source of the shots fired. *Where was Price?* Crowe called the Navajo on the radio. *No response.* Again, but louder, he repeated, "Will?" but was still met with silence.

As they cautiously approached the back wall of the building once again, Crowe listened to his flanks, hearing scattered rifle fire and the other chaotic noises that accompany the fog of war. *This thing was almost over. What a fucking mess.* Factor placed himself at the broken window, peeking quickly into the room, but was unable to see what was going on. Crowe readied himself in the doorway and then burst into the room in a low crouch, weapon ready and scanning.

It took Crowe a second to process what was happening. Will must have been surprised by a Skorpion who had come through the front door. A monstrously large Serb, probably close to seven feet tall, was holding Will Price against the wall. The woman and the screaming child were pressed with their backs to the wall on the floor next to Will. Crowe caught a brief glance of Will from around the massive right arm of the Serb. Resignation could be seen on Will's face. He had been shot; blood was spreading from the hole in his upper chest. As Crowe tried to decide if he had a shot, the Serb thrust a large knife into the gut of Will Price, ripping upward and taking what was left of Will's life in a painful dance.

As the Serb pulled the blade from the Navajo scout, he turned and sneered at Crowe. He held his arms out, his bloody bayonet dripping and howling a hoarse challenge directly at the Lakota, "I am Serb!" Crowe did not wait for the man to finish his declaration. He dropped his rifle on the floor and launched himself at the monster. He hit the giant at the neck, wrapping his arm around the man's throat and twisting in a quick circle to the left. His momentum slammed the Serb to the floor, forcing him to lose his grip on his knife. The man pulled instinctively at Crowe's arms to free himself from the choke hold, but to no avail. The Serb then placed his giant hands over his head and clawed at Crowe's face, doing everything he could to break Ethan's grip before he lost consciousness. Crowe held tight on the choke hold, but the giant was unbelievably strong. He was hit hard in the ribs by the man's elbow strike, causing him to lose his breath momentarily. Another blow struck him on the other side of his ribs, and he felt his grip loosening.

The Skorpion made a final push after the two elbow strikes, managing to break Crowe's hold on him and roll simultaneously to the right. He gained his feet and squared off to attack Crowe where he lay on the floor. He wasn't there. Crowe came at him from an angle, striking him with his fists at lightning speed. Ethan moved fluidly counterclockwise. Each of his blows struck the Serb's vital areas: the throat, the temples, and the solar plexus. The Serb was big enough that he could absorb a lot of punishment, but Crowe's attack was relentless.

Crowe stepped back after his hand assault and then moved quickly to deliver a lightning fast front kick to the groin, moving forward at the same time. Crowe reached up to the back of the head of the swarthy attacker and grabbed the back of his head with both hands, all the time moving his right knee to strike upward into the downturned face of the staggering giant. The man fell backward, stunned, and hit the floor so hard it shook the room.

Crowe was on the man, straddling him before the giant could even regain his focus on the room. To the Serb, Crowe was only a blur. Had he been able to focus, he would have seen the lean Sioux warrior pull his bowie from over his head and plunge it downward into his black heart. Crowe leaned heavily on the hilt of the blade, fiercely thinking of his friend Will and all the other poor people who had died here today. Looking up, he saw the eyes of the woman, wide-eyed from the battle she had just witnessed. Slowly the woman brought her sad eyes back to the lifeless body of her savior, Will Price.

A few moments later, the lieutenant entered the house, followed by his first sergeant, two Rangers, and a medic. Inside, some of his men were dragging out the bodies of the militiamen. In a corner stood the Seminole scout, a cold visage, a statue watching over the body of the Navajo. Behind Factor stood a small boy, taking comfort from the fierce protection the black scout offered.

On the floor, with Will Price's head in his lap, sat Crowe. He looked up at the lieutenant, pain etched in every feature of his handsome face. The lieutenant met his eyes and nodded knowingly. He spoke quietly to the medic, "Stay with him."

Crowe looked up at the medic, who was holding a blanket to place over Will's body. The medic hesitated, seeing that Crowe was making no effort to move out of the way. He seemed lost in thought. Then slowly, in a voice barely audible, he began to sing a Sioux death song.

Crowe remained motionless after the chant, slowly coming back from the rite. He felt something touch his left shoulder, a light sensation, moving gently back and forth. That touch was joined by two small hands pressed against his back. He looked up, puzzled by the sensations. Behind him was the woman and her child, both crying silently as they sought to ease the grief of this strange man whose words they could not understand.

CHAPTER 4

One month later, Butmir Base, Sarajevo

It was Sunday and the NATO base was relatively quiet. Most of the soldiers were making the most of their day of rest. Many hustled between the Norwegian, Italian, and American commissaries, all in search of products that reminded them of home. Some of the Americans, particularly the Southern boys, went to chapel. Bulgarian sentries still stared outward from behind sandbags and razor wire, stone-faced and humorless, while the Italians and the Spanish used the parade ground for their weekly *futbol* match.

Most of the men and women were part-time soldiers on short deployments, sent here as part of their country's NATO obligation. Few of them had ever seen combat and never would. They would remain safely behind the wire, happily going about their jobs, oblivious to the tragedy that surrounded them. For those men who had to fight, the world outside the walls was close and real. They stayed apart from the others, preferring their own company. They had no desire for chapel. For them, Sunday was just another day closer to the end of their deployment. If they gave any thought to religion, it was only in their letters home. God had left this place long ago.

Ethan sat on the ground, leaning against the outside wall of the American PX. To his left, Isaac sat on the edge of a concrete bench. Ethan stared straight ahead while Isaac's head hung low, his words spoken to the ground.

"It's hard to believe. In my mind he's still here. I always thought it would be one of us, not him."

Crowe kept staring into space, shaking his head. "Yeah. Will was always making sure nothing happened to us. Now I keep thinking that it was all one-sided. I should have been looking after him. It's just that it always seemed to work out the other way around."

Silence overtook the men, both lost in their own thoughts and memories. Crowe looked away, clearly trying to rein in his emotions.

Isaac broke the silence. "Would you do it again?"

"Do what?"

"Would you do this whole thing again? The army. Would you enlist, go through all this shit for the whites?"

Crowe thought about it for several beats. He sighed. "Yeah. I would. I didn't do this for the whites. The army was my way into the world. I like the old ways. You know that. But there isn't much use for those ways now. There sure wasn't much waiting for me back on the rez."

Factor grudgingly agreed with a nod. "I wonder if Will would feel the same way."

"Can't go down that road, brother. It is what it is. We can't turn back the clock. Will was a full-grown man. He knew why he was here. We talked about it."

"Yeah, but it sure seems a waste to lose that man for a bunch of folks we know nothing about. Folks that probably wouldn't do the same for our people."

Crowe nodded in agreement. "I know what you're saying, but I think its just about doing right. There's a lot of people back in that village, kids, old people, who are sure happy we were there."

"Well, I guess there's some truth in that. But I still wonder what I'm doing here."

Crowe chortled. "Almost past tense now. We go back to the world in ten days. Got some serious deciding to do."

"What you gonna do?"

Crowe paused a moment. "Well, I've got over a month of leave coming to me. As soon as we get settled back at Bragg, I figure to go out to Arizona to see Will's family. Wanna tell them about what kind of man he was, what he did."

"Count me in for that. Though I don't look forward to it. Are his folks still living?"

"Yeah. His mom lives on the Navajo rez, along with a younger brother and two sisters. The brother's name is Moses. Just a little guy now but he worshiped Will. Gonna be really hard on the kid, that's for sure."

Isaac shook his head sadly. "And then?"

"I was talking to the colonel. Says there's some spots opening up in the DIA. He thinks I'd be a good candidate."

Factor chuckled dryly. "What the hell is the DIA?"

"It's some kind of intelligence service. Sort of like the CIA but run by the military."

"You really want to stay in? Some kind of James Bond?" Factor raising his eyebrows questioningly.

Crowe smiled. "I don't know anything about James Bond, but for now it works for me. What about you? You staying in? I'm sure you could find a good spot, maybe even come with me."

Isaac exhaled loudly through his nose. "No. Sounds interesting but I'm going home. Back to my Glades. Miss those gators barking in the night."

Crowe smiled in agreement, and both men fell into an easy silence. After a few minutes, Isaac stood. "Well, I'm heading back to the barracks. Got some laundry to do and some letters to write. You coming?"

Crowe thought a minute. "No, I think I'll sit here awhile and enjoy the sun. It's been raining so long I almost forgot what clear skies look like."

Watching his friend walk away, Crowe considered Isaac's firm decision to go home and his own future. Inevitably, his thoughts returned to why he had chosen this life in the first place.

*****

As a child growing up on the Pine Ridge Reservation, life had been perfect. He had been happy and secure. His family was close and the entire tribe an extended family. As he grew older, he began to notice the poverty and despair that had been invisible to him as a young boy. He learned that life on the rez was a totally different than the white world outside the boundaries of Pine Ridge. He also came to realize that he would have to decide to enter the outside world or live a simple life on the rez.

His father had told him that his white blood would always stir within him and that he would have to find a balance. When Ethan had questioned what he meant, his father had smiled. "The ways of the Lakota and the whites are different. But I knew many white men during the war. They were not what I had expected. They felt happiness, pain, and sorrow just as we do. They longed for home just as I did. As for blood, theirs bled red just like ours."

Ethan had done his best to learn about both worlds. He had received a good education from the Jesuits, but much to their dismay, he had never chosen to embrace Christianity. The religious principles of his people were enough for him. After graduation, he had followed in the footsteps of his father and grandfather into the military. He had been a natural fit for the army and, later, the Delta Force, where at least ten Native American trackers were utilized in support of field ops worldwide. The special forces had recognized their extraordinary tracking and fighting skills, affording them special status within the elite unit.

When the US had finally committed troops to the Balkan war, Crowe and two of his fellow trackers had been seconded to the Ranger company to work as scouts. He had been in Bosnia for six months now, all that time spent scouting for the company out of Fort Bragg. Since his arrival, he had witnessed things he had never thought possible—all done in the name of religion. The last few weeks had been the worst. Two villages slaughtered by the Serbian strongmen. Innocent people senselessly raped and murdered and, worse yet, the loss of his friend Will Price. He pondered the sanity of this situation. If this was really about God, he could see no divine hand in any of this.

He didn't know which religious beliefs were being fought about out here or what the differences were that drove these people to such cruelty.

But in the end, these were white people's religions, and this would probably never make sense to him.

*****

Like all combat soldiers, he forced himself to stop thinking about it. *It is what it is.* He leaned back against the Quonset hut, closed his eyes, and let his mind travel back home to the Black Hills. He could hear the screech of a red-tailed hawk as it slowly rose from its perch in the dark forested mountains. He could see the wild mustangs racing across the plains, the wind lifting their manes and making them appear to fly across the endless prairies. Even the smell of the sweet grass came to him as he imagined himself sitting quietly on the high rocks, far from this poisonous yellow air and killing.

Thoroughly relaxed now, Crowe's thoughts were suddenly interrupted by a group of soldiers bursting loudly through the doors of the American PX. He opened his eyes and turned his head to find the source of the noise. Glancing briefly, he saw a group of young American soldiers talking animatedly. He dismissed them quickly and closed his eyes once again, hoping to return to his land of horses and hawks.

Sergeant Peet muscled his way through the door of the PX, handing two bottles of Scotch to one of his companions. He was busy bragging loudly to some of the men in his squad about the girl he had met in a bar back in Texas just before they had shipped out to Bosnia. His shaved head sat on a thick neck and massive shoulders, a tattoo of a rebel flag clearly visible on his left forearm. Private Smith, crouched and struggling to put the two bottles of Scotch into his pack and keep up with the group, looked up at Peet in awe.

As members of the 418th Transport Company out of Fort Hood, they had arrived only a month ago. Technically, this was the first combat deployment for all of them. Realistically, they would never be in harm's way. Their day was spent loading and unloading trucks, all done under the protection of the Bulgarians at the gate and the perimeter walls topped with concertina wire. This had worked out perfectly for Peet, who, in spite of all his bluster, was in no hurry to see any action. He would continue to live his life the way he had always lived it, letting his size and menacing persona see him through the day.

Off to their left, another member of their team exited the Italian PX, his left hand tucked firmly into the handle of a case of Heinekin. "Guys, wait for me." The young E-4 running to catch up to the group. "Hey, Sarge, when are we going to drink all this stuff?"

"We're going to bring it to the party the Norwegians are throwing Friday night. Should be lots of women. Have you seen some of those Italian nurses?" Peet enjoying the spotlight as always. "Maybe we can even find one of those big Bulgarian girls for Smith," Peet chiding the young soldier while putting a friendly hand on the kid's shoulder. "You don't mind a girl with a mustache, do you, Smitty?" Smith looked down, face flushed, smiling in silent admiration for the older, worldly sergeant.

The four soldiers, laughing and sharing an open package of Oreos, started across the grounds on the way back to their barracks. Sergeant Peet suddenly stopped, causing his followers to clumsily stumble into each other, one of them dropping his packages.

"Jesus, Sarge." The boy squatted to pick up his things.

Looking up, the young soldier saw that the sergeant was staring off to his right. He was focused on a soldier sitting on the ground with his arms resting on his knees, his back leaning against the wall of the PX. The soldier was dressed in American combat fatigues but wore leather moccasins and long black hair pulled back into a short ponytail. Peet sized up the seated figure for what seemed like an eternity.

Private Smith, following his sergeant's gaze, looked over at the seated figure and then said, "Sarge, what're you looking at?"

Peet ignored Smith. The hulking sergeant had grown up dirt-poor in west Texas. He knew an Indian when he saw one, and this sure as hell looked like one to him. Whatever he was, Peet was certain the guy was staring at him and his men. The cocky Texan didn't like it. He loudly asked his followers, well aware that everyone in the courtyard could hear, "What the fuck is that?" As part of his show, Peet kept moving closer to where Crowe sat calmly. Peet finally stopped, now only four feet from Crowe and pointing down at him, putting on a real performance for his friends.

Smith spoke quietly, "I think it's one of those Rangers from the Seventy-Fifth. He's wearing the patch."

Peet responded, "What the fuck does that mean? He just looks like a fucking Injun or some kind of pussy to me."

Smith cautioned quietly, "Sarge, I hear those are some bad motherfuckers..."

Peet scoffed, "Shit." Then he addressed Crowe directly, "Hey!"

No response came from the lone figure. Several Polish soldiers were now stopped and watching this potential problem among the Americans.

"Hey, you!" Peet screamed, spittle forming at the corners of his mouth.

Now Crowe was looked straight at the four soldiers.

Peet looked around, emboldened by the growing audience. "What you looking at, boy? Or should I say girl?"

The Ranger's eyes moved slightly, taking in the hulking sergeant and his silent followers, but said nothing.

"I'm talking to *you*, Tonto! What the fuck are you looking at?" Peet was edging closer to the seated figure, bolder with each insult. "What's with the fucking hair? You in some kind of beauty contest or something?"

Crowe looked up and stared intently into Peet's eyes for several seconds, then dismissed him by looking back over open ground. Peet, taking this silence as a personal insult in front of his fan club, pushed closer and kicked at the left foot of the Ranger. "Why don't you stand up like a man and answer me, or do I have to jerk you up by that pretty long hair of yours?"

Finally, the lone figure looked up. "Why don't you and your friends just move along now, Sergeant?"

Peet raised his voice, "What the fuck did you say? What is *your* rank, pretty boy? I don't see nothing on those sleeves or collars. For all I know you ain't even a soldier. Maybe you're just here to find a boyfriend."

Crowe continued to sit. He took a long calming breath.

Peet, in his best Texas drawl, continued loudly, “Hey, shit bird! I’m still talking to you!”

Quietly, the lean, muscular figure calmly looked up at the sergeant. “You really want to do this?”

Peet flashed angrily, “Fuck you! You ain’t nothin’ but some kind of rez nigger!” In a rage, he lunged forward and reached for the sitting soldier’s hair. The hair was no longer there. The soldier was no longer there either. He had spun to his right, kicking a roundhouse sweep at the legs of Peet and toppling him to the ground. Crowe seemed to move in a blur, following the motion of Peet as he fell, wrapping his left arm around the neck of the massive sergeant.

Peet instinctively grabbed for the soldier’s arm, trying to dislodge it from his throat but found it was like corded steel, stronger than a man that size should be. More surprising, Crowe’s right hand had produced a long buffalo skinner bowie knife from the small of his back, and it now rested directly against his throat.

“Now, Sergeant, we just need to decide. Do you live or do you die?” Crowe calmly speaking into the sweating soldier’s ear. Peet’s friends had backed away and were frozen in panic. Peet, unable to answer, eyes bulging with fear and lack of oxygen, appeared ready to either shit his pants or pass out.

“Crowe!” a shout from an approaching figure. The onlookers turned to see Colonel Rogers, a full bird colonel and commander of the entire American contingent, walking purposefully toward the altercation. “Crowe, enough!”

The lean scout slowly looked up, pulled the knife away from the sergeant’s throat, and released his grip, allowing the man to fall onto his side, gasping for air. Crowe rolled away effortlessly and into a standing position in one fluid movement, the knife magically disappearing to where it had come from. The colonel stood stock still and looked down at the sergeant who was now cowed, desperately looking around for a place to hide.

“Do we have a problem here, Sergeant?” The colonel looking directly at Peet. The Texan still appeared to be in shock but shook his head no, still feeling his throat, expecting it to be open and bleeding. “And you, boys?” asked the officer, now looking at the rest of the group expectantly. In unison, all nodded that they had no interest in the fight or anything that would follow. The colonel looked at Crowe for a second, turned, and just walked away. Crowe moved with him as calmly as if he had just bought a Coke at the local drugstore.

The colonel, never breaking stride and never looking directly at Crowe, asked, “What the fuck was that?”

Crowe, walking calmly, shook his head and sighed, “I guess just a bit of cowboys and Indians.”

Part Two

Present Day

The Wolf and the Apache once lived in harmony and their spirits touched.

—Chiricahua, Apache chief

CHAPTER 5

The present, Tohono O'odham Nation Reservation, Southern Arizona

Tyrell Zepeda crouched in the living room of the small stucco house on the outskirts of Sells, Arizona, a small town located in the southwest quadrant of the Tohono O'odham Nation Indian Reservation. Small though it was, Sells was the capital of the reservation and vital to the day-to-day business of the twenty-five thousand Tohono people who lived on the tribal lands.

Tyrell busied himself checking and rechecking his gear, which was neatly lined up against the wall. His wife of one month, Natalie, chided him once again from the kitchen, "Ty, your breakfast is ready. It's going to go cold. You have gone through that stuff hundreds of times already."

Natalie looked at her husband as he checked his packs with furrowed brows, mentally ticking off his list of supplies. She had been in love with Ty since they were in the fifth grade, admiring the way he always stood up for the weaker children at the Indian school. Carrying a frying pan from the stove, she slid its contents onto Ty's plate. "Tyrell, do you want the other wives to say that I'm not feeding you? Please come sit down for five minutes."

Ty turned to his wife, smiling. "Yes, dear. But what will they say when the guys find out I've turned into a timid, henpecked husband after only four weeks of marriage?"

Natalie leaned across Ty as he sat down, hugging his neck. "Let them say what they want, my love. I will do whatever it takes to keep you happy and safe. Now eat! Moses Price will have you soon enough!" said Natalie, darting playfully away as Ty turned to pull her back to him. Over her shoulder, flirting, she added, "Don't get me started or I really will make you late!"

Ty called to the kitchen as his young wife busied herself pouring juice for him. "Have you got everything you need while I am gone? You know I won't be back for four days. Have you got all the phone numbers?"

"Yes, dear. For the tenth time, I have everything I need," replied the girl, feigning exasperation.

"My mother's number?"

"Yes, of course. Do you think that she and I don't talk every day? I swear it takes two of us to keep watch over you anyway."

Ty smiled to himself. *Life couldn't be better. He loved his new job and he loved this beautiful girl.*

CHAPTER 6

The last traces of the orange-and-yellow sunset lingered over the barren landscape of the Arizona-Mexico border. The sand and dust of the vast desert were nature's paintbrush, creating colors impossible to duplicate on canvas. The heat was slowly relenting as the sun began to fall toward the horizon. The creatures that inhabited this burning land of mountains, ravines, and sagebrush desert slowly came to life as the sun surrendered to the approaching dusk. You could almost hear a collective sigh of relief as the air suddenly became breathable.

The two riders moved slowly along a high mesa that stretched for ten miles in three directions. Their horses were mustangs, "paints", so-called for the splashes of color in their coats. The short, sturdy ponies' tan-and-white coloring blended with the brown land around them, their unshod hooves leaving little trace of their passing. The men who rode them seemed to blend into the landscape as if they were a part of the horses. Some would say that they became one creature. Both riders wore the traditional clothing of their people, a combination of white-and-tan cloth, loose fitting and cool.

The lead rider, Moses Price, wore his long black hair tied back from his face. His skin was bronze, almost black from the sun. Webs of wrinkles showed around his eyes and forehead, burnt there like a brand from his time in the desert of the Arizona borderlands. His partner, Tyrell Zepeda, wore his hair short, cut in a military style. Price and Zepeda were both tribal police officers. They patrolled an area the size of Rhode Island and Delaware combined. Price was Navajo by blood, born and raised on the Navajo Nation. He came to this reservation twenty years ago through marriage, his wife coming from the Tohono O'odham tribe, or Desert People, as they were known among the other tribes of the region. Zepeda was pure Tohono, born and raised in the unforgiving furnace of the Arizona desert. This was only his second patrol with Price and really his first extended patrol as Tyrell had only recently graduated from the Arizona State Police Academy.

Ty was happy to be partnered with Moses Price. The older officer was a legend among all the tribes in the region. His grandfather had a been a Navajo code talker in WWII, and his older brother Will had been a member of the Delta Force, killed in action in Bosnia back in 1994. Moses had not pursued a life in the military, instead opting to stay home and protect the *Dine*, as the Navajo referred to themselves. Moses had started his police career on the Navajo Nation in the north but had moved to Tohono soon after meeting and falling in love with the daughter of a prominent Tohono tribal elder. He had spent the past twenty years keeping the peace on the reservation and protecting the *people* from criminals from outside the rez and from across the border.

Moses Price was well-known as a force to be reckoned with. He had tracked down several dangerous, high-profile drug traffickers over the years. In the past six months, he had intercepted two major groups of drug smugglers, both from the notorious Zeta drug cartel, an organization composed of ex-soldiers and ex-police officers from the Mexican government. They were ruthless and often killed innocents merely to demonstrate their power. Moses had cost the Zetas millions of dollars and, more importantly, prestige among the other cartels in Mexico. People were saying that there would be a reckoning. The Zetas would not take these seizures lying down. If this was something that concerned the veteran police officer, he never showed it. As Ty looked over at this partner, he found it hard to imagine that anything frightened this man.

Moses rarely spent much time worrying about what others thought of him. He knew he was quiet and was not much at making new friends. The Bosnian war had taken his best friend when his older brother had been killed fighting for the God of some crazy white people. Now his wife and two daughters were his whole life. He smiled wistfully at the thought of his girls and their beautiful mother, thinking that he missed them more each time he went into the field. He sighed quietly to himself. *Maybe it was time to think about retiring after all.* His pony brought him from his reverie, nickering at the sound of thunder in the distance. The Navajo looked sideways at his young partner. "That storm is heading north. Shouldn't come this way." He drew in a long breath through his nose. "Smell the creosote? Lightning must have set some bushes on fire."

Price slowed his horse and gazed down into the canyon from his mount, studying the trail that they had been following since dawn. He and Ty had been riding easily along the border when they had picked up sign from a group of smugglers. It was clear that a group had exited a tunnel from the Mexico side, the opening hidden in the rocky terrain. The group was moving steadily north from the border. The trail was an easy one to follow. The smugglers were on foot and carrying heavy loads, leaving deep prints in the sandy soil. Moses knew from experience that the loads were either drugs or weapons. He also knew that the "mules" were new to the desert. They had walked on through the night, unnecessarily stepping on rocks and scrub cactus along the way, risking injury and jeopardizing their cargo as well. He wondered what had been driving them to take such risks. Moses considered the best action to take, finally deciding that he and his partner would climb a side trail and follow the group from the ridge above.

The young Tohono posed the question, "How far ahead are they?"

Moses looked ahead, gently nudging his mount forward. "We'll know soon. There is an outcropping about two miles ahead. If they are close at all, we should be able to see them from there."

Thirty minutes later, Moses brought his pony to a halt five feet from the edge of the outcropping. Ty edged his mount alongside his partner, both men looking down into a widening in the canyon. Price reached down to pat his horse's neck gently, gazing silently ahead. Moses had never been too talkative, preferring to let others do the talking. To him, most conversation was just noise, and he tended to speak only when he had something to say. Ty sat perfectly still in his saddle, waiting for his partner to speak, wondering what it was they were looking at.

About one half mile ahead and at least a quarter mile below the rim on the desert floor, there was what appeared to be a makeshift campsite littered with at least thirty bodies. Several of the corpses were covered by large, ungainly black birds pulling at their flesh through the tatters of their clothing. Price silently pulled his binoculars from his saddlebag and scanned the horizon, looking for any sign of human activity. What he saw below was not done by nature or even the desert. People only died in numbers like this at the hands of other people. Judging from what he could see through his glasses, this had happened at least a day ago, but one could never be sure from this distance. He considered riding directly into the camp but resisted the impulse. *Best to be safe. There was nothing he could do for the poor souls down there at this point.*

In a voice barely above a whisper, Ty asked, "Moses, what is it?"

The older Navajo just shook his head slowly in response, puzzling it out for himself.

Moments later, Price slowly backed his horse away from the edge of the rim of the mesa. Ty quickly followed suit. Once both riders and their ponies were out of sight from the flats below, they both dismounted and moved forward on foot, finally crawling to the rocky edge on their bellies. Price pulled his 44-40 Marlin from its scabbard, deciding to use its powerful scope in place of his binoculars, which he passed over to the young police officer. Ty was doing his best to anticipate the moves of his partner, sensing that this was dangerous and unusual even for the experienced officer. Ty marveled at the effortless way that Price moved. He might have been over forty years old, but he moved like a man half his age.

The Navajo veteran remained in place for a good hour, studying the macabre scene below and regularly scanning the horizon for signs of movement. Ty remained prone next to his partner, wondering what he was waiting for and for how long they would stay in place.

After the first hour on their bellies, Ty whispered, "Should we call for backup?"

"Let's just stay still for a bit longer…"

Finally, with his eyes still fixed on the scene below, Moses got to his feet. He motioned to the rear with his head to Ty, who was already up and moving toward the horses. Both men mounted and started their journey down the side of the mesa toward the killing field below. Price rode with his reins draped over the saddle horn, both hands cradling the Marlin across his lap. The boy was a bit more cautious, keeping one hand on the reins and the other on the handle of his Glock, which was unstrapped and ready for action. The horses moved methodically down the narrow path, carefully placing their hooves between the loose rocks that littered the ancient game trail. Moses's eyes never stopped scanning the surrounding terrain, hoping that his young partner was following suit. After only a limited time with the young man, he was certain that the boy was sharp, with keen instincts that would serve him well.

They reached the flatland that stretched from the high mesa all the way to the border. Nothing but rocks, scrub grass and cactus stood between them and Mexico. It took the better part of thirty minutes to cover the remaining ground, Price content to continue at a frustratingly slow pace. As they neared the camp, the horses nickered in protest, shaken by the smell of death and the nasty vultures that hopped from body to body, strips of flesh dangling from their beaks.

Moses slipped smoothly from his saddle, letting his reins drop to the dirt and keeping his rifle in both hands as he moved through what was left of the camp. Ty followed but spread to the right, moving in tandem with his partner among the carnage. The scene was far worse up close. Many of the bodies had been ravaged by animals, faces rendered unrecognizable, clothing torn to shreds.

It was clear that these corpses were Mexican. All were men, ranging in age from fifteen to fifty years. They were short and thick of body, strong and sturdy men willing to take such risks for a paltry two hundred US dollars. They had been used by the cartels to carry contraband across the border through narrow tunnels and then across this dangerous terrain. Moses spoke for the first time, "Look at their feet." He pointed with the barrel of his carbine at the shoes of the dead men. "They all have carpet tied to their shoes. They think it prevents us from tracking them." He walked on, shaking his head slowly in disbelief.

The two men walked through the entire encampment. They counted twenty-eight bodies. Some of them were mutilated by something other than wildlife. Three had been decapitated, with no purpose other than to shock and intimidate those who found them.

Ty broke the silence. "Does it work?"

"What?"

"The carpet thing."

Moses looked up at the boy. "No."

"Then why do they do it?" Ty looking back at the feet of the bodies strewn about him.

"The Zetas are killers, soldiers and cops that have gone over to the other side. They're violent and fearsome, but they know very little of the desert or what it takes to track something. The truth is that anything that touches the ground can be tracked…anything."

"At the academy, they said that you were the best."

Moses smiled slightly. "No, there are better, much better. Get on the radio, Ty, and call for backup. If your phone gets reception, use it instead. I would rather keep this off the air if at all possible. Tell them we need transport and lots of help with this scene. We need the FBI notified. They will have jurisdiction on this. Tell them to send a forensics team from Tucson. Let 'em know it's me asking."

Ty, obviously trying to understand this thing, asked, "Moses, was this the Zetas?"

Moses thought for a minute. "I don't know. It feels like the Zetas, that's for sure, but this is still Sinaloa Cartel territory. If it is the Zetas, they don't seem to be worrying much about who they piss off."

Ty walked over to the ponies, reached into the saddlebags and withdrew the phone and the handheld radio. The phone was dead, no bars at all. The radio was old but reliable. It worked out here due to small signal repeaters that the tribe had placed strategically among the mountain ranges nearby. "Desert One to base. I repeat, Desert One to base."

An answer from headquarters, "Base to Desert One, come in."

*****

The solitary figure in desert camo moved ever so slightly, taking a calming breath. He had been lying in the narrow depression for twenty-four hours, his desert camo ghillie suit making him virtually invisible. He had waited here since the boss had ordered the execution of the *pollos*, or "chickens," as the mules were called by the cartel. He had watched as the two *policias indios* rode into the camp and walked among the dead bodies. The taller one moved slowly, with no wasted motion. It was clear that the man was working it out in his head what had happened. He followed him closely with his scope.

*****

Moses looked over at the boy as he rummaged through the saddlebags. *He would do just fine. The kid didn't rattle easily, and he was smart enough to listen and learn. If he and Annie had produced a son, he could have been like this boy.*

Ty tried to stay calm as he radioed his request to HQ. "We are on the scene of a multiple homicide, at least twenty-eight people dead." He looked at his GPS and recited the coordinates to the dispatcher.

Moses crouched over a middle-aged man who had not yet been ravaged by the birds and tried to determine how far away the shooter had been. A feeling in the back of his head kept telling him that something wasn't quite right. *Why would they do this here? So far from anywhere. There was a chance that nobody would find these bodies until they were nothing but bleached bones. What good was a message if nobody got that message? Something was wrong here.* He stood and started slowly toward the boy.

*****

The sniper took pleasure in the ultimate power that he held each time he had a victim in his crosshairs. He was as good as you could get, trained by the Americans as a member of the Mexican army's elite commando units. He had been the most talented sniper in the Mexican army. Unfortunately, the government did not pay him enough to live. It was only a matter of time before he had become a paid assassin for the Zetas, leaving behind the army and his honor. Now he killed for gold. He was known solely as Romero. He was owned totally by the leader of the Zetas, some would say the king of the Zetas—Yaotl. He was the man's personal trigger finger. Romero's reputation was now such that the mere mention of his name brought with it the fear of death.

Romero looked across the landscape. *The tall indio was thorough. He was a cautious one; he never quit scanning the horizon. This was someone he preferred to meet through a telescopic lens rather than up close. The young one was something else. It was clear he was green and relatively harmless. No matter though, he only had orders for the tall one, the one called Moses.*

*****

Moses called to the boy as he walked, "Tell them I want a chopper in the air to provide air cover ASAP."

Ty repeated the request over the radio, then said, "They want to know why? Do you think the shooters are still out there?"

Moses was looking again to the horizon. "I don't know."

The chest and back of Moses exploded at almost the same time. Ty couldn't comprehend what had happened. His partner just sank to the ground like a crumpled rag doll. The sound of the shot arrived a microsecond later. The young man fell to the ground at the feet of his pony, screaming into the radio, "We are under fire! Need backup immediately! Officer down! An officer is down!"

Ty belly-crawled across the dirt to his partner, touching his legs first, then pulling himself forward along Moses's body. "Moses! Are you okay? Moses!" Ty scrambled so that his face was next to his partner, feeling instinctively for his neck and pulse. "Moses!"

The Navajo turned his head and rasped, "I should have known."

"Shoulda known what?"

Price, in a strained, gravelly voice, "Stay down, boy! Don't move. He is out there to the west. You can't see him."

Ty moved across his partner's body, tearing away his shirt and feeling his hand come away sticky with blood. He bunched up the remains of the shirt and placed it against the hole in Price's chest. He looked desperately back to the horses who were both moving nervously, sensing danger. "Hold this in place, Moses. I'm going to get some dressings from the saddlebags."

Moses shook his head and whispered what sounded like no.

Ty jumped to his feet anyway and ran for the horses, diving at the ground next to his mount. He listened for the shot. Nothing. *Fuck!* His heart was racing against his chest.

Grabbing the medical kit, he ran back to Moses, sliding to the ground next to him. "Moses." Silence. "Moses!" feeling for his pulse again. It was there, faint but still there. He risked lifting him a bit, looking under his back to see the damage. Blood was everywhere, the sand soaking it up like a sponge. *He wasn't sure, but this was too much blood.* He hurriedly placed a compress under Price's back, then easing him gently to the ground. He then put a second compress against Price's chest, taping it in place with duct tape. He started to lift him again to do the same to his back but was interrupted.

"Boy... Ty... It's no use," said the Navajo, rasping. "I can't catch my breath."

"You'll be okay. Just let me stop this bleeding. Help is on the way!" Ty knew it was best to stay positive.

"It's Annie." A terrible sadness now in Moses's eyes.

"What?"

"Annie. Tell her and the girls..."

Ty started to ask, "What?" but Moses Price let out a final rasp of air and fell silent. The boy remained on his knees, head draped over the body of his partner and tears running down his face. His hands and arms were slippery with blood. He was no longer afraid. Instead, he felt a momentary flash of guilt, guilt for still being alive. Then thoughts of his wife, his parents, and everything he held dear. As he heard the first sounds of the chopper blades, his mind began to clear. All that remained was anger—a cold, dark anger.

CHAPTER 7

Department of Homeland Security, Washington, DC

Major General Darren Evans had been working in his office at the War College, deep into the process of submitting his paperwork for retirement. One brisk autumn afternoon, to his surprise, General Nathan Rogers, the newly appointed director of Homeland Security, appeared in his doorway. The retired four-star general had been Darren's commanding officer very early in his career in Bosnia. The director had approached Darren about accepting a position post-retirement with Homeland Security. His first response had been to shake his head no even before the four-star general had finished his pitch. But the general had held up his hand, asking him to wait. "Before you reject this out of hand, hear me out."

Darren sighed and nodded in acquiescence.

"We have a real problem on the Southern border, and I'm not talking terrorists either. It's a fucking mess. The drug cartels are moving heroin, cocaine, and meth in record amounts. Plus, they have now started trafficking in humans and weapons as if we didn't have enough to worry about."

Darren shook his head. "I guess I heard all that during the election, a boogeyman behind every cactus and a rapist behind every boogeyman."

General Rogers chortled. "Politics. You know I never gave a fuck about that and never will. I'm telling you there is a real problem down there. Innocent people on both sides of the border are dying, not to mention all the folks dying from the drugs themselves.

This isn't about some maid cleaning a house in LA or some illegals picking oranges in Florida. These Mexican cartels are making the Colombians look like fucking Girl Scouts."

Smirking, Darren shot back, "Looks like you guys need to build your precious wall ASAP."

"Fuck all that wall stuff. Let's set politics aside. We need a serious presence down there, and I need a military mind to put it into motion. I think you're the only man for the job, period. You can have whoever and whatever you need. There will be no interference. You have my word. You would have your equivalent rank in the civil service and me to handle any roadblocks you encounter."

The general paused a moment and then continued, "On my way over here, I was remembering those scouts that were assigned to your unit back in Bosnia. One in particular, Crowe, I think his name was, whatever became of him?"

Evans leaned back in his chair, putting his fingers together in front of him. "Funny you should remember him. You know, those scouts went through hell on that mission. Lots of folks in the rear with the gear did a lot of second-guessing on that." Evans stared into empty space, remembering the Bosnian nightmare. "I lost one of those boys out there. A Navajo. A hell of a man."

The old general nodded silently. "That was a shame. Those scouts were pure warriors. I seem to remember Crowe scaring the living shit out of some dumbass peckerwood from Texas outside the PX back at Butmir."

Evans chuckled quietly. "That was Ethan. Never much for being pushed by anyone." He continued, "Believe it or not, Crowe stayed on. He was swallowed up by the DIA actually. He had all those languages and was tough as nails—right up their alley for covert ops."

The general remained silent, allowing Evans to continue.

"He just retired a year or so ago. He had been working down in the jungles of Burma, partnering with the DEA on some op. Lost his wife and child in some job-related killing. I heard it broke him. To tell the truth, I don't know where he has gone. Maybe back home to the reservation."

The general finally sighed. “This is a nasty world we live in, Darren. Nothing fair about it, that’s for sure.” He then stood up and leaned his arms on Evans’s desk. “Look, this problem is getting worse every day. I think it will only be a matter of time before we do see terrorist types co-opting these cartels to bring even worse things to our shores. It’s fucking bad, Darren, really bad. All I ask is that you consider it. I need you. I hate to get patriotic on you. God knows you’ve done more than your share. But your country needs you.” He turned to leave and paused once more in the doorway. “Call me soon with your answer. And reach out to Crowe. We need men like him to make this fight.”

CHAPTER 8

Arizona

General Evans took a sip of coffee from his chair in the Homeland Security Learjet. He had accepted the job with Homeland Security two weeks ago and was on his way to Tucson, Arizona. There had been an assassination of a tribal police officer and the mass killing of almost forty Mexican men in the desert on the US side of the border. In his mind, he needed to personally have "eyes on" to see what had happened and get the lay of the land. He was already tired of the politically correct reports that were coming across his desk. Nobody in government wanted to be the bearer of bad news, somehow fearing they would be tainted with the *stink* of the news themselves. Perhaps this was the biggest difference he had found since moving to the civilian side of things. The military had trained people to be leaders, and naturally, when they were promoted, they had the training to actually lead people. They also took responsibility when things went wrong. In the civil service side of things, it seemed like mediocre had become the new gold standard. He shook his head and decided that he was probably just getting old and grumpy. His thoughts were interrupted by the flight attendant who politely informed him that they were getting ready to land.

The general was met on the tarmac by a delegation from the FBI Resident Office in Tucson. The FBI had jurisdiction on all Indian reservations when it came to homicides. The tribal police were only there to assist the federal agents in their investigations. In this case, the FBI boss was a female agent. She stood ramrod straight next to the driver's door of her white Suburban, waiting for the door of the general's plane to open. Her short blond hair framed an all-American face, tanned by the Arizona sun. She was dressed in a pair of khaki cargo pants, tan FBI-issue tactical boots, and crisply pressed white oxford-cloth shirt. On her hip was a nylon holster with a .40 caliber Glock, two spare magazines, and her gold FBI shield.

Today she had assigned three of her best agents to accompany her to meet the general. It wasn't every day that a deputy secretary of Homeland Security paid a visit. They had arrived in two-armored Suburbans, and she intended to impress upon him that the FBI was doing everything possible in the recent border killings. She watched as the government Learjet popped its door and a fit and trim middle-aged man descended the stairway. He was not accompanied by aides or other minions and moved with an energy that belied his years and experience.

Her eyes followed the man as he reached the last step and moved toward the Suburbans. He was dressed in army desert fatigues and boots. Under his jacket was a tan T-shirt, also army issued. Over his broad shoulders was a desert camo army duffel bag, which he carried effortlessly. Watching him, she could imagine him stepping onto similar tarmacs in Iraq or Afghanistan. *He might be a big shot desk jockey at Homeland now, but she would prefer him to any of her young agents if she was ever really in the shit.*

She met the general about fifty feet from the jet. "Sir, it's an honor to meet you. I'm the resident agent in charge of the FBI office in Tucson, Jane King. I hope your flight was a pleasant one."

"Just fine, Agent King, just fine. Are we set to go?"

"General, after we get your team and your bags secured, we can head over to your hotel."

"No need, Agent King. I'm afraid this is it," General Evans said, nodding to his duffel bag. "Nobody else, just me."

"You have no team?" the agent's eyes questioning and darting back to the Lear.

"No," General Evans smiled. "For the next few days, your people will be my team."

As the FBI team settled into the two government SUVs, Agent King turned around to General Evans in the back seat. "Sir, we have you booked at the Marriott downtown. I am sure you will like it. It's really the best place in town, and, most importantly, it has good air-conditioning. We can get you settled in and let you unpack. If you want, we can then head over to the office for a briefing."

The general was looking out the window to his right. "How far are we to where this happened?"

"About three hours, sir. It's a bit of a ride, most of it through reservation lands. The roads can be a bit dicey. I'm afraid it's not a pleasant ride."

The general pushed the button to lower his window. "If it's all the same to you, I'd prefer to head there now. Is there lodging on the reservation that we can utilize?"

"Well, sir, I'm sure there is, but it won't be what you are accustomed to. I mean…"

"I'll be fine, Agent King. I think we can adapt. If the Tohono can manage to live out there, I think we can rough it out in our air-conditioned, bulletproof vehicles for a few days." The general smiling wryly into the heat of his open window.

*****

General Evans sat back for what indeed became a very bumpy ride. The armored vehicles had not been a good choice for the trip although he knew the agent meant well. Even with the enhanced suspension, the upscale SUVs were never built to handle the extra weight of the armor over rough terrain. Once they had actually entered the reservation, the landscape had become even more bleak than it had been in Tucson. From time to time, they passed a modest adobe ranch house, a horse occasionally tied to a front post, or small herds of cattle grazing on stretches of grassland. As they neared Sells, Arizona, the scene changed to rows of wood-framed houses and eventually the central business district.

As the dirt road gave way to hard pavement, the general took in the surrounding town. It looked much like any other small community set out in the dry and brown American Southwest. The business district served as the commercial and governmental center for the surrounding countryside. It was here that the farmers and ranchers would do their banking and shopping, relying on the town for their communication to the outside world. He watched as the citizens went about their normal activities, moving busily from one shop to the next, all of them turning to watch the Suburbans as they passed.

The road through the downtown area was covered in some spots with dust and sand. The wind seemed intent on reclaiming the town for the desert. One business owner could be seen doing his part to stem the tide, slowly sweeping the entranceway to his shop. The man stopped mid-stroke to stare at the strange sight of two shiny government SUVs with black windows cruising purposefully down main street.

Agent King had started the trip making pleasant small talk but had eventually drifted into a comfortable silence. She wasn't sure what her visitor was looking for, but it was obvious he was not a typical bureaucrat. As they entered the town of Sells proper, Agent King called back over her shoulder, "Do you want to go to the scene directly, sir?"

"Actually no. I think I would like to go to the police department. Could you call ahead to see if Officer Zepeda is available. I understand that he was the only survivor out there."

Agent King looked into the rearview mirror at the general. "Sir, my agents in the rear car worked the case from the beginning, and I'm sure they can brief you on anything you need." She paused a beat. "Of course, we'll do anything you want."

"I think we will talk to Officer Zepeda first." The general continued to look out his window at the rundown buildings and the dark-skinned people who moved about the streets. *Now here's a group of people we never hear about in DC.*

*****

The Tohono Tribal Police Chief, Sam Whiteshirt, was not young. He had held a job with the tribal police for over forty years.

Now almost seventy, he was definitely thinking about retiring. He had been hoping that Moses would take his place, but everything had changed so drastically on that terrible day. His secretary, Maggie "Sees Far" Parker, stuck her head into his office to tell him that the FBI lady and some general were here to see him. Maggie had been with the chief for twenty years. She was Comanche, having come to the reservation after marrying one of the Narcho brothers back in 1996. The marriage hadn't lasted but she did, deciding to stay with the tribal police and Chief Whiteshirt. She had become his most trusted worker and a mother figure to all his officers.

Chief Whiteshirt smiled and nodded. "Call Ty on the radio and ask him to come in, but take your time. I want to talk to these people first." He walked over to his desk to pick up the file that would haunt him the rest of his life.

It had taken very little time to locate Officer Tyrell Zepeda. He was patrolling in town, checking into some graffiti that had been left on the front wall of the community center. It had been three months since the incident at the border, and he had been assigned to routine duties close to headquarters. The tribal police chief was wise enough to know that the young man was far from over the ordeal.

*****

The entrance to the headquarters of the Tohono O'odham Tribal Police Department opened with a bit of commotion. The sight of so many federal agents was a rare sight in the modest adobe building that had once housed representatives from the Bureau of Indian Affairs. The glass entry doors opened into a linoleum-covered waiting area separated from four desks by an old oak railing. Access to the inner workings was by a swinging gate, no bulletproof glass or Kevlar barrier in this forgotten corner of the world.

Agent King politely found her way to the front of the delegation as Maggie came to the gate to meet them. "Hello. I don't know if you remember me, but I'm Supervisory Special Agent King from the FBI and this is General Evans, the Deputy Director of Homeland

Security in Washington." Motioning with a sweep of her arm, she added, "These three men are also agents, and they work with me."

Maggie Parker looked over the group, smiling at how proud this woman seemed to be, a woman in charge of all these men. Her eyes returned to the man in the desert camo. *This one is a warrior.* He also appeared to be amused by the FBI lady but politely pretended not to notice her posturing. Maggie opened the gate and went directly to General Evans. "General, welcome to our humble office. Chief Whiteshirt has been looking forward to your arrival. Could you please follow me?" The general started forward, then politely paused for Agent King to go in front of him through the squeaky gate. She, in turn, gave an unspoken order for her agents to wait in the chairs outside the railing.

As Maggie made her way down the hallway, a man appeared from a doorway at the end of the corridor. He was of medium build and very dark, his Navajo complexion in sharp contrast to his bright white shirt. His weathered face, angular and lean, was softened by sad brown eyes and framed by thick, snow-white hair, which was pulled back into a long ponytail. His uniform consisted of black military-style trousers, a uniform police shirt, and a gold tribal police badge identifying him as the chief of police. His tie was a black bolo with a turquoise stone as its centerpiece. He stepped into the hallway and presented himself to the general, instantly taking on the appearance of a much younger man. "Sir, it is an honor and a privilege."

General Evans reached out his hand in greeting. "Where did you serve, Chief?"

Surprised, Chief Whiteshirt replied proudly, "Sir, I was in the First Cav, Second Battalion, Seventh Cavalry at Khe Sanh."

"That was a bit before my time, but I know that you boys had a bad time of it. What was your rank?"

"First sergeant, sir."

"Well, it's an honor to meet you, First Sergeant."

Maggie watched as the FBI lady tried not to appear left out of the conversation, looking everywhere but at the two old veterans. The chief then quickly looked over to Agent King and shook her hand. "It's good to see you again, Agent King. I hope all is well with the FBI." The chief smiled politely as he turned back to his office, welcoming his visitors with a sweep of his hand through the door, directing them toward the chairs across from his desk.

Agent King smiled politely at Maggie Sees Far as she brought a tray with a glass coffeepot and faded Fire-King mugs, setting them on the table in front of the chief's desk. General Evans reached out to help clear the table and guide the tray to rest, earning a nod of thanks from the normally suspicious Comanche. The general then remained standing, grabbing the pot and pouring out three mugs, passing them to both the chief and Agent King. As he eased back into his chair, he noticed the woman, Maggie, had remained in the doorway. She was looking at Chief Whiteshirt, waiting.

The chief looked up from his two guests and nodded to Maggie. "Send Ty in, would you please?" He then looked over at the general. "I called the young man in from the field when I heard that you were on the way." General Evans nodded his thanks and realized the chief had wanted to meet his guests first before exposing the young police officer to unnecessary stress. He then glanced over at Agent King, who was fidgeting in her seat and clearly uncomfortable not calling the shots.

Five minutes after Maggie had disappeared through the doorway, a young police officer was knocking on the doorframe, humbly waiting for an invitation to enter the room.

Chief Whiteshirt spoke, "Come in, Ty. Make yourself comfortable," pointing to the remaining empty chair. "You already know Agent King, of course, but this is General Darren Evans, Deputy Secretary of Homeland Security."

Ty nodded quietly to the guests and then settled tentatively into the empty seat, exchanging a quiet look with Chief Whiteshirt.

The chief drew a long breath and then relaxed back into his cracked leather chair. "Well, General, I assume you are here to talk about the case. I'm sure you have been advised that we have been cooperating fully with the FBI in their investigation. As you know, our role is limited by federal law, but we have been trying to do all the legwork that Agent King's office asks of us." Agent King nodded in agreement as the chief finished.

General Evans looked around the room, took a sip from his coffee, and spoke, "Which brings me to the question, where are we on this case?"

Both the chief and Agent King started to answer, but the chief paused and let the FBI agent begin, deferring to her with a polite nod.

"Sir, we have worked the crime scene with our best forensics team out of Phoenix. We left no stone unturned. Autopsies have been done on all the victims, and we have managed to identify at least twenty of them with the help of the Mexican authorities. All the victims, other than the tribal police officer, are believed to be Mexican nationals. We have confirmed that those identified were very low-level mules for the Zeta cartel. There is no reason to believe that the rest were anything but the same."

General Evans interjected, "What about the sniper?"

"We're working on that. It's tough to get good intel from across the border. Most of the good guys are really bad guys, and even our CIs tend to change sides on a regular basis." She quickly added, "CIs are confidential informants, sir."

Evans winked at the chief. "Thanks for that, but even an old soldier like me watches enough cop shows to get some of the terminology down."

King nodded quickly. "Plus we really don't have a presence in Mexico like some of our other federal agencies."

"Meaning who?" The general's eyebrows raised questioningly.

Agent King looked hesitantly around the room. "Well, the DEA for one and other intelligence agencies."

"What are those 'other' agencies telling us?" asked the general, his tone becoming a little brittle.

"Truthfully, not very much. Our people believe that this was all done by the Zeta cartel. Our own intelligence folks tell me that the Zetas have moved into this region in a big way. They have been pushing the Sinaloa Cartel out all along the border. They are moving in by eliminating the competition—mass shootings, beheadings, kidnappings. Some smuggling groups who were working for the Sinaloan group have voluntarily gone over to the Zetas, and I don't think it was for the pension plan." Jane King smiled wryly.

General Evans pressed his fingertips together in front of him. "Is the DEA working cases against these assholes?"

Jane King shrugged. "Don't know. I would have to believe that they are, but if that is the case, they are not sharing." After a brief pause, she added, "But we have been looking elsewhere. I have some unofficial contacts at the NSA and at EPIC." EPIC was the acronym for the El Paso Intelligence Center, the best database for drug intelligence in the world. King continued, "My sources are telling me that the Zetas are now being run by a guy who calls himself Yaotl. It's evidently a traditional Aztec name from the Nahuatl language, dates back to before the Spanish. Nobody knows if that's his real name or if he just adopted it. Truthfully, nobody knows who the hell he really is. One thing for sure, he has the indigenous people convinced he is doing this shit for the them. So those that aren't terrified of him think he is like a modern-day Robin Hood fighting the Europeans, and by Europeans, that includes us north of the border."

Chief Whiteshirt quickly chimed in with a twinkle in his eye, "Maybe not all of us, Agent King."

This drew a good-natured smile and a nod from the FBI agent.

Evans interjected, "You're telling me that with all our intelligence people working on the drug trade, nobody knows who this guy is?"

King nodded. "We know what he is, just not who he is. But we're pretty sure that he is sitting somewhere in the mountains of Central Mexico. He is said to be the final word in any and all big moves made by the cartel. His chief underboss is a guy named Roberto Maria Guzman. He is now thought to be the main operations guy, planning loads, moving product, and enforcing orders from above. They say he's a nasty piece of work. *If* the Zetas are good for this, then Yaotl ordered it and Guzman made it happen."

"What about the Mexican authorities? What are they saying about all this? Are they doing anything to assist you?"

"Well, sir, we have sent at least twenty inquiries to Mexico City through our legal attaché in the embassy. They have made noises about lack of resources, evidence, the usual bullshit. In my opinion, the crooked cops down there far outnumber the honest ones, and the honest ones are terrified of the Zetas." She then added, "Making matters worse, this Yaotl only conducts business in Nahuatl. Pretty much makes us listening from above almost impossible."

The general moved uncomfortably in his seat, feeling the tension in his lower back. A piece of shrapnel remained from an IED that had gone off near Tikrit. It inevitably started to hurt each time his muscles tensed. "What about the Mexican army? You can't tell me they're afraid of these assholes too."

King responded with a shrug, "I really don't know about that, sir," confirming that she thought exactly that.

Chapter 9

Venice, Italy

The solitary figure was dressed in the plain, jet-black vestments of the Jesuit order, covered with a long black greatcoat. He huddled in a shallow alcove, protected from the wind, watching the approach of the vaporetto waterbus. It was cold, more than usual for January. Venice took on a special chill when the temperatures dropped close to freezing. The damp air seemed to carry the cold through the skin and into the blood itself. Unfortunately, the weather had not deterred the tourists. The narrow streets were still clogged with pedestrians, noses pressed against store windows or busily snapping selfies on one of the many arched pedestrian bridges that spanned the canals. In one crowded café, a couple from Kansas could be heard demanding American coffee, which the Italians commonly referred to as "dirty water." The priest smiled at the hum of activity and pulled up his collar to the frosty mist, moving closer to the dock to see if the man he was looking for was indeed on this vaporetto.

As the waterbus moved along the canal, the priest could see that there were only a few passengers. At this time of night, the water-buses were mostly occupied by waiters and bartenders coming home from a long day out on the Lido. Looking closer, he could see one lone figure seated at the rear of the long, slender craft. The man was about forty-five with longish black hair, straight and coarse, covered by a black wool watch cap. His coat was also black, an old navy pea-coat buttoned to the top with the collar turned up against the chill.

The man didn't look up from his seat, but the priest knew he had been seen. Nothing went unseen by this man.

Father Patrick Flynn was here to find his friend. Both he and Ethan had gone to the Jesuit school in Minneapolis together. Ethan had been sent there under a government program to mainstream Native American children into American society and Patrick on a program for underprivileged children from Boston's notorious Irish *north-end* neighborhood. The Irishman had ultimately chosen a life as a priest, inspired by his Jesuit teachers and his embrace of the Catholic faith. Ethan, on the other hand, could never forsake the beliefs of his people and had enlisted in the army. The priest guessed it had been the ancestral blood running in Crowe's veins that had guided his choice.

The priest said a silent prayer for his friend. Ethan had served his country for most of his adult life but had never really found a place in the white man's world. First it had been the Rangers, and then the Defense Intelligence Agency, the DIA. He was always fighting the good fight, but never with both feet in the world of his people or the world outside of the rez. Ethan had retired two years ago and had not been able to find a place to rest and find peace. After a short return to Pine Ridge, he had suddenly left, bouncing around the world on his government pension. He had finally settled into a life on a quiet canal of Venice, living in total anonymity. Father Flynn had assisted with that move, hoping that he could somehow help his friend find a little peace.

The vaporetto, its roof providing cover from the cold mist, paused momentarily about fifty meters from the dock, the driver making room for a water taxi carrying some die-hard British tourists. The Jesuit looked out to see his Lakota friend patiently waiting while some of his fellow passengers mumbled insults to the taxi driver for delaying their arrival.

The Jesuit's thoughts went back to Ethan's final years with DIA, where he had been assigned to work with the DEA in Thailand. He had been seconded to the Bangkok office to help them track and capture the drug lords who were moving heroin to the west. The job there had been extremely tough and dangerous. He had spent weeks at a time in the jungles and mountains, accompanied only by DEA agents and local tribesmen loyal to the US mission.

During his downtime spent in Bangkok, Ethan had fallen in love with a Eurasian woman assigned to the American embassy as a linguist. After a brief courtship, they had married and, soon after, produced a son. It was during these seven years that Ethan Crowe had finally found true peace and happiness. He loved his wife, Lawan, with every fiber of his being and their son, Michel, beyond reason. It was his devotion to his family that had made him decide to finally retire and move back home to the Black Hills. He was eager for his mother and brothers and sisters to meet his family. It had been far too long, and he felt guilty that his mother had never seen her grandson. Tragically, this was not meant to be. Instead, days before their departure, his dream was to be shattered on a Bangkok street.

It had been two years since that terrible day, a day that changed Ethan's life forever. The priest felt a chill run along his spine remembering; that fateful day had shaken his own faith in God.

Ethan's career had begun at eighteen with a call to duty, seeing service in Bosnia and other hotspots around the world. The Delta Force and Army Rangers had been happy to utilize his skills as a tracker. He had hunted the Serb militia forces throughout the Balkans, witnessing their vicious war crimes.

When the time came to go back to "the world," the men from Washington had convinced him that there was another war that needed him. They asked him to put his talents to use for the DIA and the DEA, and so he had returned to a different battlefield—the jungles of Southeast Asia. He had been the best at tracking the movements of the major drug cartels. The rugged terrain where drug lords ran their global operations had become his world. Crowe had helped capture members of the feared Mong Tai Army as they moved raw opium and refined heroin through the remote pathways of the region. His actions had greatly disrupted the proven drug routes of the Golden Triangle. The DEA and Thailand's Special Forces had conducted operations based upon Crowe's intel, seizing huge outbound drug shipments and massive amounts of inbound cash. The fierce soldiers of the Mong Tai had attributed powers bordering on the supernatural to Ethan Crowe. To them, it was impossible for a mortal man to do what he did. They had come to refer to him as Ghostwalker, invisible and impossible to kill. Many of them believed he was already a spirit. One thing was certain: Crowe had demonstrated that the Mong Tai were vulnerable.

The priest tuned out the noises of the waterbus station, remembering the details of that dark day in Thailand as they had been told to him by an army general and friend of Ethan. Three months before Ethan and his family were to ship out to the States, his wife and son had been kidnapped by the feared drug lord, General Khun Sa. There had been a demand for money, and an exchange had been arranged on a Bangkok street. The kidnapping had only been staged to kill Ethan at the exchange. It had not gone well. Ethan had witnessed his family executed on the floor of a dirty streetcar; Ethan also shot and left for dead within inches of his wife and son.

The Jesuit let his memories fade, the chill of the watery city and the rumble of the vaporetto bringing him back to the present. Ethan had physically survived that terrible day, but a large part of him had gone dark, perhaps permanently. Only time would tell on that score.

*****

Ethan Crowe saw the big Irish bear of a man standing at the vaporetto station. He puzzled to himself, *So what has brought the Jesuit up from Rome on a night like this?* The waterbus came to a rocky stop at the station, the four other passengers quietly stepping into the aisle and onto the exit ramp. The last passenger, an old woman, struggled with two bags, both overflowing with groceries and boxes of juice. Crowe walked silently behind her, steadying her as she stumbled backward while walking up the ramp to the station. She turned and smiled at the handsome stranger, thankful for his steadying hand.

Crowe finally stepped onto the platform and turned to see the priest approaching with his hand extended, the handshake turning into an overwhelming bear hug.

After a bone-crushing embrace, the Jesuit pushed back and stared at his friend. "Ethan, it's been far too long."

Crowe smiled, stiffly nodded an acknowledgement, but kept walking, saying nothing.

"I have been looking for you for days. You're not an easy man to find."

Crowe walked silently toward the sidewalk, his mind racing worriedly as to what was coming.

The priest fell in beside him, looking sideways for a response.

Crowe kept walking for a few more paces, finally responding with one word. "Why?"

"Why what?"

"Why were you looking for me?"

"There has been a call from the US."

Crowe raised his eyebrows questioningly.

"From Washington. They said it was critical."

They continued to walk along the canal, Crowe still not engaging in any conversation. The priest took no offense. Ethan had been like this his entire life—never one to waste words needlessly. Since the tragedy he had become even more reticent, preferring the company of strangers to those who might remind him of his wife and son or any other part of his past life for that matter.

After about five minutes of walking in silence, Crowe began to feel bad about his dour mood with this good man. They had been friends for thirty years, and that would never change. They had gotten into their fair share of trouble as boys but had also earned the respect of the Jesuit fathers who valued their questioning minds and their courage to speak their own thoughts.

As they picked their way through the throngs of shoppers, Ethan thought back to his days at school and his friend. Patrick had found a home in the church albeit a renegade order like the Jesuits was not exactly the church. Looking back, Ethan realized that the Jesuits had been more Buddhist than Catholic. In spite of the order's unique, intellectual approach to religion, Ethan had found nothing spiritual in the Christian teachings. Perhaps his Sioux roots went too deep. He found spirituality in the ways of his people. He saw more of the Great Spirit in the natural world around him than anything he found in the marble and stone of the white man's churches. The guilt that was such a big part of the Christian religions seemed oppressive to Ethan. *Why would God impose guilt on a man for simply being born?*

If the years spent at the Jesuit school had accomplished anything, they had prepared Ethan for life in the white man's world. He had found an aptitude for languages, something that would serve him in later years spent at different universities and at the Defense Language Institute in Monterey, California. His ability to absorb different languages had surprised both his Jesuit teachers and, later, his military instructors.

Crowe finally seemed to come to some sort of decision. He reached out his arm and wrapped it around the shoulder of his friend. The priest stiffened a bit but then relaxed, noting the steely strength in his brooding friend.

Crowe, looking ahead, sighed audibly and smiled. "So what is so important in Washington that they would send a man in a dress to find me?"

Patrick just shook his head, knowing this was Ethan's way of saying he was ready to talk.

Ethan slowed and pointed to his left, steering the priest through a cluster of Chinese tourists. "Let's stop into Gino's place and maybe get a bite of pasta. I'm not sure if his cellar will compare to that altar wine you holy men drink down in Rome, but it should do."

"You do know that I continue to pray for you, Ethan. You can't stop that no matter how much you tell me it's all nonsense." Father Flynn poked good-naturedly at Crowe as they pushed into the cozy little spaghetteria.

CHAPTER 10

Tohono O'odham Reservation

Officer Ty Zepeda downshifted the tan-colored Humvee into first gear as he navigated the narrow, rocky road that descended from the mesa to the desert floor. His passenger was General Evans, who was obviously no stranger to Humvees or rough terrain. They were followed by one of the white FBI Suburbans occupied by Agent King and three men from her office in Tucson.

The trip to the crime scene had been quiet and short on small talk. The general had spent a lot of time on his sat phone, and truthfully, Ty could think of very little he might have in common with the military man. As they neared the desert floor, Ty's pulse started to quicken and a cold sweat gathered up and down his back. His hands tightened on the wheel while he did his best not to let his discomfort show to the general. Contrary to what Chief Whiteshirt thought, this was not the young tribal policeman's first time back to the scene. Ty wondered what the chief would think, or what Natalie would think, if they knew. He had returned here time and again, reliving the events of that fateful day. He thought back to the first time he had returned. He had ridden out here about a week after the bodies had been removed, lingering on the mesa above, reliving everything that had happened. He had gone to where the sniper had nested, sitting next to the slight impression in the desert floor and imagining the man who had waited there specifically to kill Moses. He had even sat there and watched the last of the FBI techs as they finished up their work at the scene, the city-dwelling agents unware of Ty's presence.

The young police officer swerved slightly to avoid a large hole in the road and continued his thoughts. The chief had been very protective of him since the shoot-out, assigning him to patrols in town, doing his best not to expose him to anything too stressful. Despite the chief's good intentions, it had been worse for him to be out of the action. The days and weeks of idle time just made it easier for his mind to go back to that day. Not a single hour went by when he didn't obsess over what he should or shouldn't have done out there. During the past months, he had found it increasingly difficult to sleep and was ashamed to admit that he found himself crying, alone, unable to bring his emotions back to normal. To make matters worse, Natalie worried and fussed over him constantly. When guilt wasn't overwhelming him, he tried to find some solace in imagining what he would do when he found the assassin who had killed his partner.

General Evans had been watching the boy as they drove in silence. He could see the young man's discomfort as they approached the crime scene. He looked away and gazed at the horizon. *Another good man tortured and scarred for life because he had to face evil head-on. This police officer was no different from all the soldiers who had fought for him on other battlefields. So many young men who would never be the same.*

A sudden dip jarred the Humvee and the general looked over at Ty, deciding it best for everyone to get back to business. "Where were the bodies and where was the *hide*?"

"Well, sir, we first saw the bodies from up on the mesa," said Ty, motioning with his head up to the rim behind them.

"We rode down this same path and dismounted right about here." Ty pointed through the windshield to a small area free of cacti. "Moses was examining some of the bodies, and I was over there," pointing to where the FBI vehicle was now parked. "Moses had told me to get on the radio and call it in."

The general listened intently and nodded, his hand reaching for the lever to open the door of the Humvee.

"I went back to the horses over there." Ty looked across the dirt to an empty space. "I pulled the radio from my saddlebag and turned to look back at Moses," his voice taut. "A second later…I saw him get hit…and then the sound of the rifle. At first, I didn't know where it came from. I really never did see where it came from. I stayed down…Moses told me to…"

The general could see the young man was in distress. The boy's fingers held the steering wheel in a death grip, and he was clearly fighting back tears. "Easy, son, that's the deal with snipers. They shoot from very far away and are not easy to find. Officer Price gave you good advice. Probably kept you alive."

The young officer seemed to regain his composure. "We found the hide about half a mile out. Over there," pointing to the west. "The thing is, I never saw him leave. I don't know how he could have disappeared like that."

The general was looking west. "That's what they do. That's what they're trained to do. This shooter was trained by the military." A long pause, then, "And the next question is, whose military?"

Ty perked up a bit, looking over his shoulder and nodding at the FBI team. "They tried to trail him, sir."

"Who?"

"The FBI. I was taken back to the station, but they told me that the FBI had some trackers who tried to find his trail."

The general looked sideways at the young policeman. "That was a waste of time. This guy was trained to exfiltrate so that he could not be followed." The older military officer added, "At least not by FBI trackers anyway."

"Moses could have done it!" Ty declared suddenly.

"I beg your pardon?"

"Sir, Moses could have followed his trail. He could track anything. They said he learned from his older brother."

The General looked out through the windshield, letting out a long sigh. "You're probably right, son. I knew Moses's brother."

"What?" Ty looked at the General questioningly.

"He served under me in Bosnia. He was a scout for my Ranger company. As tough a man as I ever knew. He died in my command.

I was just a wet-nosed lieutenant. He earned himself the Silver Star posthumously that day."

"I'm sorry, sir."

The general reached over and placed his hand on Ty's forearm. "It's okay, Ty. You never forget any of your soldiers, and Will Price is still with me to this day. It'll be the same for you with Moses, but it will get better. Just give it some time." He then glanced in his side view mirror to see Agent King exiting her vehicle and approaching from behind, obviously not happy to be excluded from any conversation on this case.

She called out, "General, is there something in particular that you want to look at?"

"Yes, Agent King," the General replied, stepping out onto the desert ground. "I would like to walk the ground a bit, get a sense of things."

"We can take you out to his *hide* site if you like."

"Yes. Definitely the *hide*…"

The general paused a moment. "When we're finished, I would like to go back and speak to Chief Whiteshirt one more time."

"Yes, sir." Agent King then turned to her three agents. "I know it sounds like overkill, but you guys take out the long guns and set up a perimeter. It's probably nothing, but this place gives me the creeps."

The general nodded quietly in approval. *This one's a fighter. No doubt about it.*

*****

Agent King and General Evans were once again seated comfortably in Chief Whiteshirt's office. The chief was beginning to believe that something might actually happen now that a military man was looking into the situation. He pulled his coffee mug to him, savoring the smell. "What did you find out there, sir?" then briefly glancing over at the FBI agent in time to see if she was still irritated for once again not being the top dog in the room. She wasn't. *Maybe I misjudged her. This woman might be sharp enough to know that this soldier was no ordinary man.* Smiling slightly, the chief turned back at the general to await his reply.

To his surprise, the general didn't answer his question; instead, he inquired, "How many officers do you have on your force?"

The chief did not have to hesitate. "Twenty-eight, including myself, and I don't get out much anymore."

The general quickly continued, "How often is the Border Patrol working on your reservation's border?"

"Not too often, General. They have thousands of miles to cover and generally leave the rez for us to handle." Adjusting in his seat a bit uncomfortably, he continued, "Truthfully, I don't think they have a very high opinion of us."

"Why is that, Chief?" The general's demeanor was all business.

Whiteshirt shrugged. "Maybe it's a turf thing, maybe something else..."

General Evans raised his eyebrows questioningly.

Chief Whitehorse shrugged, paused, then, with a sly smile, said, "Maybe everyone saw too many John Wayne movies growing up."

The general snorted and shook his head. "What about other federal agencies like the DEA and the FBI?"

The chief started to answer, but then hesitated, glancing at the FBI agent.

General Evans interrupted, "You can speak freely, Chief. Agent King is also interested in the situation here."

"Well, as Agent King knows, the FBI has jurisdiction over all homicides that occur on rez lands, and they do a great job. But other than that, we don't see much of the federals." He paused a second, then continued, "Of course, I'm sure they're busy in the cities with their other duties, and we are definitely isolated out here."

General Evans nodded, giving a sidelong glance at Agent King. "How do the FBI agents treat your officers?"

Whiteshirt quickly responded, "The FBI always treats us professionally, and I'm not just saying that because Agent King is here. It's the truth."

Agent King nodded in gratitude to the chief. She and her office had worked hard to establish a good relationship with the tribal police since her arrival, and she was grateful to see that it was working.

"One last question, Chief. What about local and state law enforcement? What's the situations with the sheriff's deputies and state police that surround the reservation? Are they cooperative?"

The chief replied cautiously, looking at both of his guests. "I think it varies person to person, but there is a bit of resentment that we patrol our lands with our own police force. In fairness, the old mistrust is still there on both sides when you look just below the surface."

The general paused a moment, then said, "Chief, I have been giving this some serious thought. It's time to get you some help down here, and I intend to do it. I've been considering forming a special unit on your reservation, federal agents working for Homeland Security."

The chief interrupted, "They would live and work here? White people?" He looked bewildered at the premise.

"No, Chief. Native Americans. I plan to bring together a team of trackers from all over the country. They'd be from different tribes but would all be of Native American blood, skilled in tracking and surveillance. I will make sure they are fully equipped and supported as well."

Chief Whiteshirt sat silently, staring at the general, not quite believing what he was hearing. "You would have a white person be in charge?"

Agent King quickly interjected, "Sir, I think I can speak for the FBI in that we would be willing to head up this task force. We already have jurisdiction," her eyes darting back and forth from the chief to the general, trying to judge their reactions.

General Evans held up his hands good-naturedly. "Whoa, folks, let me finish. This task force, as you call it, will not be a short-term project, and it will have an Indian boss, pardon my politically incorrect words, Chief." Chief Whiteshirt smiled back.

Looking at Agent King, he added, "This will be under the authority of Homeland Security, so I will appoint the leader who will then report directly to me."

Agent King wondered out loud, "Where will you find…?"

"Don't worry, Agent King, I have someone specifically in mind."

Agent King continued, "What about the jurisdiction? DEA and ICE will not be happy. I'm not even sure about my bosses."

General Evans exhaled a short breath. "Jurisdiction will not be a problem. This Administration will not stand in the way of better border security for the sake of bureaucracy. I can tell you that if the chief agrees, this is a done deal." He rose from his chair, slowly straightening his back, grimacing slightly. "Chief Whitehorse, I hope that this all sits okay with you. After all, we will be doing this in your backyard."

The chief smiled while moving toward the general, placing his arm around him. "General, I am very happy. My people will be happy too. Maybe for the first time we will be glad to see the cavalry coming."

CHAPTER 11

Venice, Italy

The men had left the frosty streets and settled into the warmth of the café, separated from the outside by steamy, leaded glass windows. Patrick was now wolfing down his pasta, smiling at Ethan's recollections of their time together back in Minnesota. He swallowed and reached for his glass. *Lord, how he missed this man.* He looked across the table at Ethan, who was drinking sparkling water and picking at his food. The man had changed very little over the years, still lean and hard, dark hair only barely tinged with flecks of grey. His face, however, though still ruggedly handsome, had changed. A certain coldness was there that told a story of the life Ethan had led. He then glanced down at his own ever-expanding belly and realized that he had not aged nearly as well as his Lakota friend.

Ethan waited until the priest had set down his fork. "Well, let's hear this thing. How did they know to call you in Rome of all places?"

"Ethan, you would know better than I on that count. I always assumed they know everything, and if not, they still know far more than they should."

"I guess Washington is a bit like your outfit in that way." Crowe smiled across the table. Ethan had always joked that the Jesuits had an intelligence network that rivaled the CIA.

"I told them I wasn't exactly sure where you were but that I might know where to look."

Crowe stared out the window and muttered something quietly.

The priest continued, "I tried calling your landlord but couldn't seem to reach anyone who was willing to divulge your whereabouts. So I caught the Aerostar, and three hours later, I was in Venice. I have to confess, this *dress*, as you call my frock, is a great door opener. The Italians might be total hypocrites when it comes to their religion, but they still can't say no to a priest at their door." Patrick smiled triumphantly at his childhood friend.

"So now that the Catholic church has tracked me down and spent the flock's money on a first-class train ticket, tell me what they want."

"Well, I don't know the whole story exactly, but there has been a killing."

Ethan looked at him questioningly. "A killing? That's hardly unusual back there."

"No, from what I can tell, it happened on an Indian reservation. Do they still call them that?"

Ethan dismissed him with a roll of his eyes, but his face suddenly showed concern. *Please don't tell me this is about Pine Ridge.*

He continued, "It happened along the Mexican border, and it was bad. Almost thirty people killed. They say it was the cartels."

"And they need *me* to fix this somehow?" Crowe was somewhat relieved and already dismissing the whole thing.

The priest interrupted his friend, "They killed a tribal police officer. I believe his name was Moses Price." Patrick was referring to notes he had evidently scribbled on a piece of paper that he had magically produced from the folds of his frock.

Crowe's eyes locked on the priest. He said nothing, but his face seemed frozen in a pain long remembered. "Moses," he almost whispered to himself.

"You knew this man?"

"No, but if he's who I think he is, I served with his brother, Will, in Bosnia, a long time ago. He was KIA. Saved my life more than once." Crowe was shaking his head, clearly traveling back in time. "How did it happen?"

The priest paused. "I don't have all of the details. The general told me—"

Ethan interrupted, "The general? What general?"

Father Flynn raised his eyebrows. "General Evans, I believe he said his name was."

"Darren Evans?"

"I'm not sure, but I believe that was it. He said he knew you and that you had served under him in the Rangers."

"What the hell is he doing involved in the killing of a tribal policeman?"

The priest shrugged. "He said something about Homeland Security or something."

"How did it happen?"

"What?"

"Moses. How did he die?"

"A sniper."

Crowe leaned forward, his black eyes burning, "That doesn't make sense. A sniper killing a tribal cop in the middle of nowhere. Why in the world…?"

The priest remained silent, shrugging. He had no answers to this.

"Did they catch the shooter?"

"Ethan, I don't know any more than I have told you. I only know what he told me to tell you. He said that you should know that this was a military-trained sniper and that he targeted Moses specifically. He wants you to come home. He is setting up a team of Native Americans. He was specific about that. This team would be put on the border to take the fight to the cartels." He paused but Ethan did not speak, so he continued, "I think he wants you to lead the team."

Both men sat together for some time, neither speaking a word. Patrick knew that his friend would work through this in his own time. He also knew that Ethan was tired of that world—weary, a more accurate description. But he also knew that Ethan's sense of duty was strong and a debt of honor to a dead comrade would weigh heavily on him. He took one last look at his friend and quietly slid the paper across the table. Crowe looked down at the number written in red ink. He nodded to his friend and met his eyes as the priest stood to leave.

The Jesuit placed his hand on Crowe's shoulder. "Take care of yourself, Ghostwalker."

Crowe shot the priest a quick, questioning look.

The priest smiled knowingly. "They tell me the Lakota have started to call you that now too." He paused, then added, "Think about this before you say yes. It might be time for you to leave the past in the past."

Crowe started to say something but slowly looked down and nodded. He embraced the priest one last time. He then remained in front of the restaurant, watching his old friend amble away along the cobbled street, turning his collar up against the cold.

CHAPTER 12

The State of Coahuila, Central Mexico

Roberto Maria Guzman looked out from the back seat of his Land Rover as his driver carefully negotiated the narrow roadway, climbing steadily through the upper reaches of the Sierra Madre Oriental mountains in Central Mexico. Seated next to the driver was a bodyguard armed with an Uzi machine gun, his head and eyes constantly swiveling left and right in search of threats to his precious cargo.

To the front and rear of the Land Rover were two Nissan Pathfinders, both occupied by additional heavily armed bodyguards. It was always a risk traveling through the countryside. While the majority of the citizenry and the police were absolutely terrified of the Zetas, there still remained the threat of competing cartels and the occasional government troops. Roberto was a high-ranking figure in the Zetas drug cartel, and his men were some of the most efficient and deadly killers to be found anywhere in the world. The recent incursions by the Zetas into territory controlled by the Sinaloa Cartel were causing increased conflicts between the two factions. However, there was no doubt in anyone's mind that this turf battle would eventually end in favor of the Zetas.

The truth was, the Zetas were better equipped and better trained. Most of their people were former soldiers and police officers. Their move on the Sinaloa organization had been a calculated decision. The Zetas were systematically attacking the Sinaloa assets in military fashion, utilizing displays of extreme violence and cruelty in order to leave no doubt as to their resolve. Mass killings of Sinaloan "mules" and even innocent peasants were messages that were never forgotten.

Roberto had just completed a series of these "messages" for *el jefe* (the boss), known only as Yaotl, the all-powerful leader of the Zetas. He ruled his empire with an iron fist and his orders were to be obeyed at all costs. Failure to comply meant a painful death for that person and their entire extended family. Roberto had only recently been granted access to the boss, who was slow to take anyone into his confidence. Roberto thought to himself, *Hell, the man never even speaks Spanish, demanding all his communication to be in Nahuatl, the ancient Aztec language of his ancestors.* Yaotl's true identity remained a closely kept secret. The man's personal life was a complete mystery. His inner circle was so small that details about his existence were, in truth, nothing but rumors. Some said it made him invincible, with no family or loved ones to become his Achilles' heel.

As Roberto anticipated his upcoming meeting, he thought about the trail of bodies his men had left on the American side, followed by the assassination of a police officer as well. It had all gone smoothly and had left a clear warning that would make the *policias indias* think twice before interfering with Zeta business ever again.

The Zeta caravan reached the front gate of drug lord's remote compound. A brief inspection of the three vehicles ended with a heavily armed guard motioning them through the concrete barriers. As they passed the guards, Roberto noticed a gun positioned above the gate area, a fifty-caliber machine gun tracking them as they proceeded to the main house.

Once within the safe confines of the estate, Roberto Guzman finally felt secure enough to lower his window, breathing in the fresh, pine-scented air of the surrounding forests. This was truly a magnificent place, fitting for the king of a vast criminal empire that stretched from these forested mountains to all corners of the globe. He was proud to have risen to a rank that allowed him access to the boss and the seat of power. He dared not speak of his desire to one day become the king himself, knowing that this thought, once spoken, would be a death sentence. He would just bide his time and do his job. *My time will come.*

CHAPTER 13

Venice, Italy

Ethan stirred from his sleep with the soft morning light filtering through the shutters. He heard some clattering in the kitchen, coupled with the rich aroma of espresso wafting into his bedroom. It must have been later than he thought. He could hear the piazza below coming to life with the sounds of merchants who plied their wares to the daily parade of tourists each day.

"Teresa?"

Nothing but the sound of dishes rattling came in response to his call.

"Hey, whoever is out there, if you're here to rob me, I'll give you anything, but please don't take my espresso!"

Finally, a mop of dark chestnut hair surrounding a beautiful Mediterranean face appeared in his doorway. "What would you do with your precious espresso without someone to make it for you?"

"Well, I'm just saying."

Teresa Misto went back to the kitchen, calling back over her shoulder, "What are you doing in bed so late?" Squinting in mock suspicion, she added, "What were you up to last night? Should a helpless Venetian girl start to worry?"

Ethan had gotten out of bed and was opening his shutters, looking out upon the small, picturesque piazza, a scene that he had grown to cherish these past ten months. He called back to the voice in the kitchen, "Helpless? That's a good one," smiling at the thought.

"Ethan, truthfully, where were you?"

"Well, truthfully, I was up all night with a priest."

"Very funny, *caro mio*. If you don't want to tell me the truth, I will assume it is another woman," she said, smiling wryly as she carried the coffeepot and a small plate of sugar cubes from the kitchen out onto the wrought iron balcony. "I know how you American men are—like hummingbirds in the lavender."

Ethan walked out onto his balcony, the winter sun beginning to warm the ancient stones of the Venice streets. He sat down at the balcony table, reaching back to put his hand on the beautiful woman's shapely backside. She responded by setting the coffee down on the table and wrapping her arms around his neck, letting her long hair fall across his face and chest.

Ethan spoke over his shoulder quietly. "How could I possibly have another woman? It takes all my strength to keep up with you. I'm not a young man anymore."

"Is forty-six an old man now? Maybe I should get you a cane to wobble through the streets."

"You know, with my people back in the days of Sitting Bull, I would be considered an elder, and all the young warriors would be coming to me for my wisdom. The women of the tribe would be working to make me comfortable. So maybe you should be looking for advice from me instead of all of this crazy sex."

Teresa moved to the other side of the table, looking seriously at this strange man who had captured her heart. She knew that he had spent his life working for the American government. She also knew, or sensed, that his work had been dangerous and violent. There was a sadness in him that she could never reach. One afternoon, while running her fingers over the scars on his taut body, she asked him about that part of his life. He had shrugged off her questions with a quiet chuckle. "They're no big deal. I just got a little too close to a mustang back on the rez." But she could see the pain even if he didn't talk about it.

Over the past year, she had pried from him bits and pieces of his life, but exclusively on his terms. She was aware of Ethan's Sioux ancestry. He had spoken of it in-depth shortly after they had begun their relationship. He had told her that he wanted her to know of his bloodlines in case it would pose a problem for her. She had been shocked that he could have thought it would make a difference. She remembered her response, "We are not American cowboys, Ethan! What difference could this make?" a demonstrative Italian display of hands in the air punctuating her feelings on the matter.

Teresa sat down cautiously across from Crowe, her eyes never leaving his. "What is this mystery? Who is this priest, and what does he want?" Worry was evident in her voice and eyes.

Crowe thought for several minutes, never looking into her eyes but, instead, preferring to gaze out upon the piazza. Finally, she could see that he had made a decision. He closed his eyes for a second and then looked at her.

"The priest doesn't want anything. He is a very old friend, and he just brought me a message from someone who does want something."

Teresa furled her rich brown eyebrows, then looked at him wide-eyed and questioning. "Well?" Ethan remained silent, trying to decide something. "Ethan, you are killing me. Sometimes I wish you were more like an Italian man. They are always talking. You can't get them to shut up!"

Finally, in response to Teresa's theatrics, he said, "There's been a killing back in the States, down on Tohono O'odham Reservation." Crowe was going slowly, working through this thing, seeming to decide what to say and how much to say.

Teresa waited patiently. She knew this man; he could not be rushed.

"The reservation is on the Mexican border. There were thirty people killed, including a tribal police officer. It was bad, really bad."

Teresa quietly said, "What does this have to do with you? You are retired."

Crowe pressed on. "They say it was the drug cartels. Many of the people were mutilated, sending a message. The police officer was assassinated at long range."

Teresa felt a shadow cross between them. Worriedly, she said, "Surely, they don't need you there for this," her worry turning to anger.

"It's more than that. There is a general from Homeland Security. He wants to form a special team of Native American trackers to patrol the border to fight the cartels. He wants me to head the team."

"Ethan," said Teresa in a pleading tone.

Crowe shrugged and looked back out on the piazza.

"Ethan, why does this *Generale* want you? Surely there must be someone else who *isn't* retired!"

"I served under him in Bosnia. I was one of his scouts."

Teresa reached out to touch his hand as it lay across the table. "*Mi caro*, I know you want to do what is right, but you have finished with that. Those aren't really our people. Your people live in the Dakotas. Those people in the desert are *not* your people, Ethan. This will be very dangerous, yes? The Mexican mafiosi are terrible people. Even worse than anything here," she said, her arm waving expressively toward the streets.

Ethan looked up gently but with a dark determination in his eyes. "They are still my people. *The People*. But it wouldn't matter either way. The police officer who was killed was the brother of a man who saved my life more times than I can remember."

She squeezed Ethan's hands tighter on the tabletop. "Ethan, what about your life here? What about us?"

He looked across at her face, her almond eyes imploring him to reconsider what she felt he had already decided.

"It won't be forever. If I do it, I would just do it to get it up and running. I can come back on leave, and you could visit me."

"Please, Ethan, this is not a good thing...for anyone."

"Tessa, I'm not sure about this. But I'm not sure where I fit in here either. You have your glass, your family, your people. My people are a world away no matter how much I try to pretend otherwise. I love you, and I like my life here, but I feel like I am in a holding pattern waiting for the next thing."

Teresa thought about this. She did have her glass. Her family had been blowing glass on the island of Murano for five hundred years. It was who she was and what she was. She knew where she had come from and where she would be in the future. This was her home and her life. Ethan was so far from his home in the Black Hills he might as well be on another planet. Her family had questioned her relationship with Ethan, a man part white and yet, at times, someone from a culture they could not even begin to understand. She had hoped that he would stay and become a part of her world, forgetting all the sorrow and violence. Now it was all in jeopardy. She looked back at Ethan as he pulled back his hands and stood.

"I am going to fly to DC. I have to see what this is."

"What about your life here? You're wrong about your people. We can be your people too."

"Tessa, I am not leaving you." Ethan letting out a long breath.

"So what about me, Ethan? Do I wait for you while you do this thing?"

"I hope you wait, but I don't want to be selfish either." He stroked her forearm tenderly. Ethan looked into Tessa's eyes. This was the first time that he had allowed himself to care about a woman since Lawan. At first it had felt like betrayal. But slowly, he had warmed to having someone care about him once again. Now with this call, he had to admit that maybe he was just damaged goods and not a good bet for this lovely creature on his balcony. He sighed as his hand came to rest on hers. "I do hope that you wait, *bella mia*."

Teresa stood stock-still, staring across the table. She then slowly walked around the table and wrapped her arms around Ethan's shoulders. This was something she would miss with every fiber of her being. She had never found an Italian man with a heart like this, wrapped in a frame of steel. "*Mi amor*, I will wait. I will wait here with my glass." As she pressed her face into his shoulder, all she could think was, *Please stay alive for me, or I will die myself.*

CHAPTER 14

Coahuila, Mexico

Roberto Guzman remained in the back seat of his SUV as it came to a stop in front of the Colonial-style hacienda. He looked at the four massive columns that framed the entrance and the shaded veranda that stretched around the entire house, providing a refuge from the noonday sun. His men were all out of their cars, and his personal bodyguard now leaned into the open front door, speaking over the seat to Roberto, "Boss, we're good."

Roberto smiled, thinking to himself, *Of course they were good. What else could we be? We are on the estate of the king of the Zeta drug cartel. He presides over what is now the most powerful criminal organization in the western hemisphere. The president of Mexico is not as safe as Yaotl.* The security "show" being put on by his team was exactly what is was, a show. It wouldn't do for him to appear weak or vulnerable, particularly to his boss. Weakness was not a quality admired by *Yaotl*.

Roberto started for the front door when a loud roar was heard coming from somewhere to the right of the giant residence, followed by two additional roars in rapid succession. His security team paused, arms moving reflexively inside their coats. His bodyguard chuckled at the rest of the men, "*Todo esta bien (all is well)*. It is only *El Jefe's* cats" referring to the collection of lions and tigers that Yaotl kept in cages on the grounds.

Roberto continued to the front door where he was met by two dark-skinned men, both massively built and wearing traditional

Guayabera shirts, automatic machine pistols slung across their shoulders. They both looked at Roberto, searched him, and nodded for him to enter. They then shifted their gaze to Roberto's bodyguards, sending a clear message that they were to remain outside. Roberto looked at his men. "Wait in the cars." He then stepped forward and into the home of the deadly and elusive Yaotl.

The two security men led Roberto through several cool and shaded rooms, all decorated with priceless works of art that included paintings by Picasso, Frida Kahlo, and others. The terrazzo floors were covered by finely woven Persian rugs from Iran. The string of rooms finally ended with an opening that led to another wing of the mansion. They entered a narrow corridor which, in turn, ended at a huge wooden door. The oak entryway was guarded by a fierce, heavily armed man who stepped aside as Roberto's escort knocked lightly. They waited three seconds and then turned the massive lever that served as a doorknob.

Roberto was amazed at the change in the decor as he entered a huge room that seemed a world apart from the rest of the hacienda. This room was full of furniture made from rare tropical woods. The walls were decorated with native rugs and tapestries, all indigenous to Mexico. Ancient Aztec and Toltec artifacts were placed on shelves and tables throughout the room. Turning around, Roberto observed a huge stone carving, probably Mayan, hanging on the wall next to the doorway. At the far end of the room, leaning with his backside on a huge mahogany desk was Yaotl.

Few had actually seen the Zeta leader in the past ten years. All the images in the newspapers were merely artists' renderings based upon rumored details of his appearance. The papers printed the rumors that he was believed to be a former military commander or special forces commando. Other sources said he was a former professor of history, sympathetic to the cause of Aztec rights. Truthfully, he looked nothing like those images. To Roberto, he looked like a middle-aged European businessman. His thick, jet-black hair was well coiffured, tinged slightly with streaks of grey. He was slim and fit, owing, no doubt, to daily workouts with his personal trainer. His clothing consisted of an impeccably tailored suit, tapered white shirt, and trousers that fit like a glove. His fine leather shoes were imported from Milan or Paris. The only thing that set him apart from some Mediterranean millionaire were his features. The man looked like he had been brought to life from an ancient carving of an Aztec chieftain. His strong nose and fierce, hawklike eyes exerted a power that vibrated in the air around him.

Roberto paused several feet away from his commander. "Sir, I am happy to see you again. I hope that I have come at a convenient time." Roberto was speaking carefully in Nahuatl.

The Aztec "king" continued to lean against his desk, concentrating on an obsidian knife that he was twirling in his hands. The knife was over seven hundred years old and was probably last wielded by one of Montezuma's warriors long before the Spanish conquest. Yaotl liked to keep his underbosses waiting. He knew that they all had aspirations of power. They were all princes in their own regions and over their own people. But he was their king, and they had to fear him more than God himself. He slowly moved to the back of his desk and placed the black glass knife gently on the hand-tooled leather writing pad in front of him. He then sat down at his throne and looked across the massive expanse of mahogany.

"Is the business done?"

Roberto answered quickly, never looking away from his boss, "Yes, *achautli* (boss), it is done."

"Everything?" Yaotl's eyebrows raised expectantly.

"Yes, everything. There is no question."

"The *indio*, this one they call Price, he is dead?"

"Yes, sir. He is dead and a message was sent. We left the message in blood. The message is what brought Price to us." Roberto was taking obvious pleasure in making the report.

Yaotl then pressed on, "Is the route secure? We need to keep the crossing clear because I have much more product to move to the north. I don't want a band of *indios* making trouble for me."

Roberto replied in soft tones, "*Achautli*, the *indios* will not be a problem. The one we killed was an exception. The rest are afraid."

"What about the American FBIs? Will they remain on the reservation?"

"No. My people tell me the FBI people are gone already. They don't care about the *indios*. We know that. It is no different than here."

Yaotl nodded silently but said nothing for a long minute, looking toward the floor, deep in thought, deciding something internally.

Finally, he looked up. "Good. I know that you have had a long journey. Let's have something to eat." The Aztec crossed the room and placed his right hand on Roberto's shoulder, guiding him politely to the next room.

The two men entered a lavish dining room. The walls were brightly painted in a warm tone of yellow. The outside wall was all glass, the pine forest seeming to wait discreetly at the edge of the outside terrace. The faint scent of magnolia drifted through the screens on a gentle breeze that carried a cacophony of bird calls from deeper in the lush greenery.

Yaotl motioned with his hand for Roberto to take a chair on the opposite side of the table from himself, nodding for his underling to take a seat. Roberto sat tentatively, taking in his surroundings and wondering what this invitation really meant.

"Do you like the view, Roberto?"

"Si, *Jefe*. It is truly a thing of beauty."

Two male servants, dressed in simple white cotton, were already pouring iced water and wine for both of the men. Roberto sat motionless while the servers finished the pouring and then waited for Yaotl to speak again.

Yaotl continued to stare at Roberto, watching him like a scientist would observe a bug under a microscope. He broke his silence with ease. "I'm glad that you like it here. What you see out that window is the land that was taken from our people five hundred years ago. It's a wonder that anything is left after the gringo cockroaches have finished satisfying their greed."

Roberto remained silent, knowing he was not expected to speak.

The Aztec continued, "What do you think of all this Roberto?" his arm stretching expansively in a sweeping gesture.

Roberto sat motionless, not sure what the man meant or what he should say.

"You can speak freely. What do you think of my struggle with the conquerors?"

Roberto cleared his throat nervously. "Sir, I don't know what to say. Some of these matters are beyond my understanding."

"That's okay. Just tell me what you think of my opposition to the Anglos."

Roberto shrugged. "I don't know what to say, sir. The Spanish are here so long. I don't think that I understand where they leave off and where we begin."

Yaotl nodded, smiling at Roberto as he would a child who could not grasp a particularly complex idea. "It's okay. I expect that. That is why I am going to teach the people. Teach them how their land was stolen from them. I will do this by creating the most powerful empire since the conquest. I will do whatever it takes and crush those who would stand against us."

The Aztec paused as the servants returned carrying platters heaped with meat, probably suckling pig from the aroma. They also placed platters of steaming vegetables and small bowls of sauces of different colors. A third servant entered the room carrying a large bowl of tropical fruits, placing it in the center of the table. Roberto's eyes opened wide. *Surely there must be others to join them for this feast.*

Once all the food was placed on the table, the servants stepped back and looked at Roberto expectantly.

"They want to know if you are ready to be served." Yaotl smiled benignly.

Roberto looked quickly to the man closest to him and nodded. The man stepped forward immediately, taking Roberto's empty plate and filling it with large portions from each platter. The other servant was likewise occupied with serving the boss his portions although they appeared to be much smaller in size. Once the plates were filled, they were placed in front of the two drug lords.

Yaotl nodded to Roberto. "Please enjoy your meal."

As the men began to eat, Yaotl continued his discussion, "My brother, I have put my trust in you for this important work. We need secure crossings, and we cannot have interference from the Americans or these fucking Indians who think they are police officers. They are a joke. Even the Americans think they are a joke."

Roberto watched his boss from across the table. The man was looking directly at him with a ferocity that he had never seen in a man before. Yaotl seemed to be looking directly into his soul. The part that was afraid. After a few seconds, he realized that Yaotl had stopped talking and was waiting for a response.

"Sir, what about the Sinaloans?" Roberto was thinking about the fierce rival cartel and their violent leader, Victor Torres.

"That has been handled. They will not challenge us."

The boss placed his knife and fork on the table, never taking his eyes off Roberto, fixing his gaze like a laser on his underboss. "It is important that you hear me now. We have new business to begin soon. Our customers in the north want us to start supplying women as well. It is a good move for us. After all, we don't have to mule the women. They transport themselves. I want you to start making preparations for this."

"What about our regular business?"

"Nothing will change. We are merely expanding our customer base." The Aztec was smiling broadly as he sat back in his chair. "The women will be a good thing for us. The drugs we can only sell once. We can sell the women over and over."

The younger man smiled silently in admiration, nodding his understanding.

Yaotl, restless, rose from his chair and moved to a chair directly next to Roberto. "Paco's group is working on new tunnels now. We will have more ways to cross than they can possibly watch."

Roberto was now totally relaxed. He had never been given this much access to the boss's thoughts. *Things were looking very bright. My power will increase tenfold from this meeting.* He felt free to speak. "What about this wall the gringo president keeps talking about?"

Yaotl smiled, a rare sight, Roberto suspected. "It will just make it harder for the Americans to see us dig our tunnels on this side."

Roberto nodded at the wisdom of his boss's words.

The boss became serious once again. "I want your people to send another message. This time on our side of the border."

Roberto looked up questioningly.

"Kill three policias and hang their bodies up for all to see. Take their heads and bury them before you hang them out. There can be no doubts about the signature. I don't care who they are. Just make the message clear."

Roberto knew the village where he would send the message. *The people, already terrified of the Zetas, would shrink from the sight of Mexican police officers hanging from the bridge. They would be afraid. The police would be afraid. The Sinaloans would be afraid. They would all be silent.*

Yaotl then stood suddenly. It was clear that this audience was over. He placed his hand on Roberto's shoulder as the younger man stood.

"Roberto, we will accomplish many things together. I only require one thing from you—loyalty. This must be beyond question. You must never doubt me or disobey me in anything. Can you do this?"

Roberto was already nodding but followed with an emphatic, "Yes, *Jefe*! Of course! I am your man and always will be."

The drug lord gently guided Roberto from the room and back into the office, where Yaotl's bodyguards stood vigil, faces fierce and hard as stone.

Yaotl paused, holding on to Roberto's arm. "And you have nothing to fear from our rivals. Nothing."

"Sir?"

"You have seen the last of Torres. In truth, you have *tasted* the last of Torres." Yaotl once again staring hard, measuring his words.

Roberto stood in place, bewildered at Yaotl's words and puzzled by the man's intense gaze. Suddenly he realized what had happened. The meal had been one final test of his loyalty. The whispers he had heard were true. The Aztec did feast on his enemies, literally. The young man struggled to process what he had just done. His stomach churned instantly, acids flooded into his gut at the horror of the sweet meat he had just eaten.

"Is this a problem, Roberto?" said the Aztec, challenging him with his eyes.

“No, sir.” Roberto doing everything in his power to keep his composure. “I am your man. I will always be your man.”

“Good. All is good. Please take care on the drive back down the mountain. The roads can be very dangerous as the darkness falls.” Yaotl then nodded to the bodyguards to escort the young drug commander out of the compound.

*****

The SUV moved purposefully down the mountain road. The bodyguards were once again on lookout, weapons ready and eyes scanning the edges of the roads. If they wondered at their boss’s silence, they knew better than to say anything. *He was the boss. He did what he did and talked when he talked.*

Roberto sat quietly in the back seat. He was sweating profusely. His stomach was churning terribly. He struggled to maintain control. It wasn’t working. Suddenly he grabbed the back of the seat in front of him, startling his bodyguard.

“Stop! Stop the car!” Roberto opened the door even before the vehicle could come to a complete stop. He bolted from the back seat, falling to the ground on his hands and knees, retching and vomiting on the side of the road. He remained kneeling in the dirt for a long time after he had purged the contents of his stomach. He had now forfeited what was left of his soul. He knew it. He was already feeling stronger for it.

CHAPTER 15

Three months later, Pine Ridge Indian Reservation

Crowe drove the dusty rental car down the two-lane stretch of blacktop leading south from Interstate 90 in western South Dakota. After the long flight from Europe, the flight from DC to Rapid City had seemed to pass by in a flash. He had been on rez lands for the past twenty minutes, the landscape transitioning from the barren moonscape of the Badlands to vast prairies and grassy mesas. To the west, he could make out the dark green of the Black Hills, and he opened his windows to inhale the smells of sweet grass and pine. It had been years since his last visit to Pine Ridge where his mother, brother, and extended family still resided. This final approach was always a mix of emotions—happiness at coming home tinged with guilt for staying away too long.

He approached a slight rise in the roadway and applied the brakes slowly. Ahead was a lone buffalo, standing in the middle of the road, in no apparent hurry to move. Ethan smiled to himself. *Well, a formal welcome!* He turned off the satellite radio and spoke aloud to the windshield, "*Hau thathanka*," offering a Lakota greeting to the great beast.

Sensing that the bull buffalo would take its time before moving on, Ethan stepped out of the car and put his feet back on his native soil. He couldn't help soaking in the beauty of the familiar landscape. It hadn't changed in a thousand years and might never do so. No sign of the outside world was evident; even power lines and cell phone towers were absent. Unfortunately, for his people, there was little here to nurture them or provide an income. The cash that many tribes were bringing in from their casinos was not to be found in South Dakota. The folks in the capitol had seen to that. All gaming was controlled by the whites in places like Deadwood.

The bull emitted a loud, deep snort as if to tell Crowe it was time to move along. The giant humped creature, covered in a full coat of thick fur, moved slowly onto the side of the road. He looked back at Ethan and let out a loud bellow, finally turning and settling peacefully onto a patch of green grass. Ethan smiled at the indifference of the creature to man or machine.

After another fifteen minutes of driving through the rez, Crowe finally pulled onto the road that led to his family's ranch. They had been allotted a parcel of eighty acres by the tribal council, which had later been increased to one hundred acres in honor of Ethan's service in the army. The dusty road led past a series of corrals, now inhabited by at least twenty mustangs. In the corral closest to the house, he saw a young girl of sixteen riding a painted mustang through a barrel racing course at full speed. It was clear that she was accomplished, the horse and girl moving around the barrels and into the stretches smoothly and quickly. The mustang chewed up the ground at lightning speed, its rider leaning forward with her head pressed against the side of the horse's neck. It was a thing of beauty.

He pulled the car into the driveway where there were already several pickup trucks, all with "dream catcher" decals in the windows. One truck had a sticker proclaiming "Proud Student at Red Cloud School" on the bumper just to the right of the trailer hitch.

As Crowe opened the door, he heard the stampede of footsteps before he saw the avalanche of family members descending upon him. The first to reach him was a girl of nine years. She leapt into his arms with such enthusiasm he struggled to keep his balance. "*Kimimela* (butterfly*)*? Surely this can't be you. Where is the baby, *Kimimela*?"

The girl didn't reply, her hold on her uncle was too fierce to allow her to speak. Finally, the girl's tight grip began to wane, and Ethan lifted her up above his head, causing a shriek of delight from the adoring child.

As Ethan set the girl down on the floor, she began chattering in rapid-fire English. "I'm almost ten years old, Uncle," scolding him for not noticing her advanced age.

"Is that so, Butterfly?"

"Mom says you can call me Angelina now. I'm all grown up"—looking over her shoulder—"right, Mama?" as a handsome woman of thirty-seven walked gracefully up to where the two were standing.

He looked over Angelina's head at his sister-in-law, smiling warmly. "Luisa."

"Ethan," replied the slim figure with thick, long black hair framing a strong, angular face. She moved quickly to embrace the man whose returns to the rez were nothing short of prodigal son proportions to both the family and the tribe. Sighing through her embrace, she said, "Why do you stay away from us for so long?"

Crowe pulled Luisa closer and then released his grip, gently pushing her back to get a good look at her. "You never age, Luisa. My brother is a lucky man. He will be an old man, and the young men will still be longing after his beautiful bride."

Luisa chided good-naturedly back at her bother-in-law, "Is this how you wrap those Italian women around your fingers? Always the smooth talker," smiling broadly, eyes twinkling at his compliment.

Ethan turned to the corrals, where his brother leaned against the top rail while Luisa's oldest daughter continued to work the mustang. "I see that Mina is still riding the wind." He paused as the girl pulled a particularly tight turn on the barrel, her horse moving quickly in a cloud of dust and hooves. "That girl was born 150 years too late. She's a warrior, that one." Pride was evident in Ethan's voice and face.

Louisa looked across the fences at her daughter, smiling wistfully. "Maybe one day she will ride as good as her uncle." She placed her hand on his shoulder. "Your brother says that the horses know her in the same way they know you."

Crowe started to the corral, Angelina clinging to his belt and talking nonstop. His oldest niece, Mina, finished her ride and cantered to the rails of the corral, waving wildly at Ethan as he approached. His brother Frank turned, smiling broadly at his long-lost sibling. "Well, what is this I see? I think it must be one of the old chiefs returning, maybe Sitting Bull himself!" Frank detached himself from the rail and walked briskly toward Ethan. The brothers met in a sudden clash, hugging each other so fiercely it stopped the girls in their tracks and brought tears of joy to Luisa's tanned face.

The Crowe brothers stood locked in an embrace for what seemed an eternity but slowly detached themselves, allowing Luisa and the girls to lead them to the main house. Ethan looked up at the white, Western-style ranch house, its spacious porch extending across the entire front of the house. A weathered rocking chair was positioned to the right of the front door, a gentle breeze moving it slowly back and forth on freshly painted floorboards. A wicker love seat and two sturdy Adirondack chairs were spaced out farther along the porch. Crowe's memories of his mother almost always included that rocker, either here or at the tiny government house where they had lived when he was a child.

Angelina was once again dominating the conversation while leading the group to the house. "Grandma Unci has been cooking for three days, Uncle. She is making everything that you like. I asked her to make us fry bread, but she said you don't like it."

Crowe smiled at the nine-year-old and rustled her hair.

"Why don't you like fry bread? Everyone likes fry bread! Grandma says it is because it's the white people's curse on the Lakota. Grandma is always saying things like that!" The girl rolled her eyes dramatically. Turning more serious, she added, "She says it makes us fat and the old people sick."

Luisa broke in, gently scolding her daughter, "Angelina, you're wearing your uncle out. He will never come and see us again." Luisa smiled and pulled at her daughter's hair gently.

The whole crew arrived at the front steps, the brothers still walking with arms around each other. The front door opened. Standing in the opening was a slender woman with thick, lustrous grey hair which, today, fell loosely over her shoulders and down her back. She was a handsome woman even at sixty-five years old. Her skin was only slightly wrinkled, and that was mostly around the eyes and mouth. Her eyes were dark, almost black, just as those of her oldest son. She watched as Ethan disentangled himself from the family. Her eyes drank in the fluid movements of her son as he climbed the short stairway to the porch. He had not changed at all. He still moved like a cougar, never wasting a single movement. *So different from my other children. So strong and so sad. The white world had not been kind to her boy. It had used him. It was going to use him again, perhaps use him up this time.*

The woman stood frozen in the doorway. Speaking gently, she used his name from childhood. "*Ohanzee*, shadow child."

"*Ina* (pronounced *eenah*)," Crowe responded to his mother in Lakota, clearly moved.

Luisa was quietly wiping tears from her face once again.

Crowe moved forward and gently placed his arms around his mother. "*Ina*," he repeated softly, holding his mother tenderly and continuing to speak in their native tongue. His eyes were blinking rapidly to keep from showing his deep feelings for this dear woman and making her uncomfortable.

The Crowe matriarch held on to her son for several minutes, oblivious to all those waiting on the front porch. Then quickly, she released her hold and looked up. "Well, what are we waiting for? Come in, all of you."

As they entered the living room, Angelina quickly chirped, "Grandma, Uncle Ethan said that he thought it would be a good idea if you made some fry bread," looking sideways and smiling at her uncle as he gave her a playful scowl.

The family quickly eased into a comfortable rhythm, everyone content to be in one another's company after such a long separation. Ethan's sister, Jenny, had arrived with her two boys, both eager to see their uncle Ethan and to hear stories from far-off lands. Their father had left the rez when they were just babies to face his own demons: OxyContin and heroin. He had never returned. The boys had come to view Ethan as their male role model, something that Jenny encouraged.

Dinner was eventually served. Afterward, Louisa and Jenny busied themselves cleaning up the kitchen while Frank went into the living room to tune into the evening news. The rest of the family moved to the porch. There Juana Crowe sat in her rocker and listened to the clamor of her brood of children and grandchildren, basking in the sounds of life around her. Ethan sat on the porch step at his mother's feet, his nephews and nieces clamoring for his attention with stories and questions.

As the evening drew long and the kids drifted inside, Juana noticed Ethan sitting alone on the porch rail, deep in thought and looking out upon the vast landscape surrounding the house. She wondered how much pain came with the sight of the children of his brothers and sisters. Ethan had never been a boy to forget anything. He had always carried pain with him as if it were his personal duty. She looked away, scanning the horizon. *Michel would be growing tall. This would now be his home. This would be his family. He would already be learning the ways of the Lakota. She looked back at her son and knew that he would always blame himself for the death of his family in that strange land.* Juana sighed deeply. *Ethan is such a strong man, but he was broken somewhere inside on that day, maybe forever.*

As if sensing his mother's thoughts, Ethan had crossed the porch and placed his hand on her shoulder. "You must be enjoying this—so many Crowes, all under your watchful eye."

Juana smiled and put her hand on top of Ethan's. "Yes, it is just what an old woman wants."

"I am leaving in the morning. I promised to get to the Tohono Rez by the weekend."

"So soon…"

"I know, but many of my people have been there for a month or more now. Isaac has been getting things ready for almost two months. It was a lot to ask of him."

His mother pulled his hand to bring him around to the chair next to her rocker. He dutifully sat down, remembering these talks from his childhood. It was in just this manner that she had challenged his decision to join the Army Delta Forces so many years ago. She had looked to his father to support her arguments, but he had remained silent. He had never intervened in the decisions of his boys, feeling it was a man's choice to pick his own road. The woman looked directly at her son, her eyes boring into him. "This job, it is dangerous?"

Crowe smiled reassuringly. "You know that Isaac will watch over me like a mother hen."

Juana pressed, "These men from Mexico are evil. What does Washington expect you to do, fight this war with you and Isaac Factor? It is too much!"

Crowe reached out and patted his mother's forearm. "I have a team of trackers from tribes all over the country. They are highly skilled in the old ways. It is something that we are good at, and I think we will be better than the Mexicans. Besides, Washington will not let us do this alone."

"Washington! They have been lying to our people for two hundred years. They will never stop. They do what is best for them, nothing more." She paused. "Ethan"—Juana looked earnestly into her son's eyes—"why do you do this work? Their world has trouble, too much trouble for anyone to make sense of. Why do you try to fix these terrible things?"

Ethan thought about an answer and remained quiet for some time. Then he said, "I don't know exactly, but I remember an old Bosnian woman who had lost her entire family to the war. I found her helping a neighbor to bandage a very old man. She was working desperately while others were still being shelled all around her. I wondered out loud to the woman, 'Why do you keep trying?'" Crowe was shaking his head slowly now, remembering the conversation.

Juana waited silently for Crowe to finish.

"She told me that it was better to light one candle than to curse the darkness." Crowe looked at his mother, clearly remembering that moment so many years ago.

Juana stared at her son thoughtfully. She had never spoken to him about the loss of his wife and child. It was not the Lakota way to speak of the dead. She knew it was a great sadness that hung over him. Lawan and Michel were Ethan's whole life. He had finally been coming home with them when they were taken from him by those evil men. She thought of Michel's photos, sent proudly by Ethan from the embassy in Bangkok. The boy had reminded her so much of Ethan when he was young. The photos were all she would ever have of her grandson. She would never hold him like a grandmother should or smell his hair on a warm summer day. She squinted her eyes against the tears. She reached forward, her strong hand coming to rest upon Ethan's head. "My son, will you ever find peace in this world?"

Crowe felt a chill at his mother's question. *Would he find peace? Was he even looking for it? The years of violence weighed heavy on his soul. Maybe this was all that was left of his life, and nothing would change that. He knew one thing. He had a debt to repay.*

"I told the general I would get this thing started. I also want to find the man who killed Moses Price if I can. I'm not starting another career. I will do as I promised but won't be there too long."

His mother looked at him accusingly. "The Lakota are now calling you Ghostwalker. I know it's something from your life with the *Wašíču*, but I don't like it."

Ethan smiled quietly. "*Ina*, it's not a *Wašíču* name. It's from another tribe. A fierce tribe in Burma on the other side of the world."

The woman gazed at her son for a long time, searching his face, trying to understand him. "Why did they give you this name?"

Ethan shook his head while looking into space. "I guess it was as an honor, a sign of respect." He leaned back in the chair and sighed softly, "Something I didn't deserve."

Juana looked at her son and felt his pain, something that mothers could sense deep in their chests.

Ethan continued to consider his mother's question. What had the name Ghostwalker meant for him and his family? *They are gone, and I am left with a name.* He had been thinking about Thailand and that life ever since coming home. He knew it had been his reunion with the family and the sensation of being back in his beloved Dakotas. His son, Michel, would have been so happy here, growing into a young man in the vastness of the tribal lands. Even as a little boy, Michel had talked about the Black Hills and the herds of wild horses as if he had seen them himself even though he had never left Thailand. He glanced over at his mother, thinking of how she would have loved Lawan and Michel. *What was I thinking staying in that nightmare assignment when all this was waiting for me? What was I trying to prove?* These thoughts were nothing new. He carried them with him all day every day. *Sometimes the memories are so loud I don't think I can survive them.*

He had begun the assignment in Southeast Asia like any other military deployment. He spent most of his time in the jungles and mountains along the Thai/Burma border. It was tough. He had been seconded to the DEA and was helping them to track elements of the vicious drug cartel that operated in those jungles and mountains. During the first year of his assignment, he rarely returned to Bangkok, preferring to remain in the field and do his job. On one occasion, he was invited to the US Embassy in Bangkok for the annual Marine Corps Ball. The ball was the *main event on the embassy social calendar, and his DEA colleagues had coerced him into attending. On this rare occasion, Ethan had worn his full-dress uniform, something he was always reluctant to do. He was always self-conscious of the medals, not wanting to draw attention to himself.*

He had arrived quietly in the company of the embassy military attaché and his wife. As they passed through security, he took his place in the receiving line, waiting to greet the ambassador and her senior staff. As he drew closer, he noticed a thin Eurasian woman at the ambassador's side, clearly serving as her translator. His turn arrived, and he reached out his hand, "Madam Ambassador, thank you for this invitation." Ambassador Brown looked back at Crowe. "Colonel, it is nice that you could attend. I must say it's a pleasure to see you in your uniform." She looked around conspiratorially with a bit of mischief in her eyes. "It might be good for some of these other peacocks to see some serious medals for a change," winking as she said it. Ethan was about to move on and looked directly at the beautiful woman at the ambassador's side.

"Ma'am," he said, nodding politely and extending his hand.

Ambassador Brown interrupted unexpectedly, "Colonel Crowe, this is my personal assistant, Ms. Lawan St. Pier. She is a key member of my staff and a former professor of languages at the University in Bangkok. We were lucky enough to steal her from her former position."

Crowe smiled politely at the Eurasian beauty and offered his hand in greeting. Lawan took it and both of them lingered, reluctant to break the physical contact. Crowe was clearly shaken, the woman's beauty overwhelming him. Finally, he stammered, "It is certainly a pleasure, Ms. St. Pier."

"Thank you, Colonel. It is my pleasure as well." Lawan showing a little nervousness from the obvious mutual attraction.

Both Ethan and Lawan paused awkwardly, hesitant to end the encounter. Mercifully, Ambassador Brown interjected herself. "Lawan, perhaps you could arrange to find a place for Colonel Crowe at our table this evening. I think that you should learn a bit about his mission here."

"But, Madame Ambassador, surely the seating is already arranged."

"Nonsense." She then looked over her shoulder and motioned to her chief political officer, who leaned forward within earshot. "Doug, please find a place at my table for Colonel Crowe. I think the Dutch ambassador will be just as happy at one of the tables close to the festivities. Place the colonel next to Ms. St. Pier."

With the ambassador's gentle intervention, a love affair had begun. Ethan's visits to Bangkok became more frequent, and the two found a lasting bond. They were soon married and, a year later, welcomed their son, Michel.

Over time, the presence of Lawan and Michel had changed Ethan. The normally quiet and reticent man had come out from under his protective armor. After the years of violence and death, he had come to believe he was beyond redemption. Finally, he had actually started to imagine that he might be a good man after all, something that he had long since stopped believing.

Ethan broke from his thoughts, returning to the present and apologized to his mother, "Sorry, *Ina*, just daydreaming a bit."

His mother returned his gaze steadily. "They never leave you, these ghosts. Their echoes live in our hearts." Juana stretched her hand to cover her son's once more. "*Ohanzee*, it is a normal thing. Your father visits me in my dreams too. I loved him very much. He was my life. He will be with me again in the next world. But you, you still have much life ahead of you. You must find your way without them. Keep them in your dreams, but you have a waking world to live in where they cannot follow."

Ethan nodded slowly in silent agreement, thinking back to Bangkok and the day that they were taken from him.

His mind raced uncontrollably at the thought that he could lose everything he held dear in the next few minutes. He stood in the door-

way watching the sea of humanity pass in the street. The vehicle exhaust mixed with the smell of unwashed bodies. Smoke from Thai cook stoves and the ever-present odors from the joss sticks hung in the air, clinging to his hair and clothes. It was suffocating. He felt another monsoon rain coming, but how much difference could it make? He was already soaked to the skin with his own sweat, his long hair was pressing wet against the back of his neck. He leaned back into an alcove. His eyes scanned the streets relentlessly, his pulse beating so hard he could feel his skin move on his chest. He took a calming breath.

He was alone and unarmed. They had been specific in their demands and were not to be challenged. Too much was at stake. He heard the bus approaching before it came into view, its black smoke billowing from the rear. His body tensed, his right hand instinctively reaching for the Glock that wasn't there. He shifted the canvas bag to his left shoulder, the wide strap digging into his flesh from the weight of its contents. He tried to scan the interior of the bus as it pulled to a stop, but most of the windows were fogged over with the humid breath of the passengers. He pushed away from the wall and crossed to the curb as the bus came to a stop. The back doors opened and he climbed the three steps into the aisle.

A quick glance revealed approximately twenty passengers, some of them children. They regarded him with trepidation, heads turning from him to the front of the bus. He followed their gaze to see two heavily tattooed Burmese tribesmen, AK-47s at the ready, standing at the head of the aisle. He heard sounds from the front stairwell. Suddenly, two small figures were propelled up into the main compartment. The first was his wife, Lawan. She lost her balance at the top of the stairs and fell hard at one of the gunman's feet. The second figure was his son, Michel, now five years old. The boy was being held aloft by a third man who rose from the stairwell.

Crowe's eyes fell to the woman on the floor, his heart aching at the sight. Her silky black hair was spread across the floor in front of her, framing her beautiful, exotic features. There were bruises and swelling on the left side of her face. A trickle of blood ran slowly from her ear. Her brown eyes looked up sadly at Crowe and then worriedly back to her son dangling helplessly in the arms of the Mong Tai gunman. Seeing Crowe, the boy came to life in his captor's arms, kicking and struggling wildly, shouting, "Papa!"

Crowe instinctively lurched forward but stopped suddenly, seeing the men bring their weapons to bear. He had to maintain some control and mouthed in French, "Du calme, Michel!" motioning gently with his hands to calm his son. He looked to the man holding the boy and recognized him as General Khun Sa, the man responsible for much of the world's opium trade. Sa operated in the highlands of northern Thailand and across the border into Burma, an area known as the Golden Triangle. His vast criminal empire sent opium and heroin to every corner of the globe. The general was said to be half Chinese and half Shan, and his Mong Tai Army was feared by the governments of both Burma and Thailand. He answered to no one, except perhaps the Chinese triads who ultimately controlled everything illegal that happened in Asia. Rarely seen, Khun Sa's acts of cruelty were unpredictable and infamous, striking fear in both his enemies and his partners. Crowe looked directly at Sa. "I've brought what you asked. We can end this here."

The general roughly handed the boy off to one of his gunmen. "Ethan Crowe, I will decide when is ended," he replied in a heavily accented English. "You alone now. The US Army and DEA can no help you now."

Crowe eased the satchel from his shoulder and dropped it to the floor. He kicked it forward and motioned for his family's captors to take it. Khun Sa nodded for the second gunman to retrieve the bag. The man edged forward, motioning with his rifle for Crowe to back away. Crowe complied, carefully stepping back a few paces with his arms in the air. Satisfied that the American was no threat, the tribesmen, his shaved head glistening with sweat, pulled the bag back toward the front of the bus. Crowe pointed at the bag with his chin. "The entire half million is there. Let them go and we walk away." He stole a glance at his beloved Lawan. For some reason, she hadn't made any move to get back up. She was just staring at their son, tears streaming silently down her face. A look of resignation fell like a shadow over her delicate features, transforming her as he watched. He felt an icy cold deep in the pit of his stomach.

The general's man finished looking through the satchel and nodded once. The drug lord smirked. "American government always want solve problems with the money."

"Are we through here?" Crowe eased forward, his left hand extending forward toward Lawan. To each side, three passengers had transformed themselves into additional gunmen, weapons pointed at him as he paused in the aisle ten feet from his family.

"No, we not through here!" Khun Sa spit the words. "Do you think I ever want money? I have more money than you DEA friends! This is matter of honor. Today I kill the ghost forever."

"You mention honor while hiding behind a helpless woman and a child?" This was going to hell fast. There was more going on here than Crowe could understand. He found himself yearning for the Glock. He would prefer his chances with it now. "Look, I'm one man. I'll take my family and leave this place. You will have the money and my surrender. I will no longer be any concern to you."

"You are problem wherever you are. You different from others."

"Then let my family live." Crowe's voice was pleading. "Let them walk away. This is between you and me."

The general seemed to reflect on this for a second, regarding the woman and child with cold contempt. "Do you think this is American movie with happy ending?"

Lawan was stirring. "Ethan." The beautiful figure was straining to look directly into his eyes. She was speaking softly, her French words barely audible. "Ma cher, je t'aime...toujours. I love you...forever."

"No!" He was yelling, looking directly at Khun Sa now. A handgun had appeared in the general's right hand.

Crowe lunged forward as two rounds from an AK tore into his wife's breast. He then felt a round enter his left thigh, causing him to lose his balance and fall forward. Another bullet seared across his cheek. Now facedown on the floor of the bus, he crawled forward toward his wife's prostrate form. He heard his son's cry of "Maman" interrupted by the explosion of Sa's handgun. Crowe screamed in anguish, "No!" his face twisted in agony as his breathing became more difficult. A third round struck him in the back, forcing the air from his lungs. His family was dying. He managed to reach for Lawan's hand, already turning white and cold as he covered it with his own. His last thoughts, What have I done?

The bus fell silent, the passengers and gunmen vanishing into the chaos of Bangkok's streets. The smoke and dust of battle slowly settled upon three bodies and the money satchel, its contents spilling over into the aisle of the bus, untouched. Crowe's last sensation was helplessness; then darkness.

*****

Juana had watched her son as he let forth a long, pained sigh. He leaned back and slumped in the Adirondack, his eyes staring blankly at the sky over the corral. The memories were pure agony for him. Recollections that he did his best to keep at bay every day. He didn't know how much time had passed, but he finally focused his eyes and looked once again at his mother, as if awakening from a deep dream. He began to weep. His body shaking, tears streamed down his face. Ethan did nothing to wipe them away. He cast his eyes down, closing them in pain. His mother just sat there, keeping her hand over his, quietly letting her son grieve openly, maybe for the first time.

Inside the house, Frank and Louisa watched through the window, Frank holding his wife tightly and crying silently.

A long time passed before Ethan took a deep breath and spoke quietly, almost reverently, "Whew. That's not something you want to do on a regular basis. I'm sorry about all this."

"You need not apologize for life, my son. You are a good man who has taken too much upon himself. You want to control the world around you, but that cannot be done. Whoever made this world does not share his plans with us."

Crowe spoke into the air in front of him.

"Beautiful."

His mother looked at him questioningly.

"*Lawan* was the Thai word for 'beautiful.'"

Juana said nothing, gently tightening her grip on her son's hand.

Crowe shook his head sadly, "Sometimes I can smell his little boy sweat in my mind. It is more than I can take, *Ina*."

Juana gazed steadily at her son, wishing she could make the hurt go away as she did when he was a boy. Both stayed quiet for a long time, content to be in each other's reassuring company.

Many heartbeats later, Juana addressed her son in a very serious tone, "Ethan, you are living out of time. The old ways are so strong in your blood. It is not easy for you. I worry that people are using you for your strength. I am proud of you and afraid for you at the same time."

"*Ina*, stop worrying so. What will happen will happen."

Juana stood slowly, placing her hand on Ethan's shoulder. "What will you do when this is finished, my son?"

Ethan covered his mother's hand with his own, wishing he had an answer but knowing he had none.

*****

Ethan and Juana finally left the porch and rejoined the rest of the family. Crowe allowed himself to bask in the warmth of his mother's kitchen. There wasn't a moment's silence. Everyone sensed the special nature of this gathering, and they all tried to squeeze the most from every second. They all knew that one of them was going back into the world again. Angelina hovered around her uncle like he would disappear if she closed her eyes for a second. All had exchanged memories of their childhood on the rez, and even Ethan's sister, normally the shy one, let her guard down and joined enthusiastically in the lively conversation.

Finally, they seemed to slow down collectively, each wondering how they would say their own goodbye. Ethan was always the one who had left the rez and gone back into the outside world. He had traveled far and done much. Secretly, they all wondered if he would be changed when he came home. After all, he represented a road not taken for all of them. They each took their leaving in their own time. Frank lingered the longest, afraid to show just how much affection he felt for his older brother, not wanting his wife and children to see his tears. Luisa just shook her head at her husband's foolishness.

A blind person could see through you, my husband. Men understand so little about themselves.

*****

The family had been gone for at least half an hour. Juana was busying herself in the kitchen, tidying up and refusing any help from the girls. Everyone had offered to pitch in, even the men, but they all knew that she preferred to do these things alone. Ethan suspected that she spent the time cherishing the moments of the evening all to herself.

Ethan stepped out onto the porch, seeking the cool breeze and a bit of quiet. He walked over to the porch railing and was surprised to see Mina sitting on the step, obviously waiting for him. "Mina, you surprised me. You trying to give an old man a heart attack?"

"I don't think you are so old, Uncle. Besides, they say you cannot be surprised. The men say they call you a ghost."

Ethan just shook his head with a wry smile. "I think you are too old for fairy tales. Besides, you know sometimes those old men gossip like old women."

Mina smiled back with a wisdom beyond her years. "Say what you want, Uncle. I know what they say."

Ethan held his hands up in surrender. "Mina, you are as tough as your mother already."

"I was waiting here for you, Uncle."

"Oh?"

"Yes, there is something I want to show you at the corral." Mina stood and beckoned Ethan to follow her.

Ethan walked with his niece the distance to the corral, noticing a brown mustang at the rail. The horse watched both of them as they approached. Mina walked directly up to the horse, its eyes intelligent and watchful. Ethan stayed back a few paces to let Mina settle the mare, noting that it had the long lashes of the wild mustangs, additional protection from the dusty winds of the prairies.

Mina spoke over her shoulder, "It's okay, Uncle Ethan. She already knows you."

Ethan closed the distance steadily, no sudden movements. He reached out through the corral rails and put his hand gently on its muzzle, letting the horse smell him and place him in her memory. "She's beautiful. How old is she?"

"Three years old. I caught her out on the mesa. She was just a young filly and full of spirit. It is her name, Wanagi. It really means *spirit* or *ghost*. But I forget. You speak Lakota better than our teachers at school."

"It's a good name. Will she take a saddle?"

"Only from me. And you." Mina looked knowingly at her uncle in the moonlight.

"You think?"

"I am sure. She won't let anyone else touch her. Not even my father. It's why Dad says that you and I are the same. He always says that the horses know us differently than the others."

They both stood quietly at the corral, running their hands gently over Wanagi, content to be in each other's company.

Ethan broke the silence, "Will you race her in the barrels?"

"No. She is not for that type of thing. In a strange way, I think it is beneath her. I love to ride, and I like the rodeos, don't misunderstand me. But Wanagi was never meant to perform in the white people's rodeos. She is meant for the open spaces."

Ethan thought about that for a minute before reaching over to place his hand on the top of Mina's head, feeling the warmth of the sun lingering in her black silky tresses. "Then this is a very lucky horse to have such a girl to care for her."

Mina put both her hands on the rail in front of her, cherishing this moment with her uncle. "No, I am the lucky one, Uncle."

They both reluctantly surrendered the moment and headed back to the house. Mina hugged Ethan one more time and then walked over to her Ford pickup. Ethan continued up the steps and disappeared into the house, looking back and waving to Mina as she spun the wheel to turn the truck around in the driveway.

Crowe was gone before first light.

CHAPTER 16

Two months later, the outskirts of Sells, Arizona

At first glance, the compound wasn't much to look at. At its center was an old adobe ranch house, probably built in the early 1900s by an aspiring settler, only later to be told that the surrounding land was being ceded to the Tohono O'odham tribe as part of a treaty. Recently, the house had been modernized, air-conditioned, and expanded to accommodate the new task force. To the left of the main building stood five recently erected container housing units which served as barracks for the team. Two hundred yards to the right of the offices stood a hangar and a large concrete tarmac, where a solitary Blackhawk helicopter rested in the shade of the metal shelter. A corral stood to the rear of the makeshift barracks, with eight horses standing in the shade of an overhang. Everything else was desert, with tumbleweeds as the only thing that could be counted on to move consistently during the heat of the day.

Ethan Crowe sat at his desk in the headquarters of this unique task force that had come to be known as the Shadow Wolves, a name borrowed from a legendary Navajo scout. The team was completely staffed with Native American trackers. He and his number two, Isaac Factor, had assembled an impressive team of men and women. The general had been right. The border situation was bad. Beyond dangerous. The two most powerful Mexican cartels, the Sinaloa and the Zeta cartels, were both pouring drugs and weapons across into the US in record quantities. Making matters worse, the two groups were at war with each other, resulting in bloodletting and murder on both sides of the border. Ethan was currently working through a pile of intelligence submissions from his team, shaking his head at the enormity of the situation. His office assistant, Maggie "Sees Far" Parker, stuck her head in his doorway. "You have an intelligence brief in five minutes. Can I get you something to eat?"

"Thanks, Maggie, I'm set. I'll catch something afterward."

Maggie gave Crowe a doubtful look. "That's what you said yesterday."

Crowe knew he could not escape the eye of Sees Far, a name that he now realized she had earned honestly. "Why don't you and I go over to the diner in Sells after the meeting for a late lunch? I probably need a real briefing from you so that I will know what is really going on around here." Ethan smiled broadly at the Comanche woman. Maggie nodded silently and headed back to her office, where she held nonofficial sway over the entire operation. She was part foreman, part mother, and part spiritual adviser to all who worked on the team. She was loved universally by every single man and woman in spite of her rough exterior and uncompromising demeanor.

Maggie had come to the team courtesy of the Tohono O'odham Tribal Police. She had been Chief Whiteshirt's assistant for as long as anyone cared to remember. The chief had brought her to Ethan's new office three months ago, a day after Ethan had arrived to take command. After quick introductions, the chief had told Ethan that Maggie was essential to the new task force. He went on to tell Crowe that he would never meet a more intelligent man or woman and that he would be crazy not to hire her immediately. Crowe had watched the woman throughout the chief's endorsement, and she had been unblinking, no false modesty evident.

When the chief finished listing the accomplishments of Maggie Parker, Ethan had looked her in the eye and asked, "Do you have anything to add?"

"No, Mr. Crowe, the chief is right. You do need me, and I will do the job better than anyone else." Her face showed no emotion, just confidence and strength.

"It would seem I would be a fool to let you get away. When can you start?"

"Now. I have my things in the car. I don't need a place to live. I have a very nice house in Sells. It is only a fifteen-minute drive."

"Well, Maggie 'Sees Far' Parker, the office across the hall is now yours. Is there anything else that I need to know about you?"

Chief Whiteshirt was enjoying this. Maggie was already moving toward the door but paused, deciding whether to speak. "Yes. I am the great granddaughter of the Comanche chief, Quanah Parker. I am a bit chubby and a bit old, but I have the same blood in my body. You will need me because I am a warrior and you are going to fight a war, Ethan Crowe."

Ethan took a long look at the woman, then a quick glance at Chief Whiteshirt, who only smiled at him. Ethan paused for a very long minute. "Yes, I think you're right, Sees Far. I am proud to have you here."

Ethan's thoughts snapped back to the present when Isaac Factor appeared in his doorway and asked, "Ready?"

Ethan nodded and stood up, taking his notepad and a couple of loose pens from his desktop. Seeing Crowe pick up the pens, Isaac chuckled. "I don't know why you bother bringing those. You manage to steal a pen everywhere you go."

Ethan stuck the pens in his pocket and smiled as he left his office. "What are you talking about?"

"Yeah right." Isaac walked ahead of Crowe, shaking his head good-naturedly.

Both men proceeded to the conference room. This room served primarily as a meeting room but quickly converted to a command post for complex operations. It also served as the stage for impromptu birthday and holiday parties throughout the year. As they moved along the corridor, Isaac informed Crowe that his two intelligence officers had just returned from EPIC and that they had also managed an off-the-record meeting with Agent King's contact there.

"They have all the latest on our friends down South. You aren't going to like it."

"Oh?"

"No, not a bit, boss."

Through the glass walls of the conference room, Crowe could see that his intel officers were ready and waiting for him. Ty Zepeda, the young tribal police officer, was seated at the PowerPoint projector. His senior partner was looking over his notes as Crowe and Factor rounded the corner of the doorframe. Maggie followed right behind Ethan and Isaac as she moved around to the far end of the table with a tray carrying a thermos carafe of fresh coffee along with five mugs. *It appeared that Sees Far was staying.* Ethan smiled to himself.

After all the hellos were said, Crowe began, "How was Texas?"

Tyrell, enthusiastically, was first to respond, "Great! You've got to see that place, sir! It is amazing. I think we could use—"

Tyrell was interrupted by his senior partner, smiling, "I think Ty is trying to say that the trip was profitable. We did learn some stuff that we should have been told a long time ago."

The senior intelligence officer was Michael Lighthorse, a retired lieutenant from the Milwaukee Police Department, where he had worked at their intelligence fusion center for his last ten years before retirement. He had grown up on the Lac Du Flambeau Reservation in Northern Wisconsin, attended the University of Wisconsin, and then spent a distinguished career with the Milwaukee police. He was a genius at IT, and while at Milwaukee PD, he had helped to establish one of the leading intelligence units in the entire Midwest. Crowe had heard about him from Agent King, who had met him during an assignment in the Milwaukee office. Crowe had wasted no time recruiting him to work on the Tohono. Michael had quickly set up a formidable intelligence unit within the Shadow Wolves, and his intel had already resulted in two major seizures of methamphetamine from the Zeta cartel.

Ethan had decided to bring Ty into the Shadow Wolves from the tribal police soon after arriving. The young officer was intelligent and eager. Surviving the ambush had affected the young man more than the boy realized. Upon joining the unit, he had come to Crowe asking to enter training to become a tracker. Ethan had responded by telling him that he would like him to work in the intelligence side of things for a while before being considered for a tracker position. In truth, he wanted to protect the young man and his family from the dangers of the border, at least until Ty could put a bit more space between himself and the massacre.

Once seated at the table, Crowe and Factor noted Ty's boyish enthusiasm and shared an amused look. Factor spoke. "Well, enlighten us, guys."

Ty looked at his partner expectantly and then started with the first slide. Lighthorse began the presentation in a steady, no-nonsense briefing voice, "This first map shows the current breakdown of territories controlled by the Zetas and the Sinaloa group. In truth, it's a month old, and it has probably already changed. The Zetas are knocking the hell out of the Sinaloans. They are leaving killing fields across the northern section of Mexico. From what they're telling us at EPIC, the Zetas are far better equipped and better trained. Most of their people in the field have either received formal training from the police or the army. Their weaponry is top-shelf."

Crowe interrupted, "Where are they getting the weapons and the equipment for that matter?"

"That's a matter of conjecture, sir. Some are saying it's coming from Eastern Europe, but I got a guy who works over at the Texas Rangers. His informant says a lot of the guns are coming from our side of the border."

Ethan glanced at Factor and then at Lighthorse with eyebrows raised questioningly.

"I know you don't like any of this conspiracy shit, but he tells me it's good intel."

Crowe then changed the subject. "So tell me about the Zetas. What's the latest?"

Lighthorse nodded. "Ty, go to slide fifteen."

The screen transformed to an organization chart. At the top of the chart was one man. Lighthorse began, "Boss, you know this one. Yaotl. No last name, no photo. He is still virtually invisible. He's the deadliest drug boss to emerge since the disappearance of the Colombian drug lords of the eighties and nineties." A composite sketch showed a swarthy man, probably more Aztec than Spanish by blood. A second photo showed a man on a mountain road, standing next to a Land Rover. The image was grainy and dark.

Lighthorse continued, "The photo you're looking at is from a satellite overflight taken almost three years ago. Unfortunately, nobody is certain the guy in the photo is actually Yaotl. It's an educated guess at best. The guy is extremely elusive and reports of him leaving his mountain stronghold are rare. Whatever Yaotl actually looks like, everyone basically agrees that he is calling all the shots in the Zeta organization. We don't know of anyone who has been able to get an informant anywhere near the man. The one thing that all the Feds seem to agree on is that nothing really big happens without Yaotl's finger on the *go* button."

"Where is he believed to be living again?" Crowe focused intensely, as always, when talking about the Zetas.

"He is believed to be up in the Sierra Madres. There have been no recent drone flights over the place, but only because our narco guys would prefer he doesn't know that we know."

Lighthorse looked over at Factor, who nodded for him to continue.

"The guys in the next row of the chart are the underbosses. As far as we can tell, there are three. There's Diego Porfillio Sanchez"—pointing at the screen with his red laser pointer—"and Arturo 'El Loco' Cabrejo," moving his pointer to the left. "The guy in the middle is Roberto Maria Guzman. He is the guy with the juice." He waited a second and then continued, "Right now he is in charge of all transport from the South to the US. He is also believed to be the only one that Yaotl totally trusts."

Crowe remained silent but continued to stare at the blue screen, transfixed by the names and photos. Finally, he spoke, "What does this name Yaotl mean? Is it a real name?"

They tell me it means *warrior* in Nahuatl. Again, back to the Aztec thing. Many like to see him as a return to the glory days before the whites came."

Crowe looked around the room with a dry smile. "I guess we've all thought about that scenario a few times before."

"Amen!" Maggie chimed in from the far side of the room. The rest chuckled quietly.

After a pause, Lighthorse looked at Factor, who nodded to continue. Lighthorse took a deep breath. "We believe it was Guzman who orchestrated the killings on our side of the fence. Also the assassination of Officer Price."

Crowe quickly asked, "What is EPIC saying about that?"

"They believe that the killing of the mules was just to send a message to everyone to leave them alone. The Price thing was personal. They think it came from the top. Yaotl, Warrior, whatever you want to call the motherfucker, probably gave the order. He was pissed because Price had taken off two big loads, and he felt it was an embarrassment to him personally. It was also a clear warning to the tribal police to leave them alone."

Crowe thought to himself, *Lighthorse sure didn't sound like a man raised on the rez even though he was pure-blooded Ojibwe. The last traces of the reservation were gone from Michael. That ship had sailed long ago. Now he just sounded like the tough big-city cop that he was.*

"Who did it, Michael?" Crowe looked directly at his intelligence officer. "Who came to Tohono and made it happen?"

Lighthorse shrugged, regret obvious in his face. "They really don't know. Or at least they say they don't know. The DEA guys were kind of weird about it."

"You think there is more than they are saying?"

"Well, you know me, boss, city cops never trust the Feds anyway." Lighthorse smiling a bit. "And I sure as hell don't trust them on this. There's more, probably lots more."

Crowe pressed once more. "The sniper. That was no amateur thing. That was a soldier. What are they saying about that?"

"Again, DEA said nothing. But a Texas Ranger mentioned a name. Only one name. I don't know if it's a first name or a last name. All they have heard is that the guy is called Romero. He is supposed to be a major hitter for the Zetas. But this is all off-the-record stuff, boss."

Crowe nodded and silently digested his intelligence officer's last comments in light of his past experiences. *What the fuck was DEA up to down there?*

Lighthorse was about to close the presentation when he exchanged a look with Ty. Then after a moment's consideration, he continued, "It was strange. When I talked to the DEA guy over at EPIC, he acted odd. It's almost like they have someone on the inside down there. If they do, they sure aren't going to tell us about it."

Crowe remained silent for a few seconds and then shook his head, thinking.

"Anything else for today?" Factor intruded quietly.

Lighthorse had lots more but he knew when to say when. The boss had what he wanted.

"Just one more thing," Lighthorse added. "They did tell us that we can expect an increase in meth and heroin over the next year. H is in big demand, along with all the related opioid pills being used by the idiots up here in the States. They also say that the Zetas want to increase their ownership in the skin trade. The border guys in Texas say that they are seeing women being brought over a couple of times a month, and it ain't pretty. The girls are young and getting younger."

Crowe nodded and bit down on his lower lip pensively. He then nodded to Isaac and both got up and headed back to Crowe's office. Maggie, silent throughout, gathered up the untouched coffee and left the room. Lighthorse helped his young partner to pack up their stuff, thinking how many times in his career he had navigated the touchy waters of complex intel briefings. He knew that too much conspiracy stuff only muddied the waters. He had learned long ago to only go with solid information, peppering it with conjecture only when necessary.

CHAPTER 17

Crowe dropped onto the threadbare couch in his office, slumping back with his head, resting on the faded upholstery. Factor folded his long body into the only remaining chair in the office, closing the door before he did so.

"What do you make of all that?" Isaac nodding back to the briefing room and looked expectantly at Crowe.

Crowe hesitated before replying, "I sure as fuck don't know. I guess the Feds have bigger things on their minds. But hell, keeping this stuff from us is fucked up. It's not like we're tribal police or vigilantes. We're Feds! Every one of us is a GS 13 or above. Hell, all of us have top secret clearances too."

"Yeah, but you know nobody out there takes us seriously. We're just a bunch of redskins with badges to them. With the exception of my black ass, of course." Isaac smiled ear to ear.

Crowe said nothing for quite a while, deep in thought. "If they have someone inside the cartel that is killing cops on this side and they're not telling us, I'm gonna be pissed."

"Could that be?"

"Let's hope not," said Crowe, shifting gears. "The intel about the increased shipments will help. We have already taken off three good-sized loads in the past two months, and now we know the shipments are going to become more frequent."

Factor nodded. "We still don't know whose dope it was."

"Yeah, but I think after today we can assume it belonged to the Zetas. I'm just wondering how we can lure one of these top bosses over to our side of the fence."

"Don't know about that, boss. How did you guys do that stuff in the DIA or DEA or whatever spook outfit you worked for?"

Crowe chuckled. "If I told you… You know how that line goes in the movies. All kidding aside, we have to make sure that all our people are briefed up on everything we learned today. I also want to double up on security measures for the patrols. Check and double-check on transport equipment, weapons, and communications."

Factor nodded acknowledgment to Crowe.

The boss continued, "How many patrols are out now?"

"Two. Blue Eagle and Iron Cloud just went out yesterday, and the Apaches are due in any minute."

As Factor spoke, a dusty Humvee could be seen approaching the main building. Behind the wheel was a woman in full camo, hair tied back with a cloth band, the remainder of her long hair flying in the wind. "Speak of the devil, or should I say devils?"

Crowe looked through his window to see two women stepping out of the Humvee. He said nothing, just watching the two as they moved to the back of the vehicle to unload their gear. His entire crew was Native American, but that didn't mean that they all looked or thought the same. Tribal traditions, languages, and even overall appearance varied widely from tribe to tribe. All his people were selected for their skills, courage, and intelligence, and they all took fierce pride in their own distinct cultures. These two, however, were something different. They went far beyond the rest of the team in embracing their roots. Crowe remembered their initial interviews, asking them if they spoke any Apache. They both looked at him in disbelief, insulted that he would even ask that question. They were Apache, the *Tinde*, as their people called themselves. Both of them seemed to think that was all that needed to be said.

The driver was Hannah Lone Hawk. She normally wore her black hair pulled back into a thick braid, which she often flipped over her left shoulder to fall across her chest. Her skin was bronze, cheeks high, and eyes black as onyx. She was tall and lean. Her muscles long and taut, her stomach as tight as a professional athlete. Born and raised on the San Carlos Apache Reservation, Hannah had left the rez and was educated at the University of Arizona. Upon graduation, she went to work as an ICE agent on the Mexico/California border. Hannah had lived away from the reservation since college and often found herself torn between the two worlds. Crowe had heard that she had been married to a white professor for a short time, but that had ended badly. She had learned her tracking skills from her father and grandfather back on the San Carlos reservation. She much preferred being on horseback to the things girls were supposed to do. By the time she turned ten, she could ride better than most adults and track wild game over the most unforgiving terrain. She had been flourishing in her job. But upon hearing about the Shadow Wolves, she had immediately requested a transfer. After reviewing her qualifications and speaking with her in person, Ethan had no doubts about bringing her aboard. He knew she would be an ideal partner for his other Apache tracker.

The second Apache was Nalin Chee. Nalin was thirty years old, a full-blooded Chiricahua Apache, and a warrior to the bone. Nalin had grown up on an Apache reservation in dry, dusty poverty. She won a scholarship to Arizona State and studied Spanish and criminal justice. Upon graduation, due to her fluency in Spanish, Apache, and Navajo, she had been recruited by several federal police agencies. Instead, she opted to return to the reservation to work for the Apache Tribal Police. She was a strong proponent of Native American rights and outspoken about the theft of tribal lands by the government. She believed strongly in maintaining the Apache culture, religious, practices and language.

While with the tribal police, Chee had learned to track from an old Apache whose distant ancestor had ridden with Geronimo. He had spent over a year teaching her the ways of the desert and the mountains. She learned how to find water in the harshest terrain and how to read the land and the creatures that inhabited it. He had also taught her much of her people's history and the old ways of the Apache people. The old man had reawakened the warrior blood that coursed through her veins.

Crowe watched Chee as she carefully stowed her firearms and other gear into carrying cases. She was a pleasure to watch, he had to admit. Her face was angular and, most would say, quite beautiful.

She wore her long hair in multiple braids infused with native beadwork, her locks falling loosely over her shoulders. She was shorter than Lone Hawk but equally fit, perhaps more so. Her movements were more like an untamed cat. Her full breasts strained against the desert camo T-shirt as she stretched to pull her bags from the Humvee. Crowe shook his head, reminding himself to stay focused. He looked up to see Isaac looking at him and smiling.

Crowe said defensively, "What?" feigning innocence.

"Nothing." Then Isaac said, "It does make you think that Mother Nature spent a lot more time on some things and some people."

"Factor, you're a dirty old man."

"That right there is a woman full-grown, very full-grown if you ask me."

Ethan just shook his head and turned his attention back to a file on his desk. Then sensing Factor still staring at him and grinning, he said, "Don't you have something to do?"

"You mean more interesting than this?" Isaac was now smiling broadly.

While he shuffled through his papers and Isaac exited his office, Crowe thought about the women trackers. Both women seemed unware of their natural beauty and had felt no need to impress their male counterparts. The Apache had a long history of fierce female warriors. To them, what they were was natural and to be expected. If anything, one got the sense that they pitied the other trackers for not being Apache.

*****

Nalin Chee pulled the last of her gear from the Humvee, dropping it onto the ground in a cloud of dust. She stretched from the long drive, eager to get a cool shower and some rest. She had a long weekend coming up and planned to drive north with Hannah to the rez at San Carlos. Hannah wanted to visit her mother and younger sister. Her mother was suffering from reservation sickness, alcoholism, a constant companion to families on reservations across the country. Nalin was going along for the ride and for moral support.

Nalin glanced up and saw her boss watching her through his office window. Discovered, he didn't look away; he just calmly met her stare. They both stood frozen for seconds, Ethan slowly moving away from the window and back to his desk. Nalin continued to gaze at the window, once again wondering about the man. He was clearly older than her, probably forty-five at least. She knew little or nothing about his personal life and was hesitant to ask too many questions.

The Apache scout grudgingly admitted to herself an attraction for Crowe. He was certainly good-looking enough; even Hannah thought he was hot. Whatever his exact age, he was certainly not a normal example of a middle-aged man. She also knew that he had spent an entire career fighting bad guys in places she would never see. Elias Blue Eagle said that he heard that the boss had a woman overseas. But Nalin had a feeling that nobody really knew the truth about Crowe except Isaac Factor. She smiled to herself, *Factor talked even less than the boss, so good luck with that!*

Nalin called across the hood of their vehicle, "Hey, Lone Hawk, how long before you're ready to ride?"

Hannah stood up from where she was crouched, arranging her gear. "Jesus, Chee, we just got here. I still have to check with the boss and file our after-action report. It'll be at least a couple hours unless *you* want to talk to the boss and do the paperwork," a trace of a grin accentuating her point.

Nalin responded with a grunt, immediately securing her rifle on her pack and working her arms through the straps of her backpack. "Fucking hilarious, aren't you? It's your turn to file the after-action, and I'll leave the boss to *you*, Agent Lone Hawk."

"I'll come by your quarters about six if that's okay," Hannah called out while watching Nalin's athletic stride as she crossed the parking lot toward the barracks. Nalin motioned a thumbs-up over her shoulder without looking back. Hannah turned to the office, smiling to herself as she walked up the stairs. *Forget about it, girl. That inscrutable Apache stuff doesn't get past me, at least as far as the boss is concerned.* As she stood in front of the entrance, she wondered about her own feelings for Crowe. *He does have something.* Entering and walking down the corridor to the equipment locker, she thought back to the time that she had been speculating out loud to Isaac about Crowe's love life. Factor had suddenly become deadly serious and told her that Ethan had lost a wife and son in a horrible way and that a part of him was badly broken. She had never told anyone about that conversation, including Nalin, but had always felt a sadness in him whenever she watched him from across a room. She walked past Crowe's office, glancing sideways through the door and nodding. "Boss." Crowe nodded back with a smile.

Chapter 18

Two weeks later, Southern Arizona,
north of the Tohono Reservation

Ethan tuned his iPod to his favorite playlist and turned up the volume. One perk of this new assignment had been his new G-ride, government speak, for an officially assigned vehicle. The twin-turbo Ford Raptor was more of a race car than a truck. He had just finished a torturous meeting in Tucson with the FBI, DEA, ICE, and the Border Patrol. The DEA special agent in charge, known as the SAC, had called a summit of all the federal players in the region. As usual, it was long on "let's all get along and communicate better in the future" and short on anything of substance. Everyone in the meeting clearly thought they were the most important person in the room. Unfortunately, they all pretended to be equals and open to anything that resembled cooperation.

Ethan thought back to the four GS-15s (a.k.a. big bosses) who had been sitting around the table during the meeting as Springsteen continued to blast from the eight speakers in the cabin. The federal supervisors had all been in their late thirties. They had all shot to the top of their respective agencies; most of them had not personally put handcuffs on ten bad guys in their lives. Admittedly, he was withholding judgment on Agent King, who actually seemed to know her shit. With that one exception, it was clear that the rest of the group had specialized in career enhancement over law enforcement. He laughed to himself, thinking back to the meeting. He vaguely remembered shaking everyone's hand, getting his cup of coffee, and the rest was just a blur. *Of one thing he was certain, those were three hours he would never get back.*

The music changed to Foreigner singing "Juke Box Hero," and Crowe decided to leave Tucson and the federal love fest in the rear-view mirror. A few hours of his tunes and the desert would be just what he needed to regain his sanity.

CHAPTER 19

Southern Arizona Desert

The two women looked out upon the ribbon of asphalt known as the West Tucson-Ajo Highway, headed back toward the Tohono reservation. The heat shimmered in waves across the black road stretching ahead of them. Hannah was at the wheel of her Toyota 4-Runner, deep in thought, and Phil Collins was on the satellite radio singing "I Don't Care Anymore." Nalin looked over at her friend, knowing that she was worried about her mom. They had arrived at the San Carlos to find her mom in bad shape. Hannah's sister, a high school senior, was basically taking care of the house and making sure that her younger brother, Jason, was fed and that he made it to school each day.

Within a day of their arrival, Hannah had made arrangements for her mom to be admitted to the alcohol rehab program sponsored by a non-profit organization that was actually making some good things happen on the rez. She and Nalin had then set about getting the house in order, cleaning everything and throwing out all the bottles of alcohol and pills that they could find. There was no shame in it for Hannah; she and Nalin were closer than sisters and both knew the world from which they came.

After two weeks of emergency leave, which Crowe had granted without question, they had made arrangements for her younger brother to return with them to Tohono for a few months. Maggie Sees Far, learning of the situation, had insisted that the boy stay with her whenever Hannah was in the field. She had already arranged for his transfer into the rez school, and there was no doubt that she would look after him like a mother bird.

Hannah looked in the rearview mirror at her little brother. He sat with his head leaning against the window, eyes closed. His smooth caramel-colored skin accentuated his long black eyelashes. She bit her lip, cursing the unfairness of life. Jason was only eight years old, an age that should have meant a life secure in the cradle of a loving family. He had been a baby that was unexpected. Her father had sired him during one of his infrequent visits home and then left again, promising to send money back to her mother as soon as the new job began. The money never came. Two months later, they heard he had died in a bar fight in some small roadside joint on the outskirts of El Paso. Sadly, he never even knew that he had a son. Her mother never had the chance to tell him. Her mom had battled the bottle for the boy's entire life. Hannah had been both sister and mother to Jace for most of his life. Her time away at school, and now with the Shadow Wolves, had been difficult. She had felt like she was abandoning him each time she drove away.

This trip had been a tough one. She had found her mom seated at the kitchen table, staring at a plate of food that Jace had cooked for her. Her brother had sat across the table from her, hoping she would to take an interest in eating. When Hannah and Nalin had come through the door, it had been unexpected. Her brother's worried look had instantly changed to joy at the sight of his sister and Nalin. He jumped up from the table and embraced Hannah in a death grip. Her mom had remained seated. But even through the fog of alcohol, she smiled gently at the sight of her oldest daughter and her son together.

Within a day, Hannah had made up her mind that she would keep Jason with her for the foreseeable future. She would take an apartment on the Tohono rez and have him attend school in Sells. She would find a way to make it work, knowing that the boss would do everything he could to accommodate her new situation. Her concentration must have been evident as she gripped the wheel because Nalin broke through her thoughts to pat her right forearm. In Apache, Nalin told her, "Don't worry sister, we have this."

Seconds later, the sound of a police siren startled both of them. They had been preoccupied and had not seen the police cruiser fall in behind. Nalin turned to the rear from the passenger seat. "What the…?"

Hannah checked her rear and side mirrors. "Are we on the rez yet?"

"No, I don't think so. I think we've got another twenty miles yet."

Hannah furrowed her brow. "What the hell are they stopping us for?"

Jace began to stir from the noise of the siren and the women's voices. "What's up, sis?"

"I have no idea." Hannah activated her right turn signal and slowed down to pull off the roadway.

The marked police car pulled behind the 4-Runner. Hannah rolled down her window, checking her side mirror to see if the deputy was approaching. She pulled out her credentials from the center console with Nalin doing the same.

Nalin, who was now completely turned in her seat, looking back at the police car, said to nobody in particular, "What are they doing back there?"

Hannah didn't answer but kept watching, trying to decide whether to get out of the car or wait in the Toyota. Finally, after almost five minutes of waiting, she slowly opened the door and stepped out onto the asphalt next to her car, facing the sheriff's unit. Careful to keep her hands in full sight, she dropped open her badge case which she held in her right hand, the gold shield clear to the deputies.

A sudden burst of noise came from the light bar on top of the cruiser. "You need to get back into your vehicle, ma'am. Place your hands back at your sides and reenter your vehicle now." Hannah then noticed the deputy on the passenger side had exited his side of the cruiser and stood behind his open door with his handgun in his right hand, his forearm resting on the doorframe. His gun was pointed at the Toyota in a casual way.

Nalin was getting agitated, telling Hannah to tell the deputies who she was. "Careful, Lone Hawk. I don't trust these *Indaa* (whites)."

Hannah slowly eased back into her seat and waited, wondering what was happening.

Jason was now looking back and forth from Nalin to Hannah. "What's wrong?"

"Nothing, sweetie, just a misunderstanding," she replied, not really believing her own words.

A few seconds later, the driver of the vehicle unfolded his tall frame from his cruiser, adjusted his tan cowboy hat and swaggered toward the driver's door of the Toyota. Hannah watched his approach in her side mirror, assessing the man by his movement and his bearing. The man was well over six feet tall, pale, and clean-shaven. His brown deputy's uniform fit tightly across his chest. *This Indaa is proud of his muscles. Probably lots of hours in the gym in front of a mirror.*

"Where are we headed today, Miss?" said the deputy, looking into the car behind reflective wire-rimmed Ray-Bans, his right hand resting on his service weapon.

"We're headed to the Tohono O'odham Reservation, Officer." Hannah twisting her neck to look at the officer. "Were we doing something wrong?"

The deputy didn't respond, ignoring her question. "Your driver's license and registration. And I want ID from everyone." His arm moved in a sweeping gesture that included both Nalin and her brother. "So let's get this moving."

"Why do you need their IDs, Officer?" Hannah was beginning to get pissed off but trying to remain calm. "Look, both of us are federal agents, and the boy is my brother."

The deputy leaned closer to the window. "I'm not going to ask again, Miss."

By this time, Nalin made the decision to step out of the 4-Runner. Turning to look back, she found the second deputy at the rear of the Toyota with his gun pointed directly at her, smiling. This one was short and chunky, tattoos from some military unit and a "Don't Tread on Me" flag on his arms.

"Got that ID, lady?" the second deputy piped in. "You heard my partner, didn't you?"

Nalin fired back, "Did you hear my partner? We're cops, federal agents from Homeland Security."

The tall deputy had lost his patience. "Get the kid out here too, and *now*!"

Jason looked at Nalin questioningly. "Nalin?"

Nalin reached across and opened the back door, placing her hand protectively around the boy as he exited the vehicle. She looked fiercely at the short one. "What now, Indaa?" she asked, forgetting her English and using the word for its other meaning: *enemy*.

The lead deputy motioned for Hannah to move to the other side of the car, out of the roadway. He directed her to join Nalin and Jason, who were now standing off the shoulder with their feet in the hot desert sand.

"So where are you three coming from?"

The two women exchanged a puzzled glance. It was now dawning on both of them that this was some sort of immigration stop.

Nalin looked at the deputy defiantly. "You've got our ID and you know we're not Mexican. We're Apache, and this is all bullshit."

"How do I know what you are? There's Indians south of the border too. That kid sure looks like a greaser to me."

"Fuck you!" Nalin moved toward the deputy but was held back by Hannah, who was worried that this clusterfuck could escalate further.

"Nahatse." Hannah was speaking forcefully and standing in front of her partner, doing her best to calm her.

The second deputy piped in, "Where's the kid's ID?" sneering at the eight-year-old, trying to invoke fear with every syllable.

"He doesn't have to carry an ID. He's my younger brother. You need to seriously think about what you're doing, Deputy."

The deputy threw the two badge cases belonging to the women on the roof of the 4-Runner, chortling and saying something under his breath. He then turned back to Hannah. "Lady, Apache or Mexican, how do I know that you aren't bringing this greaser kid over the border? And how do I know that *you* are legit?"

The second deputy, smirking, piped in, "Yeah, you two look like you're 'wet' too if you ask me."

The first deputy looked past the women and nodded to the Toyota. "Any weapons in the car?"

Nalin almost shouted, "Yeah. Glocks, both belonging to the federal government."

"Well, it looks like I am going to have to impound those until we can determine if you're the real deal."

"Fuck!" Nalin looked skyward in exasperation.

The smaller deputy moved slightly, pointing his weapon directly at Nalin as she voiced her objections. "Don't move another muscle, *lady*." The last word was said sarcastically, the deputy's words purposely menacing.

As the drama continued to unfold, only Jace had noticed a dark green Ford Raptor pull up behind the police cruiser. A dark-haired man dressed in tan cargo pants and a loose-fitting white cotton shirt stepped out of the jeep and began walking toward the group. The tall deputy looked up at the sound of the man's footsteps on the loose gravel. Hannah and Nalin's eyes silently followed Ethan Crowe as he approached the Toyota, his hands loose at his side.

"Stay right where you are, Mister!" the taller deputy commanded in a loud voice, holding his palm up in a gesture that said halt.

"Easy, Deputy." Crowe held his federal credentials in his left hand. "Homeland Security." He waited a second. Then he added, "Stand down, Deputy now," his voice quiet but steely.

The deputy nodded to his short partner. "Keep an eye on them." And then he lowered his handgun, holding it at his side as he walked back to meet the dark stranger. As he was walking, he began to worry that another person claiming to be a Fed showing up was maybe not a coincidence. But as he moved toward the stranger, he quickly reassured himself. *The sheriff said to be tough on anyone they found out here. Hell, the only people out here were wets, and even the Indians were probably from across the border. Fuck 'em.*

The deputy came to a stop just feet from Crowe, his chest expanded to the fullest to maximize his size advantage over the new arrival. "So what's your story?"

"No story, Deputy. You have two of my people and a young boy on the side of the road, and I want to know what's going on."

"I'm afraid that's sheriff's department business. If they're your people, whatever that means, we are in the middle of something here and you have nothing to do with it."

"He thinks we're illegals, boss!" Nalin shouted from her spot in the sand. "They say that Jason has to show ID."

The second deputy moved menacingly closer to Nalin, hissing the words quietly, "Shut the fuck up."

"Is that true, Deputy?" Crowe moving closer imperceptibly.

"Afraid so. We're gonna have to take him in until someone can show us proof that he's an American."

Crowe laughed, no humor in his eyes.

"What's so funny?" the deputy demanded arrogantly.

"Nothing really. But I was just thinking that he's a hell of a lot more American than you are."

"Well, that's the way it's going to be, Mr. Fed, if that's what you really are. That little greaser's going with us, and I haven't decided what's going to happen to the other two. You, on the other hand, can leave now. Otherwise, you can go with them too. It's all the same to me." The tall man nervously moved his gun hand toward Ethan.

Ethan looked over at his two agents. Both were pissed and ready to fight. Nalin was dressed in tight-fitting jeans, white sneakers, and a black hooded shirt. Her hair hung loose, flowing over her shoulders and around her face. Lone Hawk was dressed in a blue cotton dress, falling just below her knees. A pair of cowboy boots and a white Western-style blouse made her look like any other ranch girl in Arizona. The boy stood between the two women, his hand nervously holding his sister's sleeve. He then turned to Ethan, a look of fear and pleading on his face.

The boy would later think back to that moment in time. The world seemed to change before his eyes. In a lightning blur, the dark man had grabbed the deputy's gun hand, pulling the gun and hand to the left and twisting it back to the right at the same time. He then jerked the hand backward, eliciting a prolonged scream from the lawman as his trigger finger broke in the trigger guard, the gun then ending up in the hands of the dark stranger. Ethan threw the firearm to the ground behind him and continued to face the imposing deputy as the man gathered his wits and tried to advance on Crowe, clearly not yet subdued. Crowe moved forward quickly, firing three rapid punches, two to the face and one to the midsection. The deputy, who had, until now, equated muscles with fighting skills, collapsed in a heap, struggling to catch his breath. He reached up with his remaining good hand to stem the flow of blood gushing from his nose and mouth.

The second deputy's attention was momentarily drawn to the attack on his partner. In the blink of an eye, his own weapon was twisted from his hand while he was pulled violently backward to the ground by Nalin. Now on the ground with the woman's arm wrapped around his neck in a tight choke hold, he looked up to the sight of the taller woman holding his own firearm pointed directly at his chest.

Ethan Crowe walked calmly over and bent to pick up the first deputy's gun. He tucked it into his waistband and walked over to where his agents held the second deputy. He moved to the boy first, placing his arm around him reassuringly. "You okay, son?" The boy looked up at Crowe, nodding yes but fighting back tears at the same time. Ethan pulled him closer, looking out into the desert with his own thoughts and emotions.

Ethan held the boy closely for a few minutes and then gently released him. "Can you wait here for me?"

The boy answered quietly. "Yes, sir."

Crowe moved closer to where the second deputy remained in the grasp of Nalin and under the gun of Lone Hawk. He stood still for a moment, looking down at the deputy, who now looked petrified at his predicament. Finally, Crowe nodded to Nalin. "Let him up, Nahatse."

Nalin released the deputy, pushing him off to the side, while Hannah took two steps backward to give the man the space to stand up. The deputy slowly stood, brushing the dirt from his uniform. "You're in big trouble, Mister. You have just assaulted two sheriff's deputies in the course of their duties. You and these greaser bitches."

The man was interrupted by Crowe spinning him around. Crowe now had the deputy's hair firmly in his left hand and his right hand firmly on the front of the deputy's throat, clutching his windpipe. "Listen to me very, very carefully," Crowe seethed. "What you have done here has nothing to do with your lawful duty." Crowe was now whispering in the man's ear, his words unheard by the rest of the group.

"You need to take that pathetic piece of shit with you"—nodding in the direction of the other deputy—"and stay the fuck away from my people and anyone else from the Tohono. If I ever so much as hear about you bothering the people from this reservation, I will find you." Crowe paused. "I know that time will go by and you will start to rethink this moment. You might even think that you can deal with me if you meet me under different circumstances. Don't do that. You have never met anyone like me. In fact, you have never even imagined anyone like me." He held the man for a brief second longer and then released him, the deputy falling to the ground, gasping for breath and clearly cowed.

Crowe looked up, slowly coming back from the brink. He looked at the two agents and the boy who were all staring at him in shock. He forced himself to smile. "Are you guys, okay?"

The women nodded in unison, the boy held closely between the two. Hannah moved toward Crowe, handing him the second deputy's firearm. The gun was a Beretta 9 mm. Crowe took the handgun, ejected the mag, and jacked the remaining round from the chamber. He turned and threw the weapon into the surrounding desert. He then did the same with the first deputy's firearm. He immediately walked to the police car, removed the two shotguns from the trunk, emptied the shells, and threw them in the opposite direction. Finished defanging the deputies, he approached Hannah.

"So this is your brother." He looked to the boy and held out his hand. "What's your name young man?"

The boy stepped forward and shyly took Ethan's hand, staring at the man with wide, dark brown eyes. He seemed unable to speak.

Hannah, still in shock, jumped in, "Jason. This is my little brother, Jason, but his friends and family call him Jace." Her eyes looked lovingly at the boy at her side.

"Nice to meet you, Jace."

Hannah interrupted again, "Jace, this is Ghostwalker," her use of the Ethan's Sioux name a small sign of gratitude for what he had just done for them. The boy's eyes widened even further at the sound of his savior's tribal nickname.

Ethan continued to hold the boy's hand. "You can just call me Ethan," he said, winking at the boy. "Hannah tells me you're going to be staying with us for a while."

The boy nodded again, but smiling now.

"Well, I'm sure that we're going to be great friends, Jason Lone Hawk," Ethan said, reluctantly releasing the boy's hand.

Crowe looked around to see both deputies slowly moving back toward their cruiser. Neither seemed interested in looking for their weapons.

Ethan calmly looked at Nalin. "You sure you're okay?"

Nalin nodded slowly in the affirmative, intensely gazing at Crowe as if for the first time. She felt something move in her that she could not explain.

"Well, I guess we had better get started home. What do you think?" Ethan was acting like they had just finished a Sunday picnic.

Both agents looked at each other and nodded. Nalin, smiling, looked beyond Crowe at the two broken deputies.

Crowe suggested, "Hannah, maybe Jace would like to keep me company in the Raptor."

"Can I, sis?" asked the boy, eager to be with his newfound hero.

"Yep. But don't talk Mr. Crowe's ear off." Hannah smiling for the first time in what seemed an eternity.

The women settled into the 4-Runner, started the engine, and let the air conditioner begin to reduce the oven-like atmosphere of the interior. Hannah put the Toyota in gear and eased back onto the asphalt. She glanced back at Ethan's truck in the rearview mirror, her brother already talking animatedly in the front seat. She looked over at Nalin, paused, and asked, "What the hell was that?"

Nalin kept staring out the windshield. "I have no idea. Who can do that kind of stuff?" She spoke wide-eyed toward the windshield. "I never saw anything like that."

The women rode on in silence, both lost in thought as they headed back to the safety of the rez. Nalin replayed the events in her mind as she stared ahead. She had never seen any kind of emotion from Crowe before today and then this. Her adrenaline was still coursing through her system. She looked over to her partner and back to the road. *Shit!*

Chapter 20

Six months later
Acapulco/Mexico City/the American border

The pilot of the Mexicana Airlines flight announced final preparations for descent into Mexico City. Inez shifted in her seat and looked out the window at one of the largest cities in the world. Her left hand nervously fondled the religious medal hanging from her neck. She closed her eyes momentarily to ponder what kind of magic had taken a girl from the far south of Mexico to this place and time. It would have seemed impossible just six months ago. Her mind took her back to the start of this miracle.

Surviving a tearful goodbye with her mother and younger sisters, she had begun this epic adventure at the bus stop across from the mission church. She had traveled from her quaint, little village to the bustling tourist haven of Acapulco, where she was to start a new job. It was her first trip outside of her little village located in the lush tropics of southern Mexico. The journey had taken twelve hours, the bus winding slowly along the thin ribbon of roadway that passed through the mountains and forests of the Pacific coast.

The leaving had been hard. Inez loved her mother deeply and had shared with her every hope and dream since she was a child. As she had grown, she had become a friend to her mother as well as her daughter. Inez's father had died when Inez was just a young girl and there had been no time for her mom to find another man to love. He had left three daughters and no money. Inez blinked tears from her eyes as she remembered the look on her mother's face when they had said their goodbyes.

But it was time for her to go. Times were tough. The family needed the money, and there were simply no jobs for Inez in the village. She had made the difficult decision to go to the city for work over her mother's protests.

Throughout the trip, she had been unable to sleep, fearful from stories she had heard about the dangers of life outside her village. Her anxiety only heightened when the bus had finally pulled into the depot in Acapulco. The girl had slipped quietly from her seat, grabbed her ragged suitcase, and stepped tentatively from the steps onto the pavement. She looked around and found herself in the arrival's parking lot. The exhaust of the buses and the clamor of passengers coming and going was overwhelming. Dressed in her simple peasant dress, she shyly approached the uniformed bus driver, waiting patiently for him to finish his conversation with an agitated passenger. "Sir, could you please tell me how to find the Condesa del Mar Hotel?"

"Si chica, it is just down the street from the market. You can reach it in about ten minutes." The older driver looked the girl over. "It's quite a walk with your bag. Perhaps you should hire a taxi."

Inez smiled and thanked him, "I will be fine, but thank you very much." The girl reached down for her suitcase and turned in the direction of the hotel.

Inez walked tentatively along the wide boulevard, struggling with her bag, eyes wide as she took in the huge, opulent hotels rising like palaces along the strand of beach. Police officers patrolled in pairs along the same route, automatic rifles slung over their shoulders. Smiling politely at one of them as she passed, she was rewarded with only a stern grunt. Their mere presence was frightening to her. She had only experienced the friendly officers in her village, most of whom she had known personally since she was a little girl.

She finally came to a stop in front of her destination. The entrance to the hotel was covered with a huge canopy, luxury cars and taxis unloading their passengers in a cacophony of voices in English and Spanish. Uniformed hotel workers scurried like ants, attending to the needs of the suntanned European and American tourists.

The girl took a deep breath and started through the entrance to the hotel. She was stopped a few feet into the lobby when a kindly-looking man in uniform stepped in front of her. "Excuse me, young lady, are you looking for something?" Inez froze, unable to speak. "Don't worry, you are not in trouble," he soothed.

Stammering, she replied, "I am to work here... The friend of my mother is working here, and I am looking for her. Her name is Ana."

"Little one, you will not find your friend in here. You will need to go back outside and to the side of the hotel to the right. There you will find the entrance for the workers. Come with me to my desk and I will give you a note to show to the man at the door." When he finished his note, Inez quietly thanked the concierge and slipped from the lobby to the outside walkway leading to the side of the building.

*****

The plane suddenly hit some turbulence, jolting Inez from her memories. She looked fearfully around the cabin but found all was normal and the flight attendants were continuing to pick up empty plastic cups from the passengers. She stared at the seat back in front of her, letting her thoughts return to the events that had put her on this flight.

Inez was finishing a shift and putting her time card into the clock to be punched. She always liked this moment. It made her feel good. It was like a confirmation of a full day of hard work.

Looking back over the past six months, Inez knew that the job had truly been a blessing. Her salary had helped to support her mother and two sisters. She sent them money each week through the Western Union officer near her apartment. Her new life had given her a feeling of independence she had never thought possible. She was comfortable. She boarded the bus to work every morning in a finely pressed uniform, holding her head high and walking with dignity. She loved every minute of the work. Her devotion to the job had won her a quick promotion among the housekeeping staff, and it was there that she had joined a sisterhood with her coworkers. Even though she was barely grown, the women treated her as an equal, an adult. Of course, the other women were older and much more experienced in the ways of the world, but it didn't seem to matter. They had shared confidences that would have shocked her mother, but they also provided her insights into the lives of adults that both surprised and stirred her at the same time.

She moved toward the door but paused, hearing a clap of thunder in the distance. She hesitated a second, wondering if she could make it to the bus stop before the daily afternoon deluge hit. She felt lucky. Besides, she didn't want to wait another hour for the next bus. She was tired.

Walking quickly along the sidewalk, the first drops of rain began to fall. She looked longingly ahead to the bus stop and its tiny plexiglass shelter. Sighing, she saw that it was already crowded with others who were trying to avoid the coming onslaught. With another loud clap of thunder, the rain began to pour down. She struggled with her handbag to pull out her umbrella. The rain was already soaking her to the skin. Suddenly, she felt relief from the storm. Someone had come to her rescue, providing immediate protection in the form of a large black umbrella. Surprised, she looked up to find a handsome young man with black hair combed straight back, smooth skin, and dark brown eyes. She stared at him wide-eyed and speechless. Finally, after what seemed an eternity, he spoke, "Are you okay, Miss?"

Inez remained speechless for another beat, then said, "Yes, of course. I'm sorry if I seemed rude, but you surprised me. Thank you so much. You saved me from a real soaking, but I'm afraid that now you are getting wet."

The young man moved closer, now adequately sheltered from the wall of tropical rain. He smiled, holding out his hand. "It's perfectly all right. My name is Orlando, by the way, and I can always get dry."

Inez had just looked at him, not sure if she should offer her hand or if she should even speak. After an awkward moment, she tentatively offered her hand, still wet and slippery. She nervously apologized for getting him even wetter. "It is nice to meet you. I am Inez." Her eyes dropped self-consciously to the ground.

"Well, Inez of the Rain, it is a pleasure to make your acquaintance." Orlando now edged closer under the umbrella.

They both remained together in silence, neither seeming to know what to do next. Finally, Orlando spoke, "Are you here often?" He looked back over his shoulder at the hotel. "Do you work there?"

Inez nodded, shyly looking up at her shining knight. She noted that he was well-dressed and not some silly beachboy. He looked to be a little older than her, and she was sure that she had never seen anyone so handsome. His smile was bright white, lighting up his face like someone in the movies. Inez finally responded, "Yes."

"Yes?" That dazzling smile made gentle fun of her. "Yes what?"

The girl flushed involuntarily. "Yes, I work at the hotel, of course!"

They continued to talk in stops and starts, struggling to hear each other over noise of the traffic and the downpour. When the rain abruptly subsided as it often did at this time of year, their voices relaxed, as did Inez. Orlando reached up to close the umbrella, taking great care not to get any additional water on the girl. "Would you have time for a coffee?"

The girl looked up the street nervously, thinking about her bus.

Orlando quickly added, "I'm sure we can get you back here in time for the next bus. There is a nice little café just across the boulevard."

Inez looked down the street one more time, then across the street, and finally at the handsome young man. "Very well, but I have to be back here in one hour," she said, mentally setting the deadline for herself more than anything else.

*****

Inez's thoughts were once again interrupted by the flight attendant as she motioned for Inez to put her seatback forward for landing. She sat stiffly in the upright seat, her fingers once again absently fingered the tiny medal around her neck. As she watched the cabin crew make their final preparations, she nervously recalled how strongly her mother had been against this trip. "Who is this young businessman? How did you meet him? Why is he in such a hurry to marry?" she had pressed Inez. "If this Orlando is truly from a proper family, he would ask to meet your mother and observe the proper formalities."

Inez ran her finger across the window as the jet dropped slowly through the clouds and smog on final approach to Mexico City. *It will all be fine. Mama will see. We will send for her and the girls as soon as we're married.* She fought the pressing feelings of panic by thinking about Orlando. He was her one true love, and who could have dreamed of this? His good looks and knowledge of the world made her close her eyes in bliss. She could not wait to see him as she walked from the plane. She only hoped that she was dressed properly and that his family would approve of her. She let out a long breath and closed her eyes slowly. *All will be fine*, a final pronouncement to herself.

*****

Orlando stood waiting, flowers in hand. His black hair was combed back from his forehead, a starched white guayabera shirt open to show a smooth, tanned chest. Inez ran to him, pressing herself into his arms. She closed her eyes and reassured herself, *All will be fine!*

Pushing back from the flurry of kisses, Orlando spoke softly, "*Vamanos, preciosa* (Let's go, my precious one). We have places to see." They walked to the baggage claim as one, Inez fiercely clinging to him as if to life itself.

Leaving the terminal, Inez took in the frenetic activity around her. The air was dirty and suffocating, the people so close that there was no room to move or think. Cars sounded their horns; taxi drivers yelled from windows and tapped the outsides of their car doors with open palms through their open windows in some code known only among themselves. A group of teenage boys rushed past her, bumping her hard enough that she had to grab Orlando's shoulder to keep from falling. Her heart was racing and hands trembling as they stepped forward to the curb.

A large brown Ford sedan swerved and came to a stop in front of where Orlando and Inez waited. A large tattooed man with a long, wispy goatee jumped from behind the wheel, greeting Orlando and nodding to Inez. A second man, thin with long, dirty hair stringing down his back, remained in the passenger seat. A scar ran from the corner of his mouth to his right ear. Tattoos covered his neck and arms. He looked forward, never turning to acknowledge Orlando or Inez.

Inez's bag was placed in the trunk. The *scar* was talking over his shoulder to Orlando. "Ready, my brother?"

"Si, let's go. *A Nogales*," Inez heard Orlando respond as she slipped into the back seat with him.

"What is Nogales?" Inez asked, searching Orlando's face.

"It is a city in the north, my love. We are going there for some meetings. I have to tend to some work matters before we go to see my family. My father's business is far-reaching, and we have holdings in Nogales. A few days there and we will head back to our home in Mexico City." He leaned down to kiss her and stroked her hair. "I'm so glad that you are finally here."

Inez leaned into his chest, kissing his hand as she pressed it to her breast. "I am happy, my love," she whispered, trying her best to forget about the man in the front passenger seat. "How far is Nogales?"

"Not too far, *mi amor*, not too far," Orlando whispered softly to Inez. He then turned to the front seat and hissed a terse command to the driver, "*Vamos*!"

CHAPTER 21

Roberto Guzman eased into his desk chair, surrounded by oak and leather. The office was air-conditioned, and everything about the atmosphere said one thing: power. While not the king of the Zetas, he was surely a prince, and, maybe, even the first prince among the other princes. It was from this seat that he controlled all smuggling operations into the United States. Since his last meeting with Yaotl in the mountains, he had been given the power to increase the number of drug shipments and to establish markets for women above the border. There had been some turf wars with the Sinaloans, but even those had decreased with the overwhelming power that was wielded by the Zetas. He now had his people in the north negotiating deals with the MS-13 and Latin Kings gangs in several major American cities. *Things were good, very good.*

The boss had recently concluded negotiations with organized crime groups in Italy and China to expand the market for drugs and women there as well. This was already seeing results, particularly in Europe, where the EU's liberal obsession with civil rights made it easy for the criminals to do whatever they wanted to do.

Guzman was waiting for one of his recruiters to bring in a young woman. He was told that this was a special one, an exotic beauty fresh from a tiny village in the south. He was certain that she would bring a huge price over the border if he did not choose to keep her here for a time. The boss's decision to get into the flesh trade had been good all around. For Roberto, it was particularly satisfying. He was the first to see the girls and always had the option of sampling the goods. His decisions were final. This godlike power was intoxicating.

*****

Night pressed against the windows of the Ford as they wound their way north to the borderlands. Inez felt like she was moving underwater in some vast black sea. The only sounds were the snoring and occasional questions about the proper route to take from one of the men. Orlando held her close and stroked her hair until she finally surrendered to sleep halfway into the drive through the desert night.

Eight hours after leaving the airport, lights appeared on the horizon. A soft yellow glow was growing brighter with each mile. The tattooed passenger woke and came to life. Cigarettes were lit, and Inez felt a tenseness she had not felt before. She whispered, "Are we there, Orlando?"

"Yes, *chica*, we are here."

They entered a city that was asleep with the exception of the occasional bar or late night taqueria. It was 3:00 AM. The streets of Nogales had a dimly lit, empty feel to them. The deserted landscape was broken only by an occasional taxi picking up a drunken passenger or small groups of surly men standing on corners glaring suspiciously at each passing car. The girl shrunk into Orlando's arms, hard-looking men staring into their car as they drove past them on the street.

They drove through what seemed like miles of low-profile adobe houses with steel security bars on the windows, lights extinguished. Dogs, free of the daytime traffic, stood in the street and stared at the Ford as it passed through their neighborhoods. Chickens darted from the pavement that was still warm from the desert sun, fleeing into the dark alleyways at the sound of the approaching car. Inez looked out into the night with eyes wide. She watched as clumps of sagebrush drifted across road through their headlights like ghosts from the nothingness that surrounded the town. She had never been to the north. Everything here appeared alien and foreboding.

"Orlando?"

"*Calmate, preciosa.*" (Relax, precious one.)

As they spoke, the Ford turned the corner into a business district with neon lights and loud music pulsing from open doors. Women in short tight skirts, short and thick of body, leered and made lewd gestures at the men as the Ford slowly passed them in the street.

"What is this place, Orlando? What are those girls doing?"

For the first time, the tattooed one turned in his seat and sneered in a raspy voice, "Making money, *chica*."

The driver pulled the Ford to the curb in front of a nightclub called El Camino Azul. Blue neon flashed from the windows, and a blue moon in quarter phase glowed from a sign above the entrance. Huge clones of the fat driver stood at the doors, dull black semi-automatics on their hips. Orlando and Inez, flanked by the two men from the car, passed into the club like honored guests. Orlando slowed momentarily and leaned into the driver's ear to say something. The driver then pushed ahead, clearing a path for Orlando and Inez. They moved quickly through the throngs of young, sweaty bodies dancing to the pulsating music and flashing light show.

Inez stumbled along like a lamb, clinging tightly to Orlando's arm and shying away from even the slightest touch of any of the men whose rough appearance and massive size terrified her. They climbed a narrow staircase, the driver brushing his shoulders on each side, barely fitting through the narrow corridor. The heat was oppressive. Inez could barely breathe. The smell of sweat and cigarette smoke was overwhelming. She tried to tell Orlando, but he seemed strangely distracted, avoiding eye contact and walking more like a robot than the man she had come to love.

At the top of the stairs, they entered a hallway guarded by four rough-looking men in army fatigues. All were armed with semiautomatic rifles. One huge, imposing man stood menacingly in front of a door at the end of the hall. His head was completely shaved and covered in tattoos, much like the man in the Ford. His whole body appeared to be covered in ink. The word *Zetas* was clearly tatted in prison ink on the left side of his huge neck. The man stared, unblinking, at Orlando and his driver as they approached, ignoring Inez as if she was invisible. After a brief pause in front of the closed door, the guard received a message in his earpiece, nodded once to Orlando, stepped aside, and opened the door.

They entered the room and were hit immediately with a cold blast of air. Inez stared in wonder. This was an island of opulence in a sea of trash. The room was large and airy, with what she thought must be very expensive oak paneling. Everywhere she looked she saw beautiful paintings. There were desert scenes and even vivid images of nudes, each illuminated with indirect lighting. A desk stood in the center of the room. To the right of the entrance was a large sitting area with deep brown leather furniture. A flat-screen TV was tuned to the Mexican *futbol* match with Argentina. Behind the desk was a dark, well-groomed man of about forty years. He didn't look up as they entered, seemingly occupied by papers on his desk. The guard at the door waited with the group silently. He was evidently used to this and looked warningly at Orlando to do the same.

After almost five minutes, the man looked up from his desk and nodded to his guard, who quickly exited the room. He then rested his gaze upon Inez, looking at her with such an intensity that she felt dizzy. He asked her to sit down, motioning to the couch and directing Orlando's fat, greasy driver to help her to sit down. Strangely, the man ignored Orlando, and to her surprise, Orlando faded quietly backward toward the darker corner of the room, smiling and motioning for her to sit.

The man stepped from behind his desk to a leather chair directly across from Inez. He remained standing. His eyes moved hungrily up and down Inez's body for a full minute. Then he smiled. "So you are Inez. Orlando did not exaggerate when he said you were a real beauty." Guzman smiled briefly at Orlando and then shook his head slowly in admiration.

The girl was now shrinking back into the couch, somehow hoping to avoid this man's intense scrutiny. The man's gaze was so penetrating she felt violated in spite of the fact that he had not even touched her. She tried to glance sideways to appeal to Orlando, locating him standing in a corner next to the doorway. He did not return her glance but, instead, pointedly ignored her, a blank expression on his face. She wanted to cry out but was terrified to do so.

Roberto spoke smoothly from his spot at the arm of his leather chair. "I think that you and I are going to become very close friends, little one, so don't look so frightened. Have you ever been to the north before?" Then answering for her, he continued, "No, of course not. Have you ever *known* a man?" looking to Orlando and the fat man as much as her. Both men shook their heads negatively while Inez could only tremble beneath his relentless gaze.

Inez could bear it no longer, whimpering, "Orlando, what are we doing here? We must go to see your family." She looked desperately to where she had last seen him, but Orlando was gone. In his place was the guard from the door. *She had never heard Orlando leave. Where was he*? Turning back to Guzman, she pleaded, "We have to go. Orlando's father is expecting to see us, and he is waiting."

Guzman only laughed. "Sadly, it appears that Orlando has left us." He looked up and gave a brief order to the remaining guard, "Leave us."

As the door shut, Guzman closed the distance to the couch, standing in front of Inez and positioning himself between her legs. He parted them farther with his knee, her white cotton skirt now stretched to its limits. Her arms reached behind her in desperation to grab the back of the couch, struggling to find the leverage and strength to force this man from between her legs. Guzman leaned forward to gently stroke the young woman's hair, the palm of his hand running smoothly down the left side of her face. The girl cringed at the man's touch, crying out, "Orlando!" while thinking, *What is happening to me?*

Roberto stopped moving, his hand frozen against her face. "*Chica*, it is okay. You won't mind this. You will like it."

Inez started to sob quietly, pulling her head back to avoid Guzman's touch. Suddenly, her head was pulled violently forward, the man now fiercely holding her hair and pulling her head toward him with incredible speed and power. The man leaned forward to her ear, loudly demanding, "Stop crying, you stupid cow!"

Inez didn't stop crying but instead reached for his hand in an effort to break free. Guzman responded by violently pulling her from the couch and twisting her to the floor. The man, breathing heavily, declared, "If this is how you want it, it is all the same to me."

When Inez hit the floor, all the air was forced from her lungs, making it difficult for her to breathe or even think. The man fell upon her, straddling her at the waist. He tore at her blouse, ripping it from her body like paper. Pushing her bra up over her breasts, he began to kiss and lick her like a madman. Strangely, she could smell the expensive cologne from his face as her mind tried to detach itself from the moment.

Guzman was now like a rutting animal. She could feel his arousal through her clothes. He was struggling to pull off her panties, frantically groping beneath her skirt to find a grip. She could feel his fingernails digging into her backside as he pulled the undergarment down her legs.

With her panties now down around her ankles, the man used his knees once again to part her legs, finally entering her. She screamed and cried out, the pain beyond anything she had known. She couldn't breathe, and each of his thrusts took what was left of her breath from her lungs.

Mercifully, she slipped into unconsciousness at some point during the attack. She awoke to an empty room, clothes torn and scattered on the floor. She reflexively sat up and pulled her knees protectively to her chest. Cautiously reaching to the spot between her legs, her hand came away sticky with blood and fluids, causing her heart to flip wildly in horror. She then covered herself with the remains of her dress and looked for a place to run or hide. *What had happened? Where was she and where was Orlando? Why did he leave her? She must go home or find Orlando or do something, but what?*

Inez's thoughts were interrupted by the sound of a door opening, followed by soft footsteps. A pair of wrinkled hands softly touched her shoulders and eased her up from the floor. A woman, old and squat, wrapped her gently in a thin blanket. "Come with me, *flaca* (thin one*)*."

Inez kept looking around the room questioningly. "But Orlando…"

The old woman murmured sadly, "Your Orlando is no more. He never was, *flaca*. He never will be. *You* are now someone else, and you must learn to be someone else if you are to live at all. Come now." The wrinkled crone slowly led the battered Inez through a small door at the back of the office, one that the girl had not noticed before. Her vision blurred through a swollen eye, but she didn't have to see where she was going. *She was certain that this door was the gateway to hell.*

CHAPTER 22

Two months later, the Northern Mexico Desert

There was sparse light coming from the fire, mostly smoke that stung her eyes whenever the wind shifted. The ground was hard. The only sounds to be heard were "men sounds", a result of the camp food and too much drink. The disgusting noises were only interrupted by moans and whimpers from the young girls and women who were being mounted by the men not already lost to the stupor of drugs and alcohol.

Inez lay on the ground covered in a threadbare blanket and counted the women around the fire in her head, believing that there were at least fifteen of them, maybe more. Their ages ranged from fifteen to twenty years and all had been sent north by the Zetas. The "coyote", as people smugglers were called, was their guide, but he deferred to the tough cartel men at every turn.

The six thugs were hard and brutal criminals. They were armed to the teeth with automatic weapons and pistols, and evil emanated from them like heat rises from a desert road. Their leader was a large, swarthy man. To Inez, it was clear that he had unquestioned authority over his men and, ultimately, the whole group. Even the coyote seemed to tread lightly around this boss known only as Lobo.

Two additional gunmen always remained at the perimeter of the camp. They were different from the other thugs. They had a military bearing and were on constant watch, alert to the slightest sound and movement. They carried rifles cradled in their arms at all times and wore some sort of special goggles at night while peering into the darkness. She noticed that even Lobo treated them differently than the others.

The entire group had been transported from their hellish world in Nogales in the back of two large trucks with no windows. The women sat on the floors of the vehicles, staring into space. Most seemed resigned to their fate, not knowing or caring what was to come next. Inez had learned during her captivity that her rapist had been Roberto Guzman, a powerful leader of the Zetas, the most feared drug cartel in all Mexico. One of the women told her that Guzman had been a captain in the federal police in Mexico City before joining the Zetas. From what she could piece together from the other women, the Zetas were now selling women as well as drugs. The other girls, and there were many, told tales very similar to hers. They too had been tricked into coming north and were then forced to become sex slaves to the cartel.

The trucks had made several stops in the night to allow the women to answer calls of nature. They were given bottles of water along with oranges and bananas at each stop. At one stop, Inez saw two Mexican police cruisers parked in front of one of the trucks, the uniformed officers laughing and joking with the Zetas. At one point an older police officer was supplied with a young girl of no more than fifteen years. He stood at the front of his official car while the girl was forced to kneel in the headlights and service him. Inez watched the scene while relieving herself, letting her hiked skirts fall back into place and wondering when she would awaken from this nightmare.

Inez lay still in the shadows of the firelight, praying that she could somehow remain unnoticed and invisible. Eyes closed, she heard footsteps approaching in the dirt. Suddenly, she felt sand as it was kicked across her legs. She risked cracking her eyes open only to see one of the Zeta guards looming over her and eyeing her hungrily in the low light. She had noticed the man earlier, watching how he leered at the women day and night. He was short and thin, his shaved head added to his skeletal appearance. Tattoos covered every square inch of his body, including his head. His open shirt revealed a huge image of Jesus Malverde, the patron saint of the drug cartels.

Inez forced herself to remain motionless, hoping that he would think her asleep and move on. The man stopped directly at her feet. "Do you really think that I cannot see you? You should learn to enjoy this. It is your new life, *chica*." Inez tightened her legs together reflexively.

She slowly opened her eyes fully and looked up, pleading, "Please…I am sick. It is my time."

The man just grinned cruelly, slowly lowered himself onto Inez. His wiry arms powerfully pushed her hands back to the ground and then lifted her torn skirt. He took her, totally ignoring the cries and moans of pain and submission. She lay as still as possible, trying to block out one more humiliation, her mind disconnecting from the reality of the moment. The foul-smelling man grunted and mauled her until she thought she could no longer breathe. It was over in minutes. The Zeta's passion spent, he rolled off her and slapped her viciously on the side of her head. She instinctively brought her hand up to defend herself from further blows. Her ear hurt terribly and she felt a trickle of blood in the palm of her hand. Her attacker then stood and walked away as if she didn't exist. Inez closed her legs and curled into a ball, feeling and smelling him as his essence ran down her thighs. Her belly ached, and she detected the faint scent of copper, knowing that her blood was mixing with whatever he had left with her on the desert sand.

Twenty feet away, deep in the shadows, the coyote watched the scene unfold. His blood ran cold as he watched the attack on the young woman. His heart raced at the implications of what he was doing. He knew that he should never have agreed to guide the Zetas north. The money had been too tempting. Now he feared that he had crossed a line from which there was no return. He backed away silently as he heard the muffled sobs of the woman on the ground.

As the moments passed, the cold night breeze blew across the sweat on Inez's skin, chilling her and forcing her to reach for the sandy blanket to cover herself. She rolled onto her back, pulling the blanket to her neck. For a flickering moment, she remembered the warmth of her mother's home and the laughter of her sisters while they readied for bed. She reflexively reached for her medal of the

Virgin but then quickly let it drop from her fingers. In her heart, she doubted that the Virgin existed at all, much less heard her pleas.

As she shivered in the darkness, Inez could hear the one they called Lobo talking. They were to head north again in the morning. They were going to cross into the United States soon. Listening intently, she tried to work out the news. *Surely that must not be true. How could they go there? The police on the border would not allow this to happen. She would scream for help. Someone would save them and let them go home.*

*****

In the morning, the women were all herded together and told to get back into the trucks. The men seemed distracted and, for the most part, ignored them as they gathered in a huddle, awaiting their turn to climb into the cargo areas. While standing a few feet away from the group, she felt a tug at her clothes. Looking down in annoyance, she found a ten-year-old girl tucking herself into the folds of her skirt. The girl was tall and thin for her age, her head reaching Inez's chest. Her skin was the color of light cocoa, smooth and warm. Eyes as big as saucers looked out from under a mop of thick, black hair. When Inez reached down to disentangle herself from the child, the girl gripped Inez even tighter.

Inez looked around warily and spoke softly to the girl, "What have they done to you, child? What could they possibly want with you?" knowing in an instant the answer. A sudden chill passed through her, and she pulled the child closer to her, tears starting down her face in utter despair. Inez looked around. No one was interested in the child. Clearly each of the women were immersed in their own private hell, and this child was beyond their mercy. She considered the options and made a quick decision. Stroking the child's hair, she spoke gently, "Come." She and the child then walked slowly toward the trucks under the watchful eyes of their captors.

Settled into the first truck, the girl fell asleep with her head on Inez's lap. She hadn't spoken once. Inez sensed it was the terror of the situation that prevented the child from speaking and nothing physical. The woman seated next to Inez told her that the child had been stolen from a street in a small village the trucks had passed through the day before. Inez looked down at the sleeping child in horror. "My god, what about her family? What must they be thinking now?" The woman just shrugged. She had problems of her own.

Just then, the truck hit a large bump, the hardwood floor jarring the women and causing a series of loud complaints and cries in protest. The Zeta thugs quickly responded with kicks and slaps aimed at the women closest to them, telling them all to shut up.

The sudden rocking of the truck seemed to stir the woman next to Inez once more. She resumed her conversation with Inez. "Maybe she didn't have any parents. Many of the little ones live on their own in the streets. They make their own way." The woman gave Inez a knowing look.

Inez looked sadly down at the pile of hair on her lap and stroked the child's head gently; there was nothing else to say.

*****

After hours of jostling travel, the trucks stopped in the midst of four squat adobe buildings. As Inez stepped from the bed of the truck into the light of day, her eyes squinted at her surroundings. *What is this place? This is certainly no village. It is not even a place where people live.* The women were stepping down from the backs of the transport trucks along with Inez. As soon as their feet touched the ground, they were ordered to move directly into the crumbling structures. Once inside, Inez dropped to the floor, pulling the child quickly down to a place next to her. Her time in captivity had taught her how to survive and to draw no attention to herself. As the Zetas pushed the women into the building, she heard one of them tell his partner that the coyote was going out on foot to check the crossing. He would be back before morning, and until then, they would wait. Two large skins of water were thrown to the women in Inez's room, which they quietly passed among themselves. Inez took a short pull on the water and then made sure that the child got a full share of the water. The other women collapsed onto whatever broken furniture was in the room or onto the dusty floor, paying no attention to the ten-year-old girl. Their fear for their own lives had left no room for worrying about a child they did not know.

All the women had been abused countless times over the past month or months. They had no idea what awaited them. Most were beyond caring. The little one did not seem to have been touched, and Inez thought this odd at first. Then one of the older women explained to Inez that the child would bring a bigger price in the north if she was untouched. Inez worried that the child had heard the woman, but in truth, the child was too young to understand the woman's words anyway. *My god, this child is a lamb being led to the slaughter.*

Time passed slowly, the days stretching to almost a week. One morning, while the child was still asleep with her head on Inez's lap, Inez noticed a small, inexpensive medal attached to a thin necklace around the child's neck. She leaned closer, fingering the object to get a closer look. She fully expected it to be of a religious nature but instead found it to be a very small heart with a word engraved on the backside. It said *Colena*.

The child stirred, possibly sensing the movement of the necklace. Without moving, her eyes opened, looking straight into Inez. Inez smiled, murmuring softly to the girl, "Colena." The girl just closed her eyes again, choosing sleep over the waking nightmare.

*****

The Zetas had delayed the journey north until the coyote deemed it safe to make the crossing. The wait had been horrific for the women. Food and water were only provided sporadically. The inside of the buildings began to smell of unwashed bodies and human waste. The Zetas had occasionally forced themselves on some of the women but now seemed much more concerned with the crossing. They huddled together in groups, smoking cigarettes nonstop and talking in hushed tones. Sometimes the men would argue heatedly, looking furtively around the room afterward to see if they had been overheard.

Inez tried to protect Colena from these sights and sounds, but it was impossible. The child never left her side, clinging to her like life itself. Finally, on the fifth day, the women were all told to pack up and get ready to leave. That night, the sound of diesel engines approaching set the Zetas in motion. Orders were shouted to the women. Each of them gathered their meager belongings and walked slowly to the door and more uncertainty. Outside, on the hard-packed dirt, six late-model black four-wheel-drive pickup trucks stood, engines running. The headlights and taillights were taped over with black electrical tape, leaving only narrow slits of light to shine through. All traces of chrome trim had been removed and each truck fitted with oversized tires suited for off-road travel. The truck beds were covered with black toppers to conceal any occupants. As Inez and the child were pushed and pulled to one of the trucks, she noticed that several additional heavily armed men had joined the ranks of the existing Zetas.

Inez had brought a dress that she had found where she had been held back in Nogales, along with two pairs of tattered underwear, all of it stuffed into a small cloth bag which she tied around her shoulder and back. She was given a small water skin and told to use it only when given permission. Colena was also given a skin, but she had no clothing other than what was on her back. Inez took the water from the child, slipping the strap across her shoulder and adding it to the load already on her back. Before jumping into the back of the lead vehicle, Inez boosted the little one up onto the tailgate, taking care not to hit her head on the topper. She followed, quickly jumping in behind her.

The four-wheel-drive vehicles headed into the night, bouncing over the rough terrain. The smell of sweaty bodies mixed with the lingering odor of the Zeta's seminal juices permeating the interior of each truck bed. Inez dreaded the possible horrors that lay ahead. Her fear of what would happen next made her wish that the truck ride would never end. She tried to close her eyes and rest, gently stroking Colena's hair with her right hand. Suddenly, the faint squeak of brakes announced that the trucks were stopping. A cloud of dust enveloped them as they opened the rear tailgates. Rough hands quickly reached in and pulled the women from the truck beds and deposited them into the barren moonscape of the desert.

*****

This last stop had been the end of the line for the trucks. Now everyone was walking into the empty darkness. Inez had never been in a place like this. The ground was baked hard, like it had been in a bread oven for too long. The only smell was from the dust that was stirred by their shuffling feet as they trudged northward. Inez thought briefly of the lush green tropics of her home. The Pacific air in her village had been moist and sweet, fruits and flowers everywhere. Her mother's home had been small but clean and cool, the thick adobe walls and overhanging palm trees protecting them from the tropical sun. *How would she survive this harsh land and these brutal men?* Tears worked their way down her cheeks in spite of the surrounding dryness. Colena sensed her distress and looked up worriedly with her huge brown eyes.

Inez responded with a weak smile, "It's okay, little one. We will be okay," patting her gently and affectionately, knowing that nothing would be okay.

The moon was high in the sky before they stopped. The coyote talked quietly with the Zetas, telling them they were close enough to the border to stop for the night. Lobo listened intently to the desert guide and finally nodded in agreement but ordered that there would be no fires. The men were not happy because the desert temperature was dropping fast, but they did not argue with the Zeta boss. The man could silence the toughest of his followers with a single glance, and Inez wondered, *Just how violent must this man be to instill such fear in hard men like these?*

As the group spread out from the pathway, Inez found an open spot on the ground big enough for herself and Colena and, hopefully, far enough from the men. She knelt, placed her bag on the ground for a headrest, and fell gently on her back, pulling the child as close as possible. For her part, the little one was as helpless as a baby bird quivering after falling from the nest. Inez held her tight and told her to sleep, trying to reassure herself as much as the girl. Moments passed. Just as she thought the girl was drifting off, she felt the child trembling and sobbing silently in the night. Inez happened to glance at the one called Lobo, catching him staring hungrily at her and the child. She bit her lip, thinking what Lobo's attention foretold. *What now? They were helpless.* She tried to cry, but no tears would come. Instinctively, she thought to pray but then stopped herself. *She would not pray to a God that did not exist. Surely, he could not exist. She now realized that the stories the priests told were only fairy tales to help young girls fall asleep.*

CHAPTER 23

Tohono O'odham Nation Indian Reservation, United States

Nalin Chee stood with her back pushed into a depression in the wall of an ancient ravine. Her long black hair was pulled back and tucked under a tan head wrap, much like a Bedouin tribesman. Her untamed beauty was accentuated by the black paint that stretched in a band across her nose and eyes. She gazed out from the rocks with her eyelids half closed to minimize detection, much like the lizards of the desert. Her muscled legs flexed effortlessly, their strength allowing her to spend extended periods of time motionless and invisible. She was fifty yards south of a tunnel opening, and she could feel them coming. Maybe it was a soft vibration. Maybe instinct. But they were coming.

*****

Another lone figure waited patiently on the southern Sonoran Desert mesa, as still as the rock formations surrounding her. She was dressed in desert camouflage, government issued. Her footwear was tribal. Her moccasins were made just as those her Apache ancestors had worn for hundreds of years of war with the white man, first the Spanish and then the Americans. Her belt held a service issued Glock 40 caliber pistol and a bowie knife that was definitely not service issue. Strapped across her back was a lightweight combat backpack bearing an M4 rifle, spare ammunition, and other survival supplies. She scanned the horizon with her high-powered spotting scope, looking for signs of movement. Hannah Lone Hawk was back in the desert with her partner Nalin, hunting—hunting the evil that brought drugs and death across the border. Her clothing and brown skin blended into the earth, making her almost invisible, a mythical Golem risen from the earth itself.

From the thin sliver of shade provided by an overhanging rock, Hannah looked out upon the horizon. The desert at midday was like a mirage. The waves of heat shimmered across the landscape and made everything seem like it was moving. The ancient sandstone formations seemed to weave back and forth like dancers across a fire. Anything or anyone coming her way would appear and disappear time and again before forming a solid image. This land was only meant for the wild things of the desert and the Apache. Other tribes, like the Tohono, the desert people, had lived here as well, but only the Apache had truly ruled here. The white man had never fit in nor did his cousins, the Spanish.

*****

The two Apache women had been waiting out here for two days. During a routine reconnaissance, they had discovered the entrance to the tunnel, a small hole in the earth situated behind a series of large boulders and covered with a spiderweb of dead mesquite bushes. Nalin had explored the entrance and lowered herself down into the tunnel, listening and smelling the air for hours. She exited again through the narrow opening and nodded to her partner. "It's never been used. The last forty feet have just been dug."

"Wanna call it in?" Hannah asked with no emotion.

Nalin just shrugged. "Maybe just let them know we are sitting on a new dig. Wouldn't hurt."

Hannah reached over her shoulder for the sat phone tucked into a pocket of her backpack. She began to punch in the numbers. "At least they can be getting ready if something kicks off out here."

Nalin looked back at the entrance pensively. "Oh they're coming. I just wonder what they're bringing with them."

She watched her partner fiddling with the sat phone, pacing the area and checking for reception bars. "Well, as usual, nothing. These fucking rocks!"

Nalin meticulously searched the surrounding area and pointed to a mesa just to the west. "That would be a good observation post," she said, stretching her arm and pointing at a ledge above where they stood. "You might get lucky with the phone up there."

They decided to split up. Nalin would cover the mouth of the tunnel in order to get an early indication as to what was coming across: drugs, weapons, or women. The women were something new. The cartel was really stepping up the export of sex slaves. It was something that elevated the Zetas to a whole new level of evil. The march across the desert was never kind to these women, many of them dying of thirst or exhaustion before ever reaching the buyers farther north. Nalin and Hannah had discovered the bodies of women on two prior occasions, their dried-out corpses picked apart by birds and other denizens of the desert.

It had been difficult for all of the Shadow Wolves to watch helpless women and children being herded by these animals who called themselves men. It was even tougher for Lone Hawk and Chee who, by now, were respectfully referred to by the rest of the team merely as "the Apaches."

When deciding on the split, Hannah had known better than to argue with Nalin on who should wait at the tunnel. Her partner had become particularly protective of Hannah ever since her little brother had come to live with her. Nalin knew how much Jace counted on Hannah and had now taken it upon herself to make sure that nothing happened to the boy's new guardian.

Nalin, a full-blooded Chiricahua Apache, was a warrior to the bone. She could have fought alongside Cochise or Geronimo in the old times. She had tracked some of the most violent drug traffickers to come out of Mexico. She had fought them with guns, her hands and feet and her wits. Nalin Chee loved the desert. The sands and plants seemed to nurture her like no other.

Hannah knew that her partner could run for an entire day if needed and move through the mountains like the wildest animals in the Apache lands. She had overheard one of the men on the team once remark, "Watching Chee move is like watching a mountain cat. It's not something easily forgotten." Hannah had to admit, Nalin was certainly old school. She still carried a Marlin 44-40 lever-action rifle across her back and wore nothing but traditional tan leather clothing while on the track. Her knife was a bone-handled obsidian blade, honed razor-sharp for hours while lying in wait during stakeouts.

*****

On the third day, they came. It happened at dusk. The coyote popped his head from the opening and waited for almost ten minutes before moving out into the desert openness. Nalin watched him from the ravine. *This is not his first rodeo. He's as keen as his name implies.* Once above ground, he motioned for the group to follow him. The first out was a dark, mustachioed Mexican in complete battle camo, rifle cradled in his massive right arm. His body was thick and powerful, and he moved like a man of violence, an alpha predator.

Next out of the tunnel were women. They struggled through the narrow opening, stumbling as they were pulled forward by the coyote. Nalin remained frozen in place, her eyes taking in the scene. *Women, all women. But no...girls, mostly girls.* A slender woman of about eighteen fell as she was pushed out into the waning light of the American desert. She had been holding the hand of a young girl who remained with her head sticking out from the opening. As the woman fell forward onto the rocky ground, the child crawled frantically from the opening to reunite with the woman. The girl could not be more than ten, if that. Slowly, the woman and child both regained their feet and took a few tentative steps forward, both being bumped brusquely to the side by the parade of women now emerging from the tunnel. All the women moved forward, half staggering, looking about them as if they had landed on another planet. The little girl clung fiercely to the woman, probably out of fear more than anything else. Nalin wondered if these two were mother and child, then thought better of it. *The woman is no more than eighteen herself. Shit.*

The group that emerged looked to include fifteen to twenty women, but it was hard to tell as they were milling together and chattering quietly among themselves. There was no doubt that these women were captives, their movements hesitant, as if expecting to be punished at any moment. Their fear could be seen even in the half-light of dusk. The object of their fear was also obvious. Scattered throughout the procession were men, armed men, moving like soldiers who had seen combat and were prepared for it.

After squeezing through the narrow opening, the captives started to spread out onto the nearby ground, surrounded by rocks and cactus. They had to tend to personal needs, and Nalin saw them appealing to their captors. *Who knows how long these women have been underground?* A few of the men cuffed the pleading women with open hands, cursing them and making lewd gestures. All words were spoken in hushed tones, even the threats. They did not want to set off remote sensors or activate hidden microphones placed by the *migras* of the Border Patrol.

The women were finally allowed to drift a few yards into the scrub and rocks to tend to their needs and were then quickly rounded up and told to continue their march north. Some of the women carried homemade cotton duffels slung over their shoulders or on their backs, probably containing all their worldly goods. The men carried hydration backpacks with water for themselves and, no doubt, just enough to keep their captives alive in the harsh conditions. The women looked exhausted, a look of hopelessness and resignation evident in their every movement.

Nalin didn't move or even breathe noticeably. She watched and waited. Her instincts told her to let them get at least a mile ahead of her before she started her track. These were soldiers, maybe not American soldiers but trained nonetheless. She knew they would head north, straight into the desert. They would want to meet their American customers outside one of the small towns like Pia Oik or farther north near Gila Bend, away from the bigger cities that boasted real police departments and detachments of the Border Patrol.

With her muscular back pressed flat into the cool earth, she knew that this was how her ancestors had fought their wars, waiting and melting into the land. She also knew that this group had been walking for a long time. They would have approached the border stealthily from the Mexico desert to avoid agents of the Mexican Border Police and to reduce the chance of being spotted by the American drones that flew along the border. They would also have spent hours or even days in the tunnel, groping blindly in the dark, claustrophobic spaces with little or no air. These were trafficked women and girls. Mostly girls. The oldest was probably no more than twenty. They would be sold to the drug gangs in the US, forced to perform as many as forty sex acts a day, and receive little or no money for their humiliation. In reality, they had already received a death sentence. The life ahead of them would eventually make them welcome that death.

*****

As the last sounds of the group faded into the darkening sky, Nalin turned on her radio and put the earpiece over her left ear. She hated to use these things. The smugglers had learned to carry scanning devices and often listened to them with their own headsets. While the Shadow Wolves utilized a private frequency with limited range, designed to prevent detection, Nalin never trusted the technology. All her communications with Hannah were in Apache, a language these Mexican thugs would never understand.

"Lone Hawk," she whispered into her throat microphone. Nothing… "Lone Hawk, come in."

The radios had point-to-point capability but were often compromised by rock formations and sand dunes. A signal that might work perfectly in one location was useless in another. For now, it looked like it would be radio silence until morning when she would use one of the old ways—a mirror in the sun.

Hannah Lone Hawk's hand flashed to her ear. She was getting a call from Nalin. "Nalin." Silence. She repeated, "Nalin." Hannah tried for the better part of the next hour with no success. *Fuck!* She settled back and took a deep breath. She would wait until morning. There were now about two miles between her and the tunnel. She would remain in place. The call had meant that they were coming. She knew that Nalin would be in their shadow.

*****

The group had walked for the better part of two hours, covering about a mile, finally settling in for the night. Nalin moved to within two hundred feet of the camp, crawling quietly on her stomach. She moved so slowly her progress was almost imperceptible, yet she advanced. The group seemed quiet and exhausted. The Zetas had set up a perimeter, two men on the north and two on the south of the group, changing every half hour. Rotating from north to south prevented anyone from falling asleep while keeping their flanks more secure when they exchanged positions. *These men were trained.*

She slowly backed away from the camp. She would need some sleep. After losing sight of the group, she moved far enough to hear them but not see them. She dropped to the far side of a small outcrop and scraped a "hip hole" for her to comfortably lie down. She was asleep in minutes, knowing that any noise would not be missed while she dozed in her "field sleep."

CHAPTER 24

US-Mexico border, American side

It was morning, or close to it. The cold night air clung to the sand, but a pale yellow light was gently rising from the eastern horizon. Inez had never seen anything like this. The land had nothing. It was flat and dead. The rock formations rose like the monsters of her nightmares, transforming into sand sculptures in the light of day. *Could this be the United States? Where were the cities and the wonderful skyscrapers that she had seen in the cinema?*

Colena heard the camp coming awake. She tried to keep her eyes closed, wishing she could just stay asleep and that everyone would leave her alone. She was tired and hungry, and the ground was so hard it hurt to walk. She could do it, but she was terrified of the men. They were terrible, and they smelled so bad. The women's cries and moans confused her and scared her. She didn't understand what they were doing, but it seemed to hurt the women terribly. She looked up at Inez through half-closed eyes. This lady was kind and had kept her safe. Her soft, warm body felt like her mother's, and she held Colena close at night just as her mother did. The girl watched Inez's eyes as they darted around the camp. She closed her eyes once again. *She is more frightened than me. We cannot stay safe for too much longer.*

Suddenly Inez was violently pulled from her. The big one was dragging her up by the hair. Colena clung to her, getting pulled through the dirt and scraping her legs on the rocks. The child's eyes looked at the man imploringly. *Please don't hurt her, mister, please.*

Lobo pulled Inez's hair so viciously she thought it would come out of her scalp. He forced her face directly in front of his. "*Puta*, you think that this little one will keep you safe? Before I give you to the yankees, I will show your little friend what a man does to a woman," he snarled, spitting on her as he suddenly released his grip on her hair. Inez fell back to the ground and watched the man as he moved away, shouting angrily at several of his men as he walked through the camp. She felt Colena's hands as they gently probed Inez's scalp, looking for injuries, the child now protecting Inez in her own small way.

*****

The makeshift camp was coming to life. The Zetas were up, making noises and pissing in front of the women, enjoying the humiliation that it caused. They couldn't comprehend that these women were beyond humiliation. Lobo told them to get everyone ready to go, which resulted in kicks to the backsides of those still sleeping and insults to the rest. Dry beef jerky was passed out by the coyote, now almost embarrassed for his part in this tragedy. The captives took long drinks from the water skins, passing them reluctantly among themselves. At dawn, they set out on the same northerly course. Inez passed half of her beef stick to Colena to chew as they stepped back into the sands of the Sonoran Desert. Colena lifted her eyes silently, a soul now wise beyond her years.

*****

Nalin lay still in the sagebrush, watching the men and women move north from their camp. The men were dressed like soldiers and carried their weapons like professionals. But they were not soldiers. They were *banditos* for sure. They were herding the women like cattle, and the group was led by a coyote. She was certain they were headed toward Pia Oik. The route would take them two more days and a lot of hardship. If they were smart, they would all make it, but one could never be certain. She would have to alert Hannah soon. The group was headed into her lap.

Nalin decided to flank them to the west. To her right there was an elevated ridge dotted with Saguaro Cacti and Velvet Mesquite bushes that would provide good cover for her track. She would signal Lone Hawk from the ridge, letting her know what to expect and where to join the track.

Hannah had been up an hour before dawn. She had taken water from her CamelBak, a backpack that carried only water, and moved to a high point to wait for Nalin's signals. She only had to wait until the sun was up in the sky. The flashes from Nalin's mirror told her everything—the size of the group, their heading, and that the cargo was women. She also learned that the traffickers were likely from the Zeta cartel. *That means they will be trained.* She reflexively reached for her sat phone but paused, thinking. She would need to call in the team, but not yet. First, they needed to identify the Americans who intended to buy these women. It would not take long for backup to arrive aboard the Blackhawk. She would wait. Nalin would want to have a hand in that decision. *These Mexican outlaws, how could they sell their own women?*

Nalin watched intently as the coyote worked ahead of the group, scouting for sign and scanning the horizon. He was looking for the Border Patrol, overzealous sheriff's deputies or even vigilantes who were now patrolling the desert as some sort of political statement. Nalin grudgingly admitted to herself, *This guy is good.* He moved with a minimum of effort and watched the ground as well. No doubt he was part Indian, probably buried deep in his blood. Most likely he was descended from the Yaqui or some other tribe from south of the border. She smirked. N*ot Apache.* No tribe had ever fought better than her people in the desert or in these mountains. The warrior in her was already preparing for a fight with this coyote and the fierce one at the front of the pack.

As she glided along the ridge, she saw that the coyote had found an old, dried-up riverbed with raised sandstone banks on each side. It would allow the group to walk relatively unseen, and the afternoon sun would be blocked on the west side of the arid river bottom. The relative coolness of the shade would be a perfect place for the traffickers to rest their captives. She nodded, hating the coyote even more for his skill.

*****

The Zetas settled into the shade of the rocks. They drank generously from their packs, earning dirty looks from Lobo. Several of the men sat next to the girls, grabbing their breasts and pulling up their skirts. “Lobo, can we have a taste? We need to clear our heads,” the oldest of the Zetas called to the leader. He didn’t wait for the answer before savagely grabbing the small breast of the chubby girl trying to crawl away from him.

Lobo snarled at the man, “I don’t care what you do, but leave the little one alone. Touch her and I will cut your balls off and leave them for the lizards.” He sat down and motioned for the coyote to join him.

“How much farther do we go today?” Lobo demanded.

The coyote replied quickly, “We need to stay here until a little before dusk. It will be too hot out there in the sun. We can move again in two or three hours. We can walk until about ten and then settle in for the night. The buyers should be waiting south of Pia Oik. They will be watching. We will not be walking into any law. They will make certain of that.”

Lobo listened. He continued to stare into the desert sun, shaking his head silently.

The coyote wondered what was wrong. “Is there a problem, *Jefe*?”

The grizzled man’s black eyes bore into the coyote. “This is the first time I have dealt with these customers. I don’t know them. I was told they are men I can trust, but I do not know that. I trust very few men,” he said, his words trailing off, indicating that the coyote was not one of those men.

“What will you do?”

“What can I do? My boss says I will trust them. I will trust them.” Lobo shrugged his shoulders. “I follow my orders. It is what I do.”

A long silence followed, both men staring into the empty sunlit spaces.

The coyote broke the silence, "We will be careful, *Jefe*. We must assume the American buyers will be careful as well."

"You call these buyers Americans? Fuck. They are only a bunch of Mexicans and MS-13 assholes. They just live on the other side of the river. Fuck them. Hell, the MS-13 people are just some bandits from the jungles in the South, more like monkeys! They can die as easy as you and I. Know that and remember that."

The coyote looked sideways at Lobo. "You are not a trusting man, *hombre*."

Lobo snorted quickly, "I used to believe people until one day I caught myself lying. Then I realized I could trust no one."

The coyote smiled wryly, "So not even yourself it would seem." He waited for a reply, but Lobo was already asleep.

*****

The radio crackled in her ear. Hannah responded, "Go."

"I'm coming in," replied Nalin, using a minimum of words.

Hannah waited patiently, knowing there was no use looking for her partner. Nalin's ability to move like a ghost was as much a mystery to her as it was to the rest of the team. She knew that Nalin would suddenly appear, like a part of the rocks coming to life. Hannah pulled the sat phone from her pack, reassured by the signal strength. Minutes later, she felt, rather than heard, her partner.

"*Shik'isn*" (sister)." Nalin materialized from the rocks, her face a mask. Hundreds of generations of Apache blood stared at Hannah through eyes black as coal.

"Nahatse," said Hannah, acknowledging her partner in Apache, sensing the fire that was running hot in her friend's blood.

Nalin responded with hand signals, knowing how easy sounds carried in the desert. She sighed. "This is a bad business. These men from the South need killing."

Hannah needed to talk. Signing was too slow and too vague. She leaned to Nalin's ear. "We have to wait for the buyers. We have to get all of them. It will be a close thing. If we call in the Blackhawk too soon, we could lose the buyers, too late and we could lose the women. That's something we can't risk."

Nalin leaned back into Hannah, her hot breath burning in Hannah's ear as strongly as her words. "We should just go in and take the men down. We can call the office and have them send another chopper to look for the buyers. They are hurting those women, and a few might not make it through another day of walking."

Hannah looked down on the Zetas and the women while listening to her partner. *This was fucked. Maybe they should go down now. They could surprise them and maybe avoid a fight. But that was not likely. These were military men, twisted, but trained. They would not frighten easily. They would fight. Technically, she was the agent in charge. She was senior and held a higher rank, but Nalin was a force of nature.*

Hannah turned back to Nalin. "I need to call it in. We need to get them on the tarmac ready to go."

Nalin nodded absently, agreeing but working things out for herself at the same time.

"I need to get out of earshot to make the call. I have a good signal. I'll give Crowe our status and let him make the call." Hannah slung her pack over her shoulder and moved out without another word.

CHAPTER 25

Shadow Wolves Headquarters, Sells, Arizona

Crowe stood in the open doorway of the headquarters building, the shade of the porch providing some measure of comfort. He stared at the Blackhawk on the pad, showing no emotion but troubled about Lone Hawk and Chee. Both Apaches had been in the wind for two full days and nights. He had tried to reach them on the sat phones and their radios, but nothing. He knew that wasn't unusual in itself. He had been on countless missions and knew radio discipline as well as anyone. The worrisome thing was that the silence confirmed they were on a track and there was nothing to do now but wait. If he sent up the chopper or Humvees, he could be doing more harm than good, possibly jeopardizing his agents and compromising the mission.

He looked to his left and saw three men approaching across the tarmac. They had arrived in a shiny black suburban with dark, tinted windows, having parked next to the hangar instead of in front of the main office. *I guess they wanted their precious black ride to stay in the shade.* He recognized their walks before anything else. The first two were his supervisors. The greying figure in the lead was Tom Radcliff, the special agent in charge from the office of Homeland Security in Phoenix. Radcliff walked with a purpose, his stride brisk despite the heat rising from the asphalt. His lean figure fit well into his Italian made suits, no doubt purchased at some high-end shop in DC. Radcliff was a veteran Washington insider, having advanced quickly from fieldwork into the upper echelons of federal service. A few politically correct postings overseas, kissing the asses of foreign dignitaries and ambassadors, and voila, here he was in charge of one of the most critical Homeland Security offices in the country. *What a system.*

Radcliff's crew cut grey hair contrasted with his tan, smooth skin, the look, no doubt, cultivated by countless hours spent on the golf course. Following a step behind was his number two, Dan Hooper. Hooper had recently arrived in Phoenix after a high-profile posting in Chicago. He was the perfect adjutant to Radcliff. He had no problem bringing down the wrath of the department on anyone in the field who might challenge his boss. *His head was so far up Radcliff's ass he had a bird's-eye view of what the man had for breakfast each day.*

The third man walking across the pavement was unknown to Crowe. He was dressed casually, a loose-fitting tropical shirt covering an athletic frame. His trousers were loose and light, his shoes tan leather slip-ons. This man was a veteran of hot, tropical environs. He looked to be in his mid-thirties. He had short brown hair, slightly longer than military style and a swarthy, thick shadow of stubble evident even at a distance. He walked with the "suits" but was clearly apart. Crowe watched as the three closed the distance to his offices. He looked down and took a deep breath. *Perfect. Just fucking perfect.*

Radcliff mounted the three steps to the entrance, squinting at Crowe as he offered his hand in greeting. Sweat was already evident on his temples, running down past his ears and onto his starched white collar. His assistant's pale skin was flushed and mottled by the unrelenting sun, making him look as out of place as a polar bear.

"Agent Crowe, good to find you in your office. You haven't been answering your phones, and your secretary has been lying for you quite poorly. I should walk in there and fire the woman, but she would only say that she was following your orders, or maybe she wouldn't even admit to that. I guess you really inspire loyalty in the 'fuck the bosses' world that you live in."

Crowe released the sweaty hand of his supervisor and smiled tightly. "Special Agent Radcliff, always nice to see you too. Didn't know you were looking for me."

"Spare me the bullshit. What the fuck is going on? We hear that you have agents in the field tracking. Intel says they are following some big hitters. What do you know about it? If it's true, why am I hearing about this from El Paso instead of you?"

"Well, sir, I might ask the same question. Why is El Paso calling Phoenix with information about my people instead of calling me? I would be interested in what *you* know and also how El Paso knows so much about my people in the field."

"El Paso is not sure of anything. A drone operator thought she saw a large group of people heading north toward the border from the south several nights ago. They had nothing definitive and couldn't reacquire the targets. I did check radio logs, and two of your agents signed out on surveillance in the area three days ago. I'm told that they have not checked in by radio and have not been seen since. Am I ringing any bells, Crowe?"

Crowe left the doorway, and the men followed him inside. The temperature was not much cooler inside. The air conditioners stood still in their wall mounts. Two dark-skinned trackers, dressed in desert camo, worked at their desks, the first calmly talking on the phone, the other wiping down his assault rifle. Both agents failed to look up or even acknowledge the VIP visitors. The men seemed totally indifferent to the oppressive heat, long black hair tied back in ponytails. Radcliff's assistant, Dan Hooper, couldn't help noticing an Airborne tattoo running along the veined forearm of the one on the left. Both men were wearing traditional white tribal bone chokers stretched tightly around their necks.

Ethan entered his office, moved to his desk, and leaned back in his chair, his feet coming to rest on his desktop. He looked across to his visitors and thought ruefully about the pathetic bureaucracy that promoted such people. *These guys were responsible for supervising the apprehension of violent criminals who were a serious threat to the United States. They wouldn't know a bad guy if he walked in here and kissed them on the lips. He smiled to himself as Hooper fanned himself with a pamphlet he had picked up in the lobby. If they had to go out into the desert where his people worked, they would probably fucking melt and shit their pants the first time they saw a scorpion or a rattler. How the hell did these people ever conquer his people? I guess the Creator really was the coyote jokester. He paused in his appraisal. The third one might be something different.*

The men were still standing uncomfortably in the space in front of Crowe's desk when Maggie popped into the doorway. "Is there anything that you, gentlemen, could use?" said Maggie, accentuating the word *gentlemen* and not actually acknowledging the SAC Radcliff.

Crowe raised his eyebrows to his visitors. "Gentlemen? Anything Maggie can get you?"

The stranger spoke for the first time, "I could sure use a bottle of water, if that wouldn't be too much trouble," looking directly at Maggie Parker. "By the way, my name is Jake Webb, DEA." He turned and stepped forward to shake Crowe's hand and then nodded back to Maggie as she prepared to leave.

Radcliff quickly interjected, "Ms. Parker, I would like a Coke if I wouldn't be putting you out."

"Make that two, Miss." Hooper was clearly roasting to death in his suit and tie as he sat back in the vinyl chair.

Hooper and Webb settled into office chairs. Radcliff remained standing, scanning the room in desperation. "Where the fuck is the air conditioner? What are you doing, waiting until the paint starts to melt?"

Crowe smiled. "I'll have Maggie get it cranked up. We tend to keep it off for the most part around here. The team is out on the desert so much they are used to the heat and prefer it."

Radcliff finally eased into one of the remaining chairs. "Fuck me, it's hot!" The DEA agent smiled and shook his head, clearly amused at the sight of the two men loosening their ties and removing their coats as quickly as possible. Radcliff's sleeve became tangled, only serving to agitate him further.

While the two Homeland bosses got situated, Crowe looked over at the DEA man. "So how long have you been on the job?"

"Ten years. Mostly working in Miami and then some postings at embassies in the South."

Crowe nodded. He knew that the South was DEA parlance for countries in Latin America and the Caribbean.

Jake Webb paused, then said, "I heard that you worked for us for a while."

Ethan nodded. "Well, technically, *with* you, but yeah. I spent almost ten years seconded to DEA operations from the DIA, mostly in Southeast Asia. I retired a little over a year ago." Ethan knew perfectly well that Webb would have seen Crowe's file long before this meeting. This was all some sort of dance, but Crowe would play along for a while.

Webb, smiling, remarked, "So twenty and out. Now this. Pretty good gig."

"I had a few more than twenty, but that's about it, yeah."

Crowe continued after an awkward pause, "They reached out to me to set up this unit sometime back, and here I am." Ethan looked over at his sweaty supervisor who looked put out by the polite chatter.

Radcliff cleared his throat. "Crowe, you and Agent Webb can exchange class photos later. I want to know what the fuck is going on out here. For that matter, so does Agent Webb."

The DEA agent continued, obviously not cowed by Radcliff, "I have heard a lot about your team. We hear that they are kicking ass down here. I like the name too—the Shadow Wolves. Sounds traditional, old school."

Crowe, annoyed, gave him a dismissive shrug. "There is lots of work to be done down here. It would really be nice if you're here to tell me that you're going to help us do that." He thought about Webb's comments and now knew for certain that the man knew everything there was to know about Ethan's background. *At least whatever he was cleared to read.*

Crowe looked back and forth among his visitors. "Tom," he said, referring to Agent Radcliff, "you're right. I do have two agents in the field, and I am worried. They have followed protocols, and there must be a good reason that they haven't called in. I am just trying to decide when to send in the cavalry. We heard about a tunnel being dug about two months ago. We have been putting people out sporadically in hopes of catching someone popping out of the ground.

Up until now we haven't had any luck. Now I think someone did come through and my agents are on the track." To himself more than anything, he repeated, "I am worried. I have a team mobilized and we are ready to go." To emphasize that, another Shadow Wolf, head shaved in a high and tight haircut, stuck his head in the door. "Chopper is loaded and good to go, boss."

"Well, what are you waiting for?" demanded Radcliff, staring at Crowe expectantly.

"It's not that simple. I send our guys out too soon. It could get my trackers killed as easy as save 'em. I am walking the line, and from now on, it goes minute to minute."

"I say fuck it. Send out the chopper. If we find your trackers dead in the sand, there's going to be hell to pay. Take the smart bet, the safe bet. Who's out there anyway?"

"Lone Hawk and Chee."

"Who?" Radcliff snidely demanded. "I don't want their fucking Indian names. What the fuck are their *white* names?" spitting his words. Radcliff appeared to be in the midst of a meltdown, his face now a deep crimson. Sweat was now running down his chest profusely, darkening the front of his shirt as he waited for an answer. He quickly added before Crowe could reply, "And turn on the fucking air-conditioning!"

Ethan paused a minute. It was taking everything in his power to stop from reaching across the desk and dragging this pompous idiot out of the office and onto the tarmac. As attractive as the idea sounded, he knew it would result in his getting fired, his agents being lost, and this fool probably getting the fucking Medal of Valor.

"Agent Radcliff, those *are* their *white* names. Agent Lone Hawk and Agent Chee are their names, both in your world and in Apache. They are excellent agents, and Chee is more desert rat than anyone in my unit. She can certainly take care of herself. I trust them enough to give them some space. It's what they would expect. It's what I would expect if I were in their shoes."

Radcliff looked at Ethan like he hadn't heard a word he'd said. He had been rehearsing his speech and didn't really care what the lone wolf leader of this oddball unit thought. If he had his way, the unit would be disbanded. If it wasn't for all those politically correct liberals back in DC, the unit wouldn't exist. As far as he was concerned, their alleged skills were nothing but a lot of superstitious mumbo jumbo. *Someone at the top must have watched* Dances with Wolves *one too many times.*

"I'll be honest with you, Crowe. I'm thinking of sending out my own people. And I mean right now. I have the authority to do just that. In my opinion, you are too close to this situation to make this decision objectively." Radcliff then sat back smugly, almost wishing for a hostile response.

Crowe didn't have time for this shit. His people were either in the middle of a major bust or in trouble. He would know very soon. "Look, my team is ready to go now. We are only waiting for a call from our scouts. If they don't call in soon, we'll have to get up in the air anyway."

Radcliff shouted, "I say get up in the air right now!"

Crowe responded icily, "Look, Radcliff, if we put that Blackhawk up without the scouts knowing about it, it could get them killed. We wait."

Seconds later, Crowe's sat phone rang. The men in the room looked at the phone like it was alive. Crowe glanced at the screen as he picked up the phone, relieved to see the identifier. "Lone Hawk!"

"Boss, we're sitting on a bunch of bad hombres. We are about two days walk south of Pia Oik deep in the hot sand." Hannah rattled off her GPS coordinates from her watch.

Ethan responded quickly, writing down the coordinates on his desk blotter. "What have you got?"

"We got about ten bad guys, a coyote, and about twenty girls." Lone Hawk sounded stressed.

"How bad is it?"

"Beyond bad. They are raping these girls as they go along. They are not being gentle. It's really fucked."

Crowe sensed Hannah struggling to remain calm. It must be really bad for her to show this much stress. He prodded, "You want us in now?"

"I don't know, boss. We have another day to go to find the buyers on the other end of this deal, but I don't know. This is really fucked up. I don't think some of the women will even make it to the exchange site. They're not doing well in the sun, and the rest is hard to describe." Lone Hawk sounded like she was visualizing it all while talking.

Crowe tried to keep Hannah focused. "Tell me about the bad guys, Hannah."

"Eight. There's eight and a boss and the coyote. Ten total. They're all gunned up, and they are not playing. They put out sentries every time they sit down. They gotta be ex-military. I think we're gonna have to hit them hard."

"What about the girls? How old do you think?" Crowe was marking off his mental checklist as he assessed how he would do this.

"They are all under twenty years old. One is a baby, maybe nine or ten. I haven't seen them touch her yet, but I'm really worried about her."

Crowe had heard enough. "We need to come in. Will they be stationary for a few hours?"

"I don't think so. I think they will move in about an hour or so. As soon as the sun drops a bit more."

Crowe continued, "Okay. Where is Nalin?"

"She has the eyeball now."

"How is she doing with this?" asked Crowe, knowing that Nalin's blood would be up.

"Not good, boss. We need to get some cavalry here before she becomes the cavalry," replied Hannah dryly. She was happy this problem was now in Crowe's hands and that it would be over soon.

"How about the risks in the takedown?"

Hannah didn't hesitate. "It's high risk. If we don't take them when they're asleep, we could lose most of the women in the firefight if these hombres decide to go down in flames."

Telling Hannah to hold on, Crowe paused a long minute. He then clipped off his orders. "Send Nalin ahead to scout their next stop. Give her the sat phone and have her call in the numbers. I know she won't be sure of the location, but she needs to give us her best guess. We will get there ahead of them, drop our guys out of earshot, and walk it in. If they don't stop where we expect them to, we can tail them until they do."

"Roger that." A pause by Lone Hawk.

"Hannah?"

"Yeah?"

"Don't do anything till we get there, and keep Nalin under control. She needs to wait for us."

"We'll be waiting, I promise."

Crowe hung up the phone without another word. The two Shadow Wolves that had been in the office were already grabbing their gear. One of them used his radio to tell the rest of the team to meet at the chopper. Crowe stood and went to the locker near his desk to grab the remainder of his gear. He was moving toward the doorway before Radcliff could think of something else to say. Crowe paused on his way out, shouting for Maggie, "Mags, call up to Tucson and get an air ambulance started. Have them land out near the hangar and wait here as a forward base until they hear from us. Tell them to prepare for multiple casualties." Maggie was already picking up the phone as Ethan stepped through the doorway. As an afterthought, Ethan called back over his shoulder, "And when you call Tucson, tell them to send a second Blackhawk down here as well, just in case."

Agent Jake Webb stood in the hallway and watched the smooth efficiency of Crowe as he checked his weapons and adjusted his holster. As the man had pulled his T-shirt and Kevlar vest over his head, scars from at least two bullets and one long slash stood out against his sinewy back. He had read Crowe's jacket before coming out here. The file stated that he had earned the second highest medal possible, the Distinguished Service Cross. He had also been awarded a Silver Star and two Purple Hearts. His time spent attached to the DEA was a bit of a mystery. His file had been classified at a level higher than Webb would ever reach. One thing was certain, Crowe's people would walk through fire for him, and he for them.

Webb glanced over at Radcliff and Hooper. *What a pair of assholes. It was sad the alliances one had to make for the greater good.* He thought about asking to hitch a ride to the party but then thought better of it. There was no way Crowe was going to let him go out with his team, if for no other reason than his perceived association with Radcliff. He was just going to have to hang on around the edges of all this in order to make his assignment work.

Crowe was the last of the squad to climb aboard the Blackhawk. From his seat in the doorway, Ethan watched his number two, Elias Blue Eagle, as he checked his men to make sure that their gear was set. Satisfied, Elias quickly gave a thumbs-up to Crowe. Ethan, in turn, looked over his team, eight men in full combat gear, all of them rock hard and combat tested. These men were of two worlds. They were part modern law enforcement professional and part ancient warrior, proud blood coursing through their veins. His gaze finally rested upon Isaac Factor. The man had been his guardian angel on and off throughout his life. In spite of the fact that Crowe had moved his friend to a logistics position, Factor would never think of letting Crowe go on a mission without him.

Isaac had come to the Shadow Wolves from the tribal police in the Everglades. After his time in the army in Bosnia, Isaac had returned to his life in South Florida. His people had worked closely with the Miami-Dade Police during the Colombian drug wars, often tracking dangerous drug smugglers across unforgiving wetlands and mangrove swamps. His face still bore a six-inch scar from a Serbian blade that only made his countenance more fearsome, something that had given even the most vicious drug runners pause. He had only agreed to join the Shadow Wolves because Crowe had done the asking. Ethan had needed him, and that was all that needed to be said. Crowe looked briefly at the black scout, Factor calmly nodding in acknowledgement. Crowe smiled and nodded back, adjusting his headset at the same time. *This man was like his right arm and often his conscience as well.*

As the rotors wound up to speed, Crowe's dark eyes returned to the tarmac, where Radcliff could be seen shouting into his cell phone with his other hand placed over his ear to block the rhythmic noise from the chopper blades. Sensing that the Blackhawk was ready to lift off, he held up his left hand, demanding that Crowe wait. Hooper was standing beside his boss and crouching in fear of the chopper rotors and the flying dust. The DEA man stood apart, watching calmly. Crowe kept his gaze on the man. *There was much more to his story. But that would have to wait.*

Radcliff disconnected from his call and started yelling to Crowe with more intensity and motioning for Crowe to come back. Crowe shook his head and looked forward to the pilot, circling his right hand in the air, signaling to take off, leaving the bureaucrat and his *what-ifs* on the ground.

CHAPTER 26

One mile south of the Zetas' camp

The two Mexicans moved methodically across the sunbaked ground. It was hot, but they were carrying full water packs. They moved with a smooth efficiency, no wasted movement. Both men were comfortable in the desert. They were former Mexican army commandos, and both had received extensive training at the famous US Army-sponsored School of the Americas. This facility had come under fire in recent years because too many Latin American soldiers had gone over to the other side after completing this advanced training. These two had even attended the desert warfare training center run by the United States Marine Corps at 29 Palms. Of course, this was long before they decided to leave the Mexican army and sell their skills to the Zetas. Now they were very wealthy men.

Both of the men were trained snipers. For Romero, this was not his first trip to the Tohono Reservation. During his last trip, he had killed on the personal orders of Yaotl himself. This time, he was here to protect the "packages." If anyone tried to interfere, he had orders to kill them. He would follow the group from a distance, watchful for the American border police and also for the new "Federal Indians." The Zetas had received word that a new group of policias were patrolling the border and that they were something special. He had heard that they called themselves Wolves or something like that. He smiled. *Perhaps he would get to kill one of those indios on this trip.*

Romero's young partner had never been north of the border before, but he was no stranger to killing. He had killed countless peasants over the past two years, spreading terror wherever it was needed, further honing his deadly skills along the way.

Both Zetas had been assigned to follow the main group as a rear guard. Only Lobo knew of their presence. They had travelled through the tunnel well behind the group. They had then remained in the darkness of the tunnel for over four hours after the coyote had led the group of women north from the border. Upon finally exiting the opening in the earth, they quietly headed north, following the trail of their companions.

The two men walked silently, stealthily spreading east and west of the trail for the first hour with no sign of any Border Patrol. It had been the younger of the two who was the first to detect the tracks, just about one hundred yards to the east of the main trail. The signs were faint, but clearly fresh. The Zetas were being followed. The young Zeta called to his partner on his handheld radio, careful to speak only in Nahuatl.

*****

Hannah squatted next to Nalin, having briefed her about her call to Crowe. They only needed to track these people to their next stop and wait for the rest of the team. She told Nalin to leapfrog ahead of the group and find a good observation post.

Nalin nodded. "I think I know where they will hold up for the night. It's about three hours walk from here. By then it will be too dark to walk without goggles. They won't risk going farther, and there is usually a small spring there, *if* it still has water."

Hannah was half listening and looking intently through her handheld spotting scope. "The little girl doesn't look too good. The older one with her looks really nervous."

Nalin watched in silence, her vision sharp as an eagle without a scope.

Hannah tried to reassure Nalin. "The team should be in the air in about twenty minutes. We just have to hold tight until then."

CHAPTER 27

American airspace over US-Mexican border

Ethan stared out at the desert from his seat in the Blackhawk, the sun slowly dropping to the horizon. Despite the coming dusk, the rising thermals were making the chopper ride a rough one. The team was holding tight to their seats for balance. It would be hours before the heat would finally dissipate for the night. Everything was slowing down for Crowe now as it always did once the office was behind and the operation was in motion. They would set down a little less than two miles from the takedown site just to ensure they weren't seen or heard. The pilot would drop to the floor for the last few miles, making the chopper almost invisible to anyone more than one mile away.

Crowe felt his stomach's usual protest as the Blackhawk dove to the deck to make its final run across the desert floor. The chopper would set down west of where Nalin felt the traffickers would stop for the night. They would walk and run the rest of the way to avoid detection and minimize the danger for the hostages. He scanned the interior of the chopper. His men were ready to go, eyes cold and alert, watching him for the signal to deploy. He took a long, calming breath. *Let this go smooth.*

*****

Moments later, the Blackhawk set down on the hardpan of the desert floor. The Shadow Wolves were out and ducking under the blades in seconds. Each carried combat packs on their backs, weapons, ammo, and water. The Wolves were in fighting mode.

Now empty, the chopper lifted back into the sky, hugging the earth as it headed north and west. It disappeared into the growing darkness as if it had never existed. The men silently gathered their gear and looked to Crowe as he took his GPS readings and consulted the compass.

After a final radio check on his headset, Crowe split the men into two groups—Elias Blue Eagle taking his team to the east and Crowe his men on a western path toward the planned takedown location. Factor would go with Crowe. Both teams moved in a steady half run, effortlessly moving across the terrain just as their people had done since time began.

CHAPTER 28

Romero and his partner came to rest about three hundred yards from the two Apache trackers. They had slowed their pace in fear of being seen but were helped when they caught a brief flash of light where there should not have been one. The waning sunlight had caught the lens of the tall one's spotting scope and compromised her position.

"There they are," Romero said softly to himself as he held his hand up to signal his partner to freeze. He looked across with his binoculars, then whispered quietly to the younger sniper, "I think they are Indians. They look different to me. After another moment, he proclaimed, "I think they're women," his disbelief clear in his voice. "They can't be *migras*. Two women?" He took another prolonged look and shook his head in resignation. "Whoever they are, they are definitely watching our people."

The two snipers then separated and took up positions twenty feet apart in the rocks. After about five minutes, the younger one signaled silently to his partner, indicating that they should take both of the trackers out at the same time. Romero, never one to make sudden decisions, shook his head no. Puzzled, the younger one gave the universal shrug for "Why?" Romero scurried over to the other's position, leaned close, and whispered there was a chance that there could be more Americans. They needed to wait to be certain. "They don't know we are here, and we have nothing but time. We will wait." The younger one nodded obediently and both men settled in, watching.

Romero's confidence was misplaced. Within minutes, the shorter of the two trackers was already on the move, heading north and disappearing into the landscape like a cougar.

*****

Hannah had taken great care while using her spotting scope. She didn't want an inadvertent flash of light or reflection to give away their presence to the camp below. She took great pains to cover the sides of the eyepiece whenever she pointed it toward the camp. Unfortunately, she was totally unaware that a rear guard had been shadowing the group since the border and that she and her partner were now under the scopes of the Zeta assassins.

Nalin had tapped Hannah on the shoulder as a silent signal when she slipped away. She was now on her way to the next stopping point for the Zetas and their captives. She had taken one parting look at the little girl and her companion. The older of the two had suffered some abuse, being dragged through the dirt by the leader of the Zetas. The child had been dragged along with the older one as she clung tenaciously to her leg. Nalin knew about the trafficking of women by these groups, having found the bones of the unfortunates who didn't make it. But she had never seen it happening firsthand. This was obscene. As she crested the hill, she maintained a low profile, invisible to anyone who might glance her way. *How will Crowe take these men down without hurting the women? These were men without souls. They were going to fight.*

*****

El Lobo moved among his men, cursing and getting them ready to move. The women were slow to rise and were kicked and slapped by the men as they passed among them. Two or three of the women were crying, and several were clearly suffering from the rough treatment they had endured at the hands of their captors during the journey. The days of constant sexual abuse were now affecting their ability to walk for any length of time. Lobo had some uneasy thoughts, cursing himself for not being stricter with the men. *If these women were too damaged, he would have hell to pay.*

Inez got to her feet quickly, not wanting to trigger any further violence against herself or Colena. The girl was slipping away. She had yet to speak and now seemed to be slowly shutting down. Inez could still get the child to respond to her, but the girl's responses were lethargic at best. Even in her innocence, the child clearly sensed the menace in the one they called Lobo. Inez also felt something feral in the man as he looked at Colena. She truly worried what the next stop would bring.

"Colena, we have to go now," said Inez, half lifting the child from her resting place. "It is almost over now. Maybe the Americans will find us soon." Inez was not believing a word of what she just said.

The little one's eyes lifted slowly to look at Inez, but no hope was left under those long dark lashes.

*****

The Zetas and the women moved out, the men pushing and pulling their captives as they walked farther north into the desert.

A skinny, swarthy Zeta approached Lobo. "*Jefe*, how far do we have to go to get rid of these *putas*?"

"Soon. We will be going home soon." Then on second thought, he growled angrily, "Stop asking so many questions and do your fucking job, *cabron*."

*****

Hannah Lone Hawk watched as the group headed north. She slowly rose from her spot and started her shadowing track. She too wondered how this takedown would go and how they would protect this group of damaged and terrified women. She thought she heard a sound to her rear and stopped, listening for a full ten minutes before moving again. She heard and saw nothing more. *It must have been a coyote out looking for a meal or perhaps some leftovers from the camp below.*

*****

The two teams of Shadow Wolves arrived at the projected takedown site. The men were quickly deployed on both sides of the canyon below. Crowe scanned the area through his night vision glasses, spotting the eyes of a mountain lion that was fully aware of his team and watching silently from a high rock outcropping.

Crowe looked down from his vantage point to the logical stopping place for the Zetas and their prisoners. He spoke through his throat mike to Blue Eagle, "Can you get a good observation post on your side of the draw?"

"No problem, boss. I have Iron Cloud scouting a way down from here for the takedown. I can leave one long gun up here to cover us. He can take out any of these fuckers who want to shoot it out. I will move the rest of my team down closer before these guys arrive. We don't want them to hear us making noise getting off these rocks."

"Good. We have to work our way down over some pretty bumpy ground too. I am going to put one rifle up here as well. The rest of us will get down to the shadows of the draw as soon as possible." Crowe was interrupted by a tap on the shoulder, turning to see Nalin standing there. She had somehow materialized instantly from the rocks behind him. *Jesus, this girl freaked him out sometimes.*

Crowe whispered to the Apache tracker, "Are they coming?"

Nalin nodded.

"How long?"

"Another hour," Nalin stated flatly while looking down on the camp.

"We need to move most of the team down below before they get here. I need you or Hannah to call the takedown from up here."

Nalin nodded quietly while looking over the ground below their location. Crowe's radio clicked in his ear, Hannah Lone Hawk's radio coming into range.

"Ethan, this is Hannah. Do you copy?"

"Roger, Lone Hawk. I have you," said Crowe, speaking low into the thin microphone resting on the front of his throat.

Hannah spoke calmly, "They should be coming your way in about forty-five minutes, boss. They look tired, and they're tripping around like drunks in the dark."

"Come up along the ridgeline on the west. I need you at the observation post."

"I'm on it. Be there in about fifteen." Hannah moved quickly, now ahead of the Zetas, and disappeared into the dark lines of the rocks.

*****

The Mexican snipers were hurrying over the rocky terrain. They were frantically scanning the horizon and the rocks on all sides of their path. Now they had lost both of the American scouts. One minute they had been there and the next they were gone. The men knew that they would be dealt with severely if they failed at this.

After considering all options, Romero finally told his partner to continue on along the ridge while he worked his way down to the desert floor to catch up with the group. He needed to tell Lobo about the American trackers and give him the news that he had lost them. *He would not be happy. Fuck, he was getting too old for this shit. He already had more money than he needed. He should have quit this thing long ago. But then he just shook his head to himself. Who are you kidding? There is no retirement from this work.* He thought about Lobo once again. *You never knew how any of these narco bosses would react to bad news. Lobo was half crazy anyway. He was certainly nobody to fuck with.*

*****

Hannah Lone Hawk slid quietly into a small circle with Crowe and Nalin. They worked through the situation, Hannah giving her thoughts on the dangers that each of the Zetas presented. She clearly feared the leader the most. "He is an evil one, boss. He might kill the girls just to do it. We need to try to get him away from the group, maybe when he is taking a piss or something."

Crowe nodded. "I need one of you two to stay up here and call the takedown."

The two Apaches exchanged looks. Nalin tilted her head down toward the draw, and Hannah nodded once.

"Nalin will go down with you," Hannah informed Crowe. "Where do you want me?"

"Take up a spot next to our sniper. I want a play-by-play from you once they arrive. You just tell me what is happening and I will make the final call."

"Ethan, it could be a real mess. We could lose a lot of those girls if this goes bad." There was a worried look on Hannah's face that rarely showed itself. "I can't be sure on the timing of the takedown."

"I know. You just keep me posted and I will make the decision. It will be on me."

Darkness was settling in now, and Crowe passed Hannah a stronger set of night vision optics. He looked at Nalin and motioned for her to follow him down from the rocks.

Hannah took a long look at her Apache "sister" as she and Ethan prepared to leave and quietly mouthed to Nalin, "Nahatse."

Nalin, acknowledging her nickname, returned the look, nodded, and set off behind Crowe, ready for whatever was coming.

CHAPTER 29

Camp of the trafficked

Inez looked ahead as the group started to slow. The men in the lead were stopping and spreading out against the sheltering walls of the draw. Most of the women sensed, rather than heard, the order to stop. One girl had collapsed a mile back, and Inez was not even sure whether they had helped her or just left her to die in the desert. She had heard no gunshot, but these brutes would not risk the noise and could just as easily have slit the girl's throat.

Colena had been walking at Inez's side but was not responding to her touch. Inez had leaned down to talk to the girl but had been kicked in her buttocks by one of the men for making too much noise. Colena hadn't seemed to notice the incident and didn't really seem to take any comfort in the one-sided conversation any longer. As the group came to a stop, Inez pulled the little girl to the side, sitting her down next to her with their backs to a rock face. Her hope was to try to become invisible to these men when they started to drink and abuse the girls. So far, the threats of the one they called Lobo had been enough to keep them away from the child. But now she wasn't so sure that Lobo himself could be kept at bay.

Inez pulled Colena into her arms protectively as they sat against the rock, mothering her just as she had throughout the journey. The last time she had tried to steer the girl to the ground, she had felt limp in her arms, and Inez feared that this might be the end for the child. She thought that the girl had finally just become overwhelmed with the cruelty that had surrounded her for the past few days.

Inez paused to think about her role in this hellish nightmare. *Would she leave this desert alive? If so, would there be anything left of her soul?* In a way, caring for the child had managed to take her thoughts off her own plight. She was only nineteen, but after only three months with these brutes, she felt all used up. Could her life have changed so much? She no longer even thought of Orlando. She had been such a fool. Then she looked around the camp at the men spread out among the women. What if one of these animals had made her pregnant or given her some disease? Surely, she was going to be sold or even killed. *Maybe dying would be the better of the two.*

One of the men passed Inez and the child, throwing a few pieces of dried meat on their laps. Inez grabbed it in a flash, quickly chewing the jerky like it was the finest steak. The girl lifted hers to her mouth, absently chewing it momentarily and then setting the remainder onto Inez's lap. Inez watched, hesitated, and then hungrily chewed her own portion. *She had to survive this. She would survive this! She would see Mama again no matter what it took!*

As Inez placed her blanket over Colena, she eased back onto the ground, her head coming to rest on her cloth satchel. She risked a furtive look at Lobo, thinking that she could kill him if ever given the chance. *My god, what had she become?* Glancing back to the ground next to her, she reached for the goatskin, emptied some water into her hand, and started to wet the child's parched and swollen lips. She then took her wetted palm and gently washed the girl's face.

Thirty feet away, Lobo knelt on the ground and pulled a blanket over his head, forming a makeshift tent. He spread the map on the ground in front of him. He used a small flashlight to illuminate the map, compass, and GPS. The buyers would be here at first light. He would have the coyote scout the terrain surrounding their position to make sure they were secure. Lobo worried a bit about the money exchange but had been assured by Guzman that it would be there.

This was Lobo's first trip over the border with a shipment of women. He had been moving drugs north since he was twelve, when he had started his working life as a mule for the traffickers. He had been a hard worker and had no problem following orders. Over the years, he had killed many men and women when the orders were given. He had risen steadily through the ranks and was now one of the most feared crew leaders for the Zetas. This trip had been different for him. Moving drugs had always been easy. Drugs didn't need food or drink. These women were a lot of trouble. The men had also been more work on this trip. They couldn't keep their minds on their work, instead thinking only with their dicks. *And forgetting that the Americans were always hunting.*

He had to admit that he understood the men. Some of these women were a temptation. The child was an extra distraction. He wanted her. She was forbidden by the law and by the priests, but he had no use for either of them. His Aztec blood made him look down on all of the Christian shit that had held his country in chains since the Spanish and their robed churchmen had landed centuries ago. His time was running short. They would hand them over to the fucking MS-13 in the morning, get their money, and quickly get back to the relative safety of Mexico. He would take what he wanted tonight…before the handoff. He would still sell the child as unspoiled. *Who the fuck will know?* If someone raised the issue later, he would blame the MS-13 gangsters for violating her after the exchange. Having worked out his dilemma, Lobo lay back against his pack, watching the group settle in for the night, all the time staring at the little one and her guardian. He smiled to himself, *I will taste your fruit tonight, little one, and maybe your friend too.*

*****

Hannah spoke into the mike as she watched the group drop to the ground in the shelter of the sandstone wall. "They've stopped, and it looks like they are settling in for the night. They are eating and drinking and finding spots against the east wall of the draw."

Crowe said, "Copy that."

Seconds later, Hannah's voice came back in his ear. "Wait!"

"Hannah?"

"There's another one."

"What?"

Hannah replied rapidly, "There's another one. One we didn't count. Another bad guy."

Nalin turned to Crowe. Something was happening. She moved closer and looked questioningly at him.

Crowe kept looking forward, motioning with his hand for her to wait. "What are you talking about, Hannah?"

"There's an extra bad guy. He just came into camp and is squatting next to the boss, talking fast and waving his hands around."

"You sure you just don't have him confused with one of the other ones?"

"No, there were ten before, counting the coyote, and now all of a sudden there are eleven. He's new. I just don't know where he came from. He's carrying a long rifle with a scope. We couldn't have missed him." As soon as she said it, she remembered. *That was no coyote that I heard.* Reflexively she checked her back with the goggles but saw nothing.

Crowe covered his throat mike with his hand and whispered to Nalin, "She says that there is another bad guy. Could you have missed him?"

"No," Nalin answered quickly, her eyes moving quickly back and forth, thinking furiously about the situation and what it could mean.

Crowe removed his hand from the microphone and started to talk when Nalin reached out and grabbed his arm, interrupting what he was going to say.

"They must have had someone on our tail and we missed it," said Nalin, angry with herself for not realizing what had happened.

Hannah then interrupted them, "Whatever this new guy said to the boss did not make him happy. He is up and sending some of the men out to the perimeter. He looks pissed. They all have their guns out and look like they mean business. This could be bad. This guy was definitely watching their tail. He must have seen us tracking them."

"Just hold. Maybe they aren't sure," said Crowe, doing his best to calm the team. "All of you, heads-up. We have one or more extra bad guys out there. One might be unaccounted for. Everyone, check your perimeter. Report in when you are sure of your situation. Take your time and be sure."

*****

Lobo had been pissed off when the sniper had reported in. He was mostly pissed because these snipers had lost the trackers, *if* that was what they were. He wanted to shoot this one called Romero on the spot, but that would have been stupid. The man had been sent here by Yaotl. Lobo knew that killing the sniper without permission would mean his own life as well. As a practical matter, if they were being watched, the shot would alert the *migras*, and he might just need every gun he had before this thing was over.

He moved through the camp, hissing at the men, "Get out there and look for *migras*. I want you sure there is nobody out there." He shouted and pointed his finger emphatically at one of the Zetas. "You stay here with the women. Don't let them move! And keep them quiet!"

He looked over at the women and then stopped with Inez and Colena. Leaning over the child protectively, Inez met his stare. Lobo continued to stare her down for several more seconds. Then with an evil smile, he turned back to the men.

Meeting Lobo's cruel eyes, Inez had shuddered. *What was happening?* She pulled Colena closer and held her fast.

Romero watched Lobo as he barked orders at his crew. He also noted the man's interest in the young woman and child seated on the ground nearby. He didn't like this man. He knew that he had a reputation for competence but did not like the unspoken threat of violence Lobo had directed against him. He knew he could kill this pig if he chose to, but that was not his job. His job was to protect him. *They would meet another time.*

*****

Crowe kept getting reports from his team over the next two hours. The Zetas had originally appeared panicked, but they had not been able to detect anyone from the Wolves. Eventually, Hannah was able to report that the traffickers appeared to be relaxing and were slowly heading back to their camp. Each of the Zetas checked directly with Lobo before finally moving quietly to their resting places and settling into their dusty bedrolls. Lobo sent extra men out to stand sentry duty on the perimeter.

Crowe came over the radios. "Okay, team, they seem to be settling down. Let's lay low and let them get to bed. If we can keep them calm, maybe we can make our move in a few hours. Everyone stay put and keep the radio traffic to a minimum."

*****

The women had watched in fear as the Zetas grabbed their guns and rushed about the camp. There was something happening, but they had no idea what it was. Some of them began to cry hysterically, and others just trembled in their makeshift beds. One of the girls had cried out. A swarthy, bearded Zeta silenced her by smashing the side of her head with the butt of his rifle. When another captive reached over to touch the girl, she found her unconscious, maybe dead.

After the panic and chaos, Inez watched the men straggle back to the camp one by one. After reporting to Lobo, they quietly fell into their bedrolls. One thing was different. The men now seemed to purposely keep their distance, as if the girls were now a threat to their own safety.

*****

It was close to three in the morning when Lobo finally relaxed and returned to his spot near the women. His men were now down for the night, and the women were all quiet. He let out a tired sigh, put down his rifle, and slowly sank to the ground. He grabbed for his water skin but quickly changed his mind. He reached into his shirt and removed a small silver flask, taking a quick pull and letting out a long breath. *Maybe they had lost the Americans in the dark. Maybe they were not even the migras at all but just some reservation indios sticking their stupid noses into his business.*

Lobo looked over to the girls. Again, he caught the one they called Inez staring at him. He grinned at her, and she looked down immediately, pulling the girl closer to her at the same time. He chuckled to himself; this diversion had almost upset his plans for tonight. *He would only wait a little bit longer.*

*****

Hannah watched carefully from her perch above one of the Shadow Wolves' snipers. She had moved to a higher spot to give her a full view of the camp's perimeter and to avoid distracting the young Navajo with the long gun. She didn't know this Navajo very well. She had heard that he had served in the Tenth Mountain Division in Afghanistan. He had completed two tours before learning of the Shadow Wolves' unit. Like so many of the team, he was a highly decorated combat vet. She suspected that Ethan's general had made his transition to the team happen smoothly. It was reassuring to have him here. He would be needed tonight if her sense of things was even close to accurate.

The moon was almost full, but clouds continued to pass overhead, causing periods of total darkness. Hannah compensated by switching to her night vision to scan the scene below. In a calm, factual manner, she narrated what she saw, "Ethan, they are now spread all through the camp. Four are out on the perimeter and seven are in the camp. It's confirmed. There are now a total of eleven bad guys. Some are close to the girls, but not like they were. The rest are located on each side of where the girls are bedded down. They're about twenty-five feet away from them."

Crowe interrupted, "Is there any sign of another one of them sitting out there someplace?"

"Don't know, but I wouldn't be surprised. If he's there, he is really lying low." She then caught some motion in the camp. "The boss is back in his spot in the middle of the women. He looks like he might be going down for the night. Actually looks like he is drinking something from a flask, probably Mescal. He is really close to the little girl and the one who watches over her."

Crowe listened as he made last-minute preparations in his head. "Elias, can your team take the five on the north and east? We can take the remaining sentry and the five in the camp."

Elias Blue Eagle replied, "Roger that."

Crowe then reached out to his snipers on the rocks above. "I need the long guns to concentrate on the ones closest to the women. If they move to shoot or kill any of the girls, you have a green light to take them out."

"Roger that," came the response from the snipers.

"Okay. It's oh-three hundred now. Let's wait another hour to see if we can get some of them to fall asleep."

*****

Lobo lay awake thinking about the ten-year-old. Every minute that passed heightened his awareness of her in the camp. Most of the women had fallen asleep or lay whimpering underneath what passed for bedrolls. One or two of them were coughing and appeared to be on their last legs. He was beyond worrying about them at this point. *As long as they last until we get our money in the morning, fuck all of them.* He got up and walked a few feet away to relieve himself, looking over his shoulder at Inez and the girl. They both appeared to be quiet and possibly asleep.

Urinating loudly, he smiled in anticipation of taking the child. Finished, he shook himself, zipped his fly, and walked across the space to where the child and the other one slept. He stood over the two for a few minutes, checking to see if they were awake. He then reached down with lightning speed and grabbed the child's hair, violently pulling her to her feet. For the first time since her captivity, the child let out a bloodcurdling scream. Lobo continued to pull violently at the child's hair, lifting her so high her feet were now dangling in midair. As he pulled the little one to eye level, he noticed that Inez had come up with her, as if she was attached to the girl, clinging to the girl's waist. Lobo's mind flashed, *The bitch was waiting for this.*

Lobo kicked violently at Inez, catching her on the inside of her upper thigh, staggering her and loosening her grip on the girl. The girl continued to scream, squirming and grabbing for Inez's hand. As Lobo started to pull Colena away, he felt the weight of Inez once again. This whore was now holding both of the girl's legs just above her knees. He turned violently, the fury in the woman's eyes now matching his own. He struck out with his huge left hand, striking Inez in the face. Her nose erupted in an explosion of blood and mucus. Then in a rage, he dropped the girl and moved to where Inez lay on the ground.

CHAPTER 30

All the radios came to life at once. Hannah was shouting into her mike, "The boss is attacking the little girl. He is beating the other one and trying to drag the girl away from her bed. We need to move."

Crowe didn't hesitate and spoke clearly into the radio, "It's a go. I repeat, go!"

Crowe was moving as he issued his orders. His Glock was in his hand, and he was running full speed to the edge of the camp. He heard shots from all directions. No need to worry any longer about what was happening or what might happen. He had learned from experience that this was the point of no return and one had to trust in the gods.

Blue Eagle was the first to encounter one of the Zetas. As he was moving quickly to close the distance to where the traffickers were bedded down, one of the men came out from behind a rock, having just finished relieving himself. The man, recognizing the threat, began to pull his pistol from his belt. Blue Eagle did not hesitate, killing the Zeta instantly with one round from his pistol directly into the Zeta's forehead.

Lobo heard the first shot, his feral survival instincts coming alive. He paused a moment, looking back at the little girl lying on the ground where he had dropped her. He then turned quickly to locate the woman who knelt on the ground facing him, readying herself to fend off his pending attack. His arousal dissipating, he seethed at both of them, "You little bitches." He suddenly pulled his pistol and pointed it at the ten-year-old, who could only stare wide-eyed at the man.

A primal scream erupted from Inez. She threw herself across Colena, knocking the child onto her back. The girl's clothing was in tatters, and scratches were bleeding on her arms. Lobo reached out and grabbed Inez's hair, pulling her backward, upward from her position on top of the child. Inez glared up at him, hatred blazing in her eyes. Lobo then shot her point-blank in the face. As the woman fell from his grasp, dead, he heard a noise off to his left. Without turning, he released Inez and disappeared into the darkness, forgetting the child and his waning passion.

Crowe moved quickly across the western edge of the camp in an effort to reach the child. Looking ahead, he saw a muzzle flash, followed instantly by the noise of the gunshot. The man the Apaches called the boss had just shot the older of the two captives in the face. Crowe saw that the man now loomed over the little girl with a handgun in his right hand.

Suddenly there was movement to Ethan's right. An unseen Zeta was lifting his handgun to fire at Crowe. Two shots rang out. The man crumpled where he stood. He turned to see Nalin walking calmly across the camp, pistol in her hand, having just saved Crowe's life. Not even pausing to look, Nalin moved quickly to her right, firing multiple rounds rapidly as she engaged another Zeta who had been guarding the girls.

Crowe turned back to where he had last seen the head Zeta holding the girl. The man had disappeared. The girl was on the ground, leaning over a prostrate form next to her. He desperately searched his field of vision to try and see where the bastard had gone. Nothing. Only smoke and dust from the firefight. Suddenly, a flurry of muzzle flashes could be seen on the rocks overhead where both Hannah and the Navajo sniper had been positioned.

Crowe scanned the rocks in the dark. *What the fuck?*

*****

The younger Zeta sniper had reacquired one of the trackers just before the chaos erupted below. He hadn't been sure before, but now he was. *This is a woman! I can't believe a woman could move like this.* He saw that the tracker and another were just below the top of the ridge. The second person was now looking down on the camp through a telescopic sight on his rifle. *A sniper!* The woman was scanning the camp through a night vision scope and talking on a throat microphone. *These had to be federals.* He sighted in on the sniper and gently fingered the trigger. Just as he found a good spot to conceal himself, gunfire exploded from the camp. The Zeta sniper didn't hesitate. He took a breath, let it out, and fired, striking the one with the rifle high in his torso. Then quickly moving to the other target, he brought his gun to bear on the woman.

*****

Hannah heard the shot and could feel the force of the impact on the Navajo, who grunted and fell still. She instinctively turned and rolled for the cover of the rocks behind her. She felt a sudden hammer-like blow to her right shoulder, knocking her sideways in the direction she had been rolling. Her back slammed into a boulder, knocking the wind from her. She tried to raise her gun hand but looked down and could see that her arm was not moving. She had been shot. She tried to pull it up with her other hand, all the time crawling to the relative safety of the rocks. She could smell the blood, and her hand felt wet and slippery. She also felt a stinging sensation in her scalp but couldn't remember being hit in the head or a second shot. Reaching over with her left hand, she took her Glock from the wounded side and tried to concentrate on staying alive and forgetting the pain.

The Zeta sniper moved quickly from his perch, laying down cover fire to keep the two migras pinned behind the rocks, if they were still alive. Hannah fired off four rounds with her left hand from behind the rock, hoping to slow the Zeta's advance, but not expecting to hit anything. She glanced at her companion, and he was not moving. She rolled onto her back and put the wrist of her gun hand between her two knees, locking them around her wrist, allowing her to steady her gun hand. She looked ahead and waited.

The Zeta was taking no chances. He was a trained soldier and aware that nothing was certain in battle. He moved to flank the American sniper and the woman. He knew where the spotter was hiding and was sure he had hit her. He had three magazines on his belt and at least nine rounds left in his gun. He kept scanning left and right as he moved, ever watchful of the action down below as well. Four rounds came from the rocks, one of them just missing him and forcing him to fall to the ground and roll. *So one is still alive.* He didn't wait to return fire. He methodically emptied his gun into the rocks, purposely angling the shots to ricochet into the space where the bitch was hiding and firing her weapon.

Hannah felt a sharp pain in her head during the fusillade of shots that came from above. She was having trouble focusing and felt blood now running down her face. She tried to wipe it from her right eye, but the blood kept flowing into her line of sight. She fired again until her gun went dry, ejecting the magazine and putting in another from her belt. She felt for the opening in the base of the grip and reloaded blindly, just as she had been taught at the academy. She moved to lock her wrist between her knees again but could not seem to move her left leg. She reached over with her gun hand and tried to prop the leg up but couldn't lift it. Hannah wiped her face again with her one good arm, her gun wavering in front of her. She looked up to see the Zeta standing in front of her. His gun erupted into her eyes. Her world went dark.

In a fury, the Zeta pumped four more rifle rounds into the slender Apache, temporarily forgetting the prostrate figure to his left. Looking up and turning, the Zeta never heard the shot that entered through his left eye socket, the Navajo sniper killing him before falling back to the dusty ground and taking his last breath.

*****

On the perimeter, Elias Blue Eagle ran full speed at the fixed sentry position in front of him. He held two Army Colt .45s, one in each hand, firing them as he ran directly at the Zeta. The Mexican trafficker stood frozen, rifle in hand. Charging at him was a fierce

Pawnee warrior, his face in full war paint. The man was dead in the first four shots from Elias's guns.

When one of the perimeter guards heard the shots, he immediately started running. He was a coward and chose to flee rather than fight. His fellow Zetas were engaging the Americans, and it was going badly. He moved swiftly, but cautiously, relying on his military training and survival instincts.

Isaac had seen the fleeing Zeta and anticipated his decision to run. He moved quickly to his left and rear. He positioned himself in the Zeta's path and waited. Seconds later, the outlaw appeared twenty feet in front of him. Isaac holstered his handgun and pulled the shotgun from the sling that hung across his back. His black skin made him almost invisible in the dark of the desert. The Zeta came within ten feet of the Seminole before seeing him. He drew to a stop, staring at Factor for several seconds, frozen in fear. Finally, the cowardly soldier brought his rifle up to fire at the black apparition. Isaac Factor sent him to hell with his 12-gauge.

Having lost sight of Lobo, Crowe moved to the edge of camp and pulled on his night vision goggles, hoping to catch a trace of Lobo's movements. He scanned the area in front of him repeatedly. Nothing. The night vision flared annoyingly each time a muzzle flash entered his field of view. He looked back to the child. A pitched battle was going on all around her, but she remained bent over the shape on the ground at her side. He rushed to the child, seeing that the shape was in fact the body of a dead woman, no doubt her protector. Crowe gently pulled the girl away from the body. He then carefully guided her to the relative safety of the ground, telling her to stay put. The girl looked confused and initially thought Ethan was one of the Zetas. He switched to Spanish. "Stay here, girl. I am here to help. Please don't move. It's not safe." Satisfied that she finally understood, he stood and began moving through the camp, urging women to the ground and trying to calm them as he passed.

Crowe was moving again. He had spotted another Zeta who was running to the cover of some nearby rocks. He fired three shots and thought he had wounded the man. But the figure kept running. The Zeta dropped from sight behind cover. Crowe moved quickly to his right, hoping to flank the Zeta and find some high ground. He was suddenly struck by a round fired from someone to his rear, hitting him in his back near his left shoulder. He hit the ground hard, his breath forced from his lungs by the power of the bullet hitting his Kevlar vest. He rolled to his left and quickly loosened his vest to allow him to catch his breath more quickly.

Still flat on his back, Crowe heard movement in the rocks ahead. He saw a Zeta approaching with a pistol in his right hand. The man was limping, his gun hand wavering slightly. The man readied to fire. Crowe instinctively rolled to his left, knowing this was the percentage move with a right-handed shooter. A second later, a rapid succession of shots kicked up the dirt where Crowe had been. Crowe brought his Glock to bear and fired five shots into the chest of the Zeta, killing him instantly.

He looked to his right and saw a stocky Zeta soldier walking through the camp, firing two rounds into a woman crawling through the dirt. The woman fell still. He then saw a blur moving full speed across the dust. It was Nalin. She hit the Zeta full force in a violent collision. As they collided, Nalin wrapped her arm around the neck of the soldier in a choke hold. She kept her momentum going, twisting to her left with her arms firmly locked around the man's throat. She held her grip as they both slammed to the dirt, expertly avoiding the man's attempts to free himself. After a prolonged minute, the man's efforts slowed and finally ceased.

Crowe pushed himself to his feet as Nalin released her grip on the unconscious shooter. She moved into a position straddling the Zeta, turning his body and pushing the man's face into the dirt. In another blurred motion, she pulled her obsidian knife from her belt. She reached down, grabbed the Zeta's hair, and pulled his head backwards toward her. The Apache then placed the glass blade against his throat and paused, her rage burning like fire in her eyes. Crowe held his breath for what seemed an eternity, only to see *Nahatse* release her grip on the killer's hair, letting his head drop back to the ground, still alive. Leaning down, she spoke venomously into the man's ear in Spanish, "I should cut your heart out and eat it." She then rose and looked around, her fury dissipating. She methodically pulled flex-cuffs from her leg pocket and secured both his hands and legs. Nalin then turned and walked away without another glance. Crowe let out the breath he didn't realize he had been holding.

Hidden in the rocks above and directly west of the camp, Lobo and the coyote watched the action below. Lobo shook his head disgustedly. *How the fuck did this happen?* He considered that perhaps he should not have become witched by the child. *She had made his mind a cloud.*

A sound from behind startled him. Before he could turn and bring his weapon to bear, an unseen voice, in Spanish, came from the darkness. "Save your bullets, Lobo. You will need them for the Americans." The one they called Romero emerged from the shadows, nodding down at the scene below. "This will not go well back in Coahuila."

Lobo grunted in response, shaking his head in agreement. "Who the fuck are these Americans?"

The coyote shook his head. "I don't think they are Americans. They are like soldiers, but the Americans don't use their soldiers for this." He added, "I think these are the new *indios policias* we have been hearing about, the ones they call Wolves."

Lobo looked over at his two fellow survivors, seething. "I will come back and kill every one of these *indios*."

Romero stepped next to Lobo. "We should go. We need to go right away if we are to have a chance."

Lobo, still shaking with fury, looked at the coyote. "Which way?"

The coyote pointed to his rear. "We can't go directly south. They will look there first. We must go into the rocks above and through the desert. There is a crossing that has not been used for many years."

Lobo looked over at Romero with raised eyebrows, looking for confirmation.

Romero nodded. "We had better do something. I vote yes." He quickly checked his weapon and the extra ammo in the pockets of his vest. Looking up at his companions, he motioned with his rifle to the coyote to get moving. The coyote responded gratefully, eager to be out of this place. Lobo followed, always the survivor.

*****

The firefight had ended as quickly as it had begun. The smell of cordite hung heavy in the air. The women scattered around the campsite looked like figures from some medieval artist's rendering of hell. The dead were mixed among the crying women who were now crawling and finding any way possible to get away from the carnage. So far, including Crowe, three of the Wolves had been wounded, but none of the wounds appeared to be life-threatening. Moses Iron Cloud was already on the radio doing a roll call of the team and getting status reports.

Nalin was on the ground, holding the little girl and whispering to her in Spanish. Crowe looked over at her, choosing not to interfere. The rest of his men were tending to the women, trying to triage their injuries and assuring them that they were now safe. He put his finger to his throat and called for the Blackhawk and the medical chopper. "We have multiple injuries. Officers and civilians down. We need you here double-quick." He took note of the time—zero three thirty. It was much too long until sunup for a good track. *Both choppers will be needed for this mess.*

*****

Crowe was once again ticking off his mental checklist. Choppers and medics on the way. First aid already being applied. The head count on the bad guys was still ongoing, but it was certain that some had escaped into the desert. The roll call was finishing. Hannah and her Navajo partner had not answered up. He broke into the radio channel and called the observation post himself. Nothing in reply. He glanced up to see Isaac looking at him and listening to his attempts at radio contact. Seconds later, the Seminole was moving up the hill, sliding across the rocks like they weren't even there. Crowe was moving with him, like they had done countless time before, in places just as hellish as this. Ethan's fears were making his heart beat out of his chest as he climbed to see what had happened to his people.

Nalin was half listening to her radio earpiece while trying to calm the child when she saw Crowe and Isaac moving quickly up the rock face. Something was wrong. She looked around and found one of the newer Wolves, also an Apache, and motioned him over to the girl. In Apache, she said, "Stay here with the child. Don't let her look at the dead ones and keep her calm. Protect her!"

Nalin sprung to her feet and started running up through the rocks to where she had left Hannah Lone Hawk. Her prayers to the Great Spirit racing through her brain with each step. She came over the ridge to find Ethan on the ground, holding Hannah's hand as she lay dead on the ground. Isaac was bent over the Shadow Wolves sniper, the slender Navajo who rarely smiled. He was dead too, and Isaac had a look on his face she had never seen before. She walked over to the dead Zeta and turned him facedown into the dirt. His spirit would not go to the next world from this position.

Crowe watched *Nahatse*, the warrior, as she spat on the Zeta. She then turned and walked toward Ethan and her "sister," pain and fury in every feature of her face. He met her eyes, black as death. Nalin sank to the ground next to Crowe. She gently moved him aside and cradled Hannah's head in her arms, quietly singing her to the next world. Crowe fell back onto his haunches and covered his face in his hands while Isaac Factor stood and turned his chiseled face southward to visualize where the Zetas were running. He would follow them, and he would find them. Then he would kill them.

CHAPTER 31

US-Mexico border, American side

Lobo and Romero were moving quickly across the rugged ground, led by the agile coyote who moved stealthily in front of them. They had gone west as the coyote had advised. They had fled into the shadowy night, burrowing into the shelter of the mountains. Lobo had to fight the powerful urge to flee directly toward the border and safety from these Americans. But this coyote said that would be suicide. He explained that they would have drones up along the border in a few hours. The Americans would catch them before they even made the crossing. The coyote was right. They had to take a route that nobody expected. They would go where they couldn't be tracked. Even with this plan, Lobo feared that they had very little chance of making it home. *These aren't ordinary migras we are fighting. These indios were something different.*

Lobo and Romero stopped to rest as the sun began to light up the horizon. They looked back over their trail as the coyote walked back to join them. They probably had a good three-hour head start on their pursuers. The *indios* would have to wait for first light to start their hunt. Lobo looked over to the coyote, who was also looking back over the ground they had just covered. "Do you think they will follow us?"

The coyote replied, never taking his eyes from the horizon. "They will follow. They are coming now."

CHAPTER 32

Crowe had little time to mourn Lone Hawk. He looked up to see Factor scanning the horizon with his night vision scope, his gaze lingering along certain sight lines. Crowe's radio was alive with shouts of urgency from his people. He stood and glanced briefly at Nalin, still holding her "sister" in her arms, rocking her gently.

Crowe's hand went to his throat mike. "Blue Eagle, this is Crowe. Do you copy?"

Calmly, Blue Eagle responded, "Roger that."

"What's the status of the choppers?"

"We've got two inbound, with another due to get in the air in a few minutes."

Crowe was weighing their immediate needs. "What is our wounded count?"

Blue Eagle read from his list, "We have three of our people wounded, none life-threatening but still urgent. We have three of the women KIA, all shot dead by the bad guys. We also have twelve of the women who need immediate medical attention. Two of them might not make it. Then we have four bad guys KIA, two critically wounded, and one with minor injuries. Definitely more than we can take back on the two choppers."

Crowe was considering his options. They would need more support. "I'll call Maggie and ask her to make sure that the hospital is ready for us up in Tucson."

Blue Eagle paused a moment, then said, "Boss, we still got three bad guys out there. I guess they're rabbitin' for the border double-quick."

Crowe pressed his mike but said nothing, thinking about his response. After almost a minute, he said, "Let's get the evac straightened out first. It's still too dark to find their trail anyway." Then an afterthought, he added, "Call the Border Patrol to see if they have any drones up out here."

Crowe walked to where his friend was standing. Factor never took his eyes from his scope but, sensing his friend's presence, spoke quietly to Ethan, "It will take us some time to pick up the trail. This night won't leave us for at least another hour."

"Your best guess?" Ethan looked back at Chee who was now gently placing the body of Lone Hawk on the ground. He would need her for this track. *Was she up to it?*

Isaac Factor lowered the scope, obviously already considering the possibilities. "I don't think they will go straight to the border. They will anticipate that we will set up to intercept them there. I think they'll go another way. This coyote is no fool. If it was me, I would go west into one of the mountain passes and then south. I figure they will have a three- to four-hour lead by the time we can settle up here and begin to find their trail."

Crowe nodded in agreement. He then grabbed his sat phone from the pocket on his right thigh. The phone rang once, the voice of Maggie Sees Far answering calmly, "How bad is it?"

"Not good. Maggie, we are going to need the trauma center ready for us up in Tucson. Can you call up there and make that happen? I will need at least two more LifeFlight helicopters sent down here ASAP. Also, call Agent King and have her wave the federal flag for us to make sure everything is done. Tell her I will call her as soon as I can."

Maggie keyed the mike but hesitated for a second. Then she said, "Are all our people okay?"

"No, Maggie, Hannah and the young Navajo are dead." Crowe's voice was breaking a bit as he finally put the tragedy to words.

Maggie said nothing. The silence was heartrending.

"Maggie?"

"Yes. I was just thinking about the boy. How do we tell him about Hannah?"

Ethan pictured Jason Lone Hawk. The boy was truly an innocent. What would happen to him now? He quickly decided, "Do what you think is best. I will come to see him as soon as I get back." Then he reluctantly forced himself back to his pursuit of the Zetas. "Maggie, I need horses. Have Ty load up five of our best mounts, along with supplies and water for at least three days. I need them here as soon as possible, and make sure one of them is Wanagi." He thought for a second and then said, "Make sure that we have plenty of ammo as well."

Maggie told Ethan that Ty was standing in her office. Without hanging up with Ethan, she relayed the instructions to Ty. Returning to her conversation with Ethan, she said, "He's already on it. The ponies will be on the way in less than thirty minutes."

Crowe looked at his GPS. "Here are the numbers. He should have no trouble trailering the mounts here. Isaac thinks it will take him about two hours."

Maggie acknowledged Crowe's last remarks. She was ready to hang up but hesitated a bit.

"Maggie, anything else?"

The Comanche responded with one more question, "*Nahatse*, is she with Lone Hawk?"

Crowe looked back at Nalin, who was walking toward where he and Isaac stood. "Yes. She's okay, Mag. Call me if there is any problem on your end," replied Crowe, cutting the call short so that Nalin would not hear.

Ethan spoke to both the Seminole and the Apache, "Isaac probably overheard my end of that conversation, but I have horses and supplies on the way. We'll get things sorted as best we can down below. Then we'll head out at first light."

Both nodded agreement with Crowe, Nalin instinctively fingering her belt to count her spare magazines.

Crowe continued, "I am thinking that the three of us will do the track. Nalin, you okay with that, or would you prefer to stay with Hannah?"

Nalin looked at Crowe with dead, black eyes. "I'm going."

Crowe looked back and forth at his best Wolves. "All right, let's get below and sec what needs to be done. Nalin, I'll send Moses Iron Cloud up to sit with Hannah until the choppers get here. Come down when he relieves you," said Ethan, knowing that the Apache would not want to leave Lone Hawk's body alone and unprotected.

Factor was already picking his way through the rocks on his descent to the battleground below. Crowe nodded silently to Nalin and followed his black scout down the incline. His mind was working through the situation on the O'odham. *Who was behind all this? This was not random. First the loss of Moses Price and now two Shadow Wolves. This was new. The Mexicans did not kill American cops. They knew there would be repercussions. Normally they just fled when confronted north of the border. What had changed?* As he reached the flat ground below, he vowed silently, *I will find the head of this snake. It won't be the first time I have crossed a border to hunt. Whoever this Aztec is, I am coming for him.* His thoughts were interrupted by the sound of rotors as the choppers lowered to the ground, aided by their searchlights.

CHAPTER 33

Office of the US Attorney, Miami,
Southern District of Florida

Robert W. Hickock, ranking assistant US attorney for the Southern District of Florida, looked across his desk at the three DEA agents. He had made them wait in the lobby for almost half an hour. He did it partly because he had been fighting with his boss up in DC and partly because he had to remind these agents that he was running this operation. These agents were the best of the best, the most experienced people that the DEA had to offer. They had run operations against the most powerful drug cartels in the world in the most dangerous places in the world. They were not easily managed. They could not be manipulated. He had to work very hard to be the leader of these hard men, but he had proven to be adept at getting what he wanted. After all, he had the blessing and power granted from the highest levels in Washington. This was a matter of national security, and that fact always shattered any resistance encountered along the way.

Hickock had been transferred to Miami a year ago by the new administration to assume the reins of one of the most covert of all DEA operations. In his new job, he had been given a blank check to go after terrorists, wherever and whenever he could find them. It didn't matter what the groups called themselves or what ideology they preached. He was to root them out and destroy them. If it meant delving into grey areas to get it done, then so be it.

Rising up from his chair, Hickock came around the desk to greet the DEA men. Despite the tropical heat of South Florida, the fortyish prosecutor never seemed to sweat. He always wore a perfectly tailored Brooks Brothers suit, starched white shirt and tie. Today his bright white smile and tan skin contrasted attractively with the fine Egyptian cotton of his collar. His lean, athletic build, combined with his practiced, easygoing charm, inspired confidence in everyone he met. There was no doubt the man was an up-and-coming star. If the truth were known, Hickock was already thinking about a run for congress back home when he finished this assignment. He had made all the right connections and could easily point to his record when the time was right.

Having long ago chosen to use his middle name, William, he had quickly earned the nickname "Wild Bill" by the press, something he did little to discourage. He was known for his no-nonsense approach to prosecutions in his home state of Texas. His reputation as an evangelical Christian and "by the book" lawman brought him many friends on the right and an equal number of enemies in the liberal media. He didn't care. In truth, he loved the attention and silently believed he was doing God's work anyway.

He had been handpicked to head up this task force, a unit so secret it had no name. The unit was located in Miami but, in truth, operated across the globe, utilizing the combined resources of all the intelligence services of the US and its allies whenever necessary.

As the men sat down in the four easy chairs comprising Hickock's conversation pit, he addressed the senior agent. "So what are we hearing from Coahuila?"

Agent Rick Wendt looked at his two colleagues, who nodded in agreement that he should start the briefing. "We hear that our guy is talking to folks in Italy about a weapons shipment. The N'drangheta is getting inquiries from Pakistan to buy a big shipment of arms."

Hickock looked questioningly at Wendt who quickly elaborated, "The N'drangheta is the Mafia group working out of Calabria, Italy. That's the toe of Italy. They are some bad motherfuckers. They also don't care who they work with."

Hickock was now sitting straight in his chair. "Who are the Pakis?"

The second DEA agent, Wilcox, chimed in, "Nothing for certain on that yet but probably Al Queada. If not, then ISIS. Nobody else has the kind of money to make this kind of buy."

Agent Wendt resumed, "We will know something definitive soon. Our guy in Coahuila will reach out in a day or so."

Hickock looked directly at the three agents. "What's our status in Mexico? Does anyone suspect our ties to Coahuila?"

The agents shook their head no in unison, looking carefully at one another in the process.

Hickock pressed, "I mean anyone—the DEA attaché, State Department security, hell, the ambassador."

Wendt deferred to Agent Bob Diaz, the third man in the room. Diaz had seen years of duty in Mexico and South America. "Bob, what is your assessment?"

"As far as I can tell, nobody knows shit. We have compartmentalized this op to the max. When we're in country, we check in with the DEA and FBI at the embassy. That way we always have a pretext for being there. So far, we have kept our meetings with our source completely off the books, and he sure as hell isn't saying anything."

Hickock looked at Wendt questioningly. "Is Webb still the control agent on this?"

Wendt nodded in the affirmative. "He's the best there is at this." Wendt then paused and looked uneasily at his companions.

Hickock caught their discomfort. "What?"

Diaz was the first to speak. "Our source has been very active lately. There have been some casualties."

"What do you mean?"

Diaz continued, "Well, there have been some serious loads intercepted on our side of the border. A tribal cop was really putting a dent in their operations. Several months ago, the same cop got offed. We're hearing that it was our guy who might have put out the hit." Diaz paused to let it sink in. "I haven't asked too hard on this yet."

Hickock was silent for several minutes. The agents remained quiet as well, allowing the prosecutor to digest the intel. Hickock suddenly stood up and walked back to his desk. "Well, we knew that we were dealing with the devil when we signed on for this. This has always been about the greater good outweighing the rest. This assignment is about protecting Americans, and by God, that is what we are going to do."

Diaz started to say something but thought better of it and remained silent.

Hickock sensed that Diaz was holding something back. He looked directly at the agent. "Is there more?"

Diaz sighed. "Yeah. Homeland has formed a special unit on the Tohono O'odham Reservation to fight the traffickers. It's made up of Native American trackers. They're Feds. They call them the Shadow Wolves. They've been kicking ass. They have also been actively looking for anyone who will tell them who killed the tribal cop."

Hickock was clearly getting annoyed but doing his best to suppress it. "So where in the fuck is this Tohono Reservation?"

"Southern Arizona. All along the Mexican border," Wendt chimed in. "It's huge. Bigger than the State of Connecticut."

Hickock was shaking his head and gesturing with his hands to the ceiling. "Who came up with that bright idea?"

The DEA agents shrugged in unison.

Hickock was now thinking about how this would impact his mission. "This team of fucking Indians can't possibly be a threat to our source deep in the heart of Mexico. They have no authority outside US territory."

Wendt spoke carefully to the man across the desk, "No, it would be a real stretch for them to go outside their assigned area. But I hear that the head of the team down there is a former operator out of the DIA. We put out some feelers on the guy. His name is Crowe. By all accounts, the guy is the real fucking deal—army, decorated, Distinguished Service Cross. Hell, that's right under the Medal of Honor. Then in the DIA, once again decorated—Silver Stars, Bronze Stars, Purple Hearts, etc. They make movies about guys like him."

Wendt waited a few seconds for effect. "He also worked with us in Thailand. Went places nobody else wanted to go, tracking people nobody else wanted to track. If he gets his teeth into something, he might not let go." Wendt paused again to let Hickock take all of it in. He then continued, "Webb went to see him yesterday but hasn't called in yet to tell us how it went. He tagged along with some Homeland Security bosses on what was basically a meet and greet. You know, we're from the government and we're here to help sort of thing."

Hickock nodded thoughtfully. "Well, just to be safe, get back down to Coahuila and talk to our guy. He needs to understand that the killing has got to stop. I know he isn't going to admit to it, and for our purposes, it's best if he denies it anyway. But I don't want any half-assed, politically correct task force fucking up our mission. Get this under control. Tell our guy to find another way into the states if that's what it takes. But get this buttoned down and find out a way to keep track of this Shadow thing. Tell Webb to offer up DEA assistance, maybe some funding."

"It's the Shadow Wolves," Wendt corrected Hickock just to pull his self-righteous chain a bit.

Diaz interjected, "We are also going to need some more money to pay the source."

"How much?"

"I don't know. Two hundred K?" Diaz shrugged sheepishly.

Hickock looked at Diaz in disbelief. "This guy has more money than God. Why the fuck does he want more from us?"

Wilcox came to Diaz's defense. "This is more about appearances. The guy wants to feel he's driving this bus. Let's face it, sir, we are never going to get any higher in the food chain than him. We would be spending ten times that just to hear a rumor about the Pakistanis under any other circumstances. We all think this is money well spent." Wendt and Diaz nodded in agreement.

Hickock stood up and moved toward his desk to signal the meeting was over. "Okay, then pay the money. Let's keep our noses out of the drug stuff. We know he's a bad guy. That's a given. But we don't need to get too deep into his shit. We are only interested in him as it applies to our mandate. Let's keep that foremost in our minds."

The DEA agents were already moving through the door, visibly relieved to be out of the politically charged air. Little did anyone in that room know that the shit had already hit the fan in the Arizona desert.

CHAPTER 34

The sky was starting to lighten. Dawn would be upon them in half an hour. Ethan looked up at the sound of a diesel engine and saw two sets of headlights coming toward the encampment. He looked around him, secure in the knowledge that all the wounded were stabilized and ready for transport. The first chopper was already loaded, and the most serious of the wounded were aboard and ready to depart for Tucson. The second chopper was in the process of loading up the remaining women. A third helicopter was due momentarily to transport the remaining cartel prisoners. An FBI crime scene team was on the way to process the scene and oversee the removal of the bodies to the medical examiner in Tucson. He looked through the dim light to see who was in the second truck but couldn't make out the occupants.

As the vehicles drew near, Crowe could see that the first was a black Ram diesel pickup towing a stock trailer. It was driven by Tyrel Cepeda. The passenger was Maggie Sees Far. It seemed that Maggie felt she was needed out here with the rest of the team. He shouldn't have been surprised. As Ty slowly brought the truck to a stop to protect the horses, the second truck turned out to be a Chevy Suburban, government issue. Ethan let out a long sigh as he saw the front passenger jump from the vehicle before it came to a complete stop. *Just what I fucking need now, that dumb-ass Radcliff.*

Crowe's first inclination was to go directly to Ty and get him started unloading the horses, but he knew that Radcliff could not be avoided. He stopped mid-stride and turned to face the approaching Homeland supervisor. "Agent Radcliff."

"Enough!" declared Radcliff, holding up his hand in the universal gesture for *stop.* "I can't believe the shit storm you have caused. How many dead? How many wounded? What the fuck do you think this is?"

Crowe did his best to remain respectful. "Tom, it's a bad one. It was one hell of a firefight. I lost two of mine, and we have some others seriously wounded."

"I know. I have been getting continuous updates. This is why I should have been included in this op in the first place!" Radcliff was looking sideways at Dan Hooper, who was, as always, nodding in agreement with his boss. "We are going to sit down for a detailed debriefing now!"

Crowe looked quietly at the ground. He was sorry his people had to hear all this. "I really don't have time right now. We have three bad guys on the run, one of them the boss. We think they are trying to make their way back to the border. At first light we should be able to pick up their trail. Two of my people are already trying to find sign, which is taking extra time in the low light.

Radcliff looked over at the stock trailer, noting the young Indian in the process of unloading a group of horses, all saddled and ready to go. "Look, track or no track, this is enough. We have dead officers on the ground and wounded on the way to the hospital, not to mention a chopper full of rape victims. You are going to stand down until I am up to date on this whole operation."

Crowe continued to speak in polite tones, "I have assigned my people to handle everything. The FBI is already on the way to handle the crime scene and the officer involved shootings. I will not be needed right away. We need to track these guys. I believe one is the boss and another is the sniper that killed Officer Price."

Radcliff spit back, "Who is Officer Price?"

Crowe shook his head in disbelief. "The tribal cop who was assassinated by this group about six months ago."

Radcliff digested that for a second. "Well, be that as it may, this is over. I have the Department to consider, along with the media and their questions. All that could be done out here has been done. It's time to cut our losses. I am telling you to stand down."

Crowe moved closer to Radcliff, now only inches separating the two. "Let's get this straight, you fucking dumb-ass. One cop has been killed by a sniper sent across the border specifically to assassinate an American police officer. The same group came back across the border with over fifteen women and children to be sold as sex slaves, raping the women all along the way. When we tried to rescue those women, these assholes killed two of my people in cold blood and wounded three others. This might be our only chance to catch these guys and, more importantly, find out who really ordered these killings. And yet you want me to stand down." Crowe moved even closer to the SAC. "Not going to happen."

Radcliff took Ethan's tirade surprisingly well. He looked to his assistant for a thoughtful moment and then turned back to Crowe. "Well, then you leave me no choice but to relieve you of your command."

Crowe just looked at him, a cold anger spreading through his body as though a dam had broken. He remained motionless for what seemed an eternity. He began to shake his head slowly, visibly seething. He was about to say something when Maggie Sees Far interrupted.

"Ethan." She was walking toward him, holding her cell phone in the air.

Crowe looked over at her, just about to tell her "Later" when she looked directly at Radcliff.

"Mr. Radcliff, there is a call for you." Maggie handed the phone to the Homeland Security boss, who continued his stare down with Crowe while taking the phone from the Comanche.

"This is Radcliff." Hearing the identity of the caller, Radcliff turned to the side and could be heard saying, "Yes, sir, I am on the scene right now. I—" He had obviously been interrupted by the person on the other end of the line. "Yes, but—" He was cut off once again. "Well, if you want my—" He was cut off again, this time for an extended period of time. Finally, "Yes, sir. I understand. I will make that happen and advise."

The call then suddenly ended before Radcliff could say his goodbyes. He stood frozen for a moment before turning back to Crowe and his people.

Crowe was staring in puzzlement. He wondered who the call had been from and looked over at Maggie to get some nonverbal clue. All he received back was a stony expression as she continued to stare at Radcliff and her phone in his hand.

Radcliff stood perfectly still. His face was a mixture of disbelief and resignation. He finally spoke, addressing Crowe, "Well, it seems that you have your reprieve. I have been told to assist you and provide you anything you need to catch these suspects." He then looked over to his deputy and shook his head in disgust. "I can't fucking believe this shit."

Crowe, for his part, acted like nothing had happened. During the time it had taken for the call, he had regained his composure and was ready to get back to the task at hand. He called over to Elias Blue Eagle. "Elias, make sure that Agent Radcliff has everything he needs. I assume he will want to keep in touch with his office." He looked back to the man from Tucson, who was not nearly as pompous as before the call. "I am taking two of my people on horseback at first light, which is in about twenty minutes. I will report back in to HQ by sat phone or radio when I can. They will keep you informed." Crowe then turned and started for the horse trailer, where Ty was tending to the horses and equipment.

Halfway to the trailer, he stopped and called back to Maggie, "Mags, do you have a minute?"

Maggie walked up to where Crowe was standing, wedging her phone into the back pocket of her jeans. She looked at Ethan expectantly.

"Maggie, I'm almost afraid to ask, but who the hell was on that call?"

The Comanche didn't miss a beat. "General Evans."

Crowe looked into her eyes, a slight smile now on his face. "That's quite a coincidence, him calling at just the right time."

The woman looked back stolidly. "Yes, I guess it was."

Crowe looked over at Radcliff, who was deep into a heated conversation with Hooper, no doubt bemoaning the interference from Washington.

Crowe turned back to Maggie, but she had already moved on to help Ty with the horses. He chuckled to himself as he, too, moved toward the horse trailer. *She sure wasn't lying when she told me she was a warrior.*

Before Crowe could get to the trailer, another voice stopped him. "Agent Crowe, is there anything that my folks can do to help?" Crowe turned to see Jake Webb replacing his cell phone on his belt and walking toward him from the back door of the Suburban. Crowe had overlooked the DEA agent in his effort to minimize Radcliff.

Crowe paused and waited for Webb to get close. "What have you got?"

"Well, I can check on our sources down south, particularly in Nogales. Our people could be very helpful if these guys manage to get back across the border. Maybe we can ID them at the very least. I can also reach out to see if there is any chatter on the phones about this."

Crowe chuckled quietly. "I forgot, you guys are listening to everything."

"Not quite everything," replied Webb, winking conspiratorially. "But maybe we'll get lucky on this."

Crowe thought for a minute. "One thing that would be helpful. Can your people detect sat phone activity out there in the desert?"

Webb considered the question. "I don't really know, but I'll check. If they can, there can't be more than one sat phone within a hundred miles of that desert."

Crowe smiled wryly. "Agent Webb, anything, and I mean anything, you can do to help would be greatly appreciated. I take it you have my number." Crowe nodding and turning back to the horse trailer.

Webb called out to Crowe as he moved away, "Good hunting."

The noise of the third chopper drowned out Crowe's reply.

CHAPTER 35

The coyote dropped down into the narrow ravine and moved quickly to his right, his two companions falling into the depression closely at his heels. The sun had been up for three hours now, and the temperatures had already risen to one hundred degrees. He pressed himself into the sandstone wall on the east side of the ravine, feeling the cool of the rocks not yet touched by the sun. Lobo and Romero followed his example and fell to the ground, Lobo loudly gasping for breath.

Lobo's lips were already so dry that there were traces of blood at the corners of his mouth where his cracked skin was most affected. He licked at the fluid absentmindedly as he pulled out the wood stopper from his water skin. Romero, much thinner and in better shape, remained still and just watched the movements of his fellow fugitives. He had come to respect the coyote as their flight had continued westward over the desert toward the Ajo Mountains. The man knew his job. He had guided them through treacherous terrain, always taking care to travel over ground that would leave little or no traces of their passing. Never did he show any signs of panic in spite of constant complaints and threats from Lobo.

Romero glanced to his left and saw Lobo guzzling from the water skin. He couldn't have much left. The sweaty Zeta boss had been drinking freely from the bag throughout their trek even before the sun had risen high enough to become a factor. As he continued to stare at Lobo, the man returned his gaze with the bag still in his mouth, excess water dribbling down from the corners of his mouth.

"What?" said Lobo, spitting water as he challenged Romero.

Romero ignored the question and pulled out a bandana from his front pocket. He then took out his own water skin and wet it, careful not to spill any of its precious contents. Taking the moist cloth, the sniper gently dabbed at his lips. Once his lips and eyes had been carefully restored with the cloth, he put it into his mouth and slowly sucked out the last traces of the remaining moisture.

The coyote was also quietly assessing his two companions. Romero was different than Lobo. The sniper had kept calm and been smart enough to gather two water skins from the camp before fleeing. Romero was a soldier, and it showed. He was a survivor. The man realized that bullets would not save him from the sun.

Lobo, on the other hand, had only taken one skin, preferring to carry more ammunition and a second weapon, both of which he had taken off one of his own men lying dead on the ground. There was no doubt that the man was a powerful brute. He was clearly a deadly force, and in his own world, he was a man to be feared. But out here in this harsh land, Lobo's enemy was his own pride—and the sun. If there was no water up ahead, surely the Zeta boss would die soon afterward. The coyote did not relish that possibility. Lobo would not go quietly. He would do his best to kill his two companions before he succumbed to the desert himself. *I will have to think about this. Perhaps find a way to talk to the one called Romero without Lobo seeing it.* He reached into his boot and pulled out a small piece of folded paper—a map, worn and frayed along the edges. He smoothed it out in front of him and studied it carefully.

Lobo, seeing the map, barked a command, "Come over here and let me see that!"

The coyote looked up from the paper and considered his answer. "I'm just trying to make some calculations and some judgments," he said, hoping this would pacify the burly Zeta.

"I said bring it here!" Lobo capped his water skin and placed it on the ground to the left of his position.

Romero watched the exchange, thinking to himself that Lobo questioning the coyote's actions was stupid. The man had just as much to lose as the rest of them. He had no stake in leading them to their deaths, for surely his own death would also be a part of that equation.

The coyote shrugged and capitulated, picking up the wrinkled paper and moving to Lobo's side. He placed the map on the ground again, this time so that the boss man could see it as well.

Lobo grunted, "Where are we?"

"As far as I can tell, we are somewhere close to here." The coyote pointed at the map with his right index finger. "We started out here," moving his finger to the right on the map. "The tunnel we came through on the way north is here," once again moving his finger to make his point. He glanced sideways at Lobo, wondering what he was thinking.

Lobo took in everything the coyote had told him. He thought to himself while continuing to study the map, *This coyote is starting to think he is more than he is. He thinks there will be a great reward for what he is doing and that I am a fool. I will let him believe it—at least until he gets us across the border. But he will not live any longer than that. Men have underestimated me before.*

Lobo's thoughts were interrupted by the coyote talking again. "If we continue west, our chances get better. There should be some water directly west. The Sonoyta River runs through here, and it has pools of water that should allow us to top off our skins. It is one of the few spots where we can find water that isn't alkaline."

He saw Lobo's puzzled look. "Salt. It leaches from the ground into the water."

"Can't we just follow that river south to Mexico?" Romero questioned the coyote quietly.

"We could, but there is no telling what the river is like right now. If it's high, then we would have to fight the ground on the banks of the river, and that is dangerous."

Lobo posed the question, "What do you mean, dangerous? I think we can handle anyone that comes against us."

The coyote hid a slight grin. "I'm not talking about enemies. I'm talking about rattlers. Plus, it's where these *indios* will look first. They wouldn't have to follow our tracks. They could just leapfrog ahead of us and wait for us to walk straight into their arms. They know exactly where the river leads."

Lobo grunted menacingly. "I still think I would prefer to follow the river and take my chances against these *indios*."

Romero spoke up against Lobo, staring him directly in the eyes, "It seems to me that you haven't done so well with these *indio*s so far." He took another shallow sip from his skin. "But hell, I agree with our guide. I'll travel with him. You should go any way that you choose." Romero, for the first time, was challenging Lobo openly.

Lobo said nothing for a moment, then, "You will have your time, Romero. We will be out of this desert or we won't, but your day will come and I will be there to see it."

Romero continued to stare at the crew boss, who continued to sweat profusely. It was clear to all that Romero felt nothing but contempt for the man. Romero just sat and shook his head in disgust. *You are a long way from your crew of thugs in Nogales. Here you are nothing but a waste of precious water.* The only thing keeping this scum alive was Yaotl. He had not given Romero permission to kill him.

The coyote spoke up, partly to ease the tension. He didn't need these two killing each other. Gunshots would bring the trackers down on them. That was certain. "We will need to rest here in the shade until the sun passes overhead. We will have about two hours of direct sun in this ravine. I think we can carve out narrow depressions in the opposite wall and then remain there until late afternoon."

Lobo looked right and left in the ravine, as if he was assessing the situation himself. He was doing his best to seem like he was still in charge. "If we stay here, they will catch us."

The coyote disagreed. "No, they will have to stop as well. It will be just as hot for them. They will find a place to escape the worst of the heat. Plus, there is a chance that it took them some time to pick up our trail. We should be a good four to five hours ahead of them." The coyote tried his best to believe his own words. He was certain of one thing: *Lobo would not last two more hours in the desert sun without him.*

Lobo grudgingly agreed to the coyote's logic and started to settle back against the ravine wall. The coyote sighed to himself in exasperation. Both of these men were like vipers thrown together in a pit. He had no intention of dying for either of these gangsters. *However, if I have to take a side, it will be with the sniper. This Lobo is like a rabid dog and not to be trusted.*

A sudden gust of hot wind blew over the top of the ravine, blowing dust and dead scrub bushes into their hiding place. Romero took his still-damp bandanna and laid it across his face. Like all soldiers, he was asleep in minutes.

CHAPTER 36

Crowe walked up to Ty, who was adjusting the cinch on the saddle of one of the horses. Maggie had already gone to the trailer and was carrying out water cans to pour into a portable trough for the horses. She wanted to make sure they were fully prepared for what was ahead.

Crowe stepped over to his horse. The horse, catching the scent of Ethan as he approached, nickered a greeting. "Wanagi, hello to you too." The horse turned its head to see his master as he approached. Ethan reached up to run his palm reassuringly down the smooth side of the horse's neck, causing the Spanish mustang to shake its head with pleasure. The horse was a four-year-old mare, light brown, with a large splash of white across her entire hindquarters. Her eyes were soft and keen. Unlike a domestic horse, she could spot a prairie dog hole at a full gallop and avoid it. *Wanagi* was the Lakota word for "spirit," and she could sense danger on the wind. Ethan counted on her almost supernatural senses, knowing that she could detect any furtive approach by mountain lion or man. Sometimes he felt she was more guardian angel than horse. *Mina had known this from the start.*

Ethan's brother and his daughter, Mina, had trailered the horse to Arizona a week after Ethan had arrived. His niece had told her father that she did not want her uncle riding some government horse that didn't know how to run. Her father had made sure that she wasn't just doing this because she missed her uncle. He worried that her attachment for the horse would be too strong to let it go. She had returned her father's concerns with a flash of her dark eyes. "Wanagi is already Ethan's. She was just waiting to meet him. I know this more than anything I have ever known in my life."

Frank had not said another word, proud and moved at the same time. When they arrived at the Tohono O'odham Reservation, Ethan had been coming out the front door of his office. He had taken one look at the truck and then at the trailer. He knew immediately what his niece had intended that evening at the corral. While she and Ty unloaded the mustang, Frank filled in the gaps about the mare. He told Ethan that Mina had spent months nurturing the young horse and had gentled it to the saddle rather than breaking it by riding it into submission. Now, however, technically broken to the saddle, it only allowed Mina to ride her.

Frank sighed. "She says that horse will let you ride her too," he said, shaking his head in wonder. "And I believe her. You two are one in the same." Pride and affection was evident in his voice.

There had never been any doubt in Mina that Wanagi would take to Ethan. They both knew and understood horses, sensing an intelligence and devotion in them that others didn't. Ethan had accepted the horse gladly, knowing that this was very important to Mina and to him, if the truth were told. Besides, it would be comforting to know that he had a reliable mount when in the field. These mustangs could go places that other horses could not or would not go.

Before taking the reins from his niece, however, Ethan pulled her aside and spoke seriously with her, "Mina, you're not a girl anymore. I know that and I have to speak to you as a grown woman now. My job is not like others. I have to follow and arrest very bad people. If I ride a horse, it goes into that danger as well. It is probably not a choice Wanagi would make on her own. I know that she is special to you. Are you sure that you want this for her?"

Mina, now almost eighteen years old, looked calmly back at Ethan. "Yes, Uncle, I am not a child anymore. I know that your job is dangerous. I know much more than you think I do about you and your life." She smiled slyly. "You would be surprised what can be heard through vents and keyholes."

Ethan sat back, crossed his arms in front of his chest, and just shook his head in wonder. "Mina."

Suddenly becoming deadly serious, she said, "Uncle Ethan, I know about Lawan and Michel. I have wanted to tell you that I know. I'm old enough to know what you lost, and I am sorry." Tears ran silently down her face, her long eyelashes sticking to her skin.

Ethan was shocked. This was the first time that anyone in his family had mentioned their names out loud. Their Lakota traditions did not make that easy. But now, from this girl, it sounded right. "Mina, I'm not sure what to say." He was working hard not to let his emotions show.

Mina now firmly said, "Uncle, you will take this horse. She will protect you. I know it sounds like I am a little girl again, but I am not. This horse has magic. She senses things others do not. And she knows things...about us." The girl teared up once again with emotion.

Ethan reached out and put his arms around her, gently stroking her hair. "Thank you, Mina. This is a gift I will never forget. Wanagi and I will protect each other." Ethan held on to the girl and wished the moment would never end.

Nalin broke into Ethan's thoughts as she approached. Her combat pack was slung over her shoulder. As she greeted Ethan and the others, she could sense that the boss had been deep in thought. "Everything okay, boss?"

Ethan looked over from where he was adjusting the bridle on Wanagi. "All good. You ready to head out?" Ethan was now totally back in the present.

"Yeah. I just have to transfer some of this stuff to the saddlebags and I'll be good to go. How long do you think before we pick up their sign?"

"Don't know yet. Blue Eagle has two of his people out now. Even in this low light, they should come up with something soon. This coyote is no fool. He will pick his path carefully, at least as carefully as possible considering their hurry to get out of here. The three of us should be saddled up shortly, and then we just need the trail. Sunup is almost here now."

Nalin looked around at the horses and then back at Ethan with raised eyebrows. "Three of us?"

Crowe looked puzzled. "Yeah." He followed her line of sight and suddenly realized for the first time that there were four horses saddled and ready to go, with the fifth mount outfitted as a pack horse. He looked around at his people. Isaac had stopped adjusting the gear on his horse and met his stare. Ty Cepeda stood next to his paint, with Maggie Sees Far at his side, arms crossed and a defiant look etched on her face. It only took a few seconds to see what was afoot. "Okay, what is it I don't know? Why the extra horse?" he asked, already knowing the answer.

Ty stepped forward, obviously ready with a prepared speech.

Crowe stopped him with his palm raised. "Whoa, young man. I know what you're doing, but I have already given my assignments." He already sensed opposition from all of them.

"Sir, I need to go. I know this land better than you, if you don't mind me saying so. I can't track, but I know everything else—where the water is and where there is shade." The boy was not pleading but standing in front of Crowe like Crowe himself would have done at the same age. The young man hesitated, deciding what to say. "And this shooter, it's him. I know it." Ty twisted his reins in his fingers absently.

Crowe had started to say something. To take a hard line. But he couldn't. This was a debt of honor for Ty as well as for Crowe. Maybe more so. He was younger than Ty when he had joined the Delta Force. Tyrell was a man full grown with his own decisions to make. So when the young man finished speaking, Crowe merely nodded his approval. "Best make sure you're properly outfitted. We'll be out there for a time. No pack horses this trip either. We'll have to travel light and take what we need with us. Mags can trailer the other horse back with her."

Ty looked at Crowe, not actually believing he had relented so quickly. He looked over at Maggie who was there for moral support whether he needed or not. She just nodded. She always made it seem that everything had turned out as she had willed it. Like she had some unseen power to bend the will of others. *Maybe it was a Comanche thing.*

Factor merely turned back to his horse as if he had known the outcome long ago. Nalin Chee just stared at Crowe. Once again, he had altered her perception of him. *There are a lot of layers to peel on this man. Where does it end, and what is left at the core?* She might never find out and decided it was more than she needed to think about now. Bending to her pack on the ground, she removed the Marlin and dropped it into the sheath on her saddle. She then took two bandoliers and draped them over her shoulders, forming a perfect X across her chest. Methodically, she then packed her saddlebags with hardtack and other supplies, doing her best to keep the loss of Hannah from overwhelming her.

CHAPTER 37

Office of the US attorney, Miami,
Southern District of Florida

Robert "Wild Bill" Hickock stared at his computer screen, tapping his pen nervously on the desk in front of him. Classified emails had been coming across his desk for the past few hours. Agent Webb had been feeding intel updates throughout the morning, none of it good news. He wondered at the bad timing of this, pissed off that he had to spend his time worrying about simple trafficking cases out in the middle of fucking nowhere. He had sent for Wendt and Diaz as soon as the news started to dribble in, demanding they come to his office *forthwith* (cop talk for "with absolutely no delay").

His intercom buzzed. The agents were in the reception area. "Send them in now!" His receptionist pressed her lips together tightly, accustomed to his fits of temper, but not liking it a bit. She often wondered what the public would think of this side of God's crusader. *Probably wouldn't bother them a bit The man could roll anything into a biblical analogy.* She nodded to the agents, and they went straight for his office, both seeming as pissed off as her boss.

The door no sooner closed behind them and Hickock launched into a tirade. "What the fuck is going on out there?"

Wendt prepared to respond but was cut off instantly. "What did we send Webb out there to do? Jesus Christ! We have federal agents killed *and* a busload of women who have been raped senseless. I told you guys to put a lid on this asshole. Hell, we just had this conversation yesterday!"

Hickock stopped talking. The whole room was silent. The agents sat there wondering if the temper tantrum was over or if there was a second act. Two or three minutes passed in total quiet. Then Hickock, his composure regained, said, "Well?" now speaking in normal tones.

Wendt was the first to speak. "Just to be clear, I believe all this shit kicked off before our meeting yesterday. But secondly, we still can't confirm that this was our guy's people. Hell, the Sinaloa is still a major player along the Arizona border." He looked over at Diaz for confirmation, seeing his partner nodding in agreement.

Diaz then spoke up, "I called my CIs on both sides of the border, and nobody knows exactly who was involved in this thing on the reservation. I haven't tried to reach our guy yet. I think we need to be careful on that. Reaching out to him now might tip our hand to the embassy folks down there. I assumed you wouldn't want that." Diaz looked at Hickock with his eyebrows arched.

They were all still standing in the middle of the office. Hickock took a long, calming breath and gestured for the agents to take a seat. He followed suit by easing into his overstuffed leather wingback.

Hickock reached to his left, where he pushed the button on an extension of his intercom. "Katherine, please have some coffee sent in here." He paused a second, his finger off the button. "She's gonna run downstairs to Starbucks, so anything special?" Both indicated that anything would do, and he pushed the button once again. "Make that three regular coffees, Katherine," he said, disconnecting without waiting for a reply.

Five minutes later, Katherine was coming through the door with a metal tray, a glass pot of coffee, and a stack of paper cups. She set them down on the table in front of Wild Bill and backed away toward the door. "Anything else, Mr. Hickock?"

"No, that will be all. I'll be tied up the rest of the day, so clear my calendar. No calls please. I will let you know about tomorrow's schedule in the morning."

Once the room was clear, Hickock returned to the business at hand. "Look, I have brought the Pakistani intel all the way to the Director of National Intelligence. We have a green light on this. We can't have something like this bungled drug bust, or whatever it was, interfere with our case. We are talking about preventing mass casualties in a terrorist attack on our soil. Nothing has a higher priority."

The agents sat quietly, waiting for their next orders. This was not open for debate. They both knew that they had tied their fate to Hickock when they signed on for this assignment.

Hickock looked at Diaz. "Bobby, I need you down there now. Get Katherine to book you on a flight to Mexico City this afternoon. She will call the embassy and get you country clearance. The story will be that we are thinking of expanding the DEA footprint in Mexico and you are there to put together an assessment. You will probably have to stay there for a few weeks to go through the motions. Just make sure that you get our business finished as soon as you can without raising any questions. Can you get transport and arrange a meeting with the CI on your own?"

Diaz just nodded silently, his mind already working out the logistics.

"When you meet your man, don't let on that we suspect his people are behind this Arizona disaster. I hope he didn't order it, but I also don't really want to know. We have to keep our eyes on the prize here." Hickock took a long sip of his Starbucks brew. He continued, "I want you to pin him down on setting up a meet with the Pakis. He needs to show us that he is serious. Give him the iPhone from the tech unit. Bullshit him and tell him it's secure. It will allow us to monitor his conversation."

Wendt leaned forward from his place on the sofa. "I just wonder if we aren't pushing our guy to move too fast. He might balk if we push too hard."

Hickock fired back, "You tell this son of a bitch that we can snatch his ass right back up again if we choose. Tell him that it was only by my order that he was released and that the record of his capture was permanently erased from this Earth. If I have to, I will send in a rendition team and plunk his ass in Guantanamo."

"Well, that's certainly one approach." Wendt chuckled, thinking Hickock was just spouting so much hyperbole.

"You think I'm kidding! I'm dead serious. You take that message to him. And you tell him that if he gets involved in any of this bloodshed, our deal is off. And if you really have to sweeten the pot and kiss this guy's ass a bit, tell him that I am authorized to shell out two million dollars for his assistance."

Wendt and Diaz glanced at each other and then nodded to the prosecutor. Wendt then put his hands on his knees and pushed up from his seat. "Sounds good. I will remain in Miami to keep a line of communication with Bobby and with Webb out there in Arizona. We will keep you posted daily or more often if needed."

Hickock was now standing and stepped between the agents as they started for the door, putting his hands on the shoulders of both men. "Gentlemen, this is complicated, scary stuff, but I know that you are up to it. Remember, this is a war. A war just as deadly as any war fought by our fathers before us. Let's take this fight to the enemy."

The men said their goodbyes, and Hickock closed the door behind them. He turned back to his desk. *He would need to spend some time in prayer before he left for home. This op was going to go well. It had to.*

Chapter 38

Elias Blue Eagle was crouched west of the camp, studying the ground, when he heard the approach of horses. He had been scouring the area around the battleground in search of sign. He had tried to work through all the possibilities and was trying to put himself in the head of the three Zetas as they fled into the night. He had been forced to expand his circle because many of the tracks had been crossed and overlaid with sets of footprints caused by the firefight. He had stumbled onto this trail by chance while moving to a more likely escape route. Elias was grudgingly impressed. This coyote was very good at doing the unexpected. *This would not be an easy trail to follow.*

Elias stood as the Shadow Wolves brought their horses to a stop, Ethan sliding from his horse effortlessly by bringing his right leg over the saddle horn and dropping to the ground. The remaining three Wolves stayed in their saddles, Nalin's eyes continuously scanning the newly lit horizon.

"What have you got?" Crowe crouching to look at the sign for himself.

Elias looked over his boss's shoulder. "I think this is where they headed out. The sign is brushed over pretty good. But if you look out to the left, there are parts of a footprint. Then if you look about ten yards ahead, you can spot another print on the right perimeter." He watched as Ethan stood up and looked over the ground that Elias had pointed out. He then added, "Looks to me like he was using sagebrush to sweep their tracks. I haven't had a chance to move out farther along the track, but I can't imagine he kept it up for too long. He would have been losing precious lead time if he did."

Crowe looked up at Nalin, who, without a word, nodded and nudged her horse forward along the possible trajectory of the trail. Ethan continued to study the ground for another fifteen minutes, walking slowly forward for about twenty yards. He knew that this was the most critical point in any track. If they started out on a false trail, it would rob them of critical time, time needed to close the gap before these killers could make their way back to Mexico. He then turned back to Elias. "Good work. I think this is it."

To confirm Crowe's thoughts, Nalin came galloping back to their position. "Elias is right. About a quarter mile out, the tracks are clear. There's been no wind and the brush that he used is still there where he left it." While talking, she pulled up on the reins a bit as her horse crow-hopped to the right, eager to continue its run in the cool morning air.

"Sounds good," Ethan spoke as he threw his right leg over the saddle. "Ty, if they continue in that direction, what kind of terrain is out there?"

Ty thought for a minute. "Straight west is the Sonoyta River. They could get water there. There are pools in the river. They call them the sweet pools, and they are good drinking water. If they know what they are doing, they will find them. Beyond the river are the Agua Dulce Mountains and the Baboquivari Mountains. They are all part of the Ajo range, mostly dry and dusty. Lots of wind caves out there though. If they can make it that far and find the caves, it might be tough to find them." The young officer looked nervously at Ethan, not wanting to say the wrong thing or overreach his part in this.

"Okay." Ethan laid his reins over to the right, edging *Wanagi* around where Elias was standing. "Sounds like we have our work cut out for us. Nalin, what do you think about the desert?"

She looked back at Crowe, patting her horse's neck to calm him. "Well, I think we have about four hours of good riding before we rest the horses in some shade. Our two horses could go a lot farther, but the others will need to rest." Nalin referred to the mustangs that Ethan and she rode, knowing that the government mounts used by

Isaac and Ty would not fare as well as the wild horses in the desert heat.

Crowe, reaching with his left hand to rest on his horse's rump, spoke to Elias, "I will have the sat phone and a radio. I'm not sure if either of them will work out there, but I will try to call in periodically. I will try to relay my GPS positions when I call. I want you to be there to handle the communications. If we think we have them on open ground, I will ask for a chopper. But I'm afraid this is going to turn into a real cat and mouse thing out in those mountains and canyons." Crowe, suddenly remembering, turned around in the saddle and started feeling in his right saddlebag for the sat phone. "I won't have this on, but it'll be in my pocket. I can't risk you calling and someone hearing it at the wrong time." He paused a minute longer. "Well, I guess that's about it. Sorry to stick you with Radcliff."

Blue Eagle just smiled. "No problem, boss."

Without another word, Ethan pressed his heels into Wanagi's flanks, setting the horse into a steady ambling gait. The others followed suit, and soon the team was moving across the desert. At this speed, the mounts would be able to keep a steady pace without tiring. They would continue this throughout the morning, dropping down to a slow walk from time to time to rest the horses.

Nalin settled into the smooth motion of her horse, riding next to Crowe as they both watched the ground ahead. They kept their eyes focused on the ground four to five feet ahead of them, not concentrating on individual footprints but the overall track. If they detected any sudden change, they reined in the horses to study the terrain. At times they dismounted to inspect the trail more closely. Progress was slow, but steady. Nalin fought the urge to race forward, her heart set on finding these men and killing them. She knew the idea was foolhardy, but her hands tightened on the reins each time she thought of Hannah lying dead on the rocks.

CHAPTER 39

The coyote stuck his head out from the rocky overhang on the west side of the ravine. The three of them had been sheltering in the shade of the outcropping for the past four hours. The sun was now low on the western skyline, and the heat of the day would soon be dissipating. They had been lucky to find this spot. The coyote had scouted north and south in the ravine for an hour before discovering the natural indentation in the opposite wall of the ravine. When the sun had moved overhead, they had crossed the dry riverbed and crawled into the sheltering sandstone rocks. He looked back into the recess and saw that Romero sat propped against the back wall, resting, eyes half closed. A true soldier, he knew when to rest, careful to keep his pulse low and his body as cool as possible. Lobo, on the other hand, looked up angrily from his seat on the ground, challenging the coyote's very presence with a look of barely disguised contempt.

Cautiously, the coyote stepped across the floor of the ravine and crept up to the eastern wall, quickly plastering his back against the embankment. He then looked up, scanning the sky for telltale flashes of light. He was careful to systematically canvas the entire sky, dividing it into quadrants. All that he saw was a cloudless sea of blue. No drones or helicopters to mar the empty sky. He then turned back to face the wall behind him. Inch by inch, he slowly edged his head over the lip of the rim to check their back trail and the ground that they had already covered. Nothing. Nothing but scrub grass and solitary rock formations. The wind-carved rock chimneys stood out like ancient beings frozen in time across some mythical battleground.

The coyote was no stranger to his desolate surroundings. He had spent most of his life in the desert smuggling people to the north. As a young man, he had started out in the business by guiding migrants over the border as a way to scratch out a living. The job was relatively easy as the Norteamericanos took a very lax view of illegal migration. They used many of the illegals to pick their crops and perform domestic chores. The unofficial system seemed to work for everyone. In recent years, he had seen a change. Politicians in the north had started to base their platforms on demonizing the migrants, painting them all as drug dealers and rapists.

Razor wire and fences stood in many places that were once wide-open spaces. Drones now dotted the sky, and electronic sensors were spread along large portions of border. Border agents patrolled more vigorously, and local law enforcement had also gotten into the act, providing political capital for their elected sheriffs who preyed on the fears, real or imagined, of their constituents. Perhaps worse than the official response had been the American vigilantes, who had the tacit approval of the authorities and the protection of the Second Amendment, billing themselves as patriots protecting the homeland. In truth, they were bullies with guns, playing at being heroes.

In many ways, the drug cartels and the Latino gangs had contributed to this new environment. Over a decade ago, the Colombians had made a business decision to subcontract the transportation of drugs into America to the Mexican cartels. The Colombians were tired of dealing with forced extraditions and the intense electronic surveillance mounted against them by the Americans. Now they took a smaller cut but had no problems. Not wanting to look a gift horse in the mouth, the Mexican drug lords were more than willing to assume the business, proving to be far more ruthless and cruel than their predecessors. The increased trafficking across the border and the growing opioid epidemic and gang violence in the cities had provided the perfect excuse for American politicians to tighten up the border. *Hell, the Americans had even elected a president who promised to build a wall!*

He let out a long breath through his nose. The world was always changing. Nothing he could do about it. *The Norteamericanos would do what they would do. They always did. He would just have to dig more tunnels.*

Looking out over the desolate terrain, he did his best to compute their pursuers' progress. He tried to figure out how long it would have taken to find their trail and how long they could have traveled in the intense heat. He shook his head. *They will be showing on the distant horizon before too long unless he got lucky and the indios hadn't picked up the trail. That was always a possibility.* He made a sour face and snorted, knowing that was wishful thinking.

Lobo was standing at the edge of the overhang, watching him as he returned from the opposite wall. "Well?" the Zeta boss demanded.

"No sign of them." The coyote moved past Lobo to pick up his rifle. He looked over to Romero and nodded. "It's time to go. There's nobody on our tail that I can tell."

Lobo had returned to his spot to pick up his weapons as well. "Let's head south. Now."

Both Romero and the coyote stood silent. Finally, Romero said quietly, "Not yet. They could have already headed south to cut us off. I don't think we should be in any hurry to get to the border. I think we would be smarter to find a place to hold up for several days."

The coyote nodded his head in agreement. "He makes a good point. We only have an hour or so to the Sonoyta River. We should find good drinking water to fill the skins. We can decide then. We need to get our hands on some more water or we will all end our days as bones in the sand."

Lobo said nothing in return but picked up his rifle and pistol and stepped back out into the open ravine, heading to the pile of rocks that would get him back onto the flat ground again. Romero raised his eyebrows at the coyote and made to follow Lobo, pausing for second. "By the way, what the fuck is your name anyway?"

The coyote looked puzzled, like he had never thought about it. He hesitated, then said, "Bernardo. Nardo to my friends."

Romero just nodded in confirmation. "Nardo it is then." The sniper already taking steps to cement their alliance.

All three of the men started their westward journey again, Nardo dragging a tumbleweed on a rope behind them. He had now enlisted Romero to do the same, thus doubling their ability to erase their passing. Romero was starting to believe that they had a chance after all.

Chapter 40

The Shadow Wolves sat in the shade of the two lean-tos that they had placed against a lone rock chimney. The makeshift structure managed to make adequate shade for the trackers and their mounts. When they were first settled in and the horses had been watered, Crowe had checked in by sat phone, advising their position to Blue Eagle. After that, it had just been a matter of waiting, enduring the suffocating heat, and sleeping when it was possible.

Under one of the canopies, Isaac was sitting with his back to the stone, questioning Ty about the distance to the next water and the type of ground that they would be covering. The young Tohono was eagerly contributing to the Seminole's knowledge of the area. It was clear he was glad to be in the field again, finally doing something to avenge the massacre so many months ago.

Crowe sat under the second shelter. He and Nalin had shared duties in caring for the four horses. They had brushed their coats and removed cactus needles when necessary. Ethan had brought a fine-toothed plastic comb and used it to easily pluck out even the most stubborn needles with a quick flick of his wrist. Now they both sat with their backs to the stone chimney. Nalin was sharpening her black obsidian knife, Crowe watching with his arms resting on his knees in front of him, curious, as Nalin worked a stone over the edge of her glass blade.

Crowe broke the silence. "That's quite a blade. I've heard of them but never actually seen one. Where did you ever find it?"

Nalin chuckled quietly and smiled slightly. "Didn't find it. Inherited it. My father passed it to me quite a few years ago. He got it from his dad and so on down the line. Family legend has it that it was taken in a raid down in Mexico before the whites came. Seems the Apache didn't get along with the Aztecs too well and went down there on a reprisal raid. I guess this came home with them, I think I'm the first to actually use it again in a long, long time."

Crowe was intrigued. "Is it true they are sharper than steel?"

"Science says that these knives are sharper than any knife made in modern times. Professors say that an obsidian sword could decapitate a full-grown horse. Not a pleasant thought." Nalin made an unpleasant face. She continued to stroke the blade with the sharpening stone.

Crowe watched her for a long time and then slowly shook his head, maybe in disbelief or maybe in wonder.

Noticing Crowe's gaze, she challenged him, "What?"

"I was just thinking."

"Well? You going to keep me guessing?" Nalin continued to work the blade while talking.

"I was thinking of another time and another place actually," he replied wistfully.

"Nothing you can share?" said Nalin, a bit of humor in her eyes.

Crowe paused a moment, then spoke, "It was a woman. I was thinking of a woman I once knew. She worked with glass."

Nalin raised her eyes. "Obsidian?"

"No, but glass. It was a big part of her family history too." Ethan paused again, for several beats this time. Then he said, "Like I said, it was another time and another world."

She was now intrigued. "Where?"

Crowe looked to the ground and let out a sigh. "Someplace I once thought I could have a life…"

Nalin said nothing. She could see he was done with it. She felt odd. *What were her feelings for this man? Was it respect, sadness, or something else? It was something she had never felt before. It was unsettling.*

Crowe leaned back and closed his eyes, thinking about Teresa. *What would she think of this world that I inhabit? Surely her family would consider his life barbaric: horses, guns, and bandits. Can I go back to her civilized culture and be happy? Maybe not. Maybe I really belong in this place.*

*****

Nalin and Ty were busy breaking down the tarps. It had been a hot five hours, but much less so under the shade of their makeshift lean-tos. Crowe had used his sat phone to call in their position but had passed on the chance to talk to Radcliff. The horses had been watered from the larger skins. They would need to stop for a good watering soon. Ty was sure that they were about a two-hour ride to the Sonoyta and the pools. Nalin looked out to the west. She knew that they would be closing on these men soon, and it would alter their pursuit. They would have to be ever watchful for an ambush.

Nalin finished strapping the remainder of the gear to her horse. The Marlin rifle was last, the tracker sliding it back into its fringed leather scabbard. She swung her leg over the saddle, thinking to herself how she much preferred riding bareback. That was impossible with the provisions that had to be carried. She reined her horse to the right and joined the other three riders.

As the trackers moved westward, Crowe looked across to his long-time friend Isaac. He sat a horse well, but it was not something he was born to; his people were more at home in the wetlands of Florida, where water was king. Ethan knew this job out here in Arizona was not an easy adjustment for the proud Seminole, but nothing would deter him from seeking the killer of Will Price's brother and from watching over Ethan. About one mile into their ride, the trail disappeared. All four riders stopped and studied the ground, spreading out north and south in an attempt to reacquire the traces of the fugitives.

A search of two hundred yards to each side produced nothing of value. Nalin was off her horse and moving across the ground, searching in earnest for signs that the trail had been swept. Crowe told Isaac to stay with her. He took Ty forward to see if they could pick up the trail again farther along their westward trajectory.

Nalin was now on her knees, looking carefully at the sand. "They wiped their trail. That's for certain. I just don't know if they turned south or kept going toward the river."

Factor was standing over Nalin and looking both south and west. "I guess it depends on their water supply. If they took enough canteens or skins, they could have decided to make their break for the border. That is, *if* one of these is the coyote. We're still not sure on that. If he is leading them, they will make the right decision. If it is one of those Zeta thugs, anything is possible. Either way, I get the feeling that we're involved in a no-win chess match."

"What do you mean?" Nalin stood up again and brushed the dust from her legs.

"Well, we're trying to think several moves ahead of these guys, but they might not be making rational decisions. So we end up playing a chess game with nobody on the other side of the table, basically playing against ourselves and outthinking ourselves in the process."

Nalin walked back over to her horse, getting ready to mount. She turned back to Isaac. "I guess I'm more a traditionalist. I think that we just follow the sign. It's the only thing that is certain."

"I agree. Now we just have to find the tracks again." Factor smiled ruefully.

*****

Ethan and Ty had been riding for fifteen minutes when they came across a field of rocks. It might have been an ancient river but was now just a fifty-foot-wide ribbon of rock stretching north and south in the middle of the sand and dirt. Crowe dismounted and walked carefully to the edge of the rock bed, crouching to examine the rocks. It was there—sign. The rocks had scuffs from the men's boots. He walked slowly out over the smooth, sunbaked stones, bending and examining a rock closely, lifting it to hold it closer.

Ty called out to Crowe, "Find something?"

Crowe didn't answer right away, continuing to study the rock. Finally, he wet his finger and rubbed it on the rock. Taking the finger away, he rubbed the wet tip between the finger and his thumb, smelling the residue. Finally, he spoke, "Yeah, blood. Just a small drop, but blood. Dropped within the past day anyway. Someone in our little group is bleeding."

Ty leaned forward in his saddle. "Think one of them is wounded?"

"Hard to say. Not much blood and no actual blood trail. If they're wounded, they're bandaged up pretty good. But this could be something else. Maybe they scraped themselves up along the way. My guess is it's not a wound but something minor." Crowe was now walking back to his horse and wiping his hand on his pants. "Plus, they're making too good of time to be wounded very seriously. What's important is that we are back on their trail. I don't think they're that far ahead. Let's ride back and tell the others."

CHAPTER 41

The Sonoyta was low. The dry season had turned it into a sluggish, shallow river. This mattered little to the Zetas, who were now standing on the west bank, skins replenished and clothing soaked from the crossing. Lobo was once again haranguing the coyote to plot a course south along the riverbank.

"How far to the border from here?" Lobo challenged.

"Don't know exactly. This isn't the Sonoyta, actually. More of a wash that runs off the Sonoyta. The Americans don't even call it a river. But if I had to guess, it's about thirty miles to the border." The coyote looked south as he spoke.

"Well, I still think it's better to head home than wander around in the desert just waiting for some gringo *policia* to find us."

Romero, listening to the exchange, spoke up, "Bernardo, what are you thinking we should do?"

Lobo looked from one to the other. "What is this Bernardo shit? Now you two are the best of friends?" Lobo hissed threateningly. "You would both be wise to remember who is in charge here. Roberto is the boss, and I am his man. When we return, there could be a reckoning."

Romero looked directly into Lobo's eyes. "*If* we return, *Jefe, if* we return." He then looked back at Nardo like they had never been interrupted.

Bernardo paused a second, then said, "I have been thinking about that. I think if we panic and run to the border, these *indios* will find us. I don't know what they will do if they catch us. They might just kill us. If that's the case, they just have to get close enough to shoot us."

Romero cut in, "But if they want to capture us, they have to face us head-on."

"True. But I think we should assume the worst." He paused for effect, noting that Lobo was listening intently.

Romero interjected quickly, "Okay."

The coyote continued, "I think we should do what they don't expect. Go north."

At this point, both Lobo and Romero looked questioningly at each other and then at the coyote.

The coyote raised his hands defensively. "I know that sounds insane, but hear me out. They are going to expect us to run south to the border or west into the mountains. Either way, I think they can run us to ground before we can get back across the border. I think we should go north along the river. There are some caves about five miles to the north, several of them. If we can reach them without leaving any tracks, I think we might be able to wait them out. I've still got some jerky in my pack, and I think we can last for three or four days."

"What if it doesn't work?" Lobo was now warily interested.

"Well, this whole thing has been a roll of the dice from the start. I don't know much about these *indios*, but they are not gringos. They know the desert, I think, better than me."

All three of the men remained silent while considering their options.

Romero was the first to speak. "I agree with Bernardo," he said, now using the coyote's name just to piss off Lobo. "But I think we should consider one more thing." Now it was Romero's turn to puzzle his companions. He picked up a stick and moved to a place in the dirt where he began to make a crude drawing. Both Lobo and the coyote moved closer to see what Romero had to offer.

The sniper spent some time making his rough sketch in the soil. When he was finished, he began, "This is the river here," pointing to the winding line in the dirt. "This is the ground we have just covered to get here." Romero waved to the empty expanse in the drawing east of the river. "Now we are going to move north along the river. If they are as good as Nardo thinks they are, they will follow our trail right to the river."

Lobo interjected sarcastically, "So what's new? We already know this shit."

Romero replied impatiently, "If you wait, I'll tell you," the sniper now glaring at the Zeta boss.

"I think they will try to kill us. These people are different. Since they are *indios*, we don't know what they are thinking. I do know that we have killed some of their own. I wouldn't expect mercy. Not out here." He waved broadly in a sweeping gesture. He could see he had their attention now. He continued, "I think we should even the odds."

Lobo now posed the question. "We don't even know what the odds are! We haven't seen anyone on our trail ever! Which is why I say—"

The coyote interrupted, "They are following us. I am certain. I can feel it."

Romero was quick to side with his newfound friend. "I agree. What I'm saying is that I can wait on one of the rock formations to the east and kill one or two of them with my rifle." He looked into the faces of his companions and could see that they had nothing to say. "I think that if I can manage to kill or wound even one, it will slow them down long enough for us to make our run south."

Lobo was now stroking his whiskers thoughtfully. "How far out can you reach with that fancy rifle of yours?"

Romero considered the question. He had never pushed himself to the limit. He didn't really know how far he could reach out. Records by American Marines showed confirmed kills from over two miles away. Romero had never tried to reach those distances. In truth, he had never been in actual combat. His shooting scores had all come from the shooting range. His confirmed kills all involved unsuspecting victims who had no idea they were under his scope or even in a battle for that matter. This would be different. This was combat. If he missed, they would do their best to kill him. The thought of it stirred something in him. *Maybe this was finally going to be my war.*

"Well?" Lobo loudly interrupted Romero's thoughts.

"Half a mile." It was more a pronouncement than anything else. "Maybe farther on a good day. If I'm lucky, I could take down two of them." The sniper spoke with growing confidence as he thought to himself, *Why couldn't I do this? I have hit targets at the army range that were close to that distance, maybe even farther than that.*

Lobo sat back and thought about Romero's idea. *It could work. That he disliked Romero, there was no question. But he had to admit that he had heard the man was a stone-cold killer. His skills were well-known. If he did take out one or two of the indios, they could stay out here and finish it with the others, if the indios chose to fight. They might just run back to their reservation and stop fighting for the gringos.*

The coyote watched as Lobo worked through the proposition in his head. Romero remained hovered over his drawing expectantly. The guide knew that he had no say in this. He would have to do what these men decided. To go his own way would just mean postponing his death until he returned home. He wondered at the wisdom of seeking out a fight with the *indios*. He had dealt with the reservation *indios* in the past. Most of the time, they minded their own business, reluctant to get involved in gringo problems. This had been changing recently, though, with the *indio* they called Price. He had started to intercept loads, refusing to look away. He looked over at Romero again. *Could this be the Zeta killer who had gunned down Price?*

Lobo stood up and made a pronouncement. "I agree. We should go north and dig in. Do you think you can get us to those caves without leaving a trail?"

The coyote nodded.

"Then let's go. Once we get settled in, Romero can come back here and wait for the *indios.*" He then turned to Romero. "We will wait for you. They still won't expect you to come north after you kill some of them." Lobo paused as he worked it out in his head. "We've got plenty of water, and it'll be a good place to go to ground if that is what we need. Might be a little short on food, but we can eat again when we get back to Nogales."

The coyote raised his eyebrows and looked at his companions, hoping they were both in agreement. He looked to Lobo. "So are we ready?"

Lobo just nodded.

"Okay, let's get started. We are going to have walk out toward the middle of the river so they can't see our footprints in the shallow water." He looked at both of them. "Tie what you can over your shoulders. You will need your hands free to keep your balance. If you fall, it might leave a trace. It's unlikely, but we should take precautions."

Both Lobo and Romero busied themselves removing their shirts and tying them into makeshift slings. Lobo took his rifle and used the leather sling to put it over his left shoulder while his shirt, holding his bulging water skin, was draped over his right shoulder. He then tucked his pistol into his belt just below his protruding belly. All that remained were his four extra magazines, which he meticulously placed inside of his undershirt. He was forced to tuck the already stretched fabric tightly into his pants to prevent them from falling into the river. Finished, he looked over at Romero who was already wading into the water. His rifle rested across the back of his neck, his hands holding onto the weapon at both ends.

The coyote waited for the men to get into the river before taking a mesquite bush and erasing all evidence of their presence. He had no belongings other than his water skin. He backed into the water, still using the mesquite as a broom. He would take it down river for a bit before jettisoning it. He had chosen a good rocky entry point to enter the river so there should be little or no trace of them entering the water. If the *indios* did think they went into the river, they would hopefully decide that they had fled south, the natural deduction. He took his place in front of the other two, and they slowly made their way north in the river. *Now if he could just keep them from stumbling into a nest of snakes, they might just have a chance.*

CHAPTER 42

Romero looked calmly through the Leupold MK 4 fixed-power scope mounted firmly on his rifle. His M-24A3 sniper rifle was the same rifle that had been used by the US Army during the war in Afghanistan. With the enhanced .338 ammunition, it was capable of at least one thousand six hundred yards. He could see the shapes of four horses far out on the horizon. They were not yet in his range and were spread out with at least ten feet between each horse and rider. He gave some thought to the dimming light, thinking that he would need to wait another hour before switching to his clip-on sniper night sight. They would come into effective range during the *tween*, as he liked to call it—that time when it was neither day or night. He couldn't wait for the night. By then they would be too close. He leaned his head back from the sight and lowered the rifle, letting the barrel rest on the bipod. He thought about his options. *I have one round in the chamber and five in the magazine. Four riders. He would try to kill two. Maybe he would get lucky and they would panic. Then he would kill them all.* He rolled over on his back and took a series of calming breaths, staring at the shadows of night as they crept across the sky.

He thought of his two companions. He had stashed them in the caves upstream. They would be safe for the time being. But truthfully, if this ambush didn't work, he was fairly certain that they would be found eventually. These *indios* were no normal policemen. This was something entirely new. He had come up against some pretty tough Border Patrol agents over the years, but nobody like these *indios.* This was the first time that he was truly afraid of the Americans. He wondered aloud in a whisper to nobody in particular, "Where did these *indios* come from?"

CHAPTER 43

Lobo stood in front of the opening to the shallow cave, pissing into the passing water. He broke wind in a loud rap, laughing to himself at his bodily functions as if they were something unique to him. The coyote lay on the ground at the back of the cave. He had been happy to find the caves. Lobo had made it clear that if he had been wrong, he would have killed him. Now trying to fall asleep, he opened his eyes to look over at the source of the disgusting noises. *This Lobo is a greasy fucking pig.* He called out to the man, "You know, we take our drinking water from that."

Lobo zipped up and turned. "If anyone is going to drink that piss, they will be down in Mexico somewhere." He chuckled to himself as he walked slowly back into the temporary hideout. "Why the fuck don't you mind your own business anyway?" Then visibly growing angrier, he said, "You need to shut the fuck up, Bernardo." He was sneering as he said the coyote's newly learned name. "I won't tell you again. Even I can find my way back to Mexico now. All I do is follow this river. Maybe I'll just follow the smell of my own piss!"

The coyote didn't respond. He just laid his head back and closed his eyes once again. *This bastard couldn't find his way to his favorite taco stand without one of his men to take him there. Unfortunately, that didn't make him any less dangerous.* He reached down to his boot, finding comfort in the hilt of the stiletto concealed there. *Maybe I should just stick this pig here when he falls asleep and put an end to it.* He just didn't know if Romero would back him up in this. He restlessly turned on his side and let out a long breath, wondering if Romero would be successful in his battle with the *indios*, then wondering how long they would have to wait to find out.

CHAPTER 44

Romero had waited ten minutes before looking through his sights again. The *indios* were almost in range. He made some minor adjustments on the scope and adjusted the stock into his shoulder several times, finding the best fit. He could now see all four figures fairly clearly. It was definitely the *indios.* He couldn't tell which of them was the leader. They rode four abreast, equally confident in their saddles. He scanned back and forth with the glass, trying to decide which one he would shoot first, trying to predict what they would do once the first one went down.

*****

The Shadow Wolves had kept a steady pace over the desert, dismounting and walking alongside their horses periodically to rest their mounts. All of them were experienced trackers, with the exception of young Tyrell, and he was born to the saddle and the desert. They had worked out a rotation system so that none of them had to watch the trail for a long period of time. Isaac had wrapped his head completely in the Arab fashion, with only his eyes exposed, making him appear more like a warrior from the edges of the Sahara than an American special agent.

The sun had dropped below the horizon. They would have another two hours of usable light before they would have to stop for the night. They would reach the river long before that. The tracks had been clear, the Zetas were heading straight for water. The Zetas would have been there for at least three hours by now. They were closing the gap. Crowe scanned the landscape, looking ahead for anything that would indicate the presence of the Mexicans, but nothing stood out. The ground was flat, dotted with cacti and scattered rock chimneys rising to the sky. He glanced to the south along the horizon, trying to visualize the country through which the Sonoyta River would travel. The soldier in him hated crossing this empty space with no cover. *These were no ordinary criminals. They were capable of anything and had no conscience. He had faced men like this before. It had not always ended well, and good people had paid the price.* He looked to his right as Nalin suddenly pulled back on her horse, bringing it to an abrupt halt.

Crowe and the rest of the team followed Nalin's lead. Crowe hissed tersely, "What is it?"

Nalin was now leaning forward, her head now even with her horse's, straining to see across the desert.

Crowe was now concerned. "Nalin?"

The Apache hesitated a few more seconds, then sideways to Crowe. "I don't know… Something… Something is bothering my horse."

Just then, Wanagi put his ears back and nickered, his eyes wide.

*****

Romero had made his decision—the rider farthest to the right. He looked familiar. He chuckled quietly, speaking out loud to himself, "I have seen you before, boy. You were with the one they call Price. I guess I should have killed you then." He scanned quickly to the rider next to the boy, a tall thin man with his head wrapped in some sort of scarf. *This would be his second target.* He returned to the boy, his finger beginning the methodical process of tightening on the trigger, his breathing now reverting to his countless hours of practice. Suddenly, the group came to a stop. Reflexively, he looked up from his eyepiece to see if there was something he had missed.

*****

Wanagi's sudden alarm could be felt through the saddle. Crowe didn't hesitate. "Dismount!" he shouted, sliding off the mount and pulling his rifle from the scabbard as he did so. He held fast to the reins and wrapped them back around Wanagi's head, pulling her to the side and down, whispering to her to lie down. Nalin did not have to watch Ethan to know what to do. She followed suit, pulling her mount to the ground as well. Ty and Isaac were a few seconds behind them, and Ty was having trouble getting his mount to cooperate. He pulled at his horse's reins, causing it to turn his head to the left, toward the young tracker. It was then that a tremendous thud shook Ty's gelding, the helpless beast screaming in agony as it fell sideways onto its rider.

Crowe yelled to the team, "Down! Stay down. Get behind the horses."

Nalin never hesitated upon hearing the screams of the horse. She was crawling over her horse, unbuckling the cinches. She looked back over her horse's belly at Crowe, who was working quickly at the buckles of his own saddle. He then called back to the other two men, "Ty, Isaac? You two all right?"

Ty said nothing. Factor quickly responded, "The horse landed on Ty. He's pinned."

Crowe said quickly, "Is he breathing?"

"Think so."

"We're gonna go after them. You got Ty?" he asked, knowing that his old partner did have the boy. *He would be in good hands.*

Crowe then looked back at Nalin, who was slipping her leather rifle sheath off the saddle and over her shoulder, the rifle resting across her back. He called over, "You ready?"

"Yep."

"He's almost directly in front of us. I saw the muzzle flash. I'll take the left flank. You go right."

Both moved almost simultaneously, rising with their horses, saddles left on the ground. Each was up to full speed in seconds, galloping in wide arcs in the direction of the shooter. It was impossible to discern where the outline of the horses ended and the riders began. Both were lying low across the backs of their mustangs, juking slightly from one side to the other to make themselves a more difficult target.

*****

Romero knew the shot was off as soon as he pulled the trigger. He hadn't expected them to dismount so suddenly, and the skittish horse had stepped directly into the shot. He tried to reacquire the target, but he had gone under the horse, totally out of the view through his scope. He then moved his rifle to the right, trying to find the one with the head scarf. He, too, was now down behind his horse, invisible and unreachable. He quickly traversed left to find the remaining two riders. Those two horses were also flat on the ground. He caught a glimpse of movement by the rider farthest to the left but then lost it again. He struggled to keep his composure. *This is what they trained you for, Romero. Stay calm.*

Romero stared intensely through the scope to gauge his success. He couldn't tell if he had actually hit any of the *indios*. His pulse quickened when he realized two of the horses were no longer on the ground. Both had disappeared, along with their riders. He frantically swept his rifle left and right to try to reacquire his targets. Nothing. Instinctively, he raised his head to see what was happening. It was then that he saw two of the riders galloping toward him. They had split up and were following arcs from both his right and left flanks. *Fuck!* Fear was turning his bowels to water.

The sniper realized that he had to do something to slow these *indios* down. He brought his scope back up to bring them into focus for a shot. He couldn't. They were moving too fast, and he couldn't see the riders very well. They were almost invisible, hanging impossibly on the outer sides of their horses. *Jesus.* He was certain they were on the horses but couldn't see enough of them to get a decent shot. *Well, fuck it! If they were going to hide behind their horses, he would shoot the fucking horses.* He jerked his head away from the scope, not trusting its limited field of vision. He made a decision. He returned to the scope and tried to bring the rifle to bear on one of the moving targets. He gasped involuntarily. *They're moving too fast.* In panic, he fired a quick round at the rider to the left.

*****

Nalin pressed her body flat, molding herself to the shape of the horse's back. Her face was nuzzled down against the neck of the mustang, her right hand gripping its mane tightly. She was speaking quietly to the horse as it flew across the flat ground. Suddenly she felt the whiz of a bullet as it passed inches above her head. She immediately leaned to the left, sending her and her mount on a straight line for the shooter.

Ethan heard the shot and saw Nalin change her course. He did the same, bringing Wanagi on a direct collision course with the location of the sniper. He ignored the M-4 rifle slung across his back but pulled his Glock from his belt, leveling it in front of him with his arm fully extended. He aimed high, allowing for the distance, and fired four quick rounds in succession. He had no real expectations of hitting anything, but he hoped it would distract the sniper from any further attempts at Nalin. His foremost hope was that the shooter would turn and run.

Nalin decided not to slow at all as she drove toward the shooter's position. Slowing now would only make her an easier target. The sniper was only two hundred yards away, and she was closing fast.

Ethan never saw if his shots hit anything. He realized that now he was falling back to his Ranger training. *Always charge an ambush! It was beaten into their heads. He only hoped that it worked out here in the desert with a man trained to set up ambushes.*

*****

Romero was panicking. This had turned into a giant game of chicken, and he didn't think he could stand his ground against two charging horses. He swung the rifle to the right and fired off a round at the second rider. He cursed himself when the round went high. He calculated whether to try again, nervously looking back to his left, where the second rider was within a hundred yards. He wasted no more time. Stepping back from his firing position, he moved quickly down to the water, wading into the middle of the stream with his rifle raised over his head to keep it dry. *If I can only make it past that first bend, maybe I have a chance.*

*****

Ethan felt, rather than heard, the round go over his head. He thought to himself how luck was such a big factor in warfare. He could hear Wanagi breathing rhythmically as they closed the final one hundred yards. He marveled at the mustang. It was as if she understood that she was a target. It might have been his imagination, but he could almost feel the animal running closer to the ground as they flew across the intervening distance. He looked ahead to see if he could get a fix on the shooter but could see nothing. He let go with another four rounds in the general direction of the sniper, mostly as cover fire for both him and Nalin.

Nalin reached the shooter's position first. She came in at a full gallop and vaulted from the mustang's back before the horse was fully stopped. Her rifle was out of its scabbard and in her hands when her feet hit the ground. Wanagi came sliding into the sniper's nest seconds after Nalin, with Ethan sliding off the horse and moving forward in a combat crouch, his Glock pointed ahead in a ready position. Both riders moved cautiously to where the shooter had lain, sweeping their weapons back and forth. He was gone. They looked down at the shallow river, pissed. They exchanged looks. This shooter had skills.

CHAPTER 45

Factor worked feverishly to pull Ty from under the dead horse. The young man had come to and was in a lot of pain. He was suffering in silence, but Isaac could tell that the boy was barely keeping it together. Isaac had his own horse back on its feet, rigging a rope to the saddle horn and then looping it around the carcass of the dead horse. He knew that this was going to be painful for the boy, but there was no other way to free him. He had to drag the horse off his leg.

Isaac crouched down next to Ty. "You gonna be okay with this? I am going to have my horse pull the weight off your leg. I know it'll hurt, but if you can use your arms to scoot yourself backward at the same time, it'll go quicker and easier."

Tyrell just nodded, sweat beading across his brow from the pain. Isaac put his left hand on the bridle and then slapped his horse on his backside, urging him forward. Slowly, the carcass started to move, and the lessening of the weight on Ty's leg allowed him to wiggle free. Isaac pulled back quickly on the reins, relieving his horse of the burden immediately. He then unwrapped the rope from the saddle horn and let the reins of his horse drop to the ground. He returned to where the boy was sitting, relieved to find him clear of the dead horse and his breathing easier.

"How is it now, boy?" Factor crouching to gently probe the leg with his hands.

"Better. Much better." The boy smiled in relief. "I think I can get up."

"Whoa there now. Let's not get ahead of ourselves. Can you move it?"

Ty responded by raising the leg at the knee, but not without a lot of pain. "Yeah, I can move it."

Isaac responded sarcastically, "Yeah, I can see you are just fine."

"We're going to have to get you out of here. We will call in a chopper as soon as we hear back from Ethan." Factor looked nervously across the empty spaces toward where the sniper had been.

Tyrell could sense the Factor's concerns for the other two. "Do you think they made it okay?"

Factor kept looking across the open ground. "They're fine. You don't need to worry about them."

Ty was quick to interject, "You can go, Isaac. Go ahead. I'll be fine. Just leave me with my rifle and a bit of water, and I'll be good. You need to check on them. I've got my radio after all. The signal should at least reach as far as the river."

Factor remembered the radios. He knew that he couldn't reach Ethan or Nalin. *Hell, they left with nothing but their horses and their guns.* Isaac then thought about Ethan's sat phone. He could get it from his saddlebag. It would allow him to call back to HQ to get a chopper for the kid. But then he realized that a chopper could jeopardize the safety of Ethan and Nalin. He looked back at Ty. He was in minimal pain, and there was no bleeding. He would be able to sit for more than a bit. Making up his mind, he strode over to where Ethan had left his saddle. He rifled through the gear and came up holding the sat phone. He held it up and checked the power indicator and signal strength, finding both acceptable. He then moved back to where the boy was resting and handed the phone to him.

"Ty, take this. I'm going to head out to check on them. You'll be all right here. I'm going to set you up with a canteen and some hardtack. If, for some reason, I'm not back by daylight, call it in and request a chopper and a full team of Wolves." Factor was now busying himself by gathering up supplies for the boy and putting them within arm's reach.

The young man looked up at Factor as he readied his horse to leave. "I feel pretty stupid sitting here like an old lady while you guys go off to fight."

Factor never looked back at Tyrell, preferring to adjust his cinches. "Nothing to be ashamed of, boy. You can't predict a horse falling on you, that's for certain. You did just fine. Wouldn't be leaving you here on your own if I didn't think you could handle it."

Ty remained silent, the words seeming to placate him.

Now mounted, Isaac looked down at Ty. "Keep your radio on. I will try to reach out once I know what is going on out there. I've stashed Ethan's radio in my bags. Nalin's didn't survive her horse crunching it when they laid down. But with any luck, we should all be connected again soon. If we are going to be gone for long, I will radio and let you know. You've got your GPS position?"

"Yeah, I wrote it down on my hand." Ty held up a pen in his right hand.

Factor chuckled. "Well, at least the new generation is always prepared. A pen. That's a new one. I guess maybe you can spend some of your free time writing your memoirs. Should keep you from getting bored anyway." Factor smiled and gave the boy a farewell thumbs-up before urging his horse out into the desert.

CHAPTER 46

Nalin moved carefully on the opposite side of the river. She had seen clearly where the sniper had gone into the water, but there was no sign indicating that he had left it again. She began to walk methodically up and down both banks, thinking that perhaps he had gone into the water and then come back out on the same side. He could be hoping to backtrack and escape or maybe set up a second ambush.

Ethan had spent some time studying the sniper's nest. He had found three empty shell casings. It was clear that the shooter had left in hurry. He pocketed one of the casings, sure that the prints on the metal would match with those on the shells that killed Moses Price. He would leave the rest for the crime scene folks, providing he and his people came out on the winning side of this thing. He stood where he had been examining the spot where the bipod had rested. Turning, he saw Nalin emerging from the water, her clothing soaked to just below her chest. He nodded in the direction of the river. "What do you think?"

Nalin continued walking toward Ethan, answering when she was within a few feet of him. "If I was to guess, they stayed in the water."

Ethan looked instinctively to the left, then south. "They're close. At least the shooter is."

Nalin shook her head. "I don't think they went that way." She looked south with her boss. "I think they went north," she said, pointing in the other direction with her left arm.

Crowe looked at her questioningly.

"This coyote is a slick one. It's not his first dance. Everything he's done so far makes me think he's no fool." She hesitated a beat. "If I were him, I would go north too. Anyone chasing them would assume they would take the fastest and easiest route home, especially now that we are so close. A lot of people would think that they were in panic mode and rabbiting back to Mexico."

Crowe listened closely to the Apache tracker. What she said made sense. The tracks had disappeared. Now they had to go on instinct. He thought about their options. He also wondered how Ty was doing. He absently turned to find his radio but then remembered he hadn't brought it with him. It was back there with his saddle. Almost as if on cue, he heard the approach of hoofbeat. Looking into the growing night, he saw Isaac appear, tall in the saddle, reining in his mount.

Factor dismounted, dropped his reins, and closed the distance to Ethan and Nalin. Ethan was about to pose a question, but Isaac cut him off, "The boy's fine. Probably got a broken leg but not a compound fracture. He is in some pain but nothing he can't handle. He's a tough one. I got him set up back there with a radio and the sat phone." He then added, "Left him with plenty of water and some jerky too." He looked back and forth from Ethan to Nalin. "So where's the shooter?"

"Nalin thinks he went north," Ethan said, pointing upstream. I tend to agree with her."

"And the others?" Isaac raised his eyebrows questioningly.

Ethan shook his head, indicating he didn't know. "Not sure on that one. I would assume they are upstream too, but you never know. Maybe this guy was ordered to be their rear guard. If that's the case, they are hours ahead of us, running for the border."

Nalin broke into the conversation, "I think we should start moving up the river. It's getting darker by the minute, and the moon won't be up for at least another few hours. We are really cutting it close with usable light."

Factor looked at both, waiting for Ethan to decide what to do. "If it's any help, I got night vision goggles from both of your saddlebags. Might make this a lot easier."

Ethan smiled to himself. *Isaac, you never change.*

Nalin was already lifting the flaps on Factor's saddlebags. She extracted the two sets of goggles, stretching the straps of the first pair over her head and letting the glasses hang loosely around her neck. She walked back to where Crowe and Factor were standing and handed the second pair to Ethan. The goggles now hanging from Ethan's neck as well, he looked to Isaac. "Why don't you head back to where the boy is? I would prefer to have you keep an eye on him." Isaac started to object, but Ethan cut him off, "I know, he's a big boy and all that shit, but I want him taken care of properly. Call back to HQ and let them know where we are. Have them send out a Humvee to pick up Ty. I don't want a chopper up yet."

"I brought one radio too. Nalin's was crushed when the horse laid over," Isaac continued talking as he stepped over to his horse to retrieve the radio microphone set for Ethan. "You can let me know if you need anything else or if you want the choppers up to help."

Ethan was putting his throat mike around his neck and setting the earpiece in his left ear. His left hand was now on Wanagi, the reins in the same hand. "We'll follow the river north. See what turns up. We'll be going slow. I don't know if this shooter is on the run or just laying another trap for us."

Nalin was eager to get on the track. She grabbed a handful of her mustang's mane, pulled hard, and leapt up, easily swinging her right leg over the horse's back. She then pulled back on the reins, moving the horse several steps back and holding there. Ethan mounted in the same manner. He laid the reins over to the right, and both he and Nalin cantered toward the river. Reaching the water, Ethan pointed to the other bank with is left hand and then nodded to the right, indicating that he wanted Nalin to stay on this side of the river. She nodded in agreement and waited while Ethan and Wanagi crossed to the other side.

CHAPTER 47

Lobo heard the shot and stood up first. The coyote remained still and listened for more. A minute later, two more shots could be heard. The sounds were coming from a distance, and they were coming from Romero's gun. He rose quietly, not to make any additional noise, in case more shots could be heard. He walked cautiously to the cave entrance and stood next to Lobo who was standing perfectly still, not bothering to look to his left when the coyote came to a stop at his side. The coyote was about to speak when four more shots could be heard, rapidly fired in succession. *Those weren't rifle shots.* Both men realizing that fact simultaneously.

Lobo turned and went for his weapons. "Get your shit. We need to get the fuck out of here."

The coyote turned and watched the Zeta gathering up his rifle. "Where are we going to go? We don't know what happened to Romero yet. If we head south right now, there's a good chance we could walk right into the *indios.*"

Lobo suddenly ordered, "Get your shit together. We're moving out."

The coyote looked at him, puzzled.

"I'm not asking."

The coyote grudgingly started to move to the back of the cave to retrieve his gear. Then he paused. "Why don't we wait a few minutes anyway? He could be on his way back to us right now. I would rather know what we're facing."

Lobo was silent, considering his options. There was no doubt in the coyote's mind that the only options Lobo was interested in were those that involved saving his own skin. The man cared nothing about what might happen to anyone else. Visibly torn, Lobo finally pronounced, “Okay, we wait for a little longer. If he isn't here soon, we head south. You need to be thinking of the best way out of here. Hell, it was your bright idea to come this way in the first place.”

The coyote shook his head silently in the recess of the cave. He seriously considered just quietly climbing the embankment above the hideout and leaving this pig in the dark. Lobo could never follow him. If he stayed, Lobo would probably kill him before this was over anyway. If he left now, there was a good chance that Lobo would never return to Mexico to tell his tale. *Unless these indios take him alive and bring him back to an American prison. Then he would talk, and the Zetas would know the truth within twenty-four hours.*

*****

Romero was quickly making his way up the river. He had left the water shortly after he rounded the first bend. The darkness would make it impossible for anyone to pick up his trail tonight. Speed was more important than stealth at this point. He was now nearing the part of the river where the caves were located. He couldn't recall exactly where he had left the others and the darkness had changed his perceptions considerably. He moved to the rocky ledge that was now running alongside the river. He paused, standing directly over a sharp five-foot drop which ended at the water's edge. He listened intently, turning his head in both directions. He heard nothing from where he had fired at the *indios. Maybe I will have some luck after all. Maybe they were pursuing him to the south.*

Reassured that he was alone, he hastened his step, working his way back to his partners at the cave. Fifteen minutes later, he dropped off the embankment and whistled to alert Lobo and the coyote that he had returned. The coyote didn't have to be signaled. He was sitting out front of the opening, watching and listening. He stood in welcome as Romero stooped his head to enter the hideout, the butt of his rifle dragging on the sandy floor.

“Well?” Lobo challenged questioningly.

Romero just shook his head negatively.

"What do you mean? Didn't you kill any of them?"

Romero looked back and forth at both of the men. "I tried. Missed my first shot. His horse got in the way and took the bullet instead. Something alerted them just when I was pulling the trigger. They went to the ground. Took their horses with them."

Lobo pressed further, "Horses? These *indios* have horses?" He was incredulous now. "How many of them are there?"

Romero exhaled, almost apologetically. "Four. There's four. I think that I got one of them indirectly. The horse that took my round fell on him. He wasn't getting up."

"So where the fuck are they now?" Lobo's survival senses were now in overdrive.

"I don't know. I've been checking my back trail. I didn't hear or see anything." He added quickly, "But that doesn't mean anything with these trackers. I've never seen anything like them before." He then shrugged sheepishly at the coyote, who only nodded in sympathy.

Lobo was furious. Probably more from fear than anything else. He seethed, "These fucking *indios*. They're not fucking magic. They're men like any other men. I'm not going to hide in a hole in the ground from three *indios*!"

Romero held up his hand in placation. "I think I can wait for them again. *If*, and I mean *if*, they come north, I can wait just down river around the first or second bend. In the darkness, I should be able to hear them coming and, with luck, kill them." Romero raising his eyebrows, seeking agreement.

Lobo spit in the sand. "What do we do while you make your stand, Sniper?"

"I think you should wait here. If I miss them and they kill me, you still might be safe. If you leave now, you could be walking straight into their arms. But I guess that's your call, *Jefe*." The last word was said more in mockery than respect.

Lobo glared back at the sniper. He hated Romero more with each passing minute, but the asshole made sense. He looked over at the coyote, who remained silent. Lobo turned to place his rifle against the stone wall, using the motion to give further thought to his options. No one had ever accused him of not being able make a decision when it was needed. His first reaction was to oppose Romero's plan immediately. He didn't like the idea of this sniper making decisions for him. He was the boss. *He*, and *he* alone, reported to Roberto. It had taken a lifetime to earn that status. But the more he thought about Romero's idea, the more he realized that it could suit his own purposes as well. If this arrogant fool thought that he could kill these *indios*, good. If the shooting started, he would order this coyote to take him out of here. They would take a wide arc around the action and head directly south. *Like he had said to do in the first place!*

He turned back to face Romero and the coyote. "Do it. We will wait here. If they do not come, I will decide when it's time to go home. Me!" His black eyes were full of hatred and purpose.

Romero nodded and then exchanged a worried look with the coyote. He strapped his rifle over his right shoulder and ducked his head as he exited the cave. When the sniper had left the shelter of the cave, Lobo turned to the coyote with a menacing look and growled, "Get ready to move."

*****

The two Shadow Wolves walked their mustangs slowly on each side of the river. The land on both sides was rising slowly, creating a slightly elevated ridge along the waterway. Both horses moved gracefully along the darkened ground, their instincts a valuable tool to the trackers. The combination of their unshod hooves, the sandy soil, and the slow pace allowed them to move in almost complete silence. Nalin rode with her reins resting on her horse's withers, allowing her to cradle her Marlin in both hands. She was not wearing her night vision goggles, believing that this interfered with her natural senses. Crowe, on the other hand, knew that night vision provided unquestionable superiority in battle, a veteran of too many firefights to think otherwise.

The two riders had covered almost three miles. They had not seen or heard anything yet, but both strongly believed that their quarry was not far ahead. Crowe let out a soft whistle, similar to a night bird of the desert. Nalin brought her horse to a quick halt, looking over to Crowe to see what had caught his attention. Crowe hadn't heard a thing. But Wanagi had sensed something. The mustang had stopped in her tracks, nostrils flared, straining to pick up a scent. Her ears were moving in unison, turning in every direction, trying to pick up the sound of whatever it was that she had sensed in the darkness.

*****

Romero stood stock still, his back pressed firmly into the river embankment. He was lying in wait. The sniper had found a good *hide* about three hundred yards downstream from the cave entrance. Having traveled past two bends in the river, he decided that this was as good a place as any to make his stand. After convincing Lobo that this would be the best strategy, he had moved cautiously downriver, finally stopping at this slight indentation in the sandstone embankment. He knew that they couldn't outrun these *indios*. If they were coming, it would be soon. If not, the three of them could wait it out for a few more days in the relative safety of the hideaway and then quietly make their way south under cover of darkness. If the *indios* did come, with any luck, Romero would kill them.

*****

Crowe sat perfectly still atop the mustang, making hand gestures to Nalin, which she could see clearly in the growing moonlight. She, in turn, scanned the terrain ahead, straining to focus on the shadows of the vertical river banks. Crowe continued to look down into the ravine, listening to the water moving southward over the rocky bottom. He couldn't hear or see anything out of the ordinary, but he hesitated because of the mustang. She was never wrong. Wishing that she was would not make it so.

Suddenly, a faint scraping sound. Not for more than a second. Nalin was closest, and she brought her rifle to bear. Ethan's horse was also looking across the river into the darkness, her ears pointed forward like directional radar. Ethan pulled the goggles from around his neck and fired them up, illuminating the entire landscape in the expected eerie glow. He began to scan the sandstone wall on Nalin's side of the river, in the direction that Wanagi was staring. He moved his head slowly, knowing that the night vision made everything more visible though still not the same as normal daylight.

*****

Romero could see several feet in front of him fairly clearly without his nightscope, but the moon had not risen high enough to make the entire landscape visible. He wished he had goggles rather than the limited view of the rifle-mounted scope. The air was still. No insect sound out here in the desert. Suddenly, he heard the trace of something. A man-made sound, an electronic sound. It was faint, but he knew the sound well, having heard it on countless missions. Someone had just fired up a night vision device. They were hunting him, and they were close.

He cursed himself for flinching when he had realized the *indios* were nearby. Sliding backward to stay hidden, he had inadvertently brushed a narrow shelf of rock, sending a light shower of dust tumbling toward the water's edge. He froze immediately, hoping that the sound had not been detected. His eyes desperately scanned his surroundings, forcing his eyelids as wide as physically possible in an attempt to see into the darkness. He adjusted his grips on the high-powered rifle, his index finger slipping nervously into the trigger guard. He tried to move his head slowly back and forth in an effort to detect any abnormal movements above him or on the ledge across the river. It was then that he heard the sound of a small dog barking—faint but close. He quickly lowered into the crouched position, instinctively aiming his rifle toward the sound. *It could be a den of grey foxes, but he doubted it.*

*****

Nalin alerted at Ethan's fox call. She slid soundlessly from her horse and started to move north along the ridge, watching below carefully as she moved. Ethan had a clear view of the target and wanted her to move farther upriver to cover his escape route along the riverbank. She reached her goal in less than a minute, signaling to Ethan with a killdeer call, imitating one of the desert night's most active birds.

*****

Romero turned sharply at the sound of the bird. It seemed to be coming from the direction of the cave. *Surely that must be a bird. They couldn't be behind him.* His heart was racing wildly. He had never been hunted before. All his killings had been a series of calculated exercises, the pulling of the trigger done exclusively upon orders from above. This was nothing like that. He struggled to regain control. Now he would have to fight for his life, close and personal.

"Don't make a move," a deep voice ordered from the darkness across the river. Romero turned instinctively to meet the threat. The second he turned, the voice commanded, "Freeze or die. Your choice. If you so much as twitch, you die." Romero's first instinct was to fire in the direction of the commands. It was the utter calmness of the orders that had made him hesitate. The icy coldness of the tracker had sent terror coursing through his body. His fear overwhelmed him, and he knew he was beyond shame. *After all the killing, I am now afraid to die.*

"Lower your weapon slowly to the ground. Your life is in your hands. One noise from your mouth, you die. I will not hesitate. Believe it." Crowe remained perfectly still on the ridge above.

Romero deliberately reached out with his rifle at arm's length, careful to demonstrate that his finger was out of the trigger guard. He continued to search desperately for the source of the voice but could see nothing. Once the rifle was on the ground in front of him, he backed away slowly, now treating the weapon like it was radioactive.

The now godlike voice toned again from above. "Any other weapons? If so, speak now. You are only a breath away from dead."

Romero just stood there, hands raised in the air, his body trembling visibly. He glanced to his left and saw a figure come toward him, walking calmly along the water's edge. It was a woman. But she did not move like any woman he had known. She stalked rather than walked, crossing the ground with graceful menace. In her hands was a lever action carbine, pointed directly at his heart. As she drew closer, he could feel the power radiate from her body. In spite of himself, his mind flashed, *She's magnificent.* Her eyes were black as night, challenging him to move a single muscle. He started to speak. As his lips started to move, she struck him violently with the butt of her rifle, instantly dropping him into blackness and onto the sandy ground.

CHAPTER 48

Romero woke as though emerging from a fog. He found himself lying on his back, staring at the sky as he raised his head slightly to look around him. Two figures stood motionless across from him. He pressed his back into the ground to see if his small automatic remained hidden in his waistband, disappointed to realize that it was no longer there. He briefly considered closing his eyes again, but a hand reached down and grabbed him by the hair, jerking his eyes wide open. Turning his eyes to the left, he saw the woman again, her right hand firmly gripping his hair. Her left hand held a long black object. It looked like a knife but unlike anything he had seen before.

Nalin leaned down and spoke Apache quietly in his ear, "*Góchi* (pig)," then in Spanish, "So I finally meet the killer who trembles like a child in the dark." She forcefully released her grip in disgust, causing him to lose what meager balance he had summoned. The second figure then crouched down at his feet.

"What's your name?" The voice was the one that had come from above.

The sniper considered his options. He decided he had none. "Romero." Resignation was evident in his voice.

Nalin watched as Ethan's face went cold. He continued to stare at the thin figure lying on the ground, contemplating the fate of the man who had murdered Moses Price and robbed a family of their loving father.

CHAPTER 49

Fifteen minutes after the sniper had disappeared around the first bend of the river, Lobo turned to the coyote. "We're leaving. I want to get as far south as possible before daylight."

"But what about Romero? We told him—"

Lobo cut him off by grabbing him by the shirt with a powerful right hand. He pulled the man close but said nothing. Lobo's stare was menacing enough.

The coyote looked down in submission. He would do as he was told. It would do no good to survive the American desert and be killed when he returned to Mexico, knowing that his family would also disappear in the blink of an eye. As Lobo released him with a shove, he stumbled backward a few steps. He quickly forced himself to regain his composure, considering the best way to slip south past the Americans. He opted for the western side of the river. They would climb the embankment and try to swing wide of the river and avoid contact with the *indios*. If Romero engaged them, all the better. That would keep everyone busy. His mood lightened at the thought. It was too bad for Romero, but Lobo's decision actually upped his own odds of surviving this mess.

As soon as he picked up his belongings, Lobo was at his back, growling lowly, "Let's go, Bernardo," the Zeta boss spitting his name.

The coyote turned and calmly responded, "We should stick to the west riverbank for a while. We can move slowly and use the brush that runs along the river as cover. That way, even if we come across the *indios,* there's a chance we can sneak past them. No matter what we do, it will be a close thing."

Lobo nodded. "No one is to see us, not even Romero."

The coyote looked calmly at the boss. "We can do that." The slim desert guide was now a full partner in this decision.

*****

The two Mexicans had traveled only a few hundred yards when they heard hushed voices ahead. The sounds came from the ravine, along the water. The coyote held out his hand to alert Lobo, who was walking a few feet behind him. He turned his head, placing his finger to his lips to insure quiet.

They both crouched in the mesquite bushes that grew in clusters along the river. One hundred feet ahead, they saw Romero. He lay on his back, propped up on his two elbows, looking up at two of the *indio* trackers. One was a woman, holding a cowboy rifle cradled in her arms. The second was a dark man, his rifle slung over his back. The woman was continuously scanning both banks of the river, causing the coyote to place his hand on Lobo's shoulder and press him to the ground. He leaned so that his lips actually touched Lobo's left ear. "We must back away and go out to the west before they see us."

Lobo impatiently pushed the coyote away from him. He detested any physical contact with another man. He thought briefly about the advice but was already formulating his own plan of action. As the coyote started to crawl slowly backward, Lobo grabbed his right shirtsleeve and shook his head no. He then brought his pistol forward and placed it on the ground in front of him. The coyote shook his head no, not believing that Lobo would try to challenge the trackers. He felt fairly certain that there were more of them out there. If not, more were surely on the way.

*****

Crowe had brushed aside his personal feelings about the sniper. He had a job to do. Nalin, on the other hand, was seething as she stood a few feet away, glaring down at the cold-blooded assassin. Ethan calmly posed his next question. "Where are the others?"

Romero hesitated and then let out a sigh. "Gone. I stayed behind to cover their escape."

Ethan smirked. "That was decent of you. You stayed behind to protect their asses, knowing we would find you."

Romero smiled resignedly. "Well, in fairness, this could have gone another way."

Nalin took a step closer. "I have a question for you, *asesino.* What reason can you give me for not slitting your throat right here?"

Romero didn't respond to her. He looked cautiously at Crowe, trying to assess the man who would make the decisions. The he spoke, looking directly at Ethan, "You are government agents. Am I right? You cannot kill whoever you want, even *asesinos*." The sniper was now looking back and forth at both of the trackers.

Ethan was about to respond when Wanagi nickered, long and loud, causing Ethan to turn his head quickly in the direction of the west embankment. As he turned, the air erupted in gunfire, one round whizzing past Ethan's ear. Nalin fell instantly to the ground. She lay flat and aimed her rifle toward the source of the shots. Ethan dove to his left, spinning at the same time in order to bring his gun to bear on the attackers.

The air was full of lead, travelling in both directions. Nalin laid down a wide field of fire, hoping to find her targets. Each time she fired, she rolled in one direction or the other, careful not to repeat the sequence, making it difficult for the Zetas to zero in on her muzzle flashes. As suddenly as the firefight began, it was over. A fog of cordite hung in the air as Nalin cautiously regained her feet. She continued to scan the horizon, searching for movement or shadows of movement. Nothing. She moved quickly to the water's edge, wading silently into the slight current, and crossed to the western bank. She edged slowly to the lip of the ridge and listened. Again, nothing. She chanced a quick peek over the edge. They were gone. Backing away, she hurried to where she had left Ethan and the sniper.

She arrived to find Ethan getting to his feet. He was moving slowly, holding his side as he stood. She moved sideways toward him, keeping her eyes facing outward and talking at the same time. "Are you okay, boss?" she asked, now taking furtive glances to the side to catch glimpses of him.

"I'm fine." Ethan's words just a bit strained. "I don't think I can say the same for our friend here." Crowe was now bending slowly to check on the sniper.

Nalin backed up to where Ethan crouched next to their prisoner. "Is he alive?"

"Barely." Ethan checking for a pulse and looking closely at Romero's face. "He shook the sniper gently. "Romero." Nothing. The man was breathing but unconscious.

Nalin knelt next to Ethan, finally lowering her Marlin and turning to him. She could see that he wore a pained expression, holding his left elbow close to his body, pressing it against his side. "Are you hit?"

Ethan took his elbow away from his body, looking down at the bloody hole in his shirt. "Feels like a through and through. Not sure though. Could you look at my back?"

Nalin set her rifle down and moved quickly to check Ethan's side and back. She gently pulled up his shirt, noting that there were indeed two holes, front and back. It was a clear through and through. *But what did it hit when it traveled through his body?* She quickly pulled off her shirt. No modesty now. She threw the shirt to the ground, now ripping her T-shirt over her head. Not bothering to cover back up, she took out her knife and expertly dissected the shirt, creating two square patches and a strip to tie around Crowe's torso to hold them in place. Throughout the process, she remained silent, concentrating on her battlefield dressings. Finally finished, she leaned back to examine her work, turning Crowe gently to see both dressings and to make sure they were firmly in place. She was reassured to see that the bleeding had slowed considerably, a good sign. She took a deep breath. "I think that should hold." She then leaned over and picked up the first shirt from the ground, pulling it back over her head with no sense of embarrassment or awkwardness.

Crowe watched Nalin as she tended to his wound. He had never met a woman like this before. He had never served with anyone, man or woman, who was braver or tougher in a fight. Her body was lean and muscular. A sculptor could not improve on what he saw as she worked the obsidian blade, slicing through her tan military-style T-shirt. His eyes caught hers as she turned to place the compresses against his bullet holes. They both paused for a microsecond, some sort of connection passing through them that felt like lightning. The flash of recognition, or maybe attraction, passed, the Apache resuming her first aid. As Nalin finished tying the knot to hold the compresses in place, Ethan was already reaching for his radio mike to call Factor. He needn't have bothered. Isaac was already on his way.

Chapter 50

Factor heard the shots. Sound carried a long way out here in the desert, the sand acting as a conductor for the vibrations. It was a long exchange of gunfire. He heard rifles and handguns. It was a firefight or an ambush. He looked over at Ty who was listening just as intently.

"Call into HQ. Get the Wolves out here now. If the chopper is not back yet, tell them to head out in the Humvees. Make sure they have a medic onboard. Iron Cloud will do if he is closest. He was a corpsman back in the day." Ty began punching in the numbers on the sat phone.

Isaac was already mounted and reining his horse, turning it back toward the river. "Tell them I will advise on an exact GPS position as soon as I rendezvous with the boss."

Ty heard Isaac's orders and acknowledged him with a single thumb in the air. He was already talking with HQ and mustering the rest of the Shadow Wolves. He watched as Factor galloped into the night, thinking that he had already lived this once before.

Factor's radio sounded in his ear. "Isaac?" Crowe called calmly.

Isaac shouted into his throat mike to compensate for the overlapping sounds of a horse at full gallop, "Copy you, boss."

"We're going to need you out here. We are about three miles from our original position, down on the riverbank, just below a sandstone embankment. Do you copy?"

"Copy that."

"We have one bad guy in custody, wounded. The other two are on foot and in the wind. Copy?"

"Copy. Are you and Nalin okay?"

"Roger that. But we need you here so we can pursue the other two. What's your ETA?"

Before Factor could answer, Nalin, hearing the approaching hoofbeat, smiled, and turned to Ethan. "He's here."

Ethan looked up to see Factor working his horse down the embankment, finding a spot about a hundred yards south of their location. He slowly walked his horse the remaining distance, calmly addressing both of them. "I knew if I left you two alone, you would get yourselves into trouble." There was a sly grin on his face as he dismounted and surveyed the scene. Just as he reached the two scouts, the man on the ground started moaning, his mind emerging from wherever it had been.

Ethan, hearing the man moan, pointed in his direction and informed Factor, "That is Romero."

Factor nodded knowingly. "He's the one that did Moses." It was more a statement more than a question.

Crowe just pursed his lips and said nothing.

Nalin stooped down next to Romero. "Who are your friends? And don't tell me you don't know. The last time you lied to me, they came and shot you all to hell!"

Romero gasped for breath. He had been hit several times. One round had grazed his head, causing him to lose consciousness. The troubling wound was in his side, midway down his right rib cage. It burned like hell, and he couldn't seem to catch his breath. He looked up at the woman. *Did he know her?* He tried to speak, but no words came out. She leaned closer. "Can you tell me who they are?"

Romero reached out and covered her hand with his. She allowed it. "Hombre, you don't have much time left, I'm afraid," she said, now speaking to him in Spanish. "You have a lot to answer for in the next world." She paused to let the words sink in. The man was struggling to suck air in, unable to get the energy to speak.

Nalin reached over with her other hand and gently brushed the hair back from Romero's face. "We all make bad decision in this life. Some carry over to the next. Maybe you can make it easier on yourself where you are headed."

Romero rasped a reply she could not hear, nodding his head weakly that he understood.

"Who are they, hombre?" she repeated softly and gently, still caressing his forehead with her fingers.

Romero summoned all his strength and raised his hand, motioning Nalin with his finger to come closer. He was trying to form words as she leaned in. She waited patiently, Crowe and Factor content to watch her work.

Romero whispered one word, "Lobo," looking to the Apache for acknowledgement.

She looked him in the eyes questioningly. "Lobo?" She repeated the word again, this time in English. "Wolf?" She gently squeezed his left hand. "What does that mean?"

"Lobo," Romero rasped once more. "He is Lobo. He is the boss. It is him that is running."

"And the other?" she asked patiently.

"Nobody," said the man, falling silent. Nalin thought him dead for a second. Suddenly he opened his eyes again. "He is the coyote, nothing more."

"Is Lobo the one who killed the woman with the child?"

Romero could only nod.

"Where are they going now?"

Romero smiled weakly. *The woman was a vision. So beautiful.*

She repeated her question, "Where do they go?"

Romero continued to smile, a tear running down his cheek. "Home." His eyes closed for the last time.

Chee continued to hold Romero's hand for a few seconds. She had felt his spirit leave his body in that last moment. She wondered to herself where he had gone. Did they all go on to the next world, or would he go to the Christian hell that they all obsessed about? They had a complicated relationship with their bearded God. She released his hand, sure that she would waste no more time thinking on the spirit of such an evil man. She stood and looked at her companions expectantly.

Ethan spoke first, "We need to get on the trail of the other two. Now that we know the coyote is one of them for sure, we can figure that he will not make this easy. He looked southward. Couldn't be more than thirty minutes ahead. We'll make that up with the horses in no time. We just have to figure out if they are clinging to the river or widening out into the desert.

Factor looked at Ethan, nodding to the bandages. "How bad is that?"

Nalin answered for him, "I think it's a clean through and through, but not sure."

Factor nodded. "Maybe best if I take up the trail with Nalin."

"No. I'll be fine. Maybe an ace wrap over the dressings and a quick jab of antibiotics wouldn't hurt."

Nalin was already moving to Factor's saddlebags, extracting the medical kit. She walked over to Ethan. "Take your shirt off." The Apache held a sterile dressing package in her teeth and ripped it open. She then squeezed out triple antibiotic cream onto the gauze pad and plastered it to the wound. She repeated the process on the exit wound. After closely inspecting her placement, she started wrapping an elastic bandage around Crowe's torso, covering the dressings several times over.

Ethan squirmed a bit. "Hey, leave me some space to breathe."

"Oh, don't be a baby," Nalin responded in Apache in a mock scolding tone. She finished her ministrations by sticking a hypodermic smoothly into Crowe's arm, sending a megadose of antibiotics into his system.

Finished with her doctoring, she placed the kit back into Factor's bags, turned, and moved quickly to where she had laid down her rifle. She proceeded to check the magazine, working the lever to eject the two remaining rounds. She bent down to pick them up and began to reload them into the side port, following that with additional rounds taken from her bandoliers. She then took her knife from her right moccasin and wiped away any remaining fibers from the cutting of her shirt. After a close inspection of the edge, she replaced it in one smooth motion to the sheath secreted in her moc. Looking up, she was surprised to find both men staring at her. "What?" She looked at both of them questioningly. "Are you ready to ride?"

Ethan nodded. "Yeah. If I can manage to get up on Wanagi wrapped up like the mummy." Ethan smiled at Factor as he said it.

Nalin was already jumping onto the back of her mustang. "And I thought that you Lakota warriors were so tough." She reined over to where she had seen Factor descend into the ravine and eased her horse down into the riverbed. She carefully urged him across the river and started searching for a way to climb back up where Ethan's horse was waiting for him.

Ethan looked at Factor. "Once the team gets here, reach out to me on the radio. If I have reception, I will give you my GPS coordinates, and maybe you can get them to leapfrog ahead. Have them set down just inside our border."

"Roger that. And you watch that side of yours. If it starts to pumping blood again, pull up and call for backup. These fuckers aren't worth dying for needlessly."

Making light of Factor's concerns, Ethan replied, "I think we should be able to run them down in short order considering they are on foot."

Factor added, "I'd tell you to be careful, but with that Apache up there and that horse you're riding, you'll be safer than I am." Isaac flashed a toothy smile.

"Yeah, that's twice today that mustang has saved my bacon. Maybe my niece is right about that magic stuff." He started to wade across the water to the western bank, holding a fist in the air as a farewell.

CHAPTER 51

Office of the US Attorney, Miami,
Southern District of Florida

Robert "Wild Bill" Hickock was still pacing in his office, listening as the intelligence came in from Arizona. Agent Webb had been reporting in regularly on the operation underway in the desert on the Tohono O'odham Reservation. Webb was on the ground out there, waving the DEA flag of assistance. He was at the Shadow Wolves headquarters with the Homeland Security SAC Radcliff. This was both good and bad. It was great because Radcliff was an open book with all the radio communications. It was bad because, according to Agent Webb, Radcliff had become unhinged, ranting and raving about the Shadow Wolves in general and Ethan Crowe in particular.

Wendt was on the phone now, getting the latest from Webb. Hickock could hear Wendt closing out the conversation. "Okay, Jake. Good. Just keep us in the loop. We really need to know if they catch up with the rest of them." He nodded twice more, receiving additional information. "Do you think they are going to run them to ground?" He waited, nodded again, then said, "Uh-huh. Okay, just call as soon as you hear anything."

As Wendt ended the call, Agent Wilcox appeared in the doorway, carrying a cardboard tray with three Starbucks lattes. He held them up for all to see and then set them on the table, reading the labels and handing them out accordingly. He looked to his partner questioningly, "Any good news?"

Wendt started to say something, but Hickock interrupted, "Not really. The Zeta sniper is dead. We're not sure, but he might have been killed by his own people. There are two more in the wind, but there is every reason to believe that our fucking Indian friends are going to run them to ground any minute now."

Wilcox looked at Wendt questioningly. "This is a bad thing?"

Again, Hickock broke in, "Fuck yes, it's a bad thing! Look, I don't care how many fucking drug dealers these people catch or how many drugs they seize. I just can't have our guy jeopardized before this introduction is arranged with the Pakis. If these guys reach our guy, we've got a problem."

Wendt tried to placate Hickock. "Look, Bill, our guy is sitting safe down in Mexico. As long as he stays down there, it doesn't matter what happens with the crews up in Arizona. Webb tells me that he is working his way into their hearts now. I've authorized him to promise the Shadow Wolves all the equipment they need and access to our databases. As far as I'm concerned, he's the perfect trip wire for us. If they even begin to get close to our guy down south, we will know in plenty of time to put a blanket on the whole thing. You know, in the interest of National Security and all that goes with it."

Hickock turned deadly serious. "Don't fucking joke about that. This *is* a matter of national security, and we have backing at the highest levels. This is a major breakthrough for us. We've never got this close to the weapons guys in Pakistan before—ever!" He looked expectantly at the two DEA agents, challenging them to disagree. Instead, they both nodded in agreement.

Wendt interjected, "I'll be in constant communication with Webb out there until we have a conclusion. I told him that we are in your office and will remain here until the end."

Hickock was deep in thought. He walked to the window, looking out on the Bayside Shopping Mall jutting into the blue waters of Biscayne Bay. "If they pick up this Lobo character, I will move to supersede. Someone in DC will call the prosecutor in our Phoenix office and tell them that the case is ours. We will then bring Lobo back to Miami. I will want that done immediately before he talks to anyone and offers any kind of assistance. Make sure that the Lear is ready for one of you to go out there personally ASAP."

All three of them let out a collective sigh, falling back into the easy chairs and taking tentative sips from their Starbucks paper cups.

CHAPTER 52

They were moving so fast through the darkness, the coyote feared one or both of them would stumble and fall. Lobo was struggling with the exertions, his excess weight and lack of wind evident. He was wheezing loudly and demanding with increasing frequency that they stop to catch their breath. It was taking all his self-control to stay with the Zeta boss, his instincts telling him to leave him and head out into the desert alone.

They had covered a great deal of distance. The coyote was hopeful that the border was only about eight miles ahead, but that might as well be a hundred miles if the *indios* picked up their trail. He hadn't mentioned it to Lobo, but even he was traveling blind. He had only been in this part of the desert once before and had no clear memory of what they would be facing as they moved southward. The moon was up and the light was usable, making their steps a bit easier. But it would also allow their pursuers to see better. He noticed that there were big shapes looming just ahead. He couldn't make out what they were but was hoping that they might be rocks. It would be the only thing that could save them.

*****

Chee sat atop her horse, leaning forward to study the ground. She was leading, with Crowe just a few yards back and to the left. She was spotting the occasional sign, but in the moonlight, it was not possible to follow a trail effectively all the time. They were relying on "best guess" logic and the occasional sign of the Zetas' passing in order to stay on their trail. Progress was slower than they would have liked, but they had to remain aware of the possibility of another ambush. Nalin was also worried about Crowe's condition. She had kept a wary eye on him as they rode south. His forehead showed beads of sweat, and he was obviously suffering a great deal from the bullet wound. At one point, she had insisted they stop to look at some tracks in the dirt, and she had demanded to check his dressings. It hadn't been good. Blood was seeping through the dressings. She really didn't think that he should go on much farther and told him so. "Ethan, we need to get you back. You don't look too good."

Ethan had listened, checked his ace wrap with his fingers, and shook his head. "I'm fine for now. We're close." Sensing her worry, he added, "I'll speak up if it gets any worse, I promise."

Nalin stared at him silently but finally nodded in agreement.

*****

The coyote crossed himself in thanks to God. They had indeed arrived at a stretch of hills and rocks. Upon reaching them, they immediately moved up into the narrow openings in the boulders, which, in turn, led to a labyrinth of trails winding up and around the windswept stone formations. After fifteen minutes of climbing on pathways normally traveled by wild predators, they found a good spot to rest and look back over their back trail.

The coyote turned from his lookout perch and spoke to Lobo, "I can see over the crest. The moonlight is only fair, but I think that these rocks go south for a couple of miles. We can crawl over the rocks, drop down on the south end, and make our run to the border. The *indios* can't follow us on horseback. They either have to swing around these rocks or go after us on foot. With any luck, by the time they ride around these rocks, we will be on our side of the border."

Lobo was finally catching his breath. Seated on the ground, he wiped his forehead with his sleeve and looked around him at the trails leading farther into their rocky refuge. He leaned his head back on a large granite boulder. "Or we can stay here and fight."

The coyote couldn't believe what he was hearing. *Why would he want to stay and fight these indios?* He suspected that Lobo knew he couldn't travel any farther. He looked down at the Zeta and confirmed that the overweight man was spent. Most of the man's brash, confident manner had disappeared. He was now clearly in a fight for his life, and it was probably the first time in his life that he was truly afraid. He spoke again in a reasonable tone, "I do think we have a better than average chance of getting away, *Jefe*," showing respect in an effort to sway his opinion toward reason.

Lobo remained seated and spoke into the air in front of him, "I am tired of running from these *indios.* I am not afraid to face them, and I am not some rabbit running for his hole in the ground." His statement was more of a proclamation than a response to the coyote's remark. Lobo brought his pistol out from his belt, dropping the magazine to check his rounds. Finished, he set it down and brought up his rifle, holding it in front of him and showing it to the coyote. He set the rifle butt on the ground and hooked his thumbs in the bandolier around his chest. He had four spare magazines attached in pouches, which he proudly pointed out to the coyote. He lifted his chin toward the guide. "How many rounds do you have left for that pistol of yours?"

Bernardo felt his belt automatically. There were two extra magazines in an old leather holder. He pulled his pistol from his belt and checked the mag. It was half full, perhaps eight rounds remaining. He looked up again at Lobo. "Maybe forty rounds, total," he replied, thinking this might dissuade the Zeta boss.

Lobo received the news and grunted. "Good. It is enough. We will stand and fight these fucking *indios* here." He looked at Bernardo for an argument. None came.

The coyote, resigned to the course of action, began to think about where they should make their stand. He was no soldier but, then again, neither was Lobo. He didn't really know how many *indios* were coming. There had been only two, but they could have called for more by now. He looked around the little clearing where they now stood. They were surrounded on all sides by huge boulders. There were two paths in addition to the one by which they had arrived.

One led south and the other farther west. From his vantage point, on a rock facing north and east, he could see much of their back trail and any approach from that direction. He felt that they had two choices: fire down from the elevated observation perch or hunker down in the clearing and wait for the trackers to stumble into the opening. Both had negative sides, but they would have to make a choice.

Lobo listened to the coyote's propositions. They made sense. After a moment's consideration, he declared, "We will do both. We will stay up on the lookout point and try to pick them off before they get into the rocks. If we manage to kill one of them, the other might run. If not, we will wait here for whoever comes through that opening in the rocks. Then we can finish it."

Bernardo listened and agreed. This was going to be a close thing no matter how they played it. He thought back to the countless people he had guided across the border. Some had been captured by the American *migras* after he had dropped them off. Others had spread across the US, meeting up with family and blending into the massive population north of the border. This had been his first work for the Zetas. His greed had brought him to this point. He sat on his rocky perch and shook his head at his own folly. *I have never killed a man, and now I am going to face an enemy that has no fear.*

*****

Ethan and Wanagi had finally found a comfortable rhythm as they moved slowly along the trail of the Zetas. His side had stopped throbbing, and the bleeding had slowed to a trickle. The extra-strength Tylenol that Nalin had provided from the medical kit were doing a pretty good job. *Maybe he could do a commercial when this was over*, smiling to himself. He looked ahead to see Nalin reining back on her horse, waiting for Ethan to draw alongside.

"Rocks ahead. Lots of 'em." The Apache was speaking in a low whisper.

Ethan stroked Wanagi's neck while he looked ahead and off to the west where the rock formations stretched for several miles. "Pretty good place to hole up. Too good."

Nalin looked sideways at Ethan. "What do you think?"

"I think they're waiting for us up there." Ethan sat back and continued to survey the landscape.

Nalin nodded but said nothing, waiting to see what Crowe would decide. *He's seen much worse than this. He'll know what's best.*

She heard a slight noise and realized that Crowe had quietly slid from his mustang's back and was now standing on the ground, starting to remove Wanagi's bridle. Nalin looked at him questioningly.

Ethan spoke over his shoulder quietly, "We need to turn the horses loose and walk in. They'll be expecting us on horseback. We can edge over to the west and come in on foot instead."

Nalin jumped from her mount, working on the bridle of her horse as well. She knew this was for the sake of the mustangs. If something happened to her and Ethan, the horses would be free to look after themselves. They would either be found by the Shadow Wolves or rejoin a wild herd. She glanced over at Ethan, whose horse was nudging him in the back in protest, clearly not wanting to be separated from her rider. She shook her head slightly, *That is some kind of horse...*

Horses freed, both trackers headed west away from the river for about two hundred yards before turning south. They would be in the rocks in about fifteen minutes.

*****

Lobo sat on the ground cradling his rifle in his lap. He looked up at the coyote. "See anything?"

Bernardo replied in hushed tones, hoping Lobo would follow suit, "Nothing yet."

"Maybe they aren't coming. You know, I killed that fucking Romero. Or at least he should be dead. I pumped at least three rounds into his chest back there."

Bernardo dropped down from his spot on the rock. "Why did you do that?"

"Business. Just business." Lobo looked intently at the coyote. It would only have been a matter of time before he talked. Once they got him back to one of their cities and told him that he would spend the rest of his life in a federal prison, he would talk." He chuckled to himself. "Hell, even I would talk. In this life, everyone makes decisions that are best for themselves. I have no intention of having the Americans looking for me for the rest of my life because that sniper served me up on a platter."

Bernardo could only nod in silent agreement. *There were no trusted friends in this business. If he had thought that there were, he thought it no longer.*

Lobo grunted. "Get the fuck back up there, they could be down there now!"

The coyote paused for a moment, considered a retort, but decided to leave it alone. He shook his head sullenly as moved to climb back into the rocks.

*****

Lobo was right. They were down there now but not where they were expected to be. The trackers had slipped into the rocks farther north of the Zeta's position. They were moving stealthily through the winding paths that led southward. This was Nalin's land. She was more at home in the dry rocks than in her mother's womb. This was the land of the Apaches and always would be. The sound of a cougar broke the silence, causing both Nalin and Ethan to pause for a second. Ethan looked over at his partner and nodded. They started moving once again.

After about ten minutes of slithering through the rocks, Nalin paused. She motioned with her right hand to get Ethan's attention. She had heard something ahead. It was a scraping sound, like metal on rock. She wasn't sure what it was exactly, but she knew it was not a natural sound or that made by an animal. Ethan used the pause to pull up his night vision goggles. He looked ahead to a sight that resembled a moonscape more than someplace on earth. It reminded him of his own Badlands in South Dakota. After a few seconds of scanning, he saw movement. He then motioned quickly to Nalin. *They had found the Zetas.*

Crowe tried to determine what exactly he was seeing through the goggles. He started to signal Nalin but was shocked to find her at his side. *Jesus!* he thought to himself. *I don't know who freaks me out more, her or that damn Wanagi!*

"What do you see?" Nalin whispered directly into Crowe's ear, her lips brushing his skin, her warm breath carrying a sensuality Crowe could not ignore in spite of the situation.

Crowe spoke in hushed tones, "There's one lying flat on the rock just to the right," pointing and allowing Nalin to look along his forearm to follow the direction of his finger. "It's got to be the coyote. The other one couldn't climb up there."

Nalin nodded in agreement.

Crowe pulled his goggles from his eyes, blinking rapidly and looking directly at his partner. "I think we should try to work around them and come up from behind. That one is looking for us on horseback."

"Do you think the fat one is nearby?" Nalin now turned around with her back resting against a massive rock, protected from the view of the coyote.

"Yeah, I do. This coyote is not a soldier. Hell, probably not even a shooter, truth be told. This Lobo is an animal with survival instincts. He has somehow convinced this coyote to be his lookout. My guess is that he is waiting in the shadows, using the coyote as bait."

Crowe looked at Nalin. "Do you think you can find us a way to get up over these rocks and drop down behind them?"

Nalin nodded in the affirmative, glancing twice at Ethan's bandages. "How's your side doing?"

Crowe let out a short breath, more a sigh than anything. "Let's finish this."

Nalin was on her feet immediately, stepping effortlessly around Ethan. In seconds, she was up and over a massive boulder and onto a narrow pathway leading to the rear of the Zetas' hiding place. Crowe shook his head in wonder and followed in her wake.

*****

The coyote was tiring of his vigil. The past hours had sapped his strength and endurance. There were times he felt it would be much easier to just surrender to the *indios. At least I would be alive. Following this fucking Lobo is probably going to get me killed.* He had begun to worry about the trackers. They should have been here by now, particularly if they were still on horseback. He had remained alert, scanning the moonlit night for shadows or silhouettes coming from the north. So far, nothing. Perhaps they had been lucky and killed the trackers. Or maybe Romero hadn't died and they had remained with him, satisfied with the capture of the infamous killer. He looked back to the clearing and Lobo, who was now asleep, snoring quietly but loud enough to be heard from nearby. *Fuck!* He let out a long breath and slid back down the rock. He had to wake Lobo. His snoring was going to get them both killed.

He stepped quietly over to where the Zeta was leaning against a rock wall, cradling his rifle with his finger in the trigger guard. Careful to approach the man from the side, he gently touched him on his shoulder, nudging him from his sleep. Lobo, awakened in a panic, squeezed the trigger reflexively. Fortunately, the safety was on and the sound of a wildly fired shot would not be heard. Lobo looked around frantically, still startled from what must have been a deep sleep borne out of exhaustion. Seconds later, when his wits returned, he looked up at the coyote. "Are they here?"

The coyote shook his head quickly. "No. Nothing yet. We might have gotten lucky after all. They should have been here already."

Lobo was heartened by the coyote's words. He sat up straighter, reached down for his water skin, and took a long gulp. He tilted his head back and held the water bag long enough so that the water dripped around the edges of his mouth and down his chin. He lowered the bag and looked back at the coyote. "So what now?"

The coyote started to answer but was harshly interrupted.

"Don't anyone move. Don't anyone even breathe." Crowe's voice calm and controlled, speaking in clear Spanish. He had appeared from the path behind the Zetas, his Glock leveled directly at Lobo. Nalin moved into the clearing from the second path, appearing from behind a huge rock that was surrounded with dried-up mesquite bushes. Both the Zeta and the coyote stood frozen in a bizarre tableau, staring at the trackers in disbelief. The coyote held his hands out from his sides, slowly moving them above his head. He was eager to let his captors know that he would comply with their orders.

Lobo just sat there, transfixed. Staring directly at Crowe, a sneer starting to creep across his grizzly features.

Crowe retained his calm demeanor. "Take your hands of that rifle, Lobo. This is over. Just let it go. Now." Crowe's voice was hard and direct. He was being careful not to add additional stress to the situation.

Lobo was weighing his options. He could just go with this *indios.* Spend some time in their fucking American prisons. *Maybe the bosses would get him released. Who knows?* His thoughts were a jumble, jarred by the *indio*'s use of his name. *How does he know my name?* Time seemed to be slowing down for him. His eyes darted in all directions but settled once again on the lean figure in front of him. He continued to weigh his options. *Maybe I can kill him. He is too civilized. He would not be quick to shoot.*

Crowe slowly closed the distance between himself and Lobo. He was now only five feet from the man. "Think about this. Do you really want to play this out? Even I don't think there's a place for you in the white man's heaven."

Lobo's mind was clearing. *He was not going to surrender to this indio. That was not an option. He had a better than average chance of killing him. And the woman, fuck her. I will kill her afterward.* He spoke for the first time, "I will drop my weapon, *indio.* You have me. I have no choice." He moved to release his rifle, but in a flash, he turned the barrel outward, the barrel moving directly at Ethan's chest.

*****

Nalin was watching Lobo intently as she moved along the rock wall next to where she entered the clearing. She glanced at the skinny one repeatedly, but it was clear he wanted no trouble. His hands were high and empty. She was sure of one thing though: the fat one was not going to surrender. Ethan was taking too big a chance. She had closed to within three feet of the Zeta boss, listening to the interaction between the man and Crowe. She reached down silently to her moccasin, withdrawing the glass blade.

Ethan's attention was briefly drawn to the coyote, who started pleading, "I am surrendering. Please don't shoot me. Please…"

"Just shut up and stand there. No one is going to kill you," Crowe ordered, his eyes swinging back to Lobo. Unfortunately, he had missed the lightning-quick movement of Lobo. He started to bring his Glock back to bear when Nalin flashed across his field of fire. She slid across the dirt on her knees, settling behind Lobo, her left arm around his head and her right hand drawing the obsidian blade across his throat. Crowe watched as the man stared into space, surely aware that he was already dead without the rest of his body realizing what had happened. Lobo's right hand, which had let go of the rifle to defend Nalin's attack, groped desperately at the gaping hole in his throat. His hand came away red and slippery, unable to grab the rifle or anything else. He started to speak but could only produce gurgling sounds through his severed windpipe.

Nalin released her hold on Lobo and let his lifeless head fall forward, the man's chin coming to rest on his chest. The coyote stood like a stone, unable to comprehend what he had just seen but relieved to have the man called Lobo gone from this world. He would no longer threaten his existence or the lives of his family back home. He cautiously watched the *indio* standing in front of him. The man turned to him, quietly ordering in Spanish, "Get down on your knees. Keep your hands up."

The coyote did as he was told, ignoring the pain to his knees caused by the rocky ground.

"Now place both your hands on your head. And keep them there."

Crowe moved around the coyote and approached him from behind, placing his left hand on top of the coyote's. He then reached smoothly to the prisoner's waist and removed the pistol, tucking it into his own waistband. He then did a thorough pat down and told the coyote to sit down right where he was kneeling. Crowe then looked over to Nalin, who had already stood up and was now pulling up on the dead Zeta's hair, taking the measure of the monster she had seen shoot the girl point-blank in the face back in the camp. She then released his hair with a shove, forcing the body to fall to the side and onto the ground. She turned to exchange a look with Ethan, a fire still burning hot in her eyes.

CHAPTER 53

Crowe had removed the coyote's shirt, and Nalin had cut it into strips of cloth. They had used the strips to bind the coyote, hand and foot. He now rested against the stone wall directly across from Lobo. The once powerful drug boss lay facedown in the dust, flies already gathering in the blood-soaked folds of his clothes. Nalin had taken Ethan's radio and called in their location. Their GPS had broken during the melee, but she gave them a clear description of their route and all the relevant landmarks. A chopper was on the way, along with a team of the Wolves, who were already driving south along the river in a Humvee.

The coyote was slowly relaxing. He had been watching the movements of the two *indios* closely. They had been talking on the radio and asking for support. These were not the actions of people who were going to kill him. *He was going to live. That was something.*

Crowe was leaning with his back to a rock, his shirt off. Nalin unwrapped his ace bandage. She picked at the gauze dressings, careful not to pull them from the wounds. "It looks pretty good. The bleeding's stopped. I don't want to pull it away to check further. It could start it pumping again."

Crowe nodded in agreement. "Good. I guess we can just wrap it back up for now."

As the Apache intently wound the bandage back around his torso, Ethan called over to the coyote, "This isn't going to go easy on you." Curling his lip up in a grimace, he added, "Lots of dead folks back there. Then there's the human trafficking, the rapes, torture, you name it. That's a hell of a load to land on your shoulders alone."

Crowe paused for effect and watched the discomfort grow on the Mexican.

Chee continued to work on Crowe's dressings, acting like she wasn't a part of the conversation.

Crowed continued in a casual tone, "My thoughts on this are a bit different. We've figured you're the guide. Maybe not even a Zeta. Am I right?"

The coyote was nodding vigorously, hoping to distance himself from the events of the past weeks. "I'm not a Zeta. Never worked for them before. I swear on the Virgin herself!"

Crowe shook his head and let out a derisive breath. "Tough to make the prosecutors believe that one. To be honest, it's tough for me to believe."

"It's the truth! I'll do anything to prove it." Desperation was creeping into his voice.

"What's your name anyway?" Crowe was playing his part to the letter.

"Bernardo. My friends call me Nardo," the coyote offered quickly.

"Bernardo what? Surely you have a last name."

"Bernardo Gonzales. I am from Nogales. I have a wife and family." His eyes were pleading. "Yes, I am a coyote. It is how I make my living."

Crowe commented casually, "Not much of a living, is it?"

The coyote was not to be quieted. "I have always just helped people across for jobs or to be with their families in the North. I never did this before."

"If that's true, why now?" Crowe was now free of Nalin's bandaging efforts.

The coyote just shook his head. "I don't know. The money. It was going to be a lot of money." His head was now hanging and his eyes were staring at the ground.

Crowe let the man stew in his own juices for a bit. He called over to Nalin, who was trying to look busy but not doing a great job of it. "Nahatse, what do you think about going to check on the horses. They are probably getting lonely by now."

She nodded quickly. "Want me to bring them up? I can tie them up just below. Make sure they are watered." She paused a second. "You two going to be okay?" She knew that was a foolish question but smiled as she asked it.

"I think we'll be just fine, won't we, Nardo?" The coyote continued to stare at the ground.

Nalin quickly disappeared among the rocks.

Crowe called out to the coyote by name, "Nardo." A pause as the coyote kept staring at the ground. "Nardo! Look at me."

The coyote slowly raised his head.

"Yeah. You need to look at me and listen. This might be the most important moment of your life."

The coyote waited. *What is coming? What is the indio going to propose?*

Crowe began. He had made these types of offers in terrible places all around the globe. He was good at it. People trusted him. Most of the time, the people agreed. Crowe felt he was successful because he was a man of his word. He did what he said he would do. He would do the same now. "I am going to give you the opportunity to help yourself out of this mess."

The coyote started to talk. Crowe stopped him.

"You need to listen. Don't talk. You can talk afterward." The coyote nodded in agreement.

"I want you to tell me who ordered all this. Not Lobo. I want the man who did all this. The man who turned Romero loose and the man who backed Lobo's play." He paused for a second. "That is all that I want. But I want the truth, and I don't want to have to sit here for hours convincing you." He then waited another five minutes in silence, letting his words sink in.

Finally, the coyote spoke, "What happens to me if I do it? If I tell you, what happens to me?"

Crowe responded immediately, "You go free."

"What? This can't be," replied the coyote, shaking his head in disbelief.

"It can be. I want the name of the man who is the author of all this." Crowe then added, "And his boss too. That's the deal. Then I will walk over there, cut your ties, and send you home."

The coyote had heard of the tricks used by the police. They would tell you anything but give you nothing. But the more he looked at the *indio* in front of him, the more he realized this man was different. "Can I ask you your name, sir?" he asked, trying to remain respectful.

"Crowe. Ethan Crowe."

The coyote nodded. "It was Roberto who made this happen. Roberto Guzman. He is in Nogales. He is the boss of all this."

"The boss of the Zetas?"

"No, not of all the Zetas. That is someone else. But Roberto is the man who sends the drugs and the women. No one can say no to him."

Crowe asked calmly, "Did he send Romero to the North to kill?"

"*Si.* But it is said that Romero answers only to Yaotl."

Crowe prodded gently, "Tell me about Yaotl. Who is he?"

"I am sorry, but I know very little about Yaotl. He is king of the Zetas. He is the man who commands Roberto." The coyote fell silent, clearly terrified that he had even spoken Yaotl's name to the *indio*.

Crowe sensed the man's apprehension. "You're doing good, Nardo. Very good. I think that you and I can talk for a bit longer. I would like some more details of these men. You can be sure that no one will ever know what you and I have talked about here in the rocks in the middle of the desert.

*****

Thirty minutes later, Nalin walked back into the clearing. The horses were tied safely below. The team would be there soon. As she emerged from the rocks, she found the coyote standing, face pressed against the rocks. Ethan was cutting the cloth strips from his wrists. They both turned at the sound of Nalin's voice.

"All is good down below," said Nalin, trying to digest what was happening.

Crowe responded, "Good. Thanks, Nahatse." He then turned back to the coyote. "You are free to go. We will not follow you." It was clear that the coyote was terrified, not sure if this was really happening.

Nalin watched in silence. She trusted Ethan with every fiber of her being.

Crowe leaned closely to the coyote. "Remember, you are to go directly back to Guzman. You are to tell him everything. Tell him what happened down on the desert and up here. Tell him that I know who he is and where I can find him. Tell him that I am not like the others. I am coming for him. He can be certain of that."

The coyote was nodding vigorously now, hoping to be free of this man's company soon. Something about the man turned his blood to ice.

Ethan stepped back, spreading his left arm out to indicate the coyote was free to go. The Mexican took his first steps, heading to the opening in the rocks that would lead him south and home to Nogales. "And one more gift for Mr. Guzman. Tell him that I am also coming for Yaotl." Ethan paused a few seconds. "And make sure he understands that the border means nothing to me in this."

The coyote replied once, "Yes, sir. I will do as you say. I swear by the name of the Blessed Virgin."

Ethan shook his head silently. "Let's leave your Virgin out of this, coyote."

The man nodded and disappeared into the rocks. He knew this was the last time he would ever step foot across the border.

Nalin stepped forward to stand with Crowe. "That was something new. Never saw anything like that in the manual." The Apache stared at the space where the coyote had disappeared. After a moment's silence, she spoke again, "You weren't completely honest with him."

Crowe looked at her questioningly.

"You told him that you were coming for them. That wasn't entirely true."

Crowe stood still, knowing she would finish in her own time.

Nalin spoke into the space in front of her, "*We* are coming for them. You are not going alone."

EPILOGUE

Banner University Medical Center, Tucson

Ethan stared absently at the television in his hospital room. CNN was droning on about Breaking News, which sounded a lot like the same news he had heard earlier this morning. He flicked the clicker, finally landing on a black-and-white episode of *Bewitched*. He set the remote back in the holder and returned to his daydreams, the television just white noise for his musings.

Nalin and Factor appeared in his doorway. "You awake?"

Crowe smiled at the interruption. "Yep, just catching up on all the shows I missed back in the '60s."

"We heard that you were breaking out of here today. Is that true?" Nalin was standing at the foot of the bed, fiddling with the covers and straightening them absentmindedly.

"Yeah, the doc is due any minute." Crowe reached over to turn down the sound on the remote.

There was another knock on the metal doorframe. Crowe looked up, and the two trackers turned in unison. Standing there was Jake Webb from the DEA and a second man, obviously another agent.

Crowe spoke, "Webb?" puzzlement evident in Ethan's face.

"Yeah, it's me." Webb held up a pile of magazines as an offering. "Thought you might be tired of reading *Cosmo* by now." The agent walking up to the bed, crowding Nalin and Factor to stand closer to Ethan. Webb quickly turned to his partner. "This is my partner from back in Miami, Special Agent Rich Wendt."

Everyone nodded to one another in greeting, Factor and Nalin declining to reach out to shake hands. Both stood there warily, wondering what had brought these agents to Ethan's room this morning.

Nalin was the first to speak, "What brings you here?" The Apache looked at both men suspiciously.

Jake Webb was quick to reply, "I meant to get here sooner but couldn't break loose. We've been trying to dig up some intel to provide you guys on the crew that you took down. Thought it might be of some help. Rich here was in the office and asked if he could tag along and congratulate you on the job you did."

Wendt chimed in immediately, "Yeah. They're even talking about this back in Miami. This was a major takedown. One hell of a job. It sounds like you wrapped it up tightly. No real loose ends." The agent smiled broadly.

Factor and Chee stood silent, not sure how Ethan would respond to the DEA men. It was clear they were here for information, not to give it. Crowe pushed the button to let his bed recline a bit more, using the activity to consider his response. Finally, he said, "I wouldn't say it's all wrapped up. There's still the men behind all this."

Webb asked, "What do you mean?"

Ethan replied, "You know, the guy who ordered all the killings, rapes, kidnappings. That guy."

Wendt interjected, "Well, I would guess the FBI or someone will take up that baton when the time is right. I think you have reached the end of your tether down there on the rez."

Crowe chuckled. "No, my tether reaches just as far as the FBI's or, for that matter, even yours."

Webb and Wendt stood there in awkward silence. They shared a questioning glance, clearly trying to decide what to do or say next. Wendt then pushed forward. "Well, I hope if you decide to take this to the next level, you count us in. We can do plenty to help. Our contacts down south are quite extensive."

Crowe looked over at Factor, then at Chee. They all exchanged looks, Isaac and Nalin finally looking down. Crowe turned his head back to the DEA guys. "Look, let's be honest with each other. You are only here to see what we're going to do next. You could give a shit how I am or what fucking magazine I'm reading." Crowe was now sitting straight up in bed. "How about you get the fuck out of this room and leave me the fuck alone. We've got badges that work just as good as yours. Maybe better from what I've seen. We'll be fine without you or your friends in Miami."

Silence enveloped the room. Nalin was already facing the men challengingly.

The DEA men said nothing more. They turned and started for the door. Halfway there, Wendt stopped and turned. "I'm flying back to Miami, Agent Crowe. Surely you realize your little group is an experiment. Nothing more. Your job is to patrol some shithole reservation in a place nobody gives a damn about. I intend to see just how strong that tether of yours really is." With that, he stepped into the hallway and disappeared.

Silence enveloped the room. Factor and Chee slowly turned from the empty doorway back to the bed.

Crowe winked at Nalin. Factor just shook his head.

About the Author

Jake Kaminski is the pseudonym for the author of *The Shadow Wolves*. In real life, he is a retired police lieutenant with twenty-eight years of experience. Highly decorated, he spent the majority of his career working undercover and then supervising undercover operations in Miami, Latin America, and the Caribbean. He is an expert witness in US courts on the subject of undercover operations and drug trafficking.

Following his police career, he has spent fourteen years as an international adviser for the US Department of Justice, assigned to post-conflict countries in the Balkans. His job was to advise foreign police and prosecutors on the following topics: undercover operations, war crime investigations, fugitive tracking, organized crime, and human trafficking.

Jake is well equipped to tell the story of the Shadow Wolves. He has seen the firsthand the tragedy of ethnic cleansing and human trafficking in Eastern Europe and has ran successful undercover operations against both the Cali and Medellin drug cartels.

He now divides his time between writing, overseas consulting, and providing technical advice for feature films. He is currently working as executive producer on a television show called *The Murder Book* for the Oxygen Channel. He has a bachelor's degree in both Spanish and French and holds a black belt in taekwondo.

CPSIA information can be obtained
at www.ICGtesting.com
Printed in the USA
BVHW032218231121
622257BV00021B/102